HEALED FOR LOVE

BROKEN FOR WHAT YOU LONG FOR

MELVIN DAVIS

Illustrated by

JASMINE C DAVIS

ACKNOWLEDGMENTS

First, I give immeasurable thanks to my Lord and Savior Jesus Christ. I'm so glad to have You in my life. I'm truly undeserving of Your grace and mercy, yet You chose me to be one of Your servants in the Kingdom. I praise You. I worship You and love You with all my heart, soul, and mind.

Father, thank You for orchestrating all the events in my life that led to discovering one of my true gifts. For the very first time in my life, I experienced a sensation that felt better than walking across a stage to receive two degrees on two different occasions. I found something authentic and passionate! I'm at peace when I write. I'm myself when I write. God, continue to use me as a source of inspiration and encouragement to all. I'm forever available to You!

I'd like to extend my gratitude to my beloved family and friends for their unconditional support. My sister Jasmine Chenelle Davis did a terrific job designing the stunning book cover of *Healed for Love*. My brother Shimon Davis also helped with the amazing book cover. Thanks for your assistance and guidance throughout the process. I'm thankful for the friendship and the spiritual bonds that we're all developing with one another. Your prayers and words of encouragement, support of my work, and consistent reminders of the great things to come in my life have kept me focused. Thank you both. I love you! I'll always be there for you. I also want to thank my older brother Laquann Brooks. You've been there for me during hard times while writing this book. Thanks for always having my back. I love you big bro. And to my mom, thank you. Without you, I wouldn't be here. I strongly feel my creative side comes from you.

To everyone who contributed financially to getting my novel off the ground, four of whom were close family members: my father, Melvin A. Davis and relatives Desiree and David Davis and Shawn Glenn. Thank you for believing in me! Without your donations and the help of those who have been following my work on my WordPress blog (mdavis11.wordpress.com), the release of my novel would've been further delayed. Thank you all from the bottom of my heart!

Thanks to a special friend who helped shape my novel when I was learning how to write and tell a story. Manisha Reynolds, thanks for your constructive criticism, writing tips, and pointing me to invaluable resources that enriched my writing and cultivated my storytelling skills. I also appreciate you for being there for me during some of the most challenging times in my life while writing this novel. I'm eternally thankful for your friendship.

I'd also like to thank CJ Anaya for editing my novel. It was a pleasure working with you. Through our conversations, your critiques, and helpful feedback, I grew tremendously as a writer and storyteller. You didn't change my voice, thought process, or writing style. You gave me options and suggestions to improve the story, which I've taken full advantage of and watched it blossom while remaining authentic to my perspective. The developmental and copyediting skills you possess have truly gotten my novel into publishing condition. I'd also like to note how I've gained a lifelong friend in you! Thanks for reminding me that greater lies ahead for me!

Another special friend I'm compelled to acknowledge is Nelisa Lantigua. I met you in the heart of my wilderness experience in Miami Shores, FL. Sanctification and preparation for ministry happen in the wilderness. We became acquainted at a Starbucks. I blogged and worked on my novel there. I've crossed paths with many people at cafés, but Nelisa and I remain close friends to this day. Your friendship was timely. Your presence, prayers, and encouraging words held me together when I felt I could no longer bear the agony and discomfort. I prayed for help, and I met you. I thank God for you. I pray God continues to be a blessing to you, your marriage, and your family!

THE FOUNDATION

Every godly relationship has a foundation. This story rests on 1 Corinthians 13: 4-8. I hope yours does, too.

Love is patient, love is kind. It does not envy or boast; it is not proud. It does not dishonor others, it is not self-seeking, it is not easily angered, it keeps no records of wrongs. Love does not delight in evil but rejoices with the truth. It always protects, always trusts, always hopes, always perseveres.

Love never fails.

- 1 Corinthians 13: 4-8

CHAPTER 1

*J*ennifer walked demurely from behind the podium to the front of their table. She fanned her proposal up in the air, becoming glassy-eyed at the frozen faces of unbelief. "Please take a look at the statistics again." Her nostrils flared with passion. "I'm sure you'll see how badly young women in DC could benefit greatly from a Christian non-profit facility like this."

They weren't buying it. She stood still for a moment and tried to gather herself before speaking again. *God, this isn't working!*

"Can you believe that two of every five unintended teen pregnancies end in abortion?" She stopped mid-sentence and noticed some of the board members scrolling through their cellphones, probably wondering if they'd make it to happy hour in the next twenty minutes, completely unconcerned with these women or the precarious dilemmas they faced. Passionate anger rolled over her. "Fifty-six percent of women receiving abortions are already mothers trying to care for other children," she emphasized vehemently. Her mouth opened to continue until a hushing hand rose.

"Ms. Washington, we just don't think bringing teens into this facility would prevent abortions or pregnancies. When they return home or back to their neighborhoods, then what? Having sex is a decision. Using contraceptives is also a choice. We don't support religious organizations, anyway." A chairman of the board closed Jennifer's proposal.

"Ms. Jansen, you can understand, right?" Jennifer pointed to the prim-mannered woman on the left, but the lady had her head down bashfully.

I can't believe this. She's a Christian, too.

Ms. Jansen and Jennifer had worked together in a woman's ministry at a church in McLean, Virginia.

Determined, Jennifer flipped through her proposal to read more statistics, although they'd already gone through it. "Seventy-five percent of these women get abortions due to financial problems, single-parent problems, or because a teen's parents wanted them to." Jennifer swallowed hard. Her voice cracked, trying to ignore the fact that she fell into that last category. "These women don't have the financial resources or the support they need to give birth to these children; as a result, nearly twenty-one percent of them regret the abortion immediately following the procedure. That jumps to twenty-eight percent after two years following the procedure. Do you understand what that means? Of the one million women in the U.S. who get an abortion every year, two hundred eighty thousand believe their abortion did more harm than good, and fifty percent of women per year fully believe they're terminating an actual life when they have the abortion."

One gentleman gathered his belongings and stuffed them annoyingly into his briefcase. "Ms. Washington, it's clear you feel very passionate about this, but we simply . . ."

Jennifer frantically flipped through her proposal, slamming her finger on a particularly important fact. She held the page up in protest.

"And women who have undergone abortions experience an eighty-one percent increased risk of mental health issues. Now consider what this non-profit facility could do if we offered these women a place to not only receive free prenatal and pastoral care, free hospital and delivery care, free postnatal care, and professional counseling, but also connected them with prospective parents, people who want children so badly but can't have any of their own? Consider the lives saved and the families created by such a non-profit facility. If these women have this option, they *will* take it, at least twenty-eight percent of them. That's . . ." She fumbled for a moment as the head-board member gave her a sad look. ".... that's at least two hundred eighty thousand lives . . . children . . . we'd save them," she declared, fighting back the tears.

"I'm sorry, Ms. Washington. We simply cannot approve the funding for you at this time. You can file for funding again at the end of three months. And maybe if you take the God-talk out of your mission statement, it'd increase your chances of funding? Thank you for your presentation."

The sharp noise of the door shutting once everyone left amplified the acute silence in the room and unearthed a deep wound. Jennifer moved to the table and shoved her proposal aside, which fell to the floor. She put her head down as tears welled in her eyes, but the hurt was too profound for them to fall. She reached into her purse and pulled out an unforgettable memory.

Fine creases in the ultrasonogram remained like the ache in Jennifer's heart. She unfolded it just about every day.

"Kayla, you would've been nine today," Jennifer cried, tracing Kayla's cradled body where her tiny arms could be seen reaching up, appearing to grasp for something. Jennifer swore she could tell her baby would have taken on her big, round eyes, an oval face, her pointy nose, semi-high cheekbones, and dimples at the side of her plump cheeks. She got up and dropped to her knees, covering her mouth.

Aborting her had been the most heartbreaking decision she'd ever made. At eighteen she was pregnant by her high school sweetheart Robert. The reality of not being ready to mother a child wasn't the only factor that had influenced her decision. Her father had threatened to pull her from college and disown her from the family. Not only that, but she'd also faced another fear. Losing Robert. He'd threatened to leave if she kept the baby. Losing the love of her life and her family would've been too much for her. Her mother wanted her to keep Kayla, but Jennifer's father's intimidating voice and opinions held more precedence at the time. Jennifer remembered it all so vividly:

"I'm not going to have anyone, God," Jennifer screamed in fear of losing her loved ones and the life she hadn't given birth to yet. Crouched on the beige rug in the corner of her bedroom, the pink and white baby shoes that she'd bought for Kayla dangled in her hand. She gripped the white shoelaces with the same intensity she clung to her fear. "I don't want to do this, God. I want Kayla! I don't want to kill her! I can't live with this decision!" She threw the shoes against the door. They landed on the soles with the toes pointing toward her. Jennifer couldn't believe it. She thought for a moment that God was trying to tell her something. What are you trying to tell me? *She thought this was some sort of sign. A sign of what?*

Finally coming back to herself, she pushed the memories aside with tears rolling off her cheeks and got up to make her way to the parking garage. Getting into her car, she felt her phone vibrating. It was a text from Leyanie asking how the meeting went. Jennifer put her head down dejectedly.

"I failed you too, Leyanie."

Jennifer had met Leyanie when she'd moved from Miami to Washington, DC after graduating from the University of Miami at twenty-two. Jennifer wanted to get away from home and pursue a master's degree in human resources at Georgetown University. While undergoing her graduate studies, Jennifer interned at *A Leap of Joy Ministries*, a Christian non-profit in DC, and landed a permanent position as director of the non-profit after she'd graduated. Through this program, she received opportunities to work with underprivileged teens and children suffering from terminal ailments, and that's how she met Leyanie. The two of them had bonded instantly at Parson Children's Hospital.

Jennifer had access to Leyanie's case file. Jennifer learned her mother was a teen when she was pregnant with Leyanie. And twenty-eight weeks into her pregnancy, doctors discovered Leyanie had a rare blood type, which later turned into leukemia. Her mother wanted an abortion then, but the law in DC prohibited that course of action. She gave Leyanie up for adoption and moved on with her life.

Leyanie ended up in the foster care system. She bounced around from home to home. No one wanted to keep her then. No one wanted to raise a child with a high risk of living an unhealthy long life. Or worse, a short life. But one day, Jennifer passed Leyanie's room and felt God's presence. Jennifer thought the experience was odd, given she'd no idea who was in the room or why God moved within her. This continued for a week until she decided to investigate.

The nurses knew Jennifer well, which made it easier to gain access to her case file. When she read it, she was met with sadness and anger. Some conviction was there, too. Jennifer thought about her abortion, which humbled her from raising a thought or tongue of judgment for what Leyanie's mother did. This moment of humility stirred mixed emotions that didn't make her feel good. Then the thought crossed her mind that perhaps, in some way, God was giving her another chance.

Jennifer took Leyanie in as her own. She homeschooled her at the hospital by bringing tutors in and delivering some teaching herself. She also read books with her at the library frequently. Leyanie was an avid reader and an exceptional writer for her age. Jennifer believed she would be a reporter one day. They went to church together, which was an amazing experience for her. She loved the children's church and made friends with other kids there. The carnival was also a special treat. They went on rides together and traveled to Miami and New York to see The *Lion King* at the George Gershwin Theatre. Her mother and sister loved Leyanie. At the beach, building the tallest sandcastle was always a blast. As soon as the sandcastle would get nearly to the height they wanted, Leyanie would playfully push it over. Jennifer got a kick out of this adorable habit.

One day at the beach, Leyanie asked, "Who are my parents?"

Jennifer looked to the sky as if she were waiting for God to give her an answer, but she didn't get one.

"I think they're on vacation."

"Are they coming back?" Leyanie asked. "And how long is this vacation?"

"I think so." Jennifer kissed the side of her head and hugged her.

It hurt Jennifer to give her a dishonest answer. They weren't coming back. She couldn't break the bad news to a child. Her heart couldn't handle the weight of the truth. All the good times they had eventually came to a halt. Her health started to decline, and she had to stay in her hospital bed. It was only a matter of time until Leyanie met her end. Jennifer wasn't given a specific timetable of when she'd die, but she wanted to make the best of their time together while Leyanie lived. She wanted to give her something that she'd never had before.

A mother.

She legally adopted Leyanie, immediately changed her office into a bedroom, and had the walls professionally painted with blue skies and white clouds that matched the frame of the twin-sized bed. A yellow-orange sun was painted off to the side. She flooded the bedroom with different colored teddy bears and stacked the bookcases with children's books. She also stationed a desk in the room, just in case Leyanie wanted to color in the coloring books or paint with watercolors. But Leyanie never had a chance to sleep in her bed or draw imagination from the clouds that decorated her walls and ceiling. She didn't get the opportunity to hug one of those cuddly teddy bears to sleep, read a single sentence in her books, or stroke her wooden handle paintbrush against the untouched canvas. She was admitted back into the hospital. Her condition worsened.

Jennifer had spent hours watching over her sweet daughter, wishing she could take away her pain as only a mother can. As Leyanie slept in her hospital bed, Jennifer cried over her in prayer. She couldn't comprehend how God could allow a child to suffer.

Leyanie didn't ask for this, Jennifer would often say in her head.

At home, she'd yell at Him in anger or sob herself to sleep. As time went on, God opened the eyes of her understanding to see it was the innocent, jubilant fighting spirit of a five-year-old who was oblivious to how she became acquainted with leukemia or knew who her parents were that had started to heal her wounds. And Jennifer realized Leyanie needed someone else in her life, too. Besides herself, Jesus was that person. Life had filled her almond oval eyes when she'd received the opportunity to share salvation through Jesus Christ. Eventually, she'd accepted Christ into her life as Lord and Savior. That day, their bond knitted tighter than ever before.

Jennifer looked at her text again but decided to wait on responding until she visited her at the hospital, giving her emotions a chance to settle. Once she was finally home and showered, she took several moments to compose herself. It wouldn't do any good to bring grief to her bedside. Plus, someone at the agency had arranged for her to team with someone from a different agency to put an event together with the kids at the children's hospital.

"This isn't the day. I'm not in the mood to meet anyone new," she mumbled, walking into the bathroom, lamenting having to partner with someone.

After Jennifer showered and dressed, she stood in front of the mirror. She screwed her solitary diamond earrings into her ears, put her ring on, and pulled her wavy, thick, jet black hair up into a bun. Clear lip-gloss layered her lips as her hands trembled, causing her to fumble the tube into the sink. She dropped to her knees and placed her elbows against the toilet lid. She prayed and sought God for the strength to make it through the day. Just then, her mother and sister called to see how the pitch had gone.

"Hey, Jen," Her younger sister Anisha said, bursting with excitement.

"How'd things go?" her mother, Catherine, asked.

She put them on speaker. "Not so good." Jennifer's voice cracked. "They turned me down." She sighed.

They knew how badly Jennifer wanted her dream to happen. She'd been trying to establish a non-profit of her own for years.

"We're not going to let you give up. When the time is right, like all things, it'll all come together. We love you, Jen." Anisha encouraged her.

"I know. It'll eventually work out. I love both of you so much. Thanks for checking in on me! I have to get ready to see Leyanie."

When she hung up, she still couldn't get Kayla and the rejection of her proposal out of her mind. Nonetheless, she pressed through the disappointment and hurt and made her way out the door.

David sat in his car feeling frustrated, idling in the parking garage of Parson Children's Hospital in Washington, DC. He raked his fingernails through his hair. For months, he hadn't been able to come up with anything to start his next romance novel. The well of his inspiration ran as dry as his love life. He couldn't create something new from what he no longer believed in.

The thought of finding true love was as borderline fictious as his novels. He could credit that to the bitter breakup with his ex and all the other failed relationships of his past. To add to his incessant writer's block, the phone call he'd been fearing, and dodging glared annoyingly bright on his cell phone screen. His literary agent, Jason, was calling.

"What perfect timing," he muttered to himself. He answered his cell phone after the fourth ring.

"Yeah, what's up, Jay?" He paired his cell with the car speaker and tossed it on the passenger seat. "Can't talk long . . . heading in to see Max."

"How's Max?" Jason asked.

David knew this call was more business than personal. "Uh, he's hanging in there. About that book . . ." He thought he'd cut right to the chase and help Jason. Small talk irritated him. "I wrote this letter that I think could be used for the new book, but I lost it. Can't find the thing."

"David, you've been telling me for the last three months that you're nearly finished with this latest romance novel. I need to get something to Dresden Publishing soon. Ya killing me, man."

If his publisher had any idea that not only was he not finished, but he hadn't even started, he'd probably dump him on the spot, despite their ten-year business relationship. David was just so stuck. Writer's block had never been so . . . well . . . blocky.

8

About a month ago, when his drinking and writer's block had taken on new monstrous levels that he couldn't defeat, he'd gone for a stroll and found a flyer sponsored by *Life & Light* volunteers to visit the children at Parson Children's Hospital. He couldn't explain then or now why he'd felt so compelled to answer that call and become a volunteer, but he'd wondered if a change of scenery, some new experiences, and conversations with children who were generally honest and forthright might spark something within him—something that would compel him to write again and encourage him to quit drinking. His rendezvous with women certainly hadn't been working. He'd also started taking his Bible with him. And one child he connected with and visited frequently, liked when David read scriptures to him.

He was going to have to get something over to Jason, though. It wouldn't matter that he was a New York Times bestselling author if he didn't keep producing bestsellers. Authors were easily forgotten if they didn't continue to create, and currently, David had been incapable of producing anything.

"I'll get some pages to you soon, Jay. I'm just trying for an ending that really satisfies—a real tearjerker."

"I don't need Nicholas Sparks, David. I just need a romance novel —a good one at that! You have until the end of the month to get it to me."

"Jay, wait a minute." He pulled the phone away from his face and caught a glimpse of a pretty woman's high cheekbones driving by in a white Mercedes Benz coupe.

"You there?" Jason muttered, irritated.

"Uh, never mind. I saw something that may just inspire my next novel."

"Yeah. Be inspired."

"You got it. You'll have the entire thing by the end of the month." He was so getting dropped. There wasn't even a question. He ended the call and snatched his black Bible engraved with gold lettering from the back seat.

He walked to the double doors of the hospital with his finger stuck in between a scripture. He tapped the Bible nervously against his leg, fighting the urge for a drink. "God help me!" He pleaded with desperation under this breath. He stopped in his tracks and admitted, "The only thing that stops me from the drink is seeing Max." He popped a breath mint into his mouth, so Max couldn't smell the brandy on his breath and whoever Miss Smith had in mind of partnering him with today. "Don't know why she's gotta team me with someone . . . just not in the mood today."

He didn't have the slightest idea who the volunteer was or why she felt the need to make this suggestion. The last thing he wanted was to take his frustration out on a stranger. However, he couldn't turn her down. After all, she was like a mother to him and had been there during some of his darkest moments. He'd met her through a help wanted ad he'd stumbled across in a newspaper one day. She owned a woman's shelter. He'd showed up one morning to donate pillows and linens and ended up painting the dormitories. He'd also made lucrative financial contributions and continued to stop by frequently to volunteer. He eventually opened up to her about all the years that had passed, about not knowing his father up until a few weeks before his death.

His father had died of lung cancer due to smoking. David had also confided in her about his dysfunctional, now non-existent, relationship with his mother and his journey to becoming an international bestselling novelist. She found his story so compelling and inspiring that she'd invited him to lead Bible studies to pray and give motivational speeches to the shelter residents whenever his schedule permitted.

"Let's see who this person is," he sighed and headed straight to the front desk.

FINDING parking on Michigan Avenue NW was always a hassle but seeing Leyanie was worth it. Jennifer got out of her car and walked to the front desk to check in and get her visitor's badge. Before she could reach the receptionist, she saw a man standing there.

He's beautiful.

She had never called a man beautiful, but clearly she thought he was worth the compliment. He was a few inches taller than her—probably standing somewhere around five foot ten. His hair was thick and wavy, tapered at the sides of his ear. A full, thick beard gave Jennifer the impression that he was a man of nobility, scholarship, and astuteness.

He looks intelligent, too.

Jennifer didn't necessarily have a type, but his presentation solicited her attention. Something was intriguing about him. He seemed engaged in a passionate conversation with the receptionist. He talked with his hands. For some reason, he stopped mid-sentence and turned in Jennifer's direction. She felt the spirit of God instantly, slowly passing over her like an invigorating heatwave.

Lord, what's this? Why am I feeling this way?

Both of their mouths opened in shock and awe. Jennifer had never experienced this before. She didn't have time to dissect what was happening, but fear settled in swiftly. Instead of going to the front desk to check in, she took a quick left and fled to the restroom.

She paced nervously back and forth in front of the mirror.

Lord, what was that about? Are you trying to tell me something? She looked at her bun to see if it was still in place. *Maybe so, but this just freaked me out.* "Okay, I need to get myself together. I know Leyanie is waiting for me."

She walked back into the hallway, hoping that guy wouldn't be there, and he wasn't. *Whew!* That offered her some relief.

Jennifer entered the cold room and smiled at Leyanie's illuminated face. She rushed over, embraced her with a gentle hug, and lost all her resolve to remain strong, allowing a few tears to slip through innocently. Leyanie wrapped her skinny arms around her and patted her on the back.

"It's going to be okay," she said, trying to comfort Jennifer, which made her break down even more.

"I feel like giving up this vision, because this dream of mine isn't working out. I can't take any more rejection. It's too much for me,

Leyanie. I believe in God, but nothing's happening. My proposal was rejected because it's Christian-based, and they claimed it's not going to help single young women."

Jennifer started to open her mouth to say something about Kayla, but she couldn't muster up the courage. She feared the godly perception Leyanie had of her would change. She looked up to Jennifer like a role model and a woman who was living her life fully in Christ.

"I understand, Jennifer, but we can't give up. If I can fight this stinking cancer with hope and faith, you can fight your mountain with the same. I believe this is why I'm still alive."

"Oh, Leyanie." Jennifer hugged her tighter.

"Don't kill me," Leyanie pleaded, wheezing out a cough and a tiny giggle.

"I'm sorry," she replied, releasing her. "I've brought something for you." She got up and reached into her purse. She pulled out a white T-shirt with a bright yellow smiley face on it and flared it in the air. It instantly created a sparkle in Leyanie's sunken twelve-year-old eyes. She had just finished another round of chemotherapy. "I'm not done yet." Jennifer reached for a light brown teddy bear that held a heart. Stitched on the heart was "Jesus Loves You." She tucked it under the comforter next to her.

"Aw, a teddy, too." Leyanie coughed. "Thanks so much, Jen."

"You're welcome." She paused, staring at her for a few moments. She refrained from asking her how she felt when she saw the dark circles caked around her eyes like foundation. Part of the pact they'd made was to never welcome sorrow and sadness into the atmosphere. They believed by keeping the faith in Christ, healing was possible, and she'd done enough crying in front of Leyanie for one day.

Jennifer spotted a white piece of paper poking out of the cushion she was about to sit on. "What's this?" She pulled it out carefully.

Leyanie glanced at it and shrugged her shoulders. "I don't know," she commented, turning her head toward the door as it opened. A nurse came in abruptly. "Be back in a few, Jennifer . . . more tests."

"Okay," Jennifer said, nodding hello to the nurse. She gave Leyanie a supportive smile, knowing how much she hated the tests. She returned the smile with a brave one of her own and allowed the nurse to guide her out of the room. Jennifer sent a quick prayer to God, asking him to give her just a little more strength. She stared at the closed door, worrying about Leyanie until her attention returned to the envelope in her hand. Her eyebrows rose in surprise when she saw the recipient.

My Future Wife.

She bit her bottom lip, unsure as to whether or not she should open it but feeling more than a little intrigued.

I don't want to be nosy and read something private, but I need to know what this is. Maybe it's a written prayer that fell out of someone's notebook or pocket?

Before opening the envelope and slowly unfolding the letter, she swept her eyes across the room thinking someone else could see her. She shook her head, nearly laughing at herself and started to read the words.

To My Future Wife,

I pen this letter now instead of later because I want to thank God in advance for you. I already know you're going to be an amazing woman. You're going to be exactly what I prayed for. And by the time I meet you, I'm going to be everything you need me to be. So, whoever you are, wherever you are, here's an open letter I want to dedicate to you, for all to see. You are true testimony of my patience. If you gave up on love, may this letter serve as confirmation that with God, all things are possible. That it was possible to love again. I hope that your heart is open to receive these words.

Jennifer put the letter down for a moment and cupped her hands over her mouth. A tsunami of heartwarming thoughts flooded her mind.

I wonder if he specifically had someone in mind as he was writing this? This is too real. He can't possibly write these words out of empty space. "He's been hurt before." She pressed her hand against her heart and reopened it. *What if he was the guy at the front desk?* She started to kick herself.

I know that you're probably in another situation now. Maybe you're trying to work things out with the guy you're with. Maybe your heart is healing from a terrible breakup, a relationship you invested a great deal of your time and energy in. Perhaps there are some other personal issues going on in your life that are preventing you from walking into mine. Maybe we just haven't met yet. Whatever is going on in your life, there's no rush. God's timing is truly perfect. We'll grace each other's eyes and touch each other's hearts at the right time. We'll enjoy plenty of days, evenings, and nights together. We'll share memories such as waking up in the morning in bed to talk about why I took the covers away from you, engaging in candid conversation over breakfast at Holybelly Café in Paris, having water fights while I'm washing your car, feeding each other a "few" scoops of gelato pistachio ice cream after midnight, and blaming each other afterward for cheating on our diet in the morning, or checking out a live Christian music band at an intimate café. Or capturing special moments in a picture that we can relish when wrinkles form on our skin.

These are some simple yet memorable moments in life I want to share with you.

I want you to know that wherever you are in life, I'm praying for you to experience peace and wholeness. I want you to be complete and healed, full of joy before we meet each other. I'm going to look at you as a complement to my life—only to add to it, never to subtract, or divide from it.

You're not the only one who's being prepared for marriage. While I'm waiting on you, God is shaping me into the man he wants me to be for you: A protector and a provider, a great communicator, and a spiritual leader. He's molding me into a man who's transparent and vulnerable—vulnerable enough to accept you in my life without the reservation that comes from the fear of being hurt because I have experienced pain, too.

His endearing words blended into every intersection of her life. He spoke to her current healing process from a recent breakup with her ex-fiancé Robert, and how she wanted to be patient with the next guy who walked into her life. He tiptoed on the land of her longing to experience true love.

Her ex-fiancé, Robert, hadn't understood that expensive gifts and vacations could never awaken the love she wanted to receive from him and give in return. Sometimes it was the meaning behind the simple things that moved a woman and had a greater impact than luxurious living. She wanted a relationship that was transparent and held no secrets. A man that told the truth, even if it hurt. Dishonesty gave love a ceiling.

She wanted a relationship unhindered by pride and ego. Pride and ego worked like gravity. They pulled couples apart, killed the potential of love, and broke God-ordained covenants. He'd touched on her desire to build a life with a man founded on and centered on the Word of God. Robert couldn't be the spiritual leader she knew he was capable of being. He really had to want that for himself. She understood it wasn't a woman's position to mold a man into one but encourage and help water what God had already planted within him. However, if she was honest with herself, there were broken and missing pieces in her life, too. She wasn't the woman described in the thirty-first chapter in the book of Proverbs. She wasn't the virtuous wife she wanted to be just yet.

Jennifer blinked a tear onto the letter. "Wow! He's so invading my life." She forced a giggle through the raw emotions that surfaced at this moment. *Oh my gosh! I gotta fix this.*

She got up and went near Leyanie's bed to grab a tissue. She tried to pat the teardrop out, but it only made matters worse. The black ink bled into the sentence above, creating a blotch.

He's going to know I read it when I give it back to him . . . whoever he is. This is embarrassing. She fanned the letter in a panic, trying to dry the ink, but it wasn't working. The smudge of the ink could visibly be seen from the backside of the paper. *What am I going to do? It's ruined now. I guess I might as well finish reading it.* She crossed her legs, calmed herself and continued reading.

While I'm broken, God is preparing me for the very thing I long for the most: unconditional love, which is the way God loves us. He's building my trust in Him, so I can fully trust you, my love. My heart. My blessing.

I want to end this letter by saying I look forward to developing a wonderful friendship with you, a friendship that's based on open and honest communication, unyielding trust, respect, and adoration for each other. I want us to have a prayerful life because it's going to draw us closer together and open our eyes to see God in each other. Our intimate rela-

tionship with Him will prove to be enriching to our souls and to us as a whole.

I look forward to learning everything about you. I want to know the woman behind closed doors that no else sees. I want to know what's inside your heart because that's where your true treasure lies. I want to know what's in your spirit because that's where your true beauty lies. I want to know you inside and out before I propose to you. I want to find absolute security in you before I ask, "Will you?" and before you say, "I do."

Until we cross paths, don't rush love. We'll find each other soon. I know it. I can feel it. I want you to be my first and my last bride. I'll see you soon.

Love Always,

David Bradshaw

"This is truly a man after God's own heart. This was written beyond the surface. These words flowed from the Spirit."

Jennifer's head sank a little, powerfully overwhelmed by the presence of God. Just then, she heard two knocks at the door, and the nurse walked Leyanie back in tenderly. She felt slightly embarrassed, standing with one hand against her forehead and the letter in the other, along with a tissue.

"Jen, you okay?" Leyanie asked when the nurse left. "I could step back out," she offered with a grin.

I'm not okay. "No, you're fine. This letter." She fanned it in the air. "It's powerful. I wasn't ready for it." She laughed through her tears.

She'd never heard a man express himself in such a way. She thought those guys only existed in fictional romance, fairytale novels, or movies. Doubt set in, and the thought crossed her mind that the letter was pretentious—just bait used to pick up women.

"Letter? What letter?" Leyanie asked, puzzled.

Jennifer helped her back into bed, yanking the white comforter up to her neck.

"The one I found between the cushions of the chair. Some guy wrote an open letter to his future wife. It's dated back on December 11, 2008. Only a couple of months ago."

"Who?" Leyanie was now anxious to know. "And future wife? Uh-no. Maybe he broke up with somebody around that time?"

Jennifer did a double-take at the signed name on the letter. "David Bradshaw."

Why does that name sound familiar?

Leyanie pushed herself up in bed with her scrawny arms. "Now that I think of it, there's this guy who just started coming here. He visits Max. He's nice. He comes in to pray with me sometimes. His name is David. Don't know his last name, though."

"Maybe he deliberately left it in here? Sounds like he was writing this letter for someone special. Any woman longing to experience true love could appreciate this." She carefully tried to fold it back. "I gotta see if it belongs to him."

"Maybe it was meant for you to find . . . sure wasn't meant for me. I'm too old for him." Leyanie laughed her heart out until she started coughing.

Jennifer giggled back at Leyanie. "How often does he come to visit you?" She rubbed her girl's back.

"Quite often. Usually, like twice a month or something like that."

"Aw, that's so nice of him." Jennifer stuffed the letter into her purse. "Is he a priest or a chaplain?"

"Don't think so. He doesn't wear a robe or anything like that. That'd be cool if he were adorned as if he'd just left the Vatican."

"Silly." Jennifer chuckled, fighting through her concern for Leyanie. "Now that I think of it, I'm supposed to meet some volunteer through a different agency called Light & Life."

"Uh, what happened? The person didn't show up?"

Leyanie started to say something else when she heard the man's soothing and calming voice down the hallway.

"Come, Jennifer. I think that's him." Leyanie eased herself out of bed and tugged Jennifer by the hand, stealthily moving toward the door and peeping her brown, shaven head out. Jennifer followed behind her, appearing just as sneaky. "That's him," Leyanie whispered. "Get back, Jennifer; you're going to blow my cover."

"Your cover?" Jennifer snickered through her fingers, inching her head out into the hallway.

"That's him," Leyanie repeated again, causing the man to slowly look up.

Jennifer's eyes locked with his momentarily. His gaze marbled over her from head to toe. Neither waved nor spoke. Silence bound them at the moment.

"Say something," Leyanie murmured from inside the room.

I can't, she thought to herself, hiding behind a wall of fear. Eventually, he turned back to the nurse he'd been speaking to, and Jennifer stepped back into Leyanie's room.

"Oh my." She placed her hand over her chest. "Whoa! I feel something. That's the guy I saw earlier."

"Feel what?" Leyanie looked back at Jennifer, then peeked around the corner again. "And what guy you saw earlier?"

"This warm sensation in my chest," Jennifer murmured.

"Want me to call a nurse?" Leyanie teased. "Sounds like a stroke to me."

"No." Jennifer laughed loud enough for the man to hear them. She peeped her head back into the hallway and saw him raising his eyes in her direction, looking at her as if he thought she wanted to say something to him.

"Okay, but it's too late now, Jennifer. He saw us. You blew our cover!"

"What does that mean?" She jumped back, trying to smother her laugh by covering her mouth. She couldn't stop laughing.

"Why didn't you guys speak to each other? That was odd," commented Leyanie.

"Maybe he has a girlfriend? Perhaps there's something wrong or he had to use the bathroom? I don't know. But that's the same guy I saw at the front desk earlier when I was about to check in. I just felt God's presence when I noticed him. It kinda freaked me out."

"Did it cross your mind that he could be the volunteer you were supposed to meet? Hmm?" Leyanie said in a perky tone and looked up at Jennifer. "Do you know the volunteer's name?"

"Hmm. Didn't think about that, and no. I don't have a name . . . don't know if it's a guy or a woman."

"Let's go check on him." She pulled Jennifer by the hand into the hallway, but the man was nowhere in sight. This didn't seem to deter Leyanie. They tiptoed down the hallway and peeped into Max's room. Some of the nurses, social workers, and doctors they passed were laughing and shaking their heads. They were all too familiar with Leyanie's antics. Reaching the room, they spied the guy's brown hand against Max's forehead, praying for healing.

"Do you feel that? It's the presence of God." Jennifer got serious.

"Jennifer, it's like that when you pray with me, too. Him as well. You both have something special." She squeezed Jennifer's thin finger.

"Let's grab something to eat. I have to get running soon." Jennifer tugged Leyanie past Max's room. "And I need to get this letter back to him. Matter of fact, can you give it to him since he left it when he last visited you?"

"Uhhhh, no. You found it. You read it. Touched it last. Now you have to return it." Her big eyes twinkled with mirth when she laughed. "This is going to be good." Leyanie rubbed her hands together mischievously.

"The evil within you." Jennifer laughed.

Downstairs in the cafeteria, Leyanie sucked up the last bit of her apple juice. She liked to squeeze the green apple juice box and flex her muscles for Jennifer's approval. Jennifer did the same, pretending that Leyanie was stronger than she was.

"Oh. Stop faking it," she chided Jennifer. Not long after, Max and the guy walked in gingerly.

"Oh, Jennifer, there they go." Leyanie pointed her tiny finger at them with grape jelly clinging to the corner of her lip.

Jennifer bit into another celery stick layered with ranch dressing, watching Max and the guy walk over to order food. He waved to Leyanie and returned his attention to Max.

"Handsome, isn't he?" Leyanie's head bobbed up and down with her droopy eyes.

Jennifer chuckled, nearly spitting out her food. "I come here to make your day, but you always seem to make mine." She turned her attention back to David and noticed him looking at her. "Wait, he's pointing at us." Then he circled his finger around his lips and gave them a grin.

"What?" Jennifer mouthed, trying to decipher what he was drawing their attention to.

Jennifer asked Leyanie if the guy was okay. Leyanie didn't bother to answer the question. Instead, she targeted Jennifer's lips.

"You got salad dressing on your mouth." Leyanie pointed and poked fun at Jennifer.

Jennifer arched her eyebrow and wiped her mouth. "And you have jelly on yours. Look at all that jelly that missed your sandwich."

"Oh, yeah?" Leyanie reached into Jennifer's bag to get her compact mirror. "I do," she said, stretching her little tongue over to get it.

They both laughed, poking fun at each other.

"Oh my gosh. Embarrassing," Jennifer admitted, dying from amusement.

"I think you lost major cool points today." Leyanie handed Jennifer a napkin.

"Cut it." Jennifer waved to the guy and thanked him with a thumbs-up. "Someone getting turned off because you have something on your face would be silly. You know, Leyanie," she mentioned, turning serious again, "you're like medicine to my pain."

"Pain. I know you were down earlier about the proposal, but I sense there's something else bothering you. I can tell when you come to visit me. You know I can listen as well as you. Plus, you can trust me." She winked.

Jennifer gave Leyanie a side-hug. "I know I can, sweetie."

"I'm serious, Jen. I may be twelve, but I understand a lot. Would you like to talk about it?"

"That's so sweet, Leyanie." Jennifer held her hand. "You're going to make me cry in front of these people, but I'm fine. I have to get this letter to him." She pulled it out. "Be back."

Jennifer nervously walked over to the table where David and Max were eating. Although she appeared to be walking confidently with her head up, she was shaking inside.

I'm never this nervous.

"Excuse me," she barely managed to say.

The guy paused with a French fry halfway to his mouth and zeroed in on the letter. His eyes flicked to hers.

My God, this is so embarrassing.

"Are you David Bradshaw?"

He finished devouring the fry without using his hands.

Well, that's impressive, Jennifer thought to herself.

"I am." He wiped his hands off with a napkin and stood up confidently. His voice was deep, rich, and heavy.

His voice! I could give him my number now.

If she could imagine what the voice of God would sound like, this was it! He had an authoritative and commanding voice. His presence was also strong. It was surely intimidating to her, and it made her curl up inside in a fetal position.

She caught a whiff of his citrus cologne. It was smooth—not too strong or overbearing. She smiled immediately. She couldn't hide it either. It made the situation more embarrassing for her. She always kept her emotions together, but a man looking and smelling this good was a great combination for her. Add to that, he was a man of God —trifecta.

"I think you left this in Leyanie's room," she revealed nervously. As her hand slightly trembled, she handed the letter to him.

"I've been looking all over for this . . . thought I was losing my mind," he sighed in relief with a relaxed expression. He took it and opened it, rubbed down his beard and stared at Jennifer for a few seconds. His eyebrows scrunched together like an arduous detective. "Did you read it? All the ink on the page was intact the last time I saw it."

This is embarrassing. I feel so stupid.

The hairs on the back of Jennifer's neck rose, and she felt a flash of heat against her forehead. She looked to Leyanie, who was just laughing away at her.

She's no help. Lord, please get me out of this situation or give me the words to respond. When she saw his slow, teasing smile, her shoulders relaxed.

"I thought maybe you left a prayer for Leyanie. I soon discovered that wasn't the case. It's a very touching letter. I'm sure that special lady who gets to read it will be floored and honored."

"Thank you." He folded it back up. "Must've dropped it a few weeks ago in Leyanie's room. I was looking all over the place for it." He smacked it against his hand and shook his head.

"This must mean a lot to you." She couldn't help but want to hear an explanation behind the letter, as to when, why he'd written it, or if there was someone in mind. But he offered nothing other than a strained smile.

She couldn't fault him for his secrets. She also didn't mind knowing he kept it on him.

"Question." He put his chin in between his index finger and thumb. "Are you the volunteer that I was to team with today?"

"Not sure. I believe so."

"Uh, what happened?"

"I don't know," she answered in an unconvincingly innocent tone. "Just wasn't sure if it was you or not."

The presence of God stole over her again. This time it was more intense, nearly scaring the life out of her.

He gave her a knowing look. "Okay, umm. Right."

He knows I'm lying.

"Well, thanks again for returning this letter." He fanned it once more and turned back around.

"You're welcome." She quickly turned around and marched in another direction.

She rejoined Leyanie at the table and ate her last celery stick. She felt like the smallest person in the world. Leyanie didn't hold back on asking her how things had gone.

"I see the letter belongs to him. That's good. Did you get his number?"

"Get his number?" She almost choked. "No freakin' way. Besides, a man has to ask a woman for her number—not the other way around."

"You got a point." She shook her head as if she had a wealth of experience on the subject.

"I felt God's presence again when I was in front of him. I don't know if this is a good or bad thing, but it scares me a little. He's an attractive man and all, but . . ."

"Couldn't agree more, Jen," Leyanie confirmed in an ardent tone.

Jennifer nearly choked on her spit. It took a few seconds for her to gather herself together before she started laughing and blew more ranch dressing on herself.

"Maybe the Lord is telling you that you need to be open to His promptings, or perhaps He is trying to tell you David is the guy for you," Leyanie continued, giving her an assessing look. "When's the last time you've been out on a date?"

Jennifer put her hand down, trying to recall. "Hmmm."

"Right. It's been that long. You've been working hard, doing research—trying to get the proposal together."

"Yeah, you're right," she admitted. Feeling slightly uncomfortable with the topic, she decided it was time to take her leave. "Well, I have to get going now. I've got work to do, and you need to rest." She stood to her feet, taking her stuff and Leyanie's tray.

Jennifer emptied their trash and glanced over to where David and Max sat. She saw him talking to Max in a way that seemed fairly intense, but he happened to glance in Jennifer's direction right at that moment and smiled at her. She returned the same soft gesture, then reluctantly broke her gaze from his and left with Leyanie.

"I think he likes you." Leyanie playfully tugged Jennifer by the hand to the elevator.

"No, he thinks I'm a nosy letter reader," she laughed.

They both had a good chuckle over that, but Jennifer still couldn't get her mind off David Bradshaw as she walked Leyanie back to her hospital room.

David got back into his car, having an internal debate with God.

What the heck was that about? Never felt Your presence around a woman before.

You can't possibly be telling me that woman is my wife, right? I didn't even ask for her name. Besides, I just walked away from her earlier. She probably thinks something's wrong with me. I think I saw a wedding ring on her finger anyway.

"I'm stupid! This isn't a time to be pursuing anyone, anyway! I'm a borderline drunk, got a full-length novel to write in less than a month, and I'm still dealing with unresolved matters with my mom. What are you doing, God?"

He took the letter for his future wife out of his Bible. He tried reading it but couldn't stomach something so sentimental at that moment. *Had he written that?* The cold temperature in his heart didn't match the warmth channeled into the letter. He held it in the air and ripped it to shreds, shaking his head in utter disbelief. *She'd read this?* He peeled out of the parking garage and drove to Blue Café to grab a drink.

CHAPTER 2

A brisk draft wafted into the café, followed by a familiar face. David shivered as his slanted brown eyes refused to return to the article he'd been reading concerning some mystery novel titled *1994*. Apparently, his eyes preferred the beautiful female ushered in by the breeze. It was the woman from the hospital who had made his spiritual senses stand up and take notice. She was the exact woman who had read his sentimental letter and somehow found it touching.

Her five-foot seven-inch frame sashayed through the door as if a red carpet had been rolled out for her while photographers trampled on top of each other, snapping their best pictures to submit to the tabloids. His heart pummeled so hard against his chest it nearly busted through. He turned back around, dabbed his tongue against the roof of his parched mouth and took a gritty swallow. Shifting his weight from his left foot to the right, a warm churning sensation anchored deep within his soul, and peace infused his spirit. This was how he encountered the presence of God.

"I'm going to marry her," he involuntarily confessed, but not loud enough for anyone else to hear.

Why did I just say that? She's probably married or separated.

Nonetheless, it was the same feeling that had lodged deep within him when he'd first seen her in the hallway. Although that first time had led to the equivalent of a spiritual gut check to the stomach. God hadn't pulled any punches at the hospital. David scanned the café to see if anyone felt what he'd experienced, but life around him moved in slow motion as the sound of rattling blenders and a barista calling out to customers echoed like hollow background noise against the drumming of his rapid heartbeat. Everyone was engaged in conversation, enjoying their drinks and pastries. The veil had been removed from his eyes only.

"Next!" a barista called out.

David stepped to the counter. "Ah, yes. I'll have a . . . ah . . . medium chai tea latte, extra hot with . . ."

"Six pumps of chai, no water. I'll take his order from here," Monica casually interrupted. She was a barista familiar with David's regular appearances at the café. She tapped her co-worker on the shoulder. "I got it from here." She waited for the other kid to move out of the way before giving David a warm smile. "Dave, I know you all too well. Taking that newspaper, too?" Her freckled nostrils flared when she blew air through her nostrils.

He tossed the rolled-up *New York Times* on the counter. "Hadn't planned to. How's it going, Monica?" He glanced over his shoulder at the woman from the hospital. She was still there, closing in behind him in the line. He let out a shaky sigh at the overwhelming pull he felt just being near her, but not in a sexual way. He just wanted to know her. He didn't normally react to anyone like this.

He turned his direct attention to Monica, thinking back on how he'd met her. It was a pathetic attempt at avoiding his emotional turmoil concerning the compelling woman behind him. He and Monica had become acquainted outside Blue Café. Monica had been seated at one of the tables in the back. The brim of her hat had nearly covered her face, but David was able to see the tears streaming down her cheeks. He'd approached her determined to help if he could. They'd quickly developed a friendship after that. She'd opened up to him about her indifferent relationship with her mother and the breakup with her boyfriend at the time. The two had become close. They had something in common:

A toxic relationship with their mothers.

"It's going," she sighed in a dry voice.

"Things getting better at home?" He examined her closely.

Monica tended to tug down the brim of her hat and turn away when something bothered her.

"Nah. Not really." She shrugged like the situation with her mother meant nothing to her, but David knew better. Monica rarely let out her feelings, especially in public.

David knew what was up, but he didn't bother to push her. "Love your mother—no matter what." He hugged her.

The words rolled off his tongue, but not from his heart. Guilt collected over him like a mist of fog. It was easy for him to preach those words but tough for him to take his own advice. His relationship with his mother was just as torn as Monica's, and he hadn't done anything about it.

The last time he'd seen his mother was at the age of ten. They'd lived in the city of Alexandria, Virginia. He had no idea what happened to her. The only thing he could remember was being dropped off at a large brown house in Reston, Virginia, which he quickly discovered was an orphanage.

"Where did all these kids come from?" he asked one day.

Then one of the staff members confirmed, "This is home now."

He didn't know how to feel or react. He was torn between the rejection of his mother and the trauma of being abandoned and left with total strangers.

At night in his bed, he wrote stories, bringing characters to life on page, shaping them from his pain and confusion. David had found that some of the best artistic expressions came from the wounds of his soul and the revelation God had given him. Writing was cathartic for him on many days. It brought healing on some levels. However, as far as he was concerned, there was no need to look for his mother. He had no interest in searching for someone who didn't love him.

He gazed down uncomfortably and tried his best not to disclose his hurt and the disturbing distance between his advice and his actions.

"I'll try," Monica replied doubtfully.

"As long as you're trying." He snuck a peek over his shoulder, feeling distracted but incapable of focusing like he normally did. The woman was still on his radar.

Monica must have noticed him looking over his shoulder again. "You seem distracted, Dave. You okay?"

He leaned over the counter in an attempt to keep their conversation a bit more private.

"You see the woman over there with the sunglasses and pink hat?" he whispered and moved his head stiffly in her direction.

Monica tilted her head back to get a better look. "Yeah, I see her. What about her? She looks important with those huge designer glasses on. Your type," she stated teasingly. "Wait—" She paused. "Sure you wanna do this? She looks some kind of angry right now, and I see a ring on her finger, too. I don't know about this one, Dave," she whispered back uneasily.

He saw her eyes nearly roll out of her sockets. "Looks like she got an unexpected text or phone call. Maybe the guy responsible for the ring on her finger," mentioned David. "Maybe? I'm taking her tab anyway." He slid a twenty-dollar bill on the counter. "The rest is yours."

"Such a savage." She laughed, but her eyes widened when she saw the tip. "Thanks, Dave. I really needed this. Barely made it to work today. Low on gas." She tugged the navy-blue hat more firmly on her head.

"No problem. Remember, when you're walking in your purpose, God will always provide the means for you to fulfill it," David encouraged, speaking from experience. "He will send people your way to help you. Let me know if you need anything. I'm here for you."

"I will. Thanks, big bro."

"You got it." He winked.

Walking over to the counter that held the milk, sugar, and napkins, he fiddled with the stirrers. He kept his attention on the woman out of the corner of his eye. Unfortunately, he was so distracted by the sweet dimple in her cheek and her mesmerizing smile that he managed to knock over two canisters of milk. It splashed over the counter and floor.

The café grew quiet. Inside, he cringed. He could feel every eye in the room lock on to him like a group of submarines bearing heat-seeking missiles. David slowly turned around, noticing a few customers laughing into their hands. One elderly man's dentures flew out of his mouth from the force of his laughter. The elderly woman sitting with him stuffed them right back in, which might have earned her a wide grin from David if he hadn't felt like such an idiot. His ears grew steaming hot, and his cool, calm, suave persona disassembled in seconds.

He quickly tried to snatch more napkins, but they were jammed in the dispenser. Wrestling with the box for a few seconds, he thought he might be able to clean up this mess until his jerky movements caused the napkins to explode from the holder, showering the nearest patrons in the process.

What's wrong with me? I'm losing it. I'm David Bradshaw. What's that supposed to mean anyway?

"Get it together," he admonished himself under his breath. Wiping up the milk from the counter, he heard the woman place her order just next to him. He paused for a moment to eavesdrop, hoping to hear the lilting tone of her voice.

"Miss, your beverage has been taken care of," Monica advised her, biting down on her bottom lip to erase her smile.

David surreptitiously watched the young lady remove her black sunglasses and teethe the tip of the frame. She eyed Monica inquisitively.

"What? My drink is paid for?" She looked around, confused.

Monica nodded in David's direction. Since he hadn't tried to be sneaky about eavesdropping, he didn't miss her guarded glare or the beautiful flush that suffused her cheeks. She gave him a vampish stare for a moment and put her sunglasses back on casually.

David's head bowed like a defeated king who'd been expecting a triumphant day on the battlefield. He refocused on his cleaning chore, but the speed of his hand slowed. He dropped the balled-up napkins and shook his head, unsure why his attempt at charming her had no effect. He wasn't full of himself, but he'd never really had a problem catching a woman's attention and keeping it.

While cleaning up the milk, he heard a cup hit the counter next to his hand.

"Umm, is everything okay over here?" she asked.

David's eyes trailed up to a pair of dark, blue denim jeans. He tried to remain composed but erupted into nervous laughter. "Yes. I—I um —I kind of spilled some milk here." He stuttered, not daring to make direct eye contact with her.

"Kind of?" She grabbed napkins. "Uhhh, looks like you actually did." She corrected teasingly, raising her eyes. "Let me help." She leaned closer to him to wipe up the last bit of milk off the counter.

Her aromatic scent was like a breeze sweeping off the face of white and pink blossoms of the Southern Mongolia tropical forest. Her solitary round diamond earrings were positioned perfectly in her small earlobes, giving him the impression that she was a woman of refined taste.

"There. All gone. Thanks for the drink, Mr. Bradshaw." It seemed to David that she bit that one out reluctantly.

"You're quite welcome, and thanks for your help." He drifted back into reality. "And you are?" He wiped his hand with a napkin and extended it.

"The woman you didn't bother introducing yourself to at the hospital, although I did read your letter." She smiled and winked at him, grabbing a few napkins before her thin smile vanished as quickly as she did.

She left him hanging, so he had to give himself a handshake.

How stupid of me. You screwed up this time!

If he were shooting his shot, he'd definitely air-balled it. He felt like an idiot at that moment. The real reason he hadn't asked for her name at the hospital was because of the inner conflict he'd battled. His loss of faith in love and his confidence contended with the tugging from God. Although he felt the presence of the Lord when he was next to her, he still worried that he'd set himself up for failure and he figured she was totally out of his league. He'd dated super attractive women before, but there was something unique, distinctive, and special about her. He knew he had to persevere!

Well, she hadn't vanished. She'd just hightailed it away from him like he was carrying a contagious disease.

David leaned back against the counter, feeling completely floored. Confusion rearranged the muscles in his face. He watched her take a seat and pull out a book from her bag. She sipped her drink and began reading as if no one in the room existed, including him.

"I can't believe this just happened to me," he mumbled through his fingers awestruck.

I got curved.

For once, he felt as if he'd no control over the situation. He hadn't been mistaken about his feelings or his promptings, but he'd clearly messed up by not listening to that voice earlier this morning.

For a few minutes, he drank his chai tea at the counter. He tried to make eye contact with her whenever she looked up from reading, but she deftly avoided his gaze. He wasn't on her radar, and he wasn't quite sure how to salvage the situation. At one point, her attention was drawn to a man with a little girl sitting in his lap. The child struggled to hold the large cup with her small, reddish hands. The man wiped whipped cream off her nose and inched the blue straw closer to her tiny, pink lips. David saw the woman's face brighten, apparently touched by this bonding moment between what he assumed to be a father and daughter. In a flash, the blissful expression on her face vanished behind a screen of sadness, and she returned to reading.

That was interesting. David noticed the downcast expression on her face. *Maybe this isn't a good time to talk to her?*

And just who was he trying to convince here: himself or God? He considered walking out the door and just letting things happen naturally. He initially felt there was no need to put himself out there again, but as soon as the thought surfaced, it was immediately stamped out by a feeling so intense, he took a step toward her before realizing what he was doing. God was truly ordering his steps! He pondered the brief despondency he'd seen on her face and how she'd left him abruptly at the counter. Whether he was a regular at Blue Café or not, he didn't want to embarrass himself further by getting rejected point-blank again. At the same time, the Spirit was letting him know he couldn't risk losing another opportunity to get her phone number. This was his moment to capitalize on a second chance; it was a precious opportunity he probably wouldn't get again. He fixed the sleeve on his cup and thrust his chest out. Holding his chin high, he boldly made his way over to her. Moving closer to her table, he caught the specific title of the book she was reading.

"Jealousy as cruel as the grave. Its flames are flames of fire. A most vehement flame." He quoted a verse from the chapter she was reading in *Song of Solomon*. He rested his hand on the back of the chair next to her, giving her a confident grin. He knew he'd get her attention now. He waited to see if she'd respond or look up. Nothing happened. She continued reading. His legs grew heavy. The palms of his hands became clammier by the second.

She's a tough one. At least I was impressed! Awkwardness handed David's confidence a pink slip, but he refused to accept termination.

"May I join you?" he asked assertively.

With her eyes still on her Bible, she answered snarky, "If you don't spill whatever you're drinking all over me."

"Good one." He laughed halfheartedly. He was greatly relieved she hadn't sent him packing. He sat down across from her, and she finally looked up at him. He could see his reflection on her sunglasses. It prevented him from directly connecting with her, but he managed to say, "What are you studying?"

"Song of Solomon. The way King Solomon describes his love for God is impeccable." Her tone was colorless in a way to deter conversation. She crossed her legs, put her elbow on the table, one finger below her chin, and the other finger at the side of her face. "You're very calculated, Mr. Bradshaw," she said pensively. "A thinker. A strategist."

He quirked an eyebrow, a guttural laugh erupting from his belly.

He sure wasn't expecting her to say that. "What do you mean?" he asked, totally caught off guard, trying to buy time to gather himself.

"At the hospital, I noticed you pull down on your beard when something was on your mind. Your eyes squint a little, too. And at the counter, I saw them shifting left to right, which let me know you were plotting a way to have a conversation with me." She smiled a bit, which softened her analysis.

He'd never felt so exposed and vulnerable. The only thing he could do was laugh.

While she continued to talk, he couldn't hold back a grin that was followed by more laughter. He just didn't know what to say. He'd usually have a response to fire back in a situation like this. His wit had clearly jumped off the highest building and fallen to its end.

"Through your interactions with Monica, I can tell you're like a mentor to her, very much like you are to Max. It takes a certain level of sensitivity and discernment, as portrayed in your open letter to your future wife, to empathize, mentor, and play a positive role in someone's life. Quite caring." She ended her psychoanalysis of him with a quirky smile.

"Well, umm." He crossed his arms and tilted his head up astutely. *I feel naked.* He was thrown off guard and rather at a loss for words. "A psychologist?"

"Nope!" Her lips widened after the snarky remark. "A missionary and director of a Christian non-profit."

Her smile brought some relief. "You know, I'd love to see those beautiful eyes of yours while I'm talking to you. It would also be great to know your name as well." He folded his hands on the table. It was either that or leave them shaking in his lap.

"I'm sorry. Kind of rude of me, I guess. I'm in the habit of wearing them all the time." She removed her sunglasses. "My name is Jennifer. Jennifer Washington." She gave him a warm enough smile, but he noticed the tension lines around her mouth. This time, she extended her hand without hesitation.

The touch of her hand gliding carefully into his weakened him. "Your eyes are amazing." He tried to hold it firmly.

Her honeycomb brown, seraphic eyes were captivating. When he'd spotted her at the hospital, she'd looked beautiful, but that was from a distance. Up close, she was stunning. Her beauty was sublime and perfectly tailored to his preferences.

"Thank you." She blushed under his penetrating gaze. "That's a very firm grip you have there." She looked down at his hand.

"Oh, my bad." He slowly released his grasp. "You're welcome." His heart nearly jumped to his throat when he rubbed against the large ring. Was God trying to play a funny trick on him? "You're married?" he practically blurted out. He studied the princess cut diamond on her ring finger, feeling a bit sick to his stomach at the sight of it.

"No. I'm not married." Her eyes shot to her finger, and she let out an amused laugh.

Whew. He was able to breathe again normally.

"This ring represents the Bride Christ is coming back for. I want to live my life holy, separated and pleasing in God's sight. I also want to be the bride He's preparing for my husband, which is a Proverbs 31 woman."

"Whoa! Deep and yeah, you're not married," he expressed, quite relieved again. He leaned against his seat and cracked a smile he couldn't hold back. Hearing those words was like cold water from a deep well. He'd longed to hear a woman utter such devotion to God. "Spiritually profound and biblically sound. Hmm," he grunted out, approving. "That's really good."

"I'd have to agree." She tapped him on the hand, becoming just as animated as him. "Tooting my own horn, huh?"

"You're pretty much accurate," he chuckled, entertaining her humor. "Must be keeping a low profile with the sunglasses. I'm sure men are chasing after you everywhere." He cocked his head sideways, waiting for her response.

The comment took her slightly off guard. "Not at all." She enunciated each word slowly. "So, what really brought you to my table?"

David shuffled his feet back and forth under the table. It reflected a nervous tick he'd developed over the years.

It was the number one question every woman wanted to know

after a guy went out of his way to express interest in her. Nonetheless, he spoke from the heart: "I hope this doesn't scare you."

"Go for it." She slightly tilted her head to the side, ready to listen with every wakening part of her.

David circled his cup on the table for a few seconds, and stopped. He looked at her and drew his eyes back to the cup. He wasn't sure how she'd respond. He understood everyone in the body of Christ responded differently to spiritual things concerning God, depending on where they were at in their relationship with Christ, but he wasn't ashamed of what he'd experienced. If he wanted confirmation of what he felt God leading him to do, he had to act on these promptings. It was up to him to initiate this conversation.

"When I saw you at the hospital, I felt something stirring within me. It was really hard to ignore."

She leaned forward in her seat. "What did you feel?"

David gazed around the café, wondering if this was the right time and place to share this. He made eye contact with Monica. She was grinning delightedly, kind of like a little sister proud of her big brother who had accomplished some great feat.

"This urge to go talk to you," he continued. "God's presence at my back urging me forward. It's hard for people to get out of their way, get past certain fears and do things they wouldn't normally do, ya know? God must get pretty frustrated sometimes when He's doing the nudging and prompting and we're digging our heels in doubting and second-guessing. That's why I didn't approach you then. I admit, I was extremely nervous."

She lifted a brow and gave him a soft smile. "You? Nervous?" She paused. "A handsome guy like you apprehensive to approach women? No way. Not buying it." She sipped her drink and looked away for a few seconds.

He let out a low chuckle, a bit relieved, circling the cup against the table again. "Thanks for the compliment, but I'm just a guy, and most guys are afraid of rejection. That's the plain truth." He returned his attention to her. "I let my fear get the best of me once, but when you walked into the café, it was like God's Spirit was speaking right in my ear. If the Holy Spirit owned a sledgehammer, He'd have been pounding that prompting right through my thick cranium."

Jennifer's laughter was sweet and soft, gliding across David's skin like a warm, familiar blanket. "That's really cute. And just what did the Spirit have to say?"

"That it was my solemn duty to strike up a conversation with you."

Jennifer's eyes locked on to his meticulously. Her mouth opened to comment, but no words followed. She uncrossed her legs and crossed them again.

"Are you okay?" David asked. "Maybe I shouldn't have shared this with you."

"No. I'm fine. I just—" She paused. "It's just that no man has ever said that to me before." She seemed to hesitate for a moment before asking her next question. "Can I share something with you, too?"

"Go for it." David leaned back and folded his arms.

"I felt God's presence when I saw you at the front desk. I don't want to use the word weird. It wasn't weird. I'd have to say different." She looked away, appearing to be reflecting on that moment. "What do you think it means?"

He didn't want to jump out and say God was playing matchmaker. If so, guess you could *call that a divine line.* "One thing we know for sure is God stirred both of us when we saw each other. We'll just leave it at that. I'd say it was special."

They studied each other for a few moments, both doing their best to hide their blushes, yet comfortable in the companionable silence that had suddenly descended.

"Fair enough. Are you a minister, preacher, or chaplin?" she asked him, finally breaking the silence. "Leyanie said you visit Max quite a bit, praying with him and giving him comfort. How'd you come to know Max?"

"Just an author who loves God. Anyhow, it was on my heart for the longest time to visit children who are sick or terminally ill. I couldn't ignore the feeling any longer. I signed up to volunteer—even met with some of the kids' parents so they'd know who I am. They all thought it was a good idea. Some parents benefited from my visitations, too. In a lot of ways, they've been comforted and counseled by the presence of God."

"Wow," Jennifer sighed. "That's powerful. And David, that's very sweet and caring of you. I mean, it's not every day that people volunteer their time for someone with their busy business schedules."

"You got a point, but you know the saying: We make time for the things that are important to us."

"Tell me about Max. How'd you meet him?"

"One day, I walked by Max's room after visiting another patient. I saw him standing next to a nurse who I was acquainted with at the time. What caught my attention wasn't the IV in his arm; instead, it was the song he was singing."

"What song?" She scooted her chair closer to the table.

"I can't remember. I'm sorry. It wasn't something you've probably heard on the radio. The words were original. More than likely given by the Holy Spirit."

"Whew." She narrowed her lips together and blew air out. "I felt that. I've experienced it before in my own time of worship."

"Ha! You get it." He laughed.

"Right. Continue on." She tapped him on the hand.

"Then the nurse called me in and introduced me to him. When he looked up at me and asked for prayer, although I was tired and ready to head home, I couldn't refuse, so I prayed for him. Afterward, he asked if I could be his big brother because he didn't have one."

She covered her mouth in awe. She appeared deeply touched by his acts of kindness and the whole experience. "See, I was right. You're a caring person."

"It's the way the Lord made me. I've been visiting him for three years now. It's really funny how I never ran into you." His head cocked slightly sideways.

"That is odd," she expressed, deep in thought. "I was around when you started coming here. Leyanie never mentioned you. Maybe it wasn't the time to cross paths?" She shrugged one of her shoulders.

"Maybe it wasn't the right time for God to open our eyes to see each other. What about you?" David gestured his head toward her. "How'd you find Leyanie?"

Jennifer picked her cup up to take a sip but put it back down contemplatively. Her eyes shifted slowly to the little girl she'd been observing earlier, and David's attention joined her. He saw the man at the table balancing a book in one hand with the girl seated in his lap. David turned back to Jennifer. Sadness and yearning had settled in her eyes while beholding this bonding moment.

"I'm sorry, David." Jennifer drifted back into the moment. "It's kinda a long story how I met Leyanie; but as you can see, we became really good friends, and eventually I adopted her. I became her family."

"Wow! Adoption? That's a huge step, and a great act of love." Her story touched him deeply. She offered David a smile that made his heart ache just a little.

"Anyhow, you said you're an author. What have you written?" she inquired.

David didn't miss how she deftly steered the conversation away from herself. He knew there was more to the story than what she was giving. He assumed that however they met, it was too soon and too personal for her to open up about it.

"*The Simplicity of Intimacy, A Son Before His Time,* and *The Breakfast Field*," David answered.

"Those titles sound interesting. Can I find them in, let's say, Book World?" she asked.

"You certainly can," he said with pride and confidence. "They're written under my name, David Bradshaw."

"I'll have to check out those books. I could use a new read. Well, David Bradshaw, thank you for the drink, the company, and the conversation. I really appreciate it." She grabbed her book and stashed it in her bag. "Unfortunately, I need to get going. I've got a few errands to run."

He was a little disappointed to see her go, but considering the way their initial interactions had started, what they had just shared was a pretty promising start. "You're welcome. I appreciate your company, too." He got up and slowly pushed the chair in before summoning up the nerve to ask for her number. "I'd like to keep in touch with you." He stuck his hand into his pocket and pinched the edge of his cell phone.

"David, I'm going to be very forward with you." Her eyes became pensive and all the excitement in her voice evaporated.

There was enough fear emanating in the air to suck the life out of his heart. Why did it feel like she was about to break up with him . . . after they'd known each other for ten minutes?

I'm so seriously whipped right now.

Compelled to say something before all the saliva withdrew from his tongue, he interjected, "Okay." He silently sucked in a breath of air, waiting for her to speak again.

Here comes the rejection.

"Look, I'm sure you're a good person and a God-fearing man," she articulated in a gentle and kind tone. "And although I felt God's presence when I saw you, I don't feel *led* by Him to give you my number. This doesn't discredit what you shared with me about God prompting you to speak to me. Right now, I'm not looking for a boyfriend."

Yep. Rejection.

David tried to say something, but she rushed to speak first, probably seeing that he was gearing up to plead his case. "I think you're a nice guy, and I think it's admirable that you volunteer your time with Leyanie and Max, but . . ."

"Nice guy," David repeated under his breath before she could continue. He glanced down at the table in disappointment, feeling baffled by this change in her behavior. He'd heard this endearing term used on other guys before, but never toward him. He knew "nice guy" was the way a woman quietly and gently escorted a man completely out of the picture. Or worse, into no man's land: the friend zone!

She looked a bit pained as she continued to explain herself, which only made the situation worse.

"This is why I didn't want you to buy my drink. I just . . . it's the timing, you know?" she said with sadness in her eyes.

Yeah, timing.

He was more confused than conflicted. He knew God had led him to her, but what she was saying didn't confirm that. He locked aim on his next counterstatement.

"And I'm not looking for a girlfriend. I'm down with a friendship, though. Any chance we can be volunteer buddies at the hospital together? It's what we're supposed to be doing either way."

He was trying to grapple or latch on to something that would keep him in the picture, that would provide the opportunity to get to know her, but the look she gave him was filled with hopelessness so deep, it tore at his insides. She was hurting for some reason. In his gut, he just knew because it was something he could identify with totally:

Broken.

The hopelessness was soon replaced with a lifeless expression capable of sucking the hope out of any guy wanting a shot with her.

And maybe that was the front she wanted to portray?

Any other day of his life, he could have handled this kind of rejection, but not when it was preceded by a prompting so profound David felt incapable of walking away. His hand slowly loosened from his cell phone. He felt unsteady, as if he were suffering from seasickness, but he wanted to keep trying anyway. He had nothing to lose at this point. His pride and ego had already taken a hit when he summoned the courage to go over and talk to her.

"Look, David—"

"What are you drinking?" he gestured his head, nodding toward her coffee cup.

She blinked in confusion, thrown off by the change in subject. "Uh, just a skim latte. Why?" Her eyes penetrated him.

"I'll keep that in mind." He winked and gave her a gracious smile. "Just in case we happen to meet up for coffee one day. Friends buy friends coffee, right?" He shrugged his shoulders like it was no big deal.

She smirked. "And what are *you* drinking? Looks like there's a prescription written on the side of your cup or a mathematical equation of some sort." She turned her head, squinting her eyes, pretending to read the specifics on the side of his cup. "Either could work."

Hearing no inflection in her voice, he laughed harder, holding his cup high in the air, noting its specifications that had been scribbled with a black marker by Monica. He loved a woman that made him laugh. Dry humor was up his alley. "It does look like that, now that you mention it. It's a chai tea latte with six pumps of chai, extra hot, and no water."

"Cute." She let out a chuckle, looking at him a bit wistfully before her demeanor changed.

He could tell the exact moment she realized she was having fun with him. There was some hope to think she must like him a little but was fighting it . . . a lot.

"That's very specific."

"I'm just a man who knows what he wants." He winked, placing his hands on the back of his chair, preparing to head toward the exit.

Now she gotta respond to that.

She gave a half-smile. "Well, it was good chatting with you. Take care." She waved bye to him.

I died twice.

In his mind's eye, he could see himself marching off a cliff and his spirit drifting off toward anywhere but heaven. He watched her walk away, feeling torn. He couldn't believe how sideways everything had gone. Besides feeling helpless, his hopes of getting Jennifer's number had been shot down, dead in the road.

Maybe she has a special friend on the side? Maybe she's in a serious relationship or just getting out of one? Oh, that Bride of Christ ring. Right!

His thoughts ate away at him, but he quickly brushed the "maybes" off and embraced the possibility of seeing her again.

Life is all about timing.

～

THAT AFTERNOON, David lay motionless, half-asleep on the sofa, swathed in a navy throw that only reached to the knees of his sturdy frame. He stared at floating dust particles made visible by the back-light of the Apple symbol on his laptop. The possibility of Jennifer being "the one" kept him awake, including memories of her smile, eyes, and shiny black hair, along with her witty sense of humor. He couldn't stop replaying his meeting with her over and over in his mind—her coming to his rescue when he spilled all that milk, and their conversation at the table.

"Man, what the heck has gotten into me?" He was amused that he'd failed to keep his composure in her presence. "I've never been out of my comfort zone like that before."

When he sat up, a beam of sunlight pierced through the opening of the maroon oriental embroidered curtains and illuminated the edge of a picture that was face-down on the bookshelf. His body tensed, and thoughts of his mother shoved aside the pleasant images of Jennifer in his mind. He closed his eyes and remembered a time when he was five years old.

He'd crawled to the side of the sofa when he heard the pealing sound of The Guiding Light theme music. His favorite cartoon He-Man had been up next.

That day, he'd made a bold move. The mean face of his mother had never been inviting, but he'd slowly maneuvered his way onto the sofa. She hadn't looked in his direction or acknowledged his presence. He figured it was okay and leaned his head against her shoulder.

"You can't do that!" his mother snapped and pushed his head off her shoulder. "Seeing your face is like looking at your father. He disgusts me!"

He'd let himself back down onto the floor and hid at the side of the sofa for a few seconds. He'd peeked his head back out, hoping she'd give him an explanation for the push and the comment about his father. He thought, who is this man she's referring to? He'd seen many male faces around his mother from time to time, but none of them resembled him. He waited around a little longer, thinking maybe she would follow up with an apology, with a tender look that would diffuse the confusion and hurt he felt. Instead, she'd ignored him. His heart had shriveled like a plant deprived of water and sunlight. That day, abandonment, confusion, and rejection started to build a home within David.

Constant rejection over an extended time had pushed him into a corner of ruthless insecurity, shattering his perceptions of a mother's love for her son.

"I think Jennifer rejected me like my mom," he expressed, feeling even more discouraged as more painful memories reared their ugly heads, but two knocks at the door interrupted his dark moment. He blinked to dislodge the sleepiness in his eyes before grudgingly rising to his feet. "Who is it?" he asked, annoyed. He wasn't expecting company at this time of day.

"Kelsey," his friend greeted, knocking more obnoxiously.

"Coming," David yelled, hearing him cough.

He opened the door, and Kelsey barreled past him into his spacious living room. He tossed his brown newsboy hat on the coatrack and slung his gray cardigan sweater around the shoulders of the rocking chair David had bought for him. The way he was looking, he could have passed for a detective. The only thing he lacked was a pipe. He stepped over shoes, books, notepads, and loose-leaf papers.

"It's so dark in here." He coughed into a white handkerchief. "Writer turns vampire again, huh?" He went over to the bay window and drew back the heavy curtains. The sun met half of his face, illuminating eyes that were like blue oceans that had seen a million voyages. While he wasn't able to stand fully straight due to recent back surgery, he could still look over David's head. He stood about six foot three.

Two years ago, Kelsey had spotted David at Upscale—a local lounge in Arlington, Virginia. Kelsey was a bartender there. They'd struck up a conversation, finding a kindred spirit in each other. David had recognized the sense of loss, grief, and pain deeply etched in Kelsey's eyes. Without much prompting, David had opened up to him about his dysfunctional relationship with his mother and the absence of his father. At the time, David didn't know who his father was or why he wasn't around.

He just remembered his mother screaming at him when he was five, "You don't have a father!"

In return, David discovered that Kelsey had lost his son in a car accident and his wife to breast cancer. Their mutual pain had drawn them closer together. Eventually, Kelsey became a father figure to David, and David became like a son.

Before he could respond to Kelsey's sarcastic comment, his phone rang a few times until the answering machine clicked on. A sultry voice serenaded the room, like the kind you'd expect to hear on a late-night phone-sex infomercial.

"David, this is Nina...had such a great time with you last weekend, baby. Let's do it again sometime. Call me." She ended the message with a steamy kiss.

Nina was a woman he hooked up with from time to time.

David saw Kelsey's nostrils flare with anger. He shook his head as the blood beneath his face flooded the penciled lines of his ivory skin. "It's only been three months since ya broke up with Maria. Give yourself some time, man. You need to heal. Sheesh."

David's head sank low. "I am. When I broke up with Maria in December, I wrote an open letter to my future wife." He perked up. "It helped me move on. I know I deserve better."

Kelsey rubbed his eyebrows and raised his index finger. "One, you haven't moved on. Two," he asserted, lifting the next finger, "you deserving better is not so much the issue here. Three, you need to take love out of the equation and place your attention solely on Christ. Healing isn't just about overcoming emotional pain. It's about avoiding those choices that are contrary to God's will—choices that'll bring you even more pain. With the path you've been heading down lately, I doubt this Nina woman is interested in a Christ-centered lifestyle."

He couldn't argue that.

David couldn't help but laugh at Kelsey's overprotective parenting approach, even though he wasn't a teenager anymore. "Kelsey, trust me," David pleaded, spreading his fingers wide, pushing away at the air, shrugging off his wise advice. "I'm going to focus more on that. I promise you."

"Yeah," Kelsey muttered, unconvinced, waving him off with his handkerchief as he mumbled something under his breath.

David plopped on the sofa, kicked his feet up on the coffee table, and relaxed with both hands behind his head. He smiled wanly and fixed his eyes at this erstwhile Sherlock Holmes inspecting his living room for some unusual activity. Kelsey always did this when he suspected David was going through another low period. Neglecting his living space was one sign. The other was alcohol.

"Ah-ha!" Kelsey grunted, narrowing his eyes. He pointed at an empty wineglass with dried specs of red wine at the bottom. A half-empty wine bottle hid underneath the table.

"Find something, Detective Hobbs?" David yawned, preparing for the question he knew was coming.

"Hobbs? Funny. Find your mother yet?" Kelsey nearly hacked up a lung, crushing his handkerchief against his mouth.

"What?" He pretended to not hear him.

"Did you find your mother?" he asked, but this time sterner.

"Are you gonna walk away from me like my father if I don't? And why would I wanna find someone who abandoned me at some lady house who then left me at an orphanage? Why would I wanna go look for her?" he yelled, becoming so enraged at the very thought he swore he popped a few veins in his neck.

Kelsey gritted his teeth and looked away with complete disdain.

David got up and turned the framed picture face up on the book-shelf. He blew the dust off and studied his mother's face for a moment. "I'm working on it," he sighed, calming down. He pushed the picture to the far back and grabbed the photo of his father resting at the front. "I'll find her. I miss my dad, though." He heard Kelsey smother another cough into his handkerchief. "Quit smoking yet?" He turned toward Kelsey for a second.

"Don't you go getting on me now just because I'm asking about your mother." He barked. "I'm gonna quit smoking soon. Don't worry about me." He wagged his finger at him.

David walked over to Kelsey, clenching his jaws. The anger and tension shrank the space between them. David balled his hands into fists. Kelsey stood firm with his gray hairy forearms folded. He stared David down like a toddler until David's anger dissipated. Kelsey's arms dropped to his sides and his frown lines lessened for a moment.

David carefully placed the picture of his father back on the bookshelf.

"I just don't want you to end up like my dad—that's all I'm saying," David reiterated.

"And I don't want you to have any regrets like I did," Kelsey kept on him. "Man." He let out a heavy sigh. "I wish Nick had never got into that car . . . that was the last time I saw 'em. I don't have another opportunity to patch things up like you do." His voice cracked as he hacked again. "I miss my son, David." He covered his eyes with one hand and put the other on his shoulder.

"I'll work on my relationship with Jesus and get in touch with my mother before it's too late, I promise." He hugged Kelsey at the waist.

"Okay, Dave. Okay. I'll back off." Kelsey put his hands up in submission and stepped away. "You've a right to feel every measure of anger that you have towards her, but I also know God wants us to forgive—no matter how hard it is. Forgiveness frees us from the hurt caused by another and the animosity we have toward them."

"But I'm not ready to yet."

Kelsey sighed in grief. "Matthew 6:15 says, 'But if you do not forgive others their sins, your Father will not forgive your sin.' David, I believe forgiveness is blocking all the things God wants you to experience. I've been there, young fella."

David shadowed his face with his hand. He tried his best to hold back his tears, but the driving ache in his soul wouldn't let him. Although it had been nearly a decade, the wounds were still fresh and ripe.

"Dave, in God's timing. And I'm gonna quit smoking."

"I appreciate the hard truth and support."

"That's the only way I could love you, man."

"Good." David let out a chuckle. He returned to the sofa, waiting for Kelsey to take a seat in the rocking chair. "I met someone new today. A woman Miss Smith partnered me with at the hospital."

"How's she doing anyway?" There was a glimmer in his eye.

"Kelsey," David called.

"Yeah?"

"Do you have a thing for Miss Smith or something?" David watched for his response closely.

"Oh, no way, man. Come on now, Dave. Go on with your story."

"Right." David laughed for a moment before continuing. "I met someone special. I felt God's presence when I saw her. I never experienced that with anyone."

"Oh boy. What's her name?" Kelsey rolled his eyes.

"Jennifer Washington," David said, cracking up at the hard time she'd given him. He could hardly get her name out without feeling embarrassed about the way things had ended.

"What makes her more special than the woman I just heard on your answering machine? Hmm?" Kelsey laughed heartily and theatrically plopped his hands across his belly, whistling a faint tune, waiting to see what excuse he was going to paint with his storytelling skills.

David decided to tell him everything, even the embarrassing stuff. Kelsey howled with laughter here and there as he recounted Jennifer's sassy responses. He tried his best to tell him all about what he'd experienced at the hospital with Max and later at the café.

"I think I know whatcha talking about." Kelsey simmered down. "I can relate. I had the same feeling when I met Martha. Miss that woman." He mashed his hand over his face. "Haven't experienced that feeling since."

"Maybe you will again someday?" David went to the refrigerator to grab a bottle of water and offered him something to drink.

"I'm fine, but yeah, someday," Kelsey replied wistfully. "These old limbs are past their prime. Ain't no woman gonna want me." He stretched his legs out and groaned as they cracked and popped.

"Don't say that." David gave him a warm smile. "Be optimistic. Miss Smith is single." He nodded with a sinister grin. "Besides, isn't that what you're trying to get me to do?"

Kelsey ran a hand down his tired face. "Not fair to turn those life lessons back on your elders. This is a do-as-I-say-not-as-I-do situation."

David's eyes shifted tirelessly from left to right, knowing he'd never convince Kelsey to ask a woman out on a date. "Anyhow, when I ran into Jennifer at Blue Café, she didn't give me her number. Said she didn't *feel* led by God to hand out her digits. Probably seeing someone. She seemed angry at a text or call she received."

"I like her already." Kelsey let out a chuckle.

"Huh?" He was lost.

"Maybe she's particular about who she invites into her personal life? Maybe she wasn't buying the whole *God wants me to ask you out* pick-up line?" He rocked back and forth in the chair.

"It wasn't a pick-up line. Do you think she thought I was using God as an excuse to get in her pants? Unbelievable!" He paused, holding a black, casual dress boot in his hand from the night he'd gone out with Nina.

"What I'm saying, Dave, is maybe she isn't the type of woman who's going for the first handsome guy she sees? No offense, by the way."

"Uh…" David uttered, feeling stuck and a bit perplexed again.

"You may catch a woman's eye with good looks, but a woman of substance, a woman in Christ, that is, she wants to see longevity in what she discovers in your heart and spirit. That's what she'll fall in love with eventually. And your relationship with God, that's what she'll find security in ultimately. If your heart is in Christ's hands, it'll remain faithfully in hers. If she jumped at every attractive man she saw, how would that make you special?"

"Good point, but I kind of don't get it." David walked over to his bay window. He leaned his back against it and crossed his arms.

"Because it's not meant for you to get right now." Kelsey got up and walked toward David. "You are wise, but your maturity in Christ has to catch up with your spiritual gifts. You'll see what I'm talking about one day, young fella." He winked, raising the bottle of water to his lips.

"Yeah, I suppose I will. No more late nights with Nina, then, huh?"

Kelsey took a playful swing at him before enfolding him in a big bear hug. "I'm going to let you get back to daydreaming about Jennifer." He gripped his hand and shook it firmly. "Oh, before I go, how's Max doing? Gotta Lego set I wanna give to him."

"Much better." David yawned. "In good spirits. He's strong. Uh, let me know. We can go together, or I can give it to him."

"I'll let ya know. Tell him I said hello." Kelsey stuffed his handkerchief inside his pocket.

"I will. Thanks for checking up on me." David walked him to the door. "Oh, by the way, how are Alex and Susan doing? Need to pay them a visit."

"They're doing fine. You should visit them."

Alex was Kelsey's nephew and seven years older than David. He and his wife, Susan, pastored a church in Front Royal. Kelsey had introduced David to him on a road trip to Shenandoah Valley a while back. David hadn't quite taken Kelsey up on his offer of connecting with Alex. He wasn't comfortable speaking with him just yet.

"Yeah, maybe, but I'll catch you around." He stated deferentially, letting Kelsey out.

His thoughts shifted to his mother as he wondered if he should try to find her again before pursuing another relationship.

Several years after he'd been at the orphanage, he'd received an envelope in the mail from an Aunt Jamison. He'd been eleven years old at the time and peered strangely at it.

Aunt Jamison? he'd said to himself, plopping at the foot of the bunk bed. *That lady who dumped me off.*

He'd opened it and read, *I'm sure you'll have questions later. I'm here whenever you're ready to talk.*

To this day, he hadn't called the number on the note. His anger was too strong for him to care.

CHAPTER 3

*J*ennifer drove to Book World at Tyson's Corner Mall after leaving Blue Café. She looked back at herself in the rearview mirror with the cheesiest smile.

"He's beautiful! What a gorgeous smile! I can't believe I was so nervous," she admitted, blushing. "That's never happened to me. Novelist? Ha! Let's see what this guy has written."

She'd heard a lot of fictitious one-liners thrown her way, yet she couldn't deny the feeling that David had been completely sincere.

I think he's special.

She'd discerned that within a few moments of speaking to him, but it scared her, making her behavior less than welcoming when it became clear he'd wanted to get to know her better. Book World was typically crowded for a Thursday evening. It was a popular location for families, avid readers, and couples to enjoy conversation in the café area. Patrons could also converse at the four corners of the bookstore where a colored assortment of oversized bean bag chairs were stationed.

She pushed through the black double doors, spotting families gathered around board games and movies for their kids. Other people crowded the aisles to read the latest books by their favorite authors.

She maneuvered around them to the customer service desk, where a baby in a Tweety Bird onesie sat cradled in a woman's arms. As she passed by, she made eye contact with the baby. The child smiled and stared tenderly at Jennifer for a moment.

"Kayla," she murmured.

Every fuzzy feeling of joy bubbled up from within. She wanted so desperately to hold that little girl in her arms and kiss her plump ebony cheeks, but she had to quickly snap out of her daydream. Staying in this moment would only stir up the guilt she carried and damper the mood.

Waiting for the bookseller to confirm the books David had written, she started typing a text message to her mother.

"I met a novelist this time. Remember the guy I dated who said he worked with Robert De Niro in Good Fellas?"

She let out a loud laugh, startling nearby customers.

Her mother texted back. *"The fella that we never saw in the movie?"*

"He did say, if you didn't pay close attention, you'd miss him." Jennifer cringed, grabbing her stomach. *"He said you'd to look really fast."* She giggled harder, recognizing she probably looked like a lunatic laughing at her phone. *"By the way, Robert is still trying to get back with me."*

"Again? Have you been direct with him?"

"As direct as I can be." She shook her head and rolled her eyes.

"Right this way," said the bookseller. "We have a few books by David Bradshaw." The lady led her to a bookshelf and perused the books with her fingers. "I've read some myself. I think you'll love *The Simplicity of Intimacy*. It's a collection of Christian romantic short stories. His work makes me wonder if he's that way in real life." Her eyes took on the dreamy expression of a schoolteacher crushing on her favorite author. "Here you go." She reluctantly handed Jennifer the book and pretended to snatch it back, making them both burst into laughter. "The other books are back here in this area."

"Thank you," Jennifer replied, flipping to the table of contents.

I guess he really wasn't lying about being a writer. Folding Clothes, Worship, Poetry, Adoration, Touch.

"Interesting. Very interesting." She tried suppressing a grin.

She took a copy of each book and speed-walked to the bench in front of the magazine display. After an hour, she'd read all the stories that caught her eye in *The Simplicity of Intimacy.*

Wow! This man is talented. He has a gift with words. I never thought folding clothes with someone could create such an intimate moment. And Worship— to enter God's presence together would be amazing.

She returned to the register with all of David's books pressed against her chest. "Thanks for the recommendations," she uttered to the bookseller.

"What do you think?" The bookseller pushed her cherry-red eyeglasses up the bridge of her nose.

Jennifer put on her poker face. "I skimmed through a few pages. They're okay—nothing spectacular." She shrugged her shoulders. "If I read them alone, when I have some peace and quiet, maybe I'll enjoy them more."

"Ha. Right," the bookseller said, sarcastically chipper. "That's why you're purchasing them all, huh?" She nodded knowingly. She took Jennifer's credit card and verified her name on the back of it. "Whatever, Miss Washington. But remember, denial is toxic!"

The women looked at each other for a moment and burst into laughter. "Oh, my God. Ring me up, please." She was relieved to have someone there to keep her honest. "Such great customer service!" She batted her eyes.

"Sounds like you have a thing for Mr. Bradshaw already." The bookseller winked while swiping Jennifer's credit card.

"Mmm—he's not my type." Jennifer tried for nonchalance, but totally failed when the bookseller raised her eyebrows, handing Jennifer the bag of books.

"Denial is truly toxic." She fanned for Jennifer to leave the store.

THE DIM LIGHTING, the aroma of lavender-vanilla oil, and the trickling waters from the water fountain in Rejuvenation Spa immediately suffused Jennifer with peace and calm. She pampered herself there every two weeks. One of the associates who regularly took care of Jennifer saw her arrive and gave her a warm greeting, guiding her over to the red reclining chair. She stopped short when she saw *The Simplicity of Intimacy* in Jennifer's hand.

"No way! David Bradshaw is amazing. I love his books! Have you read *A Son Before His Time?*"

"No, I haven't read that one, but you're right. He's quite good." Jennifer closed her eyes when she felt the warm water pour onto her scalp.

"You're missing out!" the associate added.

"I met him this morning." Jennifer let out a sleepy sigh as the warm water worked to relax her.

"You did? You met David Bradshaw? O-M-G!" The associate megaphoned her words across the room. "Oops. I didn't say that out loud!"

"It's not that big a deal."

"Are you crazy? Not that big a deal..." Her hands stopped their soothing scalp massage as she scrutinized Jennifer as if she were some foreign-looking bug. Jennifer nearly released a sad whimper at the loss of those magical fingers.

"I just think he's a normal guy, like every other guy," she recalled in a trance.

Right. Keep telling yourself that. You feel nothing when you see him, other than God telling you to go for it. No biggie. Wow, denial really is toxic!

"Oh, no, girl! Just keep reading his books. By the end of those, you'll know for certain he isn't some ordinary guy."

Jennifer decided not to argue about it. She didn't need anyone talking her into staking out Blue Café in the hopes that she might run into David again. The fact that it wouldn't take much prodding bothered her.

Not long after Jennifer got comfortable, she felt a light tap on her shoulder. She squinted enough to see a woman with blue eyes, full lips covered in red lipstick, and blond hair that draped over her face. She could have definitely passed for the character Sharon Stone played in the movie *Basic Instinct*.

"That David Bradshaw does seem charming." The woman gushed, echoing the associate's sentiments.

Jennifer blinked her eyes, recognizing the tone of voice. "Samantha? Is that you? Wow. It's been—what? Ten years? How have you been?" Jennifer wanted to stand up to greet her, but she was still enjoying her scalp treatment. "What are you doing here in Virginia?"

"I'm doing well, Jennifer. Yes, it's been a while. I think the last time we saw each other was senior year of high school."

"All done," the attendant said, wrapping her hair up in a towel and leading Jennifer over to the hair dryer.

"I landed a modeling gig here in DC a few years ago," Samantha continued. "I didn't mind getting out of Miami, either."

"I hear that." Jennifer reached over and hugged Samantha.

Then it was time to play catch-up. Jennifer learned all about Samantha's modeling career and how she had met her husband in Paris at a fashion show. Jennifer was happy to hear about her modeling and finding love along her journey. She brought Samantha up to speed about traveling to third world countries, sharing the gospel, helping young children with literacy, and teaching young girls' etiquette at the non-profit she works at in DC.

"That's awesome," Samantha complimented her. "I always knew you would do some incredible things when you graduated from high school. Weren't you voted *Most Likely to Succeed* or something along those lines?"

"I'm pretty sure that title went to our valedictorian."

Samantha just shook her head and then grabbed the book Jen had been reading.

"You like David Bradshaw's books?" Jennifer asked with raised eyebrows as she sat down and reclined back in the chair.

"Oh yes," Samantha confessed as she glided her hand seductively against Jennifer's chair.

Jennifer jerked her head back a little. "Ohhhh-kay."

"I've read his books, including this one right here." She held up

Jennifer's copy. "The *Simplicity of Intimacy* is one of my favorites. He's so good. Mmmm, David," she moaned dreamily. "Huge fan."

"I see," she expressed emphatically with hyper sarcastic excitement. "Uh, Samantha, aren't you happily married?" Handsome or not, Jennifer always thought it best not to lust after things you couldn't have.

"You're so silly!" Samantha rolled her eyes and waved Jennifer's comment off. "Are you still seeing Robert?"

Jennifer's stomach turned, and she subtly rolled her eyes. "We were done a long time ago."

"Sorry to hear about that. Thought you guys would get married."

"Life goes on. Well, Samantha, it was great catching up with you and to hear about your fabulous modeling career. I'm really happy for you, and I'm sure you've already inspired a lot of young women out there to go for their dreams. The modeling industry is a hard one to break into."

"It really is, but I've made it work just like you have. Missionary work and ministry are probably no joke," Samantha said. "It was good to see you. Maybe we can catch up sometime? What's your number?"

"Well, I'll take yours." Jennifer opened her phone, handed it to Samantha, and went to sit under the blow dryer.

Samantha had a mischievous expression on her face as she typed in her contact information. "Here ya go!"

I'm not sure about you. Seem to be into David a bit too much. Gotta keep my distance. Jennifer eyed her warily before taking her phone back apprehensively.

"I'll be seeing you, sweetheart." Samantha sauntered out the door, leaving Jennifer to wonder what in the world that meant.

Jennifer left the spa and went to the third level of the mall to place an order for carryout at her favorite restaurant—Brown's Fine Dining. Facing a thirty-minute wait, she made use of her time browsing her favorite clothing stores and ended up stopping at a high-end jewelry store. She was instantly awestruck by the huge diamond-cluster platinum wedding ring on display. The pink diamond dazzled with yellow, orange, green, purple, and red spectrums.

"Wow. This is so beautiful," Jennifer gushed under her breath, thinking it would be perfect if she ever found the man she'd yearned and prayed to be with one day. A befitting image of David being a suitable partner popped into her thoughts. She'd felt something with him for sure. She got closer, nearly pressing her nose against the window.

"Isn't it beautiful?" Samantha popped up like a jack in the box.

"Whoa!" Jennifer flinched. "Where'd you come from?" She moved her hand over her chest to slow the heavy beating of her heart.

"Oh, I was just passing by and saw you checking out that beautiful ring. Ever plan to get married?" Samantha asked with a great sense of curiosity.

"Uhh." She sighed. "I'd love to," Jennifer confessed with a mixture of optimism and doubt.

"You don't sound too sure." Samantha inched closer to Jennifer's side, both admiring the ring.

"I hope to someday, but I don't have control over when," Jennifer answered, turning her attention briefly to Samantha. "This time around, I'm no longer making decisions based solely on how I feel about someone. I'm gonna let God tag-team this one. It has to be spiritual," she insisted with conviction. "Which I think I felt recently." She thought about David again as she returned her attention to the ring.

"Are you serious? Well, don't drop a bomb like that and then not give me the details. Who's the lucky guy?"

Jennifer turned to Samantha. "Uhhhh." She shook her head. "I'd prefer to keep that to myself," she snickered.

"I bet it's David Bradshaw. Isn't it?" There was the kind of hope in Samantha's voice that she wished he wasn't.

Jennifer looked at her in astonishment. "How do you know that?"

"Come on, Jen." Samantha crossed her arms and looked Jennifer up and down. "I was totally eavesdropping on your conversation at the spa before I came over. You always dated hot guys. I totally envied you." Her friendly smile made Jennifer relax a little. "But could you explain what you felt? Maybe I experienced the same thing when I met my husband. I could give you some much-needed validation."

"When I first saw him, I felt the presence of God stirring so strong inside of me. It was like a deep stir down in here." She put her hand over her navel. "Never felt that before, and to be honest, it kind of scared me.

"Thought I could relate, Jennifer, but I've no idea what you're talking about." Samantha expressed, looking clueless. "Never experienced that. Sounds a little weird, too."

"How can I put it? When you're a believer in Christ, the Holy Spirit enters you and is with you. He lives inside of you. The Holy Spirit was sent to lead and guide us into all truth. And, one way God confirms His will is by giving us His peace and assurance."

"Hmm. That's interesting," Samantha noted incredulously. "Don't think I'm ready for all of that, but it sounds like you're in a good place with the "Holy Spirit." It sounds like you believe in soul mates."

"Soul mates? No. I'd rather use a biblical term called being equally yoked. You can find a person who has the same foundation and moral compass as you do; however . . ." Jennifer returned her attention to the ring. She pictured someone sliding the beautiful piece of jewelry on to her finger. "Someone you're equally yoked with is someone God created for you to become one with in Him. There's a connection on a friendship level. You could listen and talk to that person about anything . . . things that aren't always too comfortable and convenient to talk about with others. It's the friendship that establishes and adds to your security with that person. A friendship builds understanding, respect, and trust in each other. There's a spiritual connection, too. You both have a relationship with the Father through Jesus Christ. With this kind of compatibility, the Holy Spirit helps you walk on the same path without tearing each other down or competing with one another. There's no insecurity and envy in love. Being with someone in Christ inspires you to go deeper in God, so you can fellowship together, worship together, so you can enter God's presence together. This is what is called being equally yoked. David touched on it in this book." She held it up with admiration. It was as if she was proud to convey what she believed to be true about compatibility.

"Uh, okay. Sounds like you're on the same page with him."

Jennifer's eyes lowered in a grateful manner.

"And you sound like a love and spiritual guru. Too deep for me, sweetie. I'm not into that God stuff. No offense." Samantha rolled her eyes and flicked her hair. "And I must've skimmed over that in his book."

Jennifer gave her a warm and friendly smile. "It took me some time to understand this. Maybe someday you'll want to learn more about it."

"I don't believe in those lofty, super-spiritual, romantic theories—like soul mates or being equally yoked . . . whatever you call it," Samantha mocked, chuckling. "That kind of love doesn't exist. You choose whomever you please." She looked at Jennifer, reveling in the ring. "Wanna try it on?" Samantha signaled to the sales associate with her head. He'd been standing off to the side as they chatted about the ring and marriage. He was an older man with a potbelly but well dressed in a tailored suit to fit the elegance of the fine jewelry store.

"Uh, sure—couldn't hurt." Jennifer smiled sheepishly.

The platinum wedding band felt cool and snug around Jennifer's slender finger. She extended her hand out in front of her, flexing her fingers, imagining the love of her life sliding it on. Her eyes grew moist. She cupped her other hand over her mouth to hide the smile she couldn't erase.

"Wow. This makes me feel like I'm actually getting married." Her wide grin beamed brighter than the ring itself.

"Is someone getting married?" The sales associate who'd brought in the ring from the display case was slightly eavesdropping on their conversation.

"Yes, very soon," Samantha teased dainty and winked at him and put her arms around Jennifer, bumping hips with her.

Jennifer blushed with embarrassment and faced the pear-shaped gentleman. "Not soon. I'm not even seeing anyone," she countered. "The ring just caught my attention." She handed it back to the salesman, who took it while simultaneously giving her an appreciative stare.

"No matter what she says, she's taken." Samantha gave the salesman a derisive snort and grabbed Jennifer by the arm, pulling her out of the store. "Ugh! That guy totally wanted to hit on you."

Jennifer chuckled under her breath. "I doubt that; but if he did, I appreciate the assist."

"Absolutely. What are friends for if not to prevent each other from getting involved with the wrong men?"

Jennifer stopped short and turned to face Samantha. She was surprised by the level of bitterness and resentment in Samantha's tone. "Why do I get the feeling you wish someone would've done the same for you?"

Samantha swallowed down a ball of emotion and took her arm again. "Let's walk and talk. I need to work off my coffee and the éclair I had for breakfast."

She squeezed Samantha's arm, feeling like she needed some reassurance. It took a moment for Samantha to speak, but when she did, it sounded like she was fighting back tears.

After Jennifer grabbed dinner from Brown's Fine Diner, they continued their conversation in the mall.

"I think I could've used a little warning about my own stupid tendencies to date men who were all wrong for me. You marry who you date, after all," Samantha continued without missing a beat.

"What do you mean?" Jennifer leaned in closer. Samantha had an edge of experience over her in the area of marriage. She thought it wouldn't hurt to get an idea of how to handle the typical ups and downs of married life. "You gave me the impression at the spa that you were blissfully happy."

Samantha huffed, letting out a sarcastic sounding snicker. "Oh, it always starts out that way. The honeymoon period doesn't last long, hun, and then years later you realize you don't really know the person you're married to. Or in my case, I do. I know who he is, but I didn't recognize him until it was too late. I'm drawn to men who are stern and controlling, just like my father."

Jennifer's heart seized a little at that, causing her to stop in her tracks. Samantha had just touched on a very sensitive subject, considering her own poor relationship with her father. She thought about the men she'd dated throughout the course of her life. They were the same, and on top of that, insensitive and cold, including her ex-fiancé Robert. *Could it be? Was it possible that her miserable experiences with men had much to do with her long-held issues with her father?*

"Are you okay, Jennifer?" Samantha asked. "You look like you've seen a ghost."

"Yeah . . . self-reflecting. I think I relate to some of the things you recalled. I think I need some fresh air. Let's go outside."

They made their way out the door and continued down the sidewalk. Jennifer felt that the weather had somehow shifted to fit the dour mood of the conversation. Tiny storm clouds drifted above, and the sweet, earthy scent of rain hung heavy in the air. She wanted to hear more from Samantha and compare experiences to see if she suffered from this pattern of being attracted to and linking up with men who were like her father. Jennifer was on to something.

"Tell me about your dad, Samantha." She watched closely for her response.

Samantha brushed back a lock of wayward hair and let out a weary sigh. "Well, for starters, he stopped my mother from pursuing her dreams. She was into fashion, much like I am, or was. He didn't want me in the fashion industry. He gave me typical alternatives like being a nurse—my mom was a nurse—a lawyer, or a schoolteacher. I didn't want those jobs. I refused to listen to him." She shook it off like a bad memory and looked at Jennifer. "Anyhow, as a result of what I've seen in my parents' marriage, and how I resented him, I was usually drawn to men who were like my father. Weird."

"Wow. Sounds like my dad and the guys I've dated. My dad didn't want me to go into ministry. Still doesn't. He felt like ministry wasn't a lucrative career. It's a calling. He thought he could dictate every single facet of my life, including decisions that never should've been his to make." Jennifer's thoughts returned to her child, even though she wanted to shy away from it, from the heartache those memories dredged up painfully.

"My Michael is nothing like he truly portrayed himself to be. I may be a model, but he runs my career, he chooses my friends, he schedules my life, and he polices all my free time. I'm pretty isolated now, and I realize he's slowly been whittling my personal life down until all I have is him. To get back at him . . . I've . . . slept with other men. I just . . . I want to feel something again. You know?"

Jennifer's soul left her body for a few minutes. Hearing Samantha confess infidelity threw her off guard.

That could be David, too.

She wasn't sure if it was her naivety, or the pure spectrum from how she viewed love that prevented her from believing what she'd heard.

"Honestly, I can't imagine cheating on my future husband, no matter how upset I get with him, but I can identify with being in a controlling relationship. My ex-fiancé was like that, but they say love is a choice."

Samantha gave her a brittle smile. "You'll see someday, Jennifer. Enjoy the single life while you can. Being married is overrated. I wish Michael was like the guys in David's books," Samantha sighed.

"Hmm." Jennifer returned the same wishful expression.

She didn't quite know what to say after that comment. She tried to enjoy the rest of her time with Samantha, but in the back of her mind she wondered if she was capable of being drawn to someone who was the exact opposite of her father. *Was it possible she had pushed David away because she was afraid to get locked into another unhealthy relationship? Was it also possible that she was drawn to David because she knew, on some instinctive level, he'd be bad for her, too?*

She tried to dismiss that last thought. *Why would God's Spirit be working so hard on her right now if David wasn't good for her?* She felt peace at the thought of seeing him again. Then fear took over, preventing her from feeling any peace whatsoever. One thing was certain: fear and faith couldn't coexist within her heart, and she wasn't sure how to let go of fear and give love a chance.

On Jennifer's way home, she called her mother, concerned and startled with this epiphany she'd just had. Catherine vaguely remembered Samantha when she was a student in high school, but she was more interested in learning about David. It had been a while since Jennifer had shown interest or even mentioned a guy. Her mom was ready to interrogate her as only moms can.

"He seems like a decent guy," Jennifer said. "I feel like we crossed paths for a reason."

"Always worth giving decent guys a chance," her mom encouraged. "But are you saying he's God-sent?"

"Mom, I'm just not sure. We were paired to volunteer together this morning. We found that out later on at the café. He seems too good to be true. You know how men are, and I brushed him off pretty good. I doubt he'd ever be interested in asking for my number again." She paused. "But I did experience something I've never felt with any other guy."

Her mother listened to Jennifer tell her about feeling the presence of God when she first saw David. It was an experience with which her mother couldn't identify.

"Look, I may have no frame of reference for what you're talking about, but it's clear you met this David guy for a reason. What you felt sounds special. Just keep your options open."

"Hmm. Maybe." Jennifer considered, feeling like she was circling back to this subject repeatedly with no real solution presenting itself. She was obsessing. It wasn't healthy. "Well, I'm home now. I'll catch up with you later. I love you."

"Love you, baby."

Jennifer wearily exited her car, walked inside her house, and dropped onto her ivory colored couch. She flipped through the channels on the television with her feet propped on the cherrywood coffee table. Searching for something interesting to watch, her attention was drawn again and again to a picture she'd violently torn in half so long ago. The half she'd held on to displayed the smiling image of her mother. Her father was glaringly absent. Every passing day, the absence of her father from her life became more vivid, more noticeable. It made her stomach sour just thinking about it.

Since she was all about eating her feelings as of late, she went into the kitchen for some much-needed ice cream in an attempt to mitigate the bone-deep sorrow overwhelming her. She bumped into the overloaded garbage can and knocked four small ice cream containers onto the floor. She dropped to her knees when a mortifying memory resurfaced.

"I'm sorry, Robert, but I can't marry you." She pulled her hand away from him as he knelt before her. *"This doesn't seem right."*

She heard the sharp intake of breath, and then her father barked out her name. When she turned to him, she saw the shock and disapproval etched across his face. Robert's family was also struggling with her response. She gave them an apologetic look before returning her attention to Robert, whose eyes had darkened in anger. His head dropped, nearly touching his bent knee.

Jennifer shook herself, blinking the memory away as she gathered the empty ice cream containers. She bit down on her lip, mustering the strength to fight through the well of oppressive emotions threatening to consume her. She lifted her hands in worship, singing a simple song about love and forgiveness, asking God to heal her heart and take away her pain.

"Your love is healing.

Your light is shining.

Shining over me.

Your presence heals me

Your love fulfills me

Oh God, please forgive me."

She hummed more words until her voice faded away by the presence of God. As she lowered her head, quiet became quiet. Still became still. Everything contending for Jennifer's attention ceased. They were no more. A peaceful presence filled her heart, enveloping her like a warm blanket.

In moments like these, it was almost as if she could hear God whispering to her, letting her know He was mindful of her struggles and ready to lend His own strength when she was at her weakest. The presence of the Lord had continued to take over and ministered to her. She couldn't have been more grateful. Once she gained her composure, she sent up a silent prayer of thanks, dabbed at her cheeks with her fingers, and went to retrieve her book from her purse. After going to her bedroom, she put on a white cardigan sweater and moved to the patio, enjoying the nippy wind and smell of impending rain as she sat down. She cracked open *The Simplicity of Intimacy* and read another short story entitled, "You Are."

Shivers went up her spine as she read. She couldn't fathom how a man could write prose with such impact and vivid imagery. His words were so touching they evoked deep emotions within her and moved her spirit. She knew the power of words. It was as if she was there with him, sitting in front of his computer screen typing away or penning her life between the blue lines of his notepad. The way David described how much a woman meant to him and how she should be seen through the eyes of God, according to Proverbs 31, was astonishing. She wondered if he was sincere, a true reflection of his writing. *Or is he just a man who has a talent for crafting stories for the sake of wooing his female audience?* Whatever discouraging thoughts clouded her perception of him, she couldn't deny what she'd felt when they'd locked eyes at the hospital. She just had to decide if she was brave enough to do anything about it.

CHAPTER 4

A few days later, there was a chill in the air, yet it was comfortable enough for Jennifer to sit outside on her patio. She spent early mornings reading her Bible, praying, and waiting quietly before God. The timing was always perfect. Either a landscaping team would arrive minutes after she was done, or neighbors would start their daily routines. She'd placed her Bible and notepad aside when an idea popped into her mind: organizing a kid's spa for the girls at Parson's children's hospital.

"Thank you, Lord. This would be awesome!" She was so psyched, she quickly hopped into the shower. After washing up, she threw on black leggings, a white T-shirt, and a black hooded jacket and drove to Rejuvenation Spa. She wanted to chat in person with the store manager about donating a few appliances and materials needed for the spa day, and perhaps the manager might offer up a volunteer member to assist her? On her way there, she thought of coordinating this spa day with David.

He could do something for the boys there, she thought.

Then it dawned on her that she didn't have his number or any way to get in touch with him. She raked her fingers through her hair, feeling irked with herself. *Would it have been so bad to exchange numbers since we are volunteering together?*

At the spa, she saw Samantha getting a pedicure. Jennifer noticed Samantha calling her over, but something else caught her attention, too. Light from the ceiling reflected off the book Samantha held in her hand. David Bradshaw's name glimmered in shining gold letters. This put a little pep in Jennifer's step. She didn't remember coming across this book at Book World.

"What's up, Sam?" Jennifer gave her a friendly smile.

"Pampering myself a little today while the hubby is on a business trip." Her eyes held a mischievous glint.

"Nice!" Jennifer replied, glancing down at the book. She thought the naughty smile on Sam's face was provoked by something she had read in David's book. "Am I interrupting a moment?"

"Not at all, Jen. Just enjoying this book. You gotta read this one." She held it up for Jennifer to catch the title.

She seemed uninterested in talking to Jennifer for sure.

"*The Quiet.* Interesting title."

"Very interesting," Samantha gushed.

Minutes later, the store manager got off a business call and was available to meet with Jennifer. She signaled Jennifer to come over and they met privately in the back to talk.

She pitched her idea of putting together a spa for the girls, and the store manager loved it. She was willing to give Jennifer whatever she needed but couldn't promise if any of the staff members would volunteer their time. Each employee had to sign a privacy clause that prohibited them from partnering with any outside organizations regarding the use of the company's products.

"That's the best I can do."

"I totally understand, Christina, but I thank you so much for providing what I need. That's enough help. These girls are going to have a good time."

"You're welcome, Jennifer. It brings joy to my heart to see you dedicate yourself to those girls. I'm sure your presence is a blessing to them. Give me a call if you need any ideas for setting things up.

I'll have everything prepared for you when you're ready to pick it up."

"Thank you. Thank you so much, and I will." Jennifer's heart filled with gratitude as they hugged.

On Jennifer's way out, the associate who usually took care of her was finishing up with another client. She went over to say hello and saw Samantha at the front desk handing her credit card to the sales associate.

Since I don't have David's number, I could ask Sam. She caught her before heading out. "Sorry for cutting our conversation short," Jennifer apologized.

"It's fine. No big deal. Is everything okay? I saw you head to the back with the store manager."

"Yeah, I'm fine. She and I are good friends. She's donating a few things I need for a kid's spa I'm hosting for the girls at the children's hospital. I wanted to know if you're available to give me a hand. I could use a little help setting up."

Samantha appeared excited. "Count me in. I could use some of the things I learned in the modeling industry." She winked.

"Great. I'm not sure if you gave me your number last time I saw you. But if so, would you mind giving it to me again?"

"Sure, Jen," she agreed, reaching into her purse.

"Thanks." Jennifer took the card from her and headed toward the exit. "I'll give you a call a week before the date."

Jennifer left feeling a bit uneasy as she considered Samantha's interest in David. *Maybe it wasn't a good idea to invite her, especially considering the way she was obsessing over him, and with the possibility of him being there to visit Max, things could go south.* Her next mission was to get in touch with David. She hoped to run into him at the hospital or the café.

TWO DAYS after Jennifer left Rejuvenation Spa, David found himself at home in his office reclining in a black leather chair. His feet were propped up on the desk beside his desktop computer. He balanced a notepad on his lap that held a few scribbles of incomplete thoughts. You probably couldn't tell if he was writing or sketching the way his borderline chicken scratch handwriting looked. That was a typical indication of his writer's block. Nothing came to mind to jump-start his next novel. *I gotta get something to Jay.* The letter was the only thing that occupied the spacious white document. He tossed a tennis ball against the white wall where a large wood portrait of a scripture hung. The background of the canvas was painted the color of dark clouds.

Illuminated in light was Proverbs 3:5. "Trust in the Lord with all your heart and lean not on your own understanding; in all your ways submit to him, and he will make your paths straight."

Painted under the scripture was a straight, narrow path of a dirt road surrounded by green grass. Miss Smith had given him the portrait a few years ago. She wanted him to meditate on it when he felt himself losing his way or getting stuck, whether spiritually or creatively. He tossed the tennis ball again and caught it.

He squeezed it, closed his eyes, and prayed, "I trust You, Lord. Guide my understanding." He hoped God would give him guidance on how to go about writing his novel, but there was a change of plans. He felt a nudge within him to go to *Hope on the Green*, a mom and pop grocery in the center of Vienna. "Guess I'll buy a few things to meal prep for the week and get back to this novel another time." At least he'd become more productive in eating healthier and building the physique he wanted.

The grocery store was located on a main street. It was a popular local gem everyone in the community loved. Some customers traveled twenty-five to thirty minutes to shop for reasonably priced organic foods. It was worth the drive for David. He held stock in the company and had come to develop a great relationship with the owners and staff. He volunteered with them to build homes and renovate others for less fortunate families. In a way, he was less famous locally than he was nationally. For many, he was just Dave.

He coasted through the sliding door, pushing a shopping cart like a kid whose mother had just given him the responsibility of driving it, and turned down Healthy Snack Avenue. Each aisle was named by a green street sign according to the contents in it, which were in white letters. He made his way to the protein bars while quickly skimming the shelves along the way. He would've surely bumped into someone if another customer was headed his way.

"Where's the chocolate peanut butter?" He reached the section. Then he heard a familiar voice call his name.

He turned his attention to none other than Jennifer, the woman he couldn't stop thinking about. His heart leaped in his throat.

They both grinned on sight. It was as if they'd been searching for one another but would never admit to it.

I found her!

"Oh, what's up, Jennifer? How are you?" he asked pretending to be unmoved, pushing his cart to the side.

"I'm good," she said excitedly. "Glad I ran into you. How are you?"

"Not too bad. Good to know all is well with you. Drove down to grab a few items, but what's up?" She noticed how he said it with extra nonchalance, accidentally bumping his cart into the shelf and disturbing a few peaceful cereal boxes.

"Is everything okay?" She placed her finger across her lips with laughter.

"I think this wheel is a little off. Old cart!"

"Right," she quipped and crossed her arms.

He tried to maintain a placid front. He just knew she was going to ask him out for lunch or coffee or any invitation that would get them together. There was an inner inclination he was getting those digits today.

"I came up with this cool idea of organizing something for the kids at the hospital. I wanna do something for Leyanie and some of the other girls. Maybe you could do something for Max and the other boys?"

Here we go, baby, he thought, giving himself a mental fist bump.

As she was talking, he was thinking *Sign me up* before she could get the rest of the details out. She could've been inviting him to crochet and he would've been down, just to be next to her.

"I like that idea," David agreed calmly and nodded his head in agreement. "What do you have in mind?" He rested his foot on the cart.

"I wanna pamper them with a mini spa." She also put her foot up on the cart.

"That's an awesome idea. I think they'd totally enjoy it, but I'm not sure what I could do for Max. I'll have to think on it."

I gotta come up with something quick. I could lose an opportunity to shoot my shot.

"It's fine. I know I put you on the spot. We could meet up this week if you're available to discuss." She pulled out her cellphone.

"Yeah, sure." He couldn't believe this was happening. This sure wasn't a date, but it was something that could put him in a position to get to know her better. On the flip side, he was interested in organizing something for the kids at the hospital. "How can I get in touch with you?" He snagged his cellphone out of his hooded jacket.

She gave him her number and asked him to text her. David tried his best to refrain from smiling. He had to tilt his head down so she couldn't make eye contact with him.

"Are you okay, David?" she asked.

"Oh, yeah." He laughed a little. "Yeah. I'm great. Just got this phone . . . still getting used to it."

Man, I need to repent for lying.

"Don't see anything funny but awesome. Give me a call and let me know what day works for you. I have to get going. It was great seeing you."

"Yeah. It was great seeing you as well."

Can you use another word besides yeah, David? You're a writer. I could blame it on my writer's block.

He could blame his loss for words on Jennifer. The guy couldn't speak. Never in his dating experiences had a woman short-circuited his intelligence. Ever! But this woman of God had that special kind of effect on him.

David finished his grocery shopping feeling ecstatic about the possibility of meeting up with Jennifer, but he needed to figure out what he could do for Max and the boys at the hospital.

JENNIFER WAS TALKING to her mom on the way to Old Town Alexandria. She told her mother about what she planned at the children's hospital and how she'd included David in it. Her mother was super excited and thrilled about this wonderful occasion.

"I bumped into him at the grocery store. That was like perfect timing. I even felt moved to go to the grocery store that morning after my devotion time with God."

"Hmm," Catherine grunted. "Sounds like your steps were guided David's way." She laughed. "And a perfect opportunity to get to know him."

"Could be, but you already know how I feel."

"I know you aren't quite ready but keep an open heart."

"I am. We were paired to work with each other anyway. Here's the chance to."

"I'm sure you two are going to put something wonderful together. Keep me posted. I need to finish cutting these onions."

"Okay, Mom. I'll be in touch. Love ya."

"Love you too, Jen."

She hung up with her mom, thinking about the possibility of something kindling between her and David, but there was some hesitance there. She wasn't ready to open up to David because of the malevolent words Robert had planted in her mind in the past.

Your insecurities will ruin your next relationship, Robert had screamed into her ear before dropping her off at her parents' house. *I hope whoever you give your time to cheats on you. You'll never be good enough!*

That day, Jennifer had jumped out of his car and slammed the door shut. She'd felt demeaned and humiliated. She'd eventually allowed what he'd said to become a reality. Every guy she'd met after him always caused her to think about the woman she wasn't. Her insecurities created problems that didn't exist. She pushed good men away, self-sabotaging some great potential relationships.

She shook her head, fighting to get rid of the toxic memories before meeting up with David. She quickly parked and got out of her car, spotting David a few cars over. She gave him a shy smile and headed toward him. They grabbed some smoothies first before getting down to business.

The boardwalk near Old Town Alexandria was a bit crowded, but David and Jennifer were able to chitchat a bit as they weaved through bodies, walking at a slow pace and sipping their smoothies until they eventually found a less crowded spot to stop and talk near a wooden rail. They paused a moment to take in their surroundings. From the corner of her eye, she discretely watched him enjoy a flock of birds jet across the sky. The right side of her lip curled up into a half-smile. She gathered that his creative side was at work while observing the scenery.

"David," she called to him.

"Yeah," he answered, breaking his attention from the skies.

"You seem like a very interesting person."

"In what way?" One of his eyebrows rose. His attention was still on the birds.

"I've never met a guy like you." She rubbed her arms because of the cool wind that passed between them.

He faced her and before responding, he took off his gray hooded jacket and helped her into it. His hand accidentally brushed against the inner part of her arm. A warm feeling came over her, producing a sweet twinkle in her eyes. She briefly smiled and finished putting on the jacket.

"Thank you, David."

"You're welcome," he said with an overtone of coolness. "You were saying you've never met a guy like me before."

She chuckled under her breath. "You seem selfless, giving, and in tune. You're able to discern what's not spoken. I picked that up in your letter. That's a wonderful gift, David."

"Thank you, Jennifer. I guess you're further expanding on your psychoanalysis of me." He winked and laughed through a smile.

"Hahaha! Right. You got me."

"I'll take that as a compliment. Jennifer, I'm not perfect. It took me some time to walk into what you see in me. I've experienced some things that calloused my heart, but also helped to make it flesh again. I don't think God is done with me yet." He turned to her for a second.

"Like what?" She focused keenly on him.

He rubbed his chin for a moment and his eyes lowered.

"You don't have to talk about it if you don't want to."

He faced her and confided, "I don't have the greatest relationship with my mother."

"Why's that?"

"Don't know. I just remember she didn't like me much and didn't spend time with me."

"There must be some reason."

"I prayed about it...haven't got an answer yet. It is what it is."

"That's so sad and unfortunate. Don't mean to cut you off, but I can relate to what you're saying in a lot of ways. I don't have a great relationship with my dad, and I'd always look for validation from men."

"Huh." He blew out some air. "Tell me about it."

"It's okay, David." She tucked her hands into her pockets, directed her attention away from him, and faced the sky that was no longer blue. The evening had set in. She wanted to place him in a category with the other men she'd dated. She couldn't, no matter how hard she tried. At this point, David had given her no reason to do so. "I've this idea about what we can do for the girls," she suggested, going into what she'd planned.

She listened to David's suggestions of teaching them how to tie a tie and thought it was a cute idea. She was eager to see him in action. They picked a day that would complement their schedules.

Getting into her car, she wondered more and more about David's relationship with his mother.

I can't imagine not knowing my mom. I'm sure that's gotta be painful for him.

She wanted so badly to console him with a hug, but that would've been totally out of line.

I don't know. Maybe I should've?

DAVID AND JENNIFER secured a room in the hospital that was designated for parties or recreational activities. Samantha didn't reply when Jennifer called and texted her, so David had the honor of carrying equipment from her car into the hospital and setting it up. She caught herself smiling at him on a few occasions as he lifted some of the heavy stuff from her trunk.

He sure is strong! He probably works out a lot at the gym. He could be my workout buddy.

She hadn't realized that some of her thoughts had escaped her mouth.

"Did you say something, Jennifer?" David asked.

"Oh no . . . talking to myself." She grabbed the last few things from her car and covered her mouth, trailing behind him. "Do it all the time."

Shut up, Jennifer.

Inside, he unfolded the white and pink tablecloth and helped spread it out on the table. They both had a difficult time hiding their smiles when they caught each other's eye. It was obvious the physical attraction was there. After David finished assisting her, she gave him a hand setting up his side of the room, which wasn't much. While he aligned a few body-sized mirrors against the wall, she took the ties out of his cardboard box and neatly lined them on the table. She smoothed the wrinkles out that were in some of them, loving the way silk felt against her skin and the way the skinny knit ties looked. She could imagine seeing David in a tailored, heather-gray suit and black skinny tie. Soon, she smelled subtle notes of rum and vanilla cologne coming from the ties.

I like his taste!

She lifted one to inhale and imagined getting cozy in his arms, cradling her face against his neck. She smiled again, returning from her daydream and looked at him in the mirror to see what he was doing, and he caught her gaze. She immediately burst out in semi-embarrassed laughter.

"Uhhhh, are you okay, Jennifer?" David said extra slow and laughed his heart out while still glancing at her in the mirror.

I'm not okay.

"Yes, I'm fine." She kept laughing, making it nearly impossible for him to understand her. "I'm good. Totally good . . . promise ya . . . just had a moment."

If you only knew what was going on in my head.

"I'm too familiar with those too . . . so yeah."

"David, have you always been into God or had a relationship with Him?" She walked closer to him and took a seat in one of the chairs, crossing her legs. She studied the course of his hair and the back of his hairline, taking notice of his small, pierced earlobes and the pronounced veins on the back of his forearms.

He's a beautiful man! She noted again.

Jennifer had always believed when you gave someone your undivided attention and your heart was solely focused on one person, you catch every minor detail of his beauty. From how a person's lip curled up at the sides when he laughed to how his eyes shifted from left to right when deep in thought, or the inflection in the voice when he talked about something he was passionate about, or how raw emotions infused his eyes when he spoke of hard times. Yes, there was beauty in resilience, healing, and overcoming.

Jennifer saw all of this in David Bradshaw.

Before turning around to answer, he made sure each mirror was perfectly aligned. "When I was separated from my mom, I started to search for God."

She moved closer to him. "Separated?" Her eyebrows arched with concern.

"My mom left me at an aunt's place. Just dropped me off. Then my aunt dumped me at an orphanage."

"She . . . she just abandoned you?" Jennifer couldn't hide her shock.

His gaze shifted down as if he couldn't believe he'd just shared that information with her.

"Let's go gather everyone up," he insisted, not even bothering to be subtle about the shift in topic.

"David, wait." She reached out and took his hand, coming face to face with him.

"Yeah." His voice dragged in apprehension, and he looked her in the eye for a moment with obscure anticipation. Then he redirected his attention to the floor.

They say the eye is the window to the soul. In some ways, she felt like he was well-practiced in hiding himself in surprisingly vulnerable times.

But it was too late. She saw him.

She grabbed his other hand and whispered, "I'm here to support you." She noticed him glance away again as if he found it hard to believe her. "Don't think I'm prying to judge you. I only want to understand you."

His eyes moved back to hers. "Thank you, Jennifer. I appreciate that. You kinda make it safe to trust again. I got a confession to make."

"What's that?" She released his hands.

"I know it seems like I'm all close with God. The truth is, I stopped spending time with Him. I just couldn't understand why He'd allow my mother to abandon me like that."

"I'm guilty of the same thing. We all struggle, but we don't have to remain there. I don't know, David, but maybe you wouldn't have such success as an author or have become the God-fearing man you are today if you hadn't gone through what you endured? I wholeheartedly believe that your past has prepared you for more."

David abruptly wrapped his arms around her and hugged her tight. She closed her eyes, returning his embrace while trying her best to not cry.

"Thank you, Jennifer. You've no idea what this means to me. Guess

God knew this moment would happen." He laughed uncomfortably. "Your presence and words are timely."

"Aww, thank you, David. Perhaps God did know you needed me at this moment." She stayed in that comfort, sensing it was important for him to be the first one to let go. When he did, she stepped back and gave him an encouraging smile. "I think it's about time to grab everyone."

~

A GRIN FLASHED across David's face when he saw Jennifer help the girls into their spa chairs. He'd never thought of having children until that very moment.

I do want a daughter so I can spoil her. And I think Jennifer would make an amazing mother.

One thing that was important to David was marrying a woman he could see himself raising a family with. He envisioned marrying a woman that would help raise their child in a godly way. Seeing their hearts filled with joy wasn't the only thing that moved him. The sparks of happiness in their eyes allowed him to see the impact Jennifer had on their self-esteem and self-worth, which was something he could testify to firsthand. He waved to them and walked the boys to their side of the room.

"Do you remember her, Max?" David asked.

"Yeah, I remember her," Max said sorting out some of the ties on the table. "When are you going to ask her out? You've been talking about finding a Proverbs 31 woman for a long time."

Max caught him off guard, making David laugh out loud.

I'm going to nail this kid next time we play dodge ball.

He saw Jennifer look up at him as she lowered Leyanie's feet into the bubbling warm water. They exchanged pleasant smiles.

"Maybe one day, Max. One day, kid." He patted him on the back like a good sport.

Max winked his eye, knowing what David was doing, and David

turned around just enough so that Jennifer wouldn't see them pounding fists in a manly sign of approval.

"Bring it!" Max put his dukes up, challenging him.

David hadn't disclosed too much to Max about his personal life. He didn't want to add any stress on the kid, given he was diagnosed with a brain tumor and was always in and out of consciousness, but he knew about Maria. He knew when David was not his joking, upbeat self. Sometimes he'd sit in the chair and not speak for the first five minutes of David's visit. David would have a finger bookmarked on the same scripture and mumble the words to himself before reading it to Max out loud. Max wouldn't say anything until David initiated the conversation.

"You know, Max, loneliness is something that many people suffer from."

"What do you mean, Dave?"

"To give yourself to someone and not receive the same effort and investment is baffling," he continued. *"Maria couldn't love me the way I wanted her to."*

Max was eight when David had ended his relationship with Maria. He understood how David had felt to some degree, as only a kid could. It wasn't in the context of a romantic relationship, but by the basic human need for love. Like Leyanie, Max didn't have parents. He didn't know who they were. He'd also been given up for adoption.

David got the boys' attention and took a tie in his hand. He threw the tie around his neck and carefully explained each step. After he showed them a few times, he had them practice in the mirror and decided to check on Jennifer.

"How's it going over here?" he asked.

By this time, Jennifer had dried the girls' feet off and began giving them pedicures.

"Well. Really well. They're loving the pampering." She beamed, exfoliating the girl's foot.

"That's the priest," Leyanie joked from three chairs over.

"Leyanie, stop," Jennifer insisted, laughing. "He's not a priest."

"My bad," Leyanie giggled. "He is, though." She uttered loud enough only for Jennifer to hear.

"Hey, Leyanie. Good to see you again." David nodded his head at her.

"Same. When are you asking the lovely Jennifer Washington out? I personally think she's an awesome and amazing person. She's totally single!" She winked at David.

He lowered his head with his palm smacked across his face. He couldn't have been more embarrassed for Jennifer and humored at the same time. Jennifer had a similar reaction. Her cheeks flushed red, and she laughed so hard she couldn't keep the girl's foot steady.

"Oh my gosh," Jennifer said laughing. "Zip it, Leyanie."

All the little girls were tickled by what Leyanie said and they all turned to David.

"Okay. I digress." She gave Jennifer a sassy wave.

When David and Jennifer were done, they walked everyone back to their rooms and finished cleaning up.

"This turned out really well." David commented, grabbing some of the mirrors as Jennifer gave him a hand.

"It really did. I'm happy we had a chance to put this together. I admire how you taught them how to tie a tie. You're very patient . . . a good teacher, too."

"Thank you." David started to say something about not having his dad around to teach him those kinds of things, but he opted to keep that to himself. He didn't want to dampen the mood, and he'd shared enough about his mom. It was enough vulnerability for one day. "I had a lot of fun. It was great to show them a few of my tying tricks and shortcuts."

"You were definitely into it."

"I got a little carried away."

She cleared all the ties off the table and put them back into the box. When she finished helping him put away all his things, he helped pack her side. As they cleaned and organized the tables, David heard someone singing—a sensual, jazzy tune near the doorway. He turned to see who it was and saw an attractive woman waltz in seductively. She appeared ready for a photoshoot rather than showing up to volunteer. She wore brown high boots, a white long-sleeve shirt, and fitted stone-wash jeans that gripped her long, curvaceous frame. Diamonds fixed befittingly in her ears, and red lipstick layered her lips. Confused, David scrunched his eyes at Jennifer. He wondered who the heck she was and where she'd come from.

"Samantha?" said Jennifer.

"Aww, I missed all the fun. I'm sorry, Jennifer. I was tied up when you called," said Samantha.

"It's okay." Jennifer continued picking things up. "No worries. Things worked out, and I got some help from David." She winked at him, the action shooting warmth straight to his heart. She looked at the other woman in confusion. "Wait, how did you know when to come? I never told you the time."

"David?" Samantha greeted him with great excitement. "David Bradshaw? OMG! Sorry, Jen. I called the front desk."

"Called the front desk?" Jennifer's eyes widened.

David saw Jennifer's eyes tighten, and she continued cleaning. He discretely exhaled a breath through his nostrils, sensing tension from Jennifer but unsure of the cause.

"Yes." David slowly took his eyes off Jennifer and faced Samantha.

"Nice to meet you, David." She whispered, extending her hand to him. "I'm a big fan of yours. I have, like, all of your books—crazy!"

"Uh, thank you." His insides twisted with unease. "I appreciate your support."

"Maybe you can do a reading at Blue Café sometime? Heard you hang out there a lot."

David's eyes widened.

Heard? How does she know that?

He turned to Jennifer, thinking she must have mentioned their coincidental run-in at the café a while back, but she looked just as surprised as he felt. This Samantha chick was clearly coming on to him, and David didn't like it one bit.

This isn't looking good at all. Jennifer is going to think something is going on.

He knew from Jennifer's expression that she was waiting for a response from him. It almost felt like someone had set him up for a fall.

Ambushed!

"I . . . umm." He mumbled, feeling uncomfortable. "It's . . . uh . . . where I often get coffee." He sheepishly stuttered.

I shouldn't have said that.

He clenched his teeth and watched Jennifer pick up one of the footbaths, carrying it out of the room. David and Samantha were now alone. He moved away from her and put all the tables and chairs back in order.

"I'm sorry, but I can't talk right now. We have to be out of here soon."

"Understandable." She came over to him and tapped him on the backside while he was bending over to lift a box.

"Hey." David jumped and moved away. *Had she seriously just done that?*

"Don't be shy." Samantha winked her eye and left the room. "I'm sure we'll have some time together soon, handsome."

He stood there scratching his head, feeling bewildered as Jennifer walked back in. She saw the panic on his face and raised her brows, appearing to be waiting for him to say something.

"You okay?" When he just stood there, failing to find the words to explain what had just happened, she gathered, "Looks like you were enjoying something. Samantha kept you entertained, huh?"

He wanted to tell her about her friend's inappropriate behavior but couldn't.

This is gonna start some drama!

He didn't want Jennifer to think he'd made a pass at her friend or had done something to make Samantha feel that it was okay to flirt on that level. He left it alone.

"Nah. Guess she's just a fan." He shrugged off her comments.

"Probably got plenty of them," she said curtly.

She sounded annoyed so he ignored that dart, too. "I had a great time. Hey, listen, I would like to get together with you. Outside of volunteering."

"David, I had a great time, too, but I don't think that's possible right now."

"A friendship never hurts, though." He gave her a gracious smile as his hands went up in surrender.

"That's kind of you, but no, thank you."

"I appreciate the honesty." His head hung low. "We got everything. I'll walk you to your car."

While heading out, a rough looking man walked into the room with a dozen roses in his hands. The guy had a determined glint in his eye as he locked on to Jennifer.

David looked at each other and saw her rolled her eyes, baffled and confused out of her mind.

"A lot of surprise guests have turned up for this event. You know him?" He nodded his head at him.

Jennifer looked absolutely horrified, bringing out David's protective instincts.

"Jen, I was in town and thought I'd stop by." The guy justified.

David's jaw tightened.

"Excuse me, Robert, but what are you doing here? We're done. And I don't want your roses. And how did you know I'd be here?"

Now I see. Ex-boyfriend.

He hesitated to leave the room in case Jennifer needed him, but he also didn't feel like this was any of his business.

What should I do?

Just then, a nurse ran into the room, looking frazzled.

"Jennifer, I need you to come with me. Leyanie isn't doing well. She collapsed while climbing into her bed." She reported, running out of breath. "She's had a seizure. We moved her into ICU."

Jennifer didn't seem to give this Robert guy another thought as she ran out of the room. David quickly followed, catching Robert's red face and dark expression out of the corner of his eye.

Yeah. That guy is upset.

His focus quickly turned to concern for Leyanie and how he could support Jennifer. The nurse brought them to the ICU, where they saw Leyanie's tiny figure dwarfed by the hospital bed. She was hooked up to an IV machine with tubes in her mouth, and her eyes were roaming about.

"Leyanie." Jennifer cried with tears rolling down her cheeks.

"This doesn't look good." David came up from behind and placed his hand on her lower back. She hardly seemed to notice as she stared at Leyanie. He wished he could do more. He wished he could hold her but held back.

He listened to the nurse explain that the chemotherapy had caused the seizure, which was the first time she'd ever responded that way to treatment. It hurt him to see her suffer.

"She will need time to recover." The nurse explained.

"Okay. Please keep me updated." Jennifer begged.

David accompanied her to the elevator, worrying about the dead look in her eyes. From the eighth floor to the first seemed like the longest ride in history. It was quiet. David looked at Jennifer from time to time but said nothing. He saw her eyes land everywhere except on him. He wasn't surprised. He could imagine the mixed emotions running through her. Samantha and Robert had popped up, followed by Leyanie's seizure—this sure wasn't a good time to talk. He kept silent and walked her to her car.

"Everything's going to be okay. I'll keep Leyanie in prayer," he assured.

Look at me, Jen. Let me be there for you like you were for me.

She kept her eyes firmly planted on her car door. "Thank you. Thanks for walking me to my car. You have a good night."

He hesitated before saying, "Good night, Jennifer."

David went straight to his patio when he arrived back home. Outside on his wicker chair, he tried to process everything that had transpired. What had unfolded seemed disjointed in a way. He felt there was some evil force at work, pulling him and Jennifer apart.

"How the heck did Samantha and that guy show up within minutes of each other? There's no way that wasn't planned." He directed his question at God.

If Samantha is friends with Jennifer, she must know all about this Robert guy. Maybe she thought it was a good idea to bring them back together? Was Samantha a well-intentioned friend making a bad call on Jennifer's behalf?

This had to be a scheme! David was on to something, but couldn't quite prove his theory was true. He knew Kelsey was going to get a kick out of this one. He rubbed his forehead, feeling guilty about not giving Jennifer more details concerning his mom. She'd been ready to connect with him, be there for him, but he'd shied away from the subject.

"Just wasn't ready to go there, God. I hope the events of this night don't set things back with Jennifer. I still hurt, Lord. Father forgive me for not spending enough time with you. I don't know why I've neglected our secret place."

CHAPTER 5

*D*avid scaled back on reaching out to Jennifer for a few days. He checked on Leyanie. She remained in ICU. He wanted to give her some space, but still wanted to see her. The week after, he visited Blue Café more often than his cholesterol warranted. He couldn't help but hope for another opportunity to talk to her. Unfortunately, there was no sign of her. Three miserable weeks passed without the sight of her beautiful face or the sound of her enchanting voice. And it didn't help his mental health when he thought about Robert showing up unexpectedly.

"That's just gotta be her ex." He thought, walking out the door for a run one afternoon. He had sought her out at the children's hospital when visiting Max, but he hadn't seen her there either, so he simply checked on the status of Leyanie, who slowly seemed to be improving. However, he never bothered to ask her about Jennifer. Wherever he went, he searched for her in crowds, at the mall, and even the local bookstores.

Nothing!

One day, during a workout at Gladiator's Gym, his search for her finally came to an end. Settling into the seat of the leg-press machine, he thought he spotted her from the corner of his eye, walking by in some light blue sweatpants and a soft pink top.

"Jennifer." He whispered ecstatically.

He released the yellow handle of the leg-press machine and watched her climb onto the orange-wheel cycle. He paced around the gym, master-planning a clever way to approach her without being intrusive. He stopped at the water fountain for a drink when an idea came to mind. Amped, he pressed too hard on the button of the fountain, squirting water into his eyes.

"Crap!"

"You all right over there, buddy?" one of the trainers asked in a chipper tone, watching David pull the end of his T-shirt up to his eyes. "Hitting those weights too hard, huh?"

"Yeah. I'm fine." David laughed at himself. He couldn't seem to get it together whenever Jennifer was around. "I'm good. I'm good." He muttered with forced assurance, walking away slightly embarrassed. "I'm losing it, man."

David popped a piece of spearmint gum into his mouth and marched with some seriously fake confidence toward the bicycle equipment.

You got this, bro. Go hard or go home, but don't go home empty-handed.

He saw Jennifer cycling away with her face buried in a Bible devotional book. He quietly sat on the cycle next to her and tried to adjust the seat, however his foot slipped off the pedal and he banged his shin against it.

"Ouch. Inappropriate word," He wailed in excruciating pain. The four-letter word nearly escaped his mouth. "I almost cursed. Lord forgive thee . . . er . . . I mean me." He let out a heavy sigh, grunting in pain. "Clearly, I need more saving today." He glanced around the room to see if anyone else had noticed. He heard one of the patrons repeat the phrase, *inappropriate word*. He couldn't help but laugh at himself. *Ah, exercise! No pain, no gain, right?* Of course the one person he didn't want to notice his predicament was the only one who actually did.

"Are you okay?" Jennifer got off the cycle and came to his side.

For a minute, hearing her voice made him forget about the pain.

"Oh hey, Jennifer." He let out a self-deprecating laugh. Still, her concern was pretty satisfying. "I didn't see you there." He cringed at how fake that had sounded.

"I'll grab some ice for you—be back."

David gently grabbed her arm and smiled. "I'm fine, I'm fine. No need to get ice for a scraped-up shin. This is nothing. I just need to be less clumsy next time."

This hurts like crazy!

"It's no trouble. You don't want to mess with swelling." She quickly headed toward the reception desk as his eyes followed her lithe form.

Jennifer's concern for him made him have a flash of the day he'd fallen off the monkey bars all those years ago.

"Bet I could hang upside down." David bragged to his childhood friend.

"No, you can't," his friend said.

"Watch me." He climbed up to the bar.

David got one foot around it, but when he tried to get the other, he slipped and fell on his back and shoulders. The impact knocked the wind out of him. He gulped in a deep breath, squinting up at the sky in pain. Every child and parent in the playground stared at him with varying looks of concern and pity. He turned to the side to see his mother sitting on the bench nearby. She moved her head away from the newspaper and sighed angrily. Their eyes met while he was still on the ground, but they weren't on the same page. Her eyes glimmered detachment and apathy. He begged for her care and comfort, but the frigid expression on her face never changed, nor did she make any move to come over to see if David was okay. There was only the voice of children and their parents checking to see if he was hurt.

"Back." She announced. "Sit over there and put your leg up. And by the way, nice save."

David returned from that aching memory with an electrical surge jolting through his body as she helped him up by the arm and guided him to a nearby bench. The warm, gentle touch of her hands comforted him. Once seated, she placed the ice on his shin.

"Save. What do you mean?"

"Inappropriate word."

He busted out laughing again. "Yeah, I caught myself."

She stood up and rested her hand on her hip. "I see we ran into each other again. Are you stalking me or something?"

"You're not stalkable," he teased dryly. "I haven't seen you at the café or hospital for weeks. It's like you're not nearly as addicted to coffee as the rest of us mere mortals." He smiled, satisfied when she returned it with one of her own. "And I didn't see you until a few minutes ago. I swear it."

"Stalkable, huh? I think pain causes you to make up words. And what do you mean by that, not stalkable?" She threw a playful punch at his arm. "I guess we keep missing each other. I'm at the hospital and café quite a bit. Can't help it if your timing stinks." She shrugged and gave him a warm smile.

"I'm already in pain and you're throwing a jab at me. Thanks, Jennifer." He rubbed his arm animatedly. "Probably so," he said, responding to her comment about them missing each other.

"That's tough love, sweetie." She winked and fixed her ponytail. "Tough love."

"Anyhow, I saw you pass by and head toward the bicycles, so I figured I'd come over to say hi."

"Wait a sec. You just claimed you didn't see me."

David quickly put his head down, covered his face with his hands, and cringed with laughter. *Can't hide anything from this woman.*

"Well, uh, you know . . . I thought I saw you but wasn't sure. You know how that is." He nodded up and down, trying to persuade her to believe him.

"Uh-huh. Right." She mirrored his movements and walked to her exercise bike and climbed back on. "I know what you mean. Are you working on anything new with your writing?"

"Thinking about crossing over to another genre. Mystery. The plots are challenging to work with, but I'm mostly known for romance novels. It might throw my readership off a bit. Hopefully, they'll be willing to cross over with me."

"I think they absolutely will. Lots of people who love romance books also love mystery."

"Got a point there. How's Leyanie?"

"They're monitoring her closely. She's been resting. I haven't been able to talk with her much. I stop by to watch her from the window."

"I've been praying for her." He started rubbing the bag of ice across his shin.

"That's very thoughtful of you," she said kindly, hopping back on the cycle and getting back to her workout. "She needs all of our prayers."

He watched her peddle for a few seconds until realizing she'd completely removed her attention away from him. He quickly glanced around, as if expecting someone to explain to him how their conversation had come to such an abrupt end. He couldn't read her. She seemed so remote and distant after being so kind and caring only a moment before.

Leyanie probably has her down lately.

Or maybe I made her nervous because she did think I was stalking her?

He released a soft chuckle under his breath. He needed to get out more often. Maybe read fewer mysteries? Either way, it was clear he wouldn't make any headway with her at this point. She'd already closed herself off to him.

"Well, thank you for the ice. I should probably get back to my workout."

She nodded. "And I should probably end mine. It was great to see you again, David. Have a nice day."

Yep, dismissal, if there was ever was one! He stood and gingerly walked away from her, hoping she'd stop him before he got too far away, but he didn't hear her angelic voice call after him. The rhythmic swish of machines worked and the grunts and weights smashing against the floor echoed in his ears instead. He shoved his gym clothes inside his bag, sensing his chances with her were nil.

I've tried, Lord. You know I have. I think I'm gonna need a little divine intervention here.

He headed back toward the leg-press, but stopped short, realizing his heart just wasn't in it today. He grabbed his water bottle and gym bag and walked out of the weight room toward the exit. He wasn't expecting to find Jennifer sitting on the bench outside when he pushed through the double doors. She was rifling through her bag, apparently looking for something, but not having much luck judging by the annoyed look on her face. He clenched the strap of his gym bag, bracing himself for another round of rejection. He just couldn't get enough of it. He approached her like he would a jumpy colt.

"Looking for something?"

He cringed at his question. Of course she was looking for something.

"My keys." She shouted in exasperation. "I swear I put them in my purse. Hope I didn't drop them somewhere in the locker room."

While she was on a mission to find her keys to get going, he interpreted the moment differently. He nearly broke out into a smile pleased under the belief the Lord was ~~buying~~ gracing him with more time to spend with her.

"May I sit down?" he asked, trying snuff out the excitement in his voice about the loss of her keys. Probably not an appropriate reaction.

"I don't mind." She scooted over, still searching through her bag.

"Do you have a specific pocket in your purse you like to place them in typically?"

Dave, really? Man, this is so terrible. Do you really want her to find her keys and leave you hanging again?

"Yes, and they aren't there." She looked up at him and blew her hair out of her face. "I even checked with the front desk and nobody has turned them in yet."

Well, that was promising. What was the likelihood that she'd consent to him giving her a ride?

"I'm sure someone from the facility will find your keys and give you a call. I could call a taxi."

"The offer is kind, but I just know I have them in here somewhere. Besides, I have a million errands to run." She went back to digging through her purse.

Well, that had tanked, but he could at least keep her company until she found them. "So how long have you lived in the area? I've never seen you around here at the gym before."

She paused and faced David. "About six years—lived in DC, but it's been two years now in Northern Virginia." She opened her bag wider. It looked like she firmly believed her keys were somehow hidden in the lining of her purse.

Determined. He liked that about her.

"Oh, really. Where are you from? Didn't have the chance to ask." He fully admitted to himself that he was trying to distract her from searching for her keys.

"Miami," she said, pulling out lip gloss, a headband, and a compact mirror.

"Oh. I was thinking from somewhere else. You have distinctive facial features."

That got her attention. She stopped searching long enough to give him a bemused look. One of her eyebrows arched up. "What in the world do you mean by that?"

"You have a very unique look: your round face, the shape of your eyes, and the wavy texture of your hair. I can also hear a Caribbean accent. That's really what gave it away."

The corner of Jennifer's lips went up and her lashes batted a few times.

"My ancestry comes from Turks and Caicos."

He just knew there was something exotic about her. It made perfect sense now. Most of the women he'd dated had looked nothing like Jennifer. David didn't necessarily have a type, although many of them could pass for models. Her features were unique, different, and new to him. He liked that.

"I was right." David cheered, earning another grin from her.

"Where are you from?" Jennifer asked.

"Born and raised right here in Alexandria." He gloated with a proud lift of his chin.

"Ever thought of relocating?" She quickly looked up at him.

He sensed the question was an important one. The thought crossed his mind that perhaps if they got together, she might be open to leaving Northern Virginia one day.

"Nah." David shook his head. "But I'm open to wherever God leads me."

"It's good to be open-minded, but to plant your roots in one place is good, too." She reached back into her bag.

"I agree." He wondered if maybe she'd been testing him to see if he was more of a nomad or a man of stability? Many authors liked to get up and travel whenever inspiration hit them.

"Ah-ha." She lifted her hand from her bag and dangling the keys in front of David while simultaneously dashing his hopes to pieces. "Found them. Thank you for keeping me company. That was kind of you." She got up to make her way to the parking lot.

"No problem, Jen," David said faintly. He wondered if it was a good idea to join her. "Same here. Hey, wait." He stood up as if he were preparing to make an announcement. All at once, his throat went dry. "Let's walk and talk," he suggested firmly with confidence.

She grinned. In some way, it seemed she took a liking to his persistence.

"Let's speed walk."

He walked beside her and cleared his throat, hoping she'd parked far away to buy time for more conversation. Unfortunately, that wasn't the case. Her car was a few steps away from where they were. She stuck the key into her white Mercedes coupe and turned around with an inquisitive expression. David bit down on his lips, gripped the strap around his shoulder bag, and took a fortifying breath.

He cleared his throat again. "I was wondering if we could link up again?"

She opened her car door and panted out a short breath. "Persistent, I see," she said with some fervor in her voice.

That gave him some hope; however, he wasn't prepared for her direct response.

"Dave, please don't take this as rejection." Her gaze shifted diffidently to the ground.

He stood still and his eyes widened a little as he braced himself for what she was about to say.

"It's not that I'm not interested in getting to know you. I just don't think the timing is right. There's too much going on right now. I hope you can understand that." She sank into the seat and pulled the seatbelt across her chest. "It was a great experience partnering with you to do something for the kids at the hospital."

He nodded his head in understanding, wanting to ask about Robert, but he knew it wasn't his place yet, although he suspected that whatever had happened between her and Robert had a lot to do with her constant aversion of spending time with him. "You got something on your car over there?" He spotted a white envelope in her windshield wiper.

"Odd." She got out of the car. "I didn't notice that up there." She removed it.

He waited to see if she was going to open it. Instead, she just got back into the car.

"I understand." He acknowledged, getting out of his head. "Whenever the time is right, I want to be the first to know." He closed her car door.

"The first?" she replied with a half-smile.

"I mean," David said playfully and shrugged his shoulders, "I'm sure other men are interested in you."

"And I'm sure you've got Samantha. Bye, David." She waved to him and drove off before he could respond to that unfounded statement.

"She's a tough one." He waved back, catching her first and last initials on the license plate.

His good looks and charisma didn't affect Jennifer Washington. It burned him deep down inside that she didn't give him much to go on. He pondered if maybe she wanted to see how determined he was, if his interest was genuine, or if he was just the typical guy who only wanted one thing.

"I hope what Kelsey said is right." He limped to his car. "But I wonder what was in that envelope. Ah . . . I don't know. Not gonna worry about that."

It'll drive me crazy.

~

SATURDAY MORNING DAVID hobbled into the cool empty auditorium of Miss Smith's women's shelter. He sat up front in one of the white folding chairs. He rubbed his hands together and cupped them, blowing warm air to generate heat. Miss Smith walked in quietly. A dimple formed on his cheek when he smelled her rose perfume and felt the gentle, motherly touch of her soft, fragile hands on his shoulders. His eyes shut, and he sighed deeply, moving his hand on top of hers. He'd yearned for that motherly touch since childhood.

"David, how are you? It's always good to see you." She kissed him on the cheek, came around, and joined him. "Did you sneak in here?" Miss Smith's Southern accent remained, even after relocating from Charleston, South Carolina thirty years ago.

"No." He chuckled and looked into her brown eyes. "I just came in for some quiet time before we get started." Before Miss Smith got a chance to ask David about his mother, he got up and limped around the auditorium.

David had found Miss Smith's shelter through a help wanted ad in the newspaper. The name of her shelter was *Woman of Virtue*. He'd shown up one morning to donate pillows and linens and ended up painting the dormitories. He'd also made handsome financial contributions and continued to stop by frequently to volunteer. He eventually confided to Miss Smith about his relationship with his mother, and his journey to becoming an international bestselling novelist. After finding his story so compelling and inspiring, she'd invited him to lead Bible studies, hold prayer meetings, and give motivational speeches to the shelter residents whenever his schedule permitted. He'd agreed without reservation.

"Oh, David, what's wrong with you? Are you okay?" She pointed to his leg.

"I hurt myself at the gym. It's nothing."

"I hope she was worth it." She joked. "I'm going to get everyone together."

"Speaking of worth it." He laughed a little. "A month ago, I met this woman, Miss Smith. I've never experienced anything like this before."

Miss Smith closed her eyes and smiled tenderly. "Go on, David."

"When I saw Jennifer, I felt God's presence come over me so strong. I can't..." He looked down at the palm of his hand, trying to gather what he felt. "I can't explain why that happened." He returned his attention to her.

Miss Smith let out a knowing grunt.

His lips twisted a little. "What does that mean, Miss Smith?"

"Sounds like you met someone special. I've been praying for your wife."

"Praying for my wife?" He was a little caught off guard, but then again, she knew certain aspects of his love life.

"I pray for you and your wife often. I believe she's a special lady. Set apart! The spirit of God will be in her, and her relationship with God is going to ignite yours in a way to go deeper in Him. She's going to understand where you precisely are in Christ and support you in getting there, but you must be prepared to court her. There's virtue in her, David, and she's been through the wringer with other men. You have to be prepared, healed, and soul-tie free. I believe that's why you felt God's presence."

He moved his hand across his heart, feeling God's presence again. "I hope that I'm prepared for her."

"In time you'll be, but as of now, you're not quite there. Be patient, David. You could delay that good thing God says a man will find." She winked.

He felt God's presence stronger, and he stood for a few seconds speechless.

"In time, young man. In time," Miss Smith reminded him.

THE CLACK of his shoes against the bamboo hardwood floors echoed throughout the auditorium as the ladies took their seats. There were about thirty people present. At the podium, David rehearsed the poem he'd prepared, but the thought of salvaging his relationship with his mother hit him square in the chest. He envisioned her sitting front and center, listening to his poem and looking completely disinter-

MELVIN DAVIS

ested. Anger boiled within him. He imagined staring at her callous face—communicating without words that there was no need to reconcile now. He'd made it this far in life without her. He dropped his head, concluding that maybe it wasn't meant for them to have the kind of relationship he thought they should have. He had prepared himself mentally and emotionally for the day that she'd pass away. He told himself he didn't care if she died. It hurt him to arrive to such a dark and unfortunate conclusion.

Love is truly tested when it's inconvenient to give it unconditionally.

The chattering voices of the women in the auditorium broke him away from his heavy thoughts. Seats filled with both familiar and unfamiliar faces staring at him with wary and curious eyes. He pulled out a canary yellow handkerchief from his brown tweed sports jacket and cleaned his eyeglasses with it. Miss Smith nodded, and he yanked the wiry neck of the microphone closer to him.

"Before I begin, I'd like to say that all of you women here are beautiful and special to me. Thank you all for allowing me to be part of your lives. I have a poem that I'd like to share with you. It's about a mother and her son who I saw at a park. The poem was also inspired by a boy who never experienced the kind of motherly love and nurturing that he needed. Is that okay with you all?"

He heard murmurs of approval and a few claps as he twisted the cap off his bottled water to take a big swig. Then he began:

"I saw a boy running with a balloon one day. His mother shouted, 'Be careful, Aden. You're going to lose the balloon I just bought you.'

"'Okay, Mommy.' He ran in circles on the trimmed green grass where other kids played, but Aden ended up letting the balloon slip out of his small hands. I observed and listened to the response of Aden's mother. 'It's okay, dear,' she said. 'When you grow up one day, there are some things that you'll have to let go of, and those things will be replaced by something greater than what you had before. You'll get another balloon, but not today.' She smiled, embracing him with a hug and a kiss on the cheek.

"'Okay, Mommy.' Aden wiped his tears.

"I was amazed that Aden's mother didn't yell at him when the balloon accidentally slipped away. Her discipline was combined with care, love, and affection. Seeing this struck a chord deep within me—inspiring this poem entitled, *The Mother I Never Had*. I hope you enjoy it."

David cleared his throat before continuing.

Who can take the shine out of the sun?

Who can take the beauty out of beauty?

Who can take the life out of life?

Only the Creator.

Only the One who spoke the universe into existence with His words.

I'm speaking of the One through Jesus Christ."

David paused, feeling God's soothing, warm presence. The women in the audience thought he was waiting for applause. They had no idea what he was actually experiencing at the moment.

"What happened to the look of love in her eyes? Only distance I see.

What does her warm touch feel like? Only cold and pain I feel.

Where's the peace in her voice? Wrath is the only sound familiar to me.

Where did her love and validation go? Only her anger and apathy I know.

Within this prose are my feelings, thoughts, and spirit.

Within this prose are my hurts and pains, rejections and confusion.

Within this prose are parched lips, unquenched thirsts, unanswered prayers, and questions.

Why not the contrary?

As space and time changed, I changed—changing in the direction of progression.

I emptied my pain into the hands of Jesus Christ.

And He in return filled me with an unmatched love.

I'm no longer haunted by a love I wish I could've received.

I have God's love."

He paused for a moment, allowing those last words to really sink in, not only for their benefit but for his as well. "Thank you."

Miss Smith and the rest of the women applauded as she approached the podium. She took her place next to David and spoke into the mic. "Wow, that was heartfelt, David." She dabbed her teary eyes with a tissue.

The women in the room clapped louder and louder until everyone gave him a standing ovation. He removed his reading glasses, bowing, thanking them silently.

Miss Smith whispered into his ear, "Don't worry. Things will get better between you and your mother."

"Thank you, Miss Smith." David stepped up to the microphone. "Remember, the deepest wounds heal when you connect with God. Spend time in His presence. Talk to Him, praise Him, and worship Him."

Several of the women in the audience nodded in admiration.

"Take time to love yourself unconditionally," he continued. "No person should be able to do what you can do for yourself. Receiving love from others should complement the love you already have within you. Mend those fractures beneath the surface, stop seeking love and validation from someone else—especially a man. Self-love is sufficient, but God's is greater. Thank you again."

David stared beyond the women and into the truth of his existential reality. He should take his own advice. He'd never released the anger and pain from his mother's cruel treatment and placed it in God's hands. Neither had he truly forgiven her.

This is why Miss Smith said I wasn't ready. Another memory seized him as he considered all the hurt he held in his heart.

"David, what are you doing over there?" His mother threw her hands up in a fit. Her voice was husky and intimidating. "Why aren't you playing with your cousins?"

With his hands gripped tightly around the blue plastic shovel, David faced his mother's familiar, sinister stare.

"You're too quiet! Why are you so quiet?" his mother yelled. "What are you thinking? You must be stupid or something. Look at how your cousins play with everyone else. Go over there with them!"

David continued to play in the sandbox while glancing at his raging mother.

"I said, go over there with them," she screamed. "Are you chicken or some-

thing? And what the hell are you drawing over there? You're always drawing those stupid maps or writing some dumb story. I'm surprised you're not talking to yourself today."

His mother stepped into the sandbox and kicked sand in the air, erasing the drawings he'd created. Some sand flew into his eyes, causing them to sting and tear up.

"I'm going to feel sorry for you when you grow up, mute boy! Everyone's going to think you're weird and retarded. You stupid idiot! You're dumb just like your father."

David's hands loosened from the blue shovel. His thoughts came to a standstill. A heaviness settled around his heart. His eyes met with his cousin, who had stopped playing with the other boys and girls. David's head lowered to his chest and a tear dropped into the sand. He was more than embarrassed and hurt. He was broken.

"David," Miss Smith said, tugging on his arm. "David?"

He shook himself and finally answered her.

"I'm sorry, Miss Smith. Yes?"

"Are you joining us for lunch?"

"No, thank you. Not this time. I have to prepare for my charity event tomorrow evening."

"How much have you raised thus far?" Miss Smith asked, taking a checkbook from her purse.

"About one point two million."

She let out a low whistle, sounding impressed, and handed him a check. "Here, take this. I know you'll put it to good use."

"You don't have to." He started to push it away.

She placed the check in his hand anyway. "You help out around here so much. Take it. Don't embarrass me out here in front of everyone," she insisted.

"Thank you, Miss Smith. I really appreciate it."

"Okay, dear." She rubbed David's back and looked intently into his eyes. "David, you know what you have to do."

"I know, Miss Smith. I know." He admitted.

"I love you." She kissed him on the cheek. "That little boy is going to be filled with so much love. The man you are today will come to know of it."

"I love you too, and I believe so as well. Thank you, Miss Smith."

The streets of DC were filled with busybodies and parades of people who looked more like tourists. Lights gleamed from the windows of restaurants, pubs, clothing, and jewelry stores. David wasn't too far from the Archtop Hotel. He parked his car in one of the parking lots nearby and speed-walked down the streets.

He pushed through the heavy, thick, tall, double glass doors with gold handles. Raking the dirt off the bottom of his shoes on the beige and hunter green oriental rug, he nodded to one of the bellhops he'd become well acquainted with throughout the years due to hosting events for writers and charities. He casually reached into his black tuxedo jacket and handed him a generous tip.

"The bellhop nodded and thanked David.

"Anytime, my brother." David nodded back, strolling into the ballroom.

Inside, men and women in the audience sat restlessly at round tables that were draped in white tablecloths. The woman spear-heading the event looked relieved upon spotting him.

Yeah, I know I'm running late. Stupid traffic.

A white glowing light in the middle of the tables offered enough lighting in the dim room for people to see each other's faces. On his way to the stage, he bypassed some familiar faces. He recognized colleagues he'd formerly met at writing conferences, business partners, and beta readers that had read his books earlier in his career. He cut his eyes at the women he'd had more than a professional relationship with at some point in his career and smiled at them. Scanning the room, he felt someone staring at him and noticed a gentleman sitting in the far back. He squinted his eyes trying to make out the clean-shaven face.

He looks familiar . . . kinda like that Robert guy.

He blocked the face out and got on stage, adjusting the lapel of his jacket.

He gripped both sides of the podium tight. His head was slightly hungover at the sight of the hundreds of people who had shown up at the charity event. It didn't matter how many times he spoke in front of people, stage fright still snuck up on him. He caught a glimpse of Kelsey in a front-row seat pointing at his watch. David laughed through his eyes. That helped ease his nerves a little. He yanked the microphone toward him, creating some feedback. He shook his head, wishing he were anywhere but here.

"Wow." He blurted out loud.

Then he spotted another familiar face in the audience. As soon as he'd pushed her from his thoughts, there she was Jennifer Washington. Legs crossed with hands resting on top of her white purse and her long hair pulled up in a ponytail. She sat pristine in a sleek black cocktail dress. She looked regal in a way a queen sat unbothered on her throne.

"Jen—." He started to say her name, completely forgetting he was in front of an audience of hundreds of people in the ballroom. Kelsey got to his feet, clapping away as if David had already given his speech.

"Excuse me." David cleared his throat, making Jennifer chuckle into her hands. "Thank you all for contributing to this wonderful cause. I'm grateful for your charitable donations. It's been about seven years since my dad passed, and we're more determined than ever to find a cure for lung cancer. We're going to move over next door to the dining room shortly. Thank you." He bowed his head in thanks. He looked around for the guy that had been sitting in the back, but he was nowhere to be found.

Kelsey, along with some of David's writing colleagues and business partners, huddled around him once he stepped off stage.

"Man, who's Jen?" one of the guys asked.

They teased him about his scatterbrained incident, but David didn't care. He beamed with happiness. All that mattered at that moment was seeing Jennifer. He saw her across the crowded ballroom. They locked eyes for a few seconds, but she turned her head and continued chatting and laughing away with a group of women. He grimaced at her nonchalance, rejoining the conversation with the people around him.

She's trying to play it off. He chuckled to himself.

Well into dinner, David gathered everyone together to propose a toast. He raised his wine glass high in the air, seeking out Jennifer in the crowd, but she was nowhere in sight. David gave a brief toast. And not long after, Jennifer returned, glancing at him from across the room. David flashed an unbothered, debonair smile before bringing the brim of his glass to his lips. He continued conversing with his colleagues. Soon after, the lively conversation about sports was winding down when he felt a light tap on his shoulder and heard his name called.

"That must have been one heck of a toast, considering all the noise you guys made over here. Did someone donate a million dollars tonight?" Jennifer asked.

David gave her a teasing smile. "Nothing much. I just told everyone that I'd finally met the woman of my dreams, and I plan to marry her soon."

She shook her head at his silly antics. "Oh really. And the lucky girl is where?" She glanced around, pretending to search for the woman in question. "She must be over there. Looks like there's a line of women ready to talk to you."

He laughed her comment off. "Right here," he said equably, never taking his eyes off her.

Why not go for it? He thought.

She playfully hit him on the arm, a gesture he found encouraging since she was initiating physical contact.

"You're quite the Casanova." Her cheeks turned a rosy tint. It was clear to David that Jennifer had a hard time accepting compliments or a man's attention, for that matter.

"I seem to need the practice with you." His eyes tried to tell her what his words just couldn't. Why was she fighting this so much? He knew she was attracted to him. He'd seen glimpses of it here and there, but he kept running into her emotional brick walls. Yet as he stood there, looking into her beautiful eyes, he thought he saw her soften just a little. The hard edge to her stare made way for something that looked a lot like longing. He couldn't give up. "It's nice to see you again, Jen."

A plethora of gratitude was behind his words.

"You as well." She'd regained her composure. "It's quite a coincidence that we'd run into one another again, wouldn't you say?" She crossed her arms.

"Maybe it's not." David quipped. He gestured to her glass. "Can I get you another? Don't think you're enjoying that."

She held up the full glass of red wine and made a sour face. "This is gross. I'm not a drinker."

David took the glass out of her hand and quickly returned it to the bar before grabbing her something he thought she might like a little better. "Here. Try this."

She took a tentative sip. "Mmm. I like. A fancy sparkling cider? Much better."

"Let's have a seat over there." He escorted her to one of the tables near the dining area of the ballroom and pulled out her chair. He was relieved when she willingly went with him

She's not running away. That's always a good sign!

Before David could get comfortable in a conversation with Jennifer, Kelsey walked over and joined them. "This is the special woman you were telling me about?" he asked, pulling a chair out next to her.

Jennifer's face grew bright turning toward Kelsey and nodded a greeting.

"This is her." A dimple formed at David's mouth as he winked at Jennifer.

"Your name again, madam?" He asked with mock formality.

"Jennifer."

In David's opinion, her bright smile gave life to the entire ballroom.

"Pleasure to meet you, Jennifer." Kelsey lifted her hand to his lips and kissed it.

"Come on, Kels." David burst out laughing. "Cut the Sir Lancelot crap."

"I taught you everything you know, kid," Kelsey said, mimicking Clint Eastwood's voice.

"Get outta here." David grinned.

"See you around, kid." Kelsey ambled away.

David eyed Jennifer through his raised wine glass. The dry red wine rested against his lips until it dashed onto his taste buds. He was thrilled that Jennifer had enjoyed Kelsey's brief company. He wanted a woman who'd accept his friends and loved ones.

"You downed that pretty fast."

That comment sure did pinch him.

"Are you a drinker?" She waited with anticipation for his response.

"Every now and then." That's all he wanted to say. "Hey, I saw someone that kinda looks like your ex."

"Are you kidding me?" She looked around the room in a panic.

"I don't know. Could be just me."

She sighed in frustration.

"Let's focus on the evening. It probably wasn't him. You look stunning tonight."

"Thank you, David. You're pretty dapper tonight. Very handsome."

"Thank you." He bowed.

"By the way, how old are you? Just thought I'd ask. You look really young." She sipped more of her cider.

"Thirty." David answered.

Jennifer quickly gulped down the last bit of the cider. "I'll have a glass of wine now," she said, pretending to signal a waiter.

"Get outta here." David laughed. "Am I too young?" He sipped and then circled the last bit of wine in the glass.

"I have two years on you." She quickly glanced away from him.

"And?" David cocked his head to the side and crossed his arms.

"You seem mature beyond your years."

Scie

Sp

Professor Mack E. Crayton III, PhD
Scientist and Christian

Urban Reader Books

440 E McCullough Dr. Ste A-130 Charlotte, NC

April 2, 2022 | 1:00 - 3:00PM

Book Tour : Book Reading, Discussion, and Signing

Using *Science* to better

ce &

irituality

h Mack E. Crayton III, Ph.D.

Coming to Charlotte, NC

Available on www.Amazon.com [Paperback and Kindle eBook] and Urban Reader Books

erstand Biblical *Scriptures*.

"I get that a lot." He raised his eyes a little, wondering where the conversation was headed. "Am I too young or something?"

"No. Age doesn't matter, but maturity does," she said, glancing at the time on her black-faced slim watch. "It's getting late."

"May I walk you to your car?"

Her eyes traveled up to his tall frame. "Sure. You're such a gentleman!"

The evening had come, and the blue in the sky was escorted away by the night. The weather was genial and perfectly conducive for a casual stroll around the city. Streetlights shined off the old cobblestone sidewalk of the narrow street. The ambiance in the air matched the romantic disposition David held in his heart. He felt like they'd been cut and pasted into a scene in one of his novels.

This seems too surreal.

"Anything exciting going on in your life?" he asked.

"I got an upcoming symposium to prepare for . . . kinda nervous about it."

"The nervousness is natural. It's a good thing."

"Why's that?"

"You can rely on your confidence and ability to accomplish whatever it is that you're trying to do. Whenever I have a major event or speaking engagement, I spend time in prayer or meditate on God's word. It eases my fear, and typically I practice at home. I envision seeing a crowd of people before me," he said, pausing for a moment. "Are you okay?" Her grin told him she was impressed with what he was saying.

"I admire your walk with Christ. It's beautiful. I appreciate you taking the time to share that with me."

"Well, thank you."

When they arrived at her car, he gallantly opened the door, eliciting a quiet chuckle from her. "You have good taste in cars." He nodded toward her vehicle.

"Thanks." She settled into her seat just as the sound of her ringtone fired off repeatedly. "Excuse me for a sec, David. This may be my mom calling." She searched for her phone in her purse and found it. She glanced up and saw David walking away.

"Wait, you're not going to say good night?" she yelled out the window, bringing the phone up to her ear.

On the other end of the line, he spoke in a suave undertone. "Not until I know that you're safe and sound in bed."

"Smooth, Mr. Bradshaw, so smooth." She giggled, smiled at him and put her tinted windows up slowly.

"Just a little." He laughed. There was a brief silence. He held the phone to his ear, smiling, just knowing he'd swooned her. "I'm going to stay on the phone until you make it securely home," he said, opening his car door and spotting a note on his windshield.

What's this? His eyes cut left to right. *Secret admirer?*

"Aww, thank you, David."

He glanced up and gave her a distracted smile. "Uh, you're welcome, Jennifer." He folded the note into his hand.

Over the phone, he tried his best to forget about the note he hadn't read yet. He didn't want it to disrupt the romantic vibe. They shared their most embarrassing moments. He told Jennifer about the time he'd stood at the top of the stairway at church while his childhood pastor had given the benediction. How his Sunday school buddy pushed him from behind, and the sole of his shoe caught on the rug. He'd tumbled down the steps and crashed into a deaconess. She dropped the communion tray on his head, and he saw the old lady's underwear, which gave him nightmares for years. Jennifer laughed hysterically, pleading for him to stop before she got into an accident.

She told David about the time of doing pull-ups in middle school. She'd anxiously waited at the back of the line, biting her nails. Other girls picked up on her fear and poked fun at her. "I jumped as high as I could and slipped from the bar. I hurt my back so much, David, I cried."

"Oh no," he empathized with concern. "I can't believe the teacher didn't help you out."

"It was okay, David. I was a tough girl, and now I'm an even tougher woman," she said.

He could hear the mental toughness of survival in her voice. He knew she was a headstrong, independent woman. Yet, his heart confessed, *I still want the honor to protect you.* That possibility danced in his head for seconds.

"I'm sure you are."

"Oh, before I forget. Remember a few weeks ago, outside the gym? And you found a letter stuck in my windshield? I don't know who wrote it, but the note read, *He's mine.*"

David became quiet. "Uh, I don't know what to say. Who do you think the person was referring to?" he asked, thinking about the one he'd received.

"Have no idea. Whoever it was—it kinda freaked me out."

"I wouldn't worry about it too much. Someone could've placed that note on the wrong car. It's hard to call it."

"I guess. I have to go now. Thanks for staying up with me, David."

"Anytime, Jennifer. Good night."

"Good night, Mr. Bradshaw." She whispered low and soft.

They had a grand time chatting on the phone. It was as if they'd known each other for years. They were like two high school students who had crushes on each other and had finally mustered up the courage to talk.

He drove in a state of disbelief, feeling mawkish at the same time. Any man who yearns for a godly woman would share the same sentiments. He had never met a woman like Jennifer Washington before. He kind of laughed a little, simply for the fact that there was some hint of surrender in her voice when she said good night.

I think she likes me. My patience has finally paid off. God, you crack me up sometimes!

JENNIFER ARRIVED HOME BEFORE DAVID. She stepped into her condo feeling excited. In a way, she hadn't felt this nervous since the first guy she had crushed on in kindergarten. But what she was feeling for David was no comparison, and she couldn't put her finger on what had changed. She did such a great job at keeping him at arm's length, but seeing him on that stage, doing something good in honor of his father . . . well . . . it'd touched her, and she'd felt something different.

Peace.

Peace accompanied the romantic feelings she was developing for him. This was something she'd never had when she met Robert, and she'd never felt it throughout their relationship.

How could I have gone so long without feeling peace in that relationship?

She removed her shoes and blurted out loud, "I like him. He's not a bad guy. Wait, what did I just say?" She laughed to herself, rushing into the shower.

God, I didn't know I could feel this way again.

After she showered and climbed into bed, she called him back to make sure he'd made it home safe too. He was delighted that she returned the thoughtful gesture.

"Hey, I was wondering if we could get together this weekend," she said. "I'd like to return the favor for the skim latte."

"What day works for you?"

"Next week on Friday evening . . . let's say five," she answered.

"Friday evening is good for me," he agreed. "I'm gonna get some writing done before bed."

"Okay. I'll let you go. Thanks for staying up with me. I appreciate it. Good night again."

"Good night, Jennifer. I'll give you a call tomorrow."

I'm not ready to hang up.

"Sounds good. Oh, by the way, I read *Intimacy* and *The Breakfast Field*. You're such a talented writer. It's wonderful that you followed your dreams. Very inspiring!"

"Oh," David sighed, taken aback by her encouragement and sincere words. "Thank you. No woman has ever said that to me."

"Well, get some rest. Happy writing. Good night."

"Good night, Miss Washington."

After Jennifer got off the phone, she stared up at the ceiling and flashed a grin. She then curled up in the fetal position, smiling, thinking about how she'd run into David after not seeing him for a couple of days.

God, what are you trying to tell me? I know running into him tonight wasn't a coincidence. Didn't realize it was David's charity event...didn't realize it was his name on the flyer.

"Robert and I never talked like this, and I never felt this comfortable with him. There's something different about David." She took the note from her nightstand that was left on her car at the gym. She smelled it once more. "This fragrance is familiar."

DAVID STAYED up a bit longer with the phone still pressed against his ear. He imagined calling her back. He cleared his throat and started to rehearse what he'd say.

"What's up, Jennifer? What do you have in mind for this weekend?" He stopped to think for a minute. "That wasn't good." He laughed. "Let me try again. Jennifer, this is David," he said in the most unnatural deep tone. "After we have a good time, may I have the honor of taking you out?" He laughed even harder. He couldn't help but have his thoughts linger on her a little longer. There was a special bond forming between them. It was like a relationship blossoming from a friendship. He'd recently realized this was something he wanted to have in his next relationship.

His experiences and time spent with God had taught him a relationship without a foundation was nothing more than an intense emotional encounter that offered the impression of love. He knew, when times would get rough, emotions would quickly dissipate under uncomfortable conditions and challenging circumstances. He believed a Christ-centered relationship and a strong friendship would provide a foundation for love to thrive and exist upon. This is what David envisioned having with the woman God chose for him.

He removed the phone from his ear and examined it in the way curious eyes fasten on a foreign object. He couldn't believe he had just gotten off a late-night intimate chat with Jennifer Washington, the woman he thought he'd never see again, let alone call. Her encouraging words touched him in a way he'd never felt before. His ex-fiancée had never told him he was a talented writer. She'd never read any of his novels, but that didn't matter to David anymore. He had another woman who was supportive of him, other than Miss Smith. He smiled and then remembered the note left on his windshield. He wiggled it out of his back pocket and parted it open. He sat up in shock as he read: *She belongs to me.*

"What the heck is this about? Who left this note on my car?" He thought about it for a moment, remembering that man who had reminded him of her ex. "Gotta be her ex, man. I think that was him sitting in the back. Don't have time for drama." He wondered if it was a good idea to say something to Jennifer about suspicious activity. "I can't. This might create conflict." He balled the note up and tossed it in the trash.

The next day he called Jennifer, but she didn't answer or respond to his voicemail. Wednesday, he tried again to confirm their date for Friday. After two rings, her phone went directly to voicemail.

Odd, he thought. *I don't understand what's happening.*

He felt lured into the gray area by her lack of communication. The gray area is a place that no one wants to be. It's hard to get a clear signal of where someone stands with you. And the possibility of being hurt or disappointed seems to be greater than things working out smoothly.

He grew a little irritated. He always liked to confirm engagements at least two days before the commitment. This was crushing his momentum of hope.

JENNIFER CUDDLED in the white comforter staring at her phone. Beside her was the sonogram picture of Kayla. Mixed emotions swarmed her heart. She had just returned home from visiting Leyanie at the hospital. She hadn't improved much, and Jennifer felt her focus on David was a distraction she couldn't afford. She'd lost a lifetime with Kayla due to Robert and her father. She didn't want history to repeat itself with David. There wasn't much of a want or a desire to speak with him, either. The thought of losing her adopted daughter completely consumed her thoughts. She got on her knees to pray for the millionth time for Leyanie's healing.

"Please heal her, God. I can't lose her!"

Faith was far from her prayer. Discouragement had taken over to the point her lips stopped moving and she became faint-hearted.

What Jennifer was battling at this moment was valid. Faith is often challenged when we sense the inevitable coming or when we can't see a positive outcome of the situation.

FRIDAY CAME. David spent most of the morning and afternoon writing. He'd finally snapped out of his writing slump and started working on his next novel. He'd come up with a thrilling idea he knew his literary agent would be hyped about. As he kept writing, he'd look over regularly at his phone to see if Jennifer had called or texted. He'd then turn the phone facedown like it'd miraculously increase the chances of hearing from her. Every fifteen minutes he looked, and after not hearing from her, he lost a little bit of hope. It was killing him that Jennifer hadn't returned any of his phone calls or given him a heads-up in advance that there had been a change of plans. He would've been understanding. Knowing how busy he'd get with writing and traveling, he wasn't going to allow the negative thoughts to run rampant through his mind. He didn't quite know what to make of this, given how well things had been going between them. Around four o'clock, he decided to get dressed anyway. He was stepping out on faith. Just then, his phone rang. Jennifer's name appeared across the screen.

"Perfect timing," he confirmed excitedly before answering the phone. "What's up, Jen?"

"I apologize for getting back with you so late."

"It's cool. Getting dressed now, so I'm about ready." He stuffed both legs into his navy-blue chinos. When Jennifer didn't say anything, he knew something was up. Anxiety pinched him. He walked into the living room, slowly maneuvering a natural colored T-shirt on and drawing back the curtains in his living room to let some light shine in. He started cleaning and organizing. This was one way he dealt with difficult conversations. He'd partially keep himself distracted to lessen the impact of bad news. "What's on your mind?" He gripped his phone tight, sitting up on the ledge of his window, staring down into the neighborhood.

"I hate to come off as hot and cold."

"What do you mean?" Concern filled his voice. He bit his top lip and braced himself for her explanation.

"I don't think it's a good idea for us to keep meeting up. Volunteering with you was a great experience. I enjoy your company, but I'm not ready yet to get close to anyone. Too much is going on in my life right now, and Leyanie needs my support."

"I enjoy your company, too, but I thought I communicated that I'm not looking for a relationship at the moment."

"You did, but I feel it's heading in that direction, you know?"

David was quiet for a moment. He hopped off the ledge and made his way out of the house, keeping the phone to his ear. She definitely had a point. He did feel like things were headed down the path of becoming more than friends.

"Yeah. I understand. I'm sure Leyanie's health is taking its toll on you."

I have nothing else to say.

After an awkward moment, he finally spoke, "Well, you've got my number. If you change your mind, I'm here."

"I do. Thanks for understanding."

"Not a problem. I hope everything's okay." He paused, thinking about the note he'd received, waiting for further explanation, but got none.

"Cool. Talk to you whenever." He quickly hung up, walked to his car, opened the door, and tossed the phone into the passenger seat. He stood there staring at it, feeling despondent and embarrassed. "I'm not buying this crap."

He got in the car and slammed the door with his head bowed in disappointment, staring at the black leather steering wheel and clenching it with both hands. He squeezed it until his knuckles cracked.

There has gotta be more than Leyanie. It's her ex, right?

He couldn't believe he was dressed to impress, peppered in his finest cologne with nowhere to go. Women canceling on him was rare. It seemed to him he'd stumbled upon a woman who was completely unaffected by what he thought were moderate good looks and chivalry. He wasn't full of himself, but he didn't think he was repugnant, either. One thing was for sure, he wasn't heading back inside with nothing to do. There was absolutely no way he'd stay home on a Friday night. His deflated ego wouldn't allow it after Jennifer's rejection. He scrolled through his phonebook and decided it was time to reach out to his lady friend who'd left him a voicemail two months ago when Kelsey had stopped by unannounced. Nina was one of the many women he neglected since meeting Jennifer. When he called, she jumped at the chance of an outing with him.

He decided to head to Tyson's Corner Mall to pass the time. He tried to make a connection between Jennifer getting back with him so late and canceling their date at the last minute. The more he pondered it, the harder he pressed on the gas pedal. *"There's gotta be someone else in the picture. There's gotta be!"*

Jennifer got off the phone with a cloud of guilt floating above her head. *What am I doing? I'm playing with this man's emotions.* At least she was honest with herself, although she hadn't fully disclosed how she truly felt.

She went into her garage and searched a stack of boxes that hadn't been unpacked yet. There was one particular box she was looking for that had red tape on it. "There it goes," she mumbled, spotting it near the bottom. She lifted each box until finding it and peeling the tape off. Inside were a pile of textbooks from college. Underneath them were pictures of her and Robert.

I don't know why I still have these pics. "Must've forgotten to throw them away."

Each photo was dated and named by a specific theme, according to the places they had vacationed and visited. Some good feelings surfaced as she went through each picture. Then she broke down and cried.

"I wanted the relationship to work so badly. It's all my fault. My insecurities messed things up."

She possessed a menagerie of insecurities about men, their opinions, and their influences.

David never would have made me choose between him and Leyanie. If I'd have asked, we could've gone to visit her together tonight, and he would've been completely fine with that. What was I thinking?

She'd been unconsciously comparing him to Robert. She'd been projecting in a way. Robert's influence had been a powerful force in her life. He'd often made it a point to tell her how much weight she'd gained at different times in their relationship. She remembered standing in front of her mirror and covering her eyes, unhappy with what she saw and always fearing Robert would find another woman. Eventually, he did. He'd cheated on her a few times. And though she'd taken him back, the relationship was never the same.

There's something fundamentally devastating about unfaithfulness. It's like striking a million lines with a permanent marker against a white T-shirt. No matter how many times you wash or scrub it out, the stain remains. She'd tried to forgive, but her heart wouldn't allow her to forget. She'd stayed with a man who had broken her. She was held captive in a toxic relationship, knowing it wasn't ordained by God. She couldn't quite figure out why she'd continued going back after the heartbreak.

It was like a soul-tie, an unauthorized relationship God hadn't ordained.

"Why did I stay?" The question had lingered in her heart for years.

And why can't I trust my judgment with David? He isn't Robert. I should give him a call back.

Just when she was about to call him, her friend Matthew dialed in frantically. Matthew had been a previous colleague of Jennifer's. A few years ago, they'd worked together at the non-profit she currently directed. They became close when Jennifer had discovered he dealt with depression, and later he became suicidal.

"Matthew?" she asked.

"Jen? I think I need you."

It was their protocol for when things got tough for him. He'd reached out to Jennifer because he was having a down moment and wanted her company. Out of the kindness of her heart, she agreed to meet up with him.

I'll catch up with David another time.

Arriving at Tyson's Corner, David parked on the upper level of the parking deck where the movie theater was located. He got out of his car and saw a white Mercedes-Benz parked in front of him, just a few rows away. The initials JW were on the license plate. He remembered seeing it on Jennifer's car the night of his charity event. "God, I hope this isn't her car," he said, making his way into the mall with a nauseated feeling.

A long line looped around the entrance of the theater. And there, standing in line with another man, was Jennifer. They were laughing, appearing to enjoy each other's company. He couldn't believe it.

This is foul. He sighed in frustration and shook his head. *She totally fooled me!*

"It's Leyanie, huh?" His steps slowed as if he were trotting through mud, losing strength. "Women come, and women go." He shrugged in anger and walked into the bookstore.

A salesman, who had previously been cordial with David and was a fan of his work, saw him studying an advertisement for the book *1994.*

"Michael Duvon's book is great," the salesman praised, walking up to David.

"Oh, yeah?" David nodded and shoved his hands into his pockets.

"Yep. It's doing pretty well. I'll show you where you can find it."

On the front cover of the book, the title *1994* appeared in fiery red against a pitch-black background. He flipped to the back cover and saw a ghostly male figure. Behind him was a fashion house engulfed in flames. David was intrigued. He read the synopsis:

The chilling, unsolved murder of fashion mogul Andre Eustache leaves the fashion industry and Paris stunned. Detectives search meticulously for his murderer but fail to gather any promising clues. Michael Duvon's ability to retell and recapture the legacy of Andre Eustache is simply remarkable—a writer's writer!

"I'll take it." He handed the book to the salesman.

David arrived at his date's apartment about thirty minutes later, still fuming over Jennifer's behavior but recognizing there was absolutely nothing he could do about it. As he saw it, his future wife had canceled on him to spend time with another man. He felt it should've been him arm to arm, shoulder to shoulder, laughing and having a good time, preparing to spend a little over two hours with her. *He* wanted to enjoy a movie with her. It should've been *him*.

He shifted gears from Jennifer and grounded himself at the moment. His date wasn't ready yet, so he reclined his seat and began reading Chapter One of *1994.* David's eyes clung to every word. The further he got into the story, the more curious he became about Andre Eustache's murder. He took his pen and pad out from the glove compartment and scribbled notes about the story as he read. About five minutes later, his phone rang. He answered from his earpiece, without looking at the caller ID.

"Nina, what's taking you so long?" David said, getting a little impatient. "I'm across the street."

"Nina. Who's Nina?" a familiar voice responded, unnerved.

His mind froze for a second.

That's not Nina's voice. His heart beat faster and faster. *Jennifer.*

His mind thawed out in a matter of seconds when he remembered what he'd seen at the movie theater. Jennifer with another guy. Silence hung in the air, providing both David and Jennifer the opportunity to explain their actions. Before he could answer, his date opened the car door and fell over him in the passenger seat.

"Let's go, handsome." She smacked a loud kiss on his cheek.

He squeezed her thigh, hoping it'd silence her for a moment.

"Jennifer now isn't a good time. Can I call you later?" he asked, telling himself the guilt he felt was irrational. She was the one who had canceled on him to be with another man. He heard no response. He glanced at his phone and realized she had hung up. He started the engine and pulled into traffic. He was perturbed that his date had spoken into the phone. He knew this made matters worse.

After David and Nina had dinner, he took her back home instead of having her stay the night. She was shocked and threw a fit. She emphasized how he'd been acting strange the entire date. He apologized for seeming quiet, distance and subdued but not for taking her back home. "I'm a changed man," he expressed to her. She rolled her eyes and slammed his car door and gave him the middle finger.

HE CONTINUED with his usual routine, which included visiting Max, writing, working out at the gym, volunteering at Miss Smith's women's shelter, and communicating with his financial advisor to discuss diversifying his portfolio and stock options. The days rolled by, and he felt that whatever he and Jennifer had developed was nothing more than a fading memory. By the next weekend, he hadn't heard from her, and he didn't attempt to reach out either. He also didn't see her at the children's hospital. However, the following week, when he headed out to get a haircut, she caught him by surprise with a phone call. He answered without any inflection in his voice. Jennifer's tone voice came across the line as if nothing was wrong. It irked him even more.

"Hey, David. I'm so sorry about canceling on you and being MIA—

things have been a bit hectic lately," she admitted, as if their awkward moment over the phone had never happened.

"Oh, really," he continued with disinterest.

"Yes, they have," she said, seemingly unaware of his indifference. "What are you up to now? I'm free. We can grab a cup of coffee at Blue Café if you want."

"Bad timing. On my way to the barbershop," he revealed quickly and curtly.

Awkwardness coasted through the air, but this time it wasn't David getting the pink slip.

"Umm. Are you going to be free after?" she asked.

"Possibly." He wasn't interested in giving her any promises since she couldn't seem to keep hers.

What does this woman want?

"Okay. Just let me know if you can. Thanks."

"Cool." He hung up and let out a heavy sigh.

I don't have time for games.

He felt Jennifer was dismissing the whole matter, but he decided to meet up with her anyway. He figured this would most likely be a painful coffee breakup.

After he got a haircut and a beard trim, he gave linking up with her some thought again.

I don't know if this a good idea or not. I hate confusion. Either you're hot or cold. I don't do lukewarm. I know what I want.

He stared at his cellphone for a moment and decided to call her. He told her what time he was going to be there, and she seemed to agree without feedback.

At the café, he found Jennifer waiting at the same table where they'd first talked. She had a placid expression over her face with her hands folded across her lap. As he walked closer to the table, the muscles in the back of his neck tightened. All he could think about was the guy he'd seen her with and Jennifer overhearing Nina's voice in the car. He just didn't know what to say or what to expect from this get-together.

"How's it going?" he inquired, feeling a bit lifeless as he swung into the chair opposite her.

"I'm well," she replied a little too cheerfully.

Her response elicited even more irritation from him. "Hard to catch you these days, huh?" He gave her a hard-stone stare.

"No. It's just things that tend to come up. You know how that goes, right?" she retorted with all smiles.

"Right," he answered snidely. *Getting together is stupid and pointless.*

He was readily anticipating an explanation of her canceling on him.

"You're having a . . . wait, don't tell me." She jumped to her feet and relaxed one hand on her hip. "An extra hot, grande chai tea latte with . . ."

"Six pumps of chai and no water." David got to his feet.

"Darn it. I almost forgot your prescription," she carried on cheerfully.

You're so funny ha-ha-ha. "Good one," he replied dismissively.

Monica came out from behind the cash register and hugged him. He asked her how she was doing.

"Pretty good," she replied, waving hello to Jennifer and returning behind the counter to take their orders.

"I've noticed that you're very affectionate." Jennifer crossed her arms as they waited on their drinks.

"Which is weird because my dad was out of the picture, and my mom was pretty much hands-off with me." He grabbed his drink and handed Jennifer hers. He felt a little less tense for some reason. "I kinda yearn for affection because of that."

After uttering those words, he wondered why he'd shared this information with her since he no longer felt she was someone he could trust with the personal details of his life. He put the halt on his train of thought and tasted his drink to see if it was to his liking. He turned to Monica and gave her the thumbs-up.

"I see. My mother was affectionate with me, but my father wasn't." She eased into her seat at the table. David was less angry now but still guarded.

"Any idea why your mom held back?" Jennifer tore open a Splenda and dumped it into the cup.

"Oh, I don't know. I don't think much of it now." He shrugged his right shoulder like he didn't care and lowered the corner of his lips.

"I've been meaning to ask you. Why are you single? That is, if you are single, ladies' man," she teased.

His eyes broadened just a little, and he snickered with sarcasm. "Single." All he could think about was the guy she'd been with two weeks ago. He couldn't believe she dared to ask him why he was single. Yet

again, he figured he'd cut her some slack with his dating history. After all, he'd broken a few hearts by choosing not to commit to the women who wanted more.

"Yes, single," she reiterated. Her eyes nearly popped out of her sockets, zeroing in on David's face.

"I don't think I'm much of a ladies' man." He stared out the window, trying to figure out where this line of questioning was headed. He heard her short laugh of derision—the first sign she'd given that maybe she wasn't ready to act as if everything was okay between them.

"I find that very hard to believe. Now that I think of it, Samantha seemed to have the hots for you. I'm sure she kept you company back at the hospital that day."

"Guess I'm single because I haven't found the right one yet. I've been single for about seven months now."

"You're going to ignore my comment about Samantha?"

"Did we meet up to talk about her? If so, I didn't." The tension grew thick in the air and he noticed it. He wouldn't have minded if this conversation was cut short. He was ready.

I have better things to do.

"Okay. That's fine. But seven months, that's not long at all." She rested her chin in the palm of her hand. "Don't you need a break?"

He studied the chai in his coffee cup, stirring it a bit and taking a sip. He felt he was being interrogated.

"Depends on how you look at it. Our relationship had been over for a while, but neither of us wanted to admit it."

"Hmm." She lifted her cup slowly to her mouth. "I can relate to that. I got a question for you. What do you think about being equally yoked? Or what do you think is an equally yoked person?" Jennifer smiled behind her hand.

David laughed because he knew Jennifer was testing him to see where he stood with love, courting, and God.

"A person who is a gift from God, sent to understand, speak, and be your love language. That person is the forever-more love letter inside the envelope of your heart and a consistent presence of trust and security. She's the evidence seen and the substance of faithfulness. Your spouse should also be your best friend, a helpmate, and someone you can fellowship with. She's God's expression of His unconditional love to you. It's humbling to be loved by someone who sees our scars and other imperfections, and yet our spouse still chooses to love us. Love is present even when you're feeling like you don't want the company.

Jennifer sank back into her seat as David's words anchored deep into her heart. She pressed her hand against her chest. "Wow, David. I felt that." She exhaled. "Powerful! I've never heard it defined that way before."

"I just believe in real love and doing things God's way. At least, I try to," he expressed, feeling frustrated again and wondering where in the world this was headed.

Jennifer crossed her legs and gave him a considering look. "Are you currently seeing someone?"

Must be playing some type of mind game with me. I know you heard Nina's voice when you called. David waited to give a response, glancing around the mostly empty café in search of eavesdropping patrons.

"I have friends."

She took a quick swig of her coffee. "Friends? There's nothing wrong with friends."

Now we're being sarcastic.

This was some sweet torture to David. At this point, he had the right to remain silent, because anything he would've said could or would be used against him in the court of Jennifer.

Pretty much.

"So why haven't your previous relationships worked out?" she said, continuing her pointed interrogation.

He shrugged. "Sometimes a person can have all the qualities you're looking for, like physical attraction, intellect, a great personality, and belief in God, yet you feel deep down inside that something's missing."

"Like what?" She was curious.

"Peace." he answered sternly.

"Why would peace be missing if everything else is there? You just described the total package." She eyed him contemplatively. "This is getting good. It's refreshing to hear how a man thinks."

"Lifestyle. You can believe in God but not have a relationship with Him. Belief doesn't always translate into intimacy. It's difficult to be compatible with someone who isn't hungry for God like you are. I mean, especially if that person isn't a believer in Christ or has no desire to grow beyond the point of when he or she first gave their life to Him."

Jennifer nodded. "Sounds like that scripture in 2 Corinthians 6:14 where it talks about being unequally yoked with unbelievers. I've never thought about being unequally yoked with another believer."

"Oh, it's possible," he said emphatically. "Not every believer is a disciple of Christ. There are more followers in the body than disciples. A disciple of Christ follows all of the truth of God's word. They've set themselves apart from the world. Followers tend to unfollow when God's revelation doesn't fit their religious paradigm or personal preferences. When you touch on the truth about sin, it offends them. The flesh doesn't like the gospel. Neither does unbelief."

David was glad to get off the subject of his past relationships and focus on Scripture, however, she moved on to David's recent ex.

"Soooo true, David. I thought I was the only one who felt that way. I'm glad we're on the same page. Why didn't things work out with your most recent relationship?"

HEADED FOR LOVE

He cleared his throat and whisked his beard. His eyes steadied on the floor.

"Perhaps we can save that conversation for another time," she suggested.

"It's cool. She was selfish and unappreciative."

"In what way?" Jennifer rested her forearms on the table with her hands crossed over one another.

David told Jennifer how he made special handmade greeting cards and handwritten notes for his ex-fiancée and left them in places she'd later find. Some messages included "I love you," "Thinking about you," "You're so beautiful," "I believe in you," and "You're an awesome woman."

"Not to take anything away from you, David. These things are great. I'm moved by them, but every expression of love doesn't speak to every woman's heart."

"Didn't think about that." He rested his index finger between his bottom lip and chin, but his pondering position didn't last long when he saw Jennifer wink. "I guess I did these things because I'm moved by words and thoughtful gestures."

"I am too, but please, continue." She touched his hand and smiled.

"One night, I arranged a Greek-style candlelit dinner on the beach in Fiji. I arranged lanterns to be planted and lit with fire into the ocean floor. I'm talking about real fire in it," he laughed. He'd felt proud of himself for planning such an occasion. "The lanterns lit the pathway to a table set out in the water, which I had covered with a white linen cloth. The table was kinda close to shore but far away to be escorted in a small boat. What I enjoyed most about that night was seeing her smile through her eyes."

Jennifer's hands collapsed over each other. "How did you two manage to get out there without getting wet?"

"We had a chauffeur." He started cracking up. "Nah, I'm joking. An islander sailed us out on his wooden raft. It was so cool."

"That's romantic, David. Sounds like you treated her like she was your everything," Jennifer commented.

"She *was* my everything. If I'm in love with you, I'm devoted to

123

you. Loving you would be like loving myself. It's my responsibility to keep a smile on your face. I want you to know that you're loved. I want you to feel special, desired, and appreciated."

Jennifer refrained from questioning and continued to listen.

He told her about the tough times when he'd helped pay for her mother's funeral and supported her during the healing process.

"I can't imagine losing my mother. She's my best friend. Must have been tough for her. That's caring of you, David."

"It's what you do for the people you love. You carry each other's burdens. You're there for them and love when the light of the candle flickers. You should never feel alone in a relationship when you're going through something. It's important to be supportive and present."

He also shared how he'd helped her get through graduate school, tutored her in English literature, and edited her research papers and essays. "I invested a lot of time and emotion in her, feeling like that relationship was headed somewhere special. English wasn't her first language, but she returned the help by tutoring me in Spanish. She cooked for me, taught me how to make a few dishes, and even helped me attempt to translate one of my books into Spanish."

"Aww. That was nice of her." Jennifer gave him a puzzled look. "It sounds like you two were doing well together."

He chuckled humorlessly at the painful memories. "That was until I returned from a book tour in Los Angeles, completely ready to propose to her. I found her on the beach in another man's arms. I was devastated." He paused for a moment before fastening the lid back on to the cup. He stared, feeling the pain from that memory return.

Jennifer covered her mouth and gasped. "I'm sorry to hear that."

"It's okay. I'm over it now." He looked away, breaking eye contact with her.

"We don't have to talk it about anymore if you don't want to."

He didn't want to talk about it anymore. He also didn't want to remember anymore, but flashbacks continued to hit him hard anyway. He remembered it like it'd happened yesterday.

Strong winds clamored against the huge window, shaking the bamboo blinds. He stood with his back turned to Maria, fiery anger coiling within his gut. He watched violet lightning rip through the dark gray sky. She stood behind him with tears in her eyes.

"I'm sorry, David, but I was never really in love with you like I thought. Things kind of changed when we moved in together. You're such a sweet guy. I mean that, but . . ."

"But what?" David faced her. His eyes grew darker than the night. "What do you mean you never really loved me?" he spat in anger. "You're nothing but a—" He caught himself before he swore at her. He'd vowed to never curse at a woman. But in that heated moment, he was almost carried away by his fury.

"I'm sorry, David." Maria covered her tearful face.

"Sorry doesn't cut it, Maria." David closed his eyes, bit down on his bottom lip, and listened to the raindrops drumming against the windowpane.

Coming out of that painful memory, David insisted, "It's okay. I learned something really important from that situation. Disobedience welcomes unnecessary pain and heartache. I should have left that relationship when God told me to. I didn't listen."

"That sounds like a good lesson to take away from that experience . . . for sure."

"You get it, I see."

"I do."

"What about you?" David continued. "How's your love life?" He pushed his cup aside.

"I've been single for about nine years now. I was engaged to Robert, who you abruptly met, but that didn't lead to the altar."

David was in shock. He couldn't believe she had been single for that long. *I know you had to be dating since you've been single. There's no way!* He couldn't fathom the idea of a guy letting Jennifer slip away so easily.

What a fool!

"Why didn't you marry him?"

Sadness cast over her, getting a faraway gleam in her eye. "He just wasn't the one, nor was he supportive of my calling to ministry. The day before I left Miami to move here, he told me that my dad was right. I needed to give up ministry and my goals for starting a non-profit."

"How long were you with him?"

"Seven years. We met our sophomore year of high school and broke up when I started college. I was twenty-one then, but after all that time spent together, he knew exactly how I felt about the non-profit organization I wanted to start one day. He realized what my life goals were. I couldn't imagine myself married to someone like that."

David sensed there was some hurt there and wondered if she'd had a chance to deal with it yet. "I mean . . . uhh . . . he showed up at the hospital. Sounds like you've been in some type of communication here, and he's in the area."

"We talked here and there, and he moved here for business and to pursue me."

"Hmm. Interesting." He rubbed the stubble on his chin, turning his head to the left. He considered how often they might have communicated.

"But trust me. I'm over him."

"I want to say something."

"Yes?" She seemed to have no idea of what he wanted to talk about, and it made him wonder if she hadn't been at all bothered by the voice of the woman on the line when she'd called him the other night. Did she not see that there were some issues to clear up?

"The day you canceled our first get-together." He noticed her shoulders tense as she swished her cup. They raised a little. She almost looked ready to be hit by some low blow. "I decided to stop by the bookstore. I saw your car outside." He saw her eyes widened in surprise and her lips flattened into a thin line. He held his hand up to postpone whatever she looked like she was about to say. "Now, I know we're not together, but I'd hoped at that moment that it wasn't your car in that parking lot. On my way into the mall, I saw you linking arms with another guy. If you didn't want to go out with me, then that's fine, but I just felt so confused. What was that about?"

She covered her face with her hands for a moment in embarrassment before peeking over the edge of her fingertips. "David, I'm so sorry. I should've explained what was going on, but I didn't think it was my place to share such sensitive information." She blew out a breath and shook her head. "Emotionally, I was in a different space when I canceled. My previous relationship with Robert has colored a lot of my faith in men. I didn't want anything, even a friendship with you, to cloud my judgment. That night, a close friend of mine called me. He struggles with depression and suicidal tendencies. He'd recently attempted suicide a month ago, and I'd promised him he could call me whenever he felt like he was going over the edge. He needed me that night. I'm sorry for the misunderstanding."

The nuts and bolts of David's earlier assumptions slowly unscrewed. He took a hard swallow and gave an inward thanks to God that she hadn't been out with another love interest.

"I'm sorry to put you on the spot like that. I just needed to know if there was another guy in the picture."

"No problem. I get it, but I think it's my turn for you to give me an explanation. I heard a woman's voice when I called you that night. I was calling to tell you why I'd canceled our get-together."

David squirmed in the way a suspect would in a small, hot interrogation room. And knowing she was adept at psychoanalyzing, he didn't want her to know how wrong he'd been.

"Umm." He cleared his throat and looked her in the eye. "She's a good friend of mine, and since our date had been canceled, I decided to give her a call."

"Hmm." She sighed in a way that let him know she wasn't buying it. "Look, David, there's no need for us to question each other. We're not in a place to. Again, I apologize for canceling on you at the last minute. I'm sure you were suspicious as to why, and I can understand that. I apologize again." She brushed her hair away from her face. "I have to get going . . . I have a symposium to prepare for."

"Is there something wrong causing you to up and go?"

"No, I'm fine." She dismissed it, brushing him off.

He wasn't buying it. "What's your topic?" He was interested to know.

With her eyes downcast, she grabbed her purse hanging off the back of the chair. David waited for a response, realizing he'd hit a nerve with his question.

"Teenage abortion." Her eyes were still on the floor.

"Heavy topic. You mind if I come out? I'd love to hear you talk."

"Maybe another time."

"Not a problem." David figured she wasn't comfortable with the thought of him hearing her speak.

She brushed her hair away from her face. "Thank you, David. I really appreciate it." She started to walk out the door. "Thanks for meeting me for coffee." She waved to him as she backed her way out the exit. "I wanna make up for last time."

"Oh, yeah?" There was some pep in David's voice. "What do you have in mind?"

"I'll leave it up to you, mister creative."

David laughed, also standing to his feet. He was tickled by her gesture. "And I'll take you up on your offer."

They lingered around for a few moments within arm's reach. His attention moved from her eyes to her lips.

She looks like a bride. Man, I wanna kiss her.

Without thinking, he stepped forward and hugged her. He didn't know if this was the right move or not. Perhaps it was an act of faith? He didn't know how she'd react. However, the risk proved worth it.

She embraced him with a long, tight hug. Her warm, nurturing touch pervaded him deep within. He lost some strength. She made him feel vulnerable. Women who had that effect possessed a tenderness and love about themselves that made it easy for a man to open up with them. In some mysterious way, with that embrace, he felt that she'd deposited something within him when he felt some of his emotional pain withdraw.

Never felt this before.

He held her tighter, not wanting to let go. He understood the power of touch. He always knew the strength and length in the time of a hug revealed the extent of someone's value, commitment, and love for you. While they hadn't reached a point of love, he was aware that they both saw something special in each other, which they'd been able to express at this moment.

She exhaled, gazing hazily into his eyes. "Wow. You give good hugs."

"We both have that in common." He followed up with a semi-smile. "I'd like to invite you to the women's shelter where I volunteer. We're having Bible study there. I'm teaching on Proverbs 31. And, I'd like you to meet Miss Smith. I believe she'd love you, and maybe you can engage her in a conversation about what it takes to start a non-profit."

"I'd love to, David, and Proverbs 31?"

"Yeah," he said excitedly.

Jennifer's eyes dimmed. "What does a man know about Proverbs 31?" She chuckled just a bit.

David laughed, cocking his head back. He could tell she was curious. "I want to understand the mind and spirit of a Proverbs 31 woman. It's my way of preparing for my bride."

"Well, all right, Mr. Bradshaw. He who positions himself for success." She clapped her hands.

"Wisdom!" He laughed from the belly again.

CHAPTER 6

*J*oy sprung up within Jennifer when she saw the *Woman of Virtue* sign in purple letters hanging above the front door of Miss Smith's woman's shelter.

This is awesome! I want something just like this for the girls!

She spotted David sitting outside on the front porch with whom she assumed was Miss Smith. She quickly waxved before parallel parking between two cars near the front. She got out of her car eagerly and tucked her Bible between her arm and hip. She was anticipating what David planned to teach. Her white T-shirt overlapped the stonewashed jeans that were cuffed slightly above her navy-blue flats. Her vibe was '90ish. She smiled nervously as she moved up the paved walkway, thinking, *Why does it feel like I'm about to meet his mother for approval?*

"Hi, David." She gave him a warm embrace.

"Good to see you again." His full lips brushed lightly against her ear.

Jennifer jolted at the warmth that stole over her. "Same," she said off rhythm.

"You must be Jennifer." Miss Smith stood up to hug her. "The special woman I heard about."

Jennifer's cheeks turned rosy red. "I am. I mean, I'm Jennifer." She laughed, feeling put on the spot. She turned to David, who was blatantly looking in another direction. "A pleasure to finally meet you. I like your sweater." She felt Miss Smith's tight, motherly squeeze. "Yellow is one of my favorite colors."

"Pleasure to meet you as well. Mine, too." Miss Smith laughed. "Makes a gal feel happy. Hear you're interested in starting a nonprofit."

"I am. I am," she exclaimed super excitedly.

"I'd love to hear about your ministry." Miss Smith rubbed her arms. "Well, it's almost time, son. You ready?" She turned to David.

"I am. After you." He put his hand out for her to lead the way.

Jennifer followed beside David with Miss Smith. As they passed through the hallway, she noticed how women called after David, waving to him.

Must be popular here. She was met with sassy looks, smiles of curiosity, and whispers of *Who's she? That's David's girlfriend.*

She waved back to them, returning graceful smiles.

They reached the auditorium, and Jennifer saw twenty or more chairs in a huge circle, which was a little intimidating for her. Most of her Bible studies were done in small groups. Nevertheless, her heart remained open to what the Lord might reveal to her.

She took a seat next to Miss Smith. David was to the right of them. Soon after, women entered and filled the chairs. Some women had to bring chairs of their own to fit in the circle. By the look on David's and Miss Smith's faces, she could tell they weren't expecting such an overflow. There was a glow of joy on David's face that enabled Jennifer to see his heart for God and people. This was rare and different for her to discern. She'd never witnessed a man's zeal for God.

That's beautiful. He's serious about the Lord. I like that!

Once the women settled in, David began to speak, and Jennifer looked up to face him.

"I'd like you to all meet Jennifer Washington. She's an

extraordinary woman with whom God has allowed me to cross paths."

"Oohs" and "ahhs" spread across the room.

Jennifer blushed red and put her head down when she saw Miss Smith and a few other women make eye contact with her and laugh in glee.

"Thank you, David," she said quietly.

"There's something else I want to say," David interrupted.

Jennifer's tongue stuck to the roof of her mouth. She just didn't know what he was about to say next.

"I know many of you have wondered why a young man like myself would volunteer his time here when he could be doing other things that people my age are doing."

"Yeah, why do you come here?" a woman called out, causing laughter to spread through the room.

Jennifer focused her attention on the woman, then back to David.

I wonder why, too.

"Shush!" Miss Smith ordered.

Jennifer and David made eye contact and shared a laugh of their own. Once the room grew quiet, he continued. "I'm going to tell you why." He aimed his attention at the woman who had asked the question. "There's something I want to share with all of you that's very personal to me. It's something that I don't talk about often, especially publicly. But for some reason, I'm inclined to today."

"Take your time, David!" another woman shouted.

"It's been years since I've seen my mother. I don't know how she's doing, or even where she is. I don't even know if she's alive. The last time I saw her, I was probably an undergrad student." He paused. "That was several years ago."

The room was completely hushed as Jennifer crossed her legs and gripped her Bible tight. All eyes were riveted on him.

"Anyhow, I believe the absence of love or, rather, the kind of love that I never experienced from my mother, has played a major part in my reason for volunteering my time here. I've been trying to patch up that hurt by keeping busy—not to say that what I do here isn't sincere."

This is all starting to make sense. I could see this in his writing, Jennifer thought.

"We love you, David!" a woman in the back called out.

Jennifer gazed around the opposite side of Miss Smith and slowly turned her back. From the corner of her eye, she saw Miss Smith handing her a tissue.

"Thank you," she whispered. "Wasn't expecting this."

"Me either," Miss Smith whispered back.

"I love all of you in the way I wish I could love my mother. You all show me the kind of love that I wish I could've received from her—especially you, Miss Smith." David faced her. "I'm forever grateful to have you in my life."

Jennifer watched the older woman bow her head humbly and begin to cry.

Lord, I can't take this! More tears flowed down her face. *Thank God I'm not wearing makeup today.*

"And now I need to let my mother know that she's appreciated, loved, and beautiful, despite our unpleasant history. I need to give her what I've been giving you," he added. "I'm sure she needs my love as much as I need hers."

Jennifer watched Miss Smith peer over at him with teary eyes and a proud smile.

"You ladies have access to a wonderful woman who has been like a mother to me for years. Here's to Miss Smith. Let's give her a hand." He ignited a burst of resounding applause.

The women shouted as they stood and applauded. The noise went on for a full minute. All the while, Miss Smith waved her hand for them to stop, looking a bit embarrassed. Finally, they did.

"Let us pray."

While he prayed, Jennifer felt a soothing, warm sensation sweep into the circle in a way she didn't immediately recognize. It was like the wind. And the room became silent for a few minutes, which felt like hours until weeping broke out solemnly.

God, this is powerful!

Jennifer couldn't hold her tears back. She wept, standing to her feet and lifting her hands in worship. Some of the other women stood up with her.

His prayer came to an end, and he told everyone to turn to Proverbs 31. He read, "Nobility and virtue are qualities that God has instilled in a woman to carry herself in a way in which He sees her. Those qualities in a woman are what makes her worth more than rubies and any other materialistic possessions. That's why a Proverbs 31 woman can't be bought. If she can be purchased and swayed by material possessions, she hasn't known the God who created her or has not yet come to know the virtue He's placed inside of her. She inhales virtue and exhales the wisdom of God. A Proverbs 31 woman is a woman a husband has full confidence in because her heart is in the hand of the Father, her mind is in Christ, and the Holy Spirit lives inside of her. A woman who's faithful to God is faithful to her husband. This is the kind of woman who brings peace and joy into her husband's life."

Jennifer was floored, shocked, and impressed at the same time.

This man is different. I've never heard a man teach this way before or on Proverbs 31, period. He's special.

She gazed around at faces. She saw the women listening intently to his teachings. He taught with such authority and confidence.

He makes me want to submit to him. I've never felt that way about a man before.

As the Bible study ended, David invited participants who hadn't given their lives to Christ to come to the circle. Everyone looked around uncomfortably at first, but ten brave women came forward and David met them there. He prayed the prayer of salvation with each woman individually as Jennifer sat back in shock.

"Awesome. Isn't it?" Miss Smith leaned over to Jennifer and said into her ear.

"It is. I've never seen this before. There's something different about him."

"There is. I noticed when he first started coming here. I always knew the Lord's hand was mightily on him. Never asked him to do any of this. He simply saw a need and stepped forward."

Jennifer glanced over at him. She didn't know what to say. After he was done, Miss Smith told Jennifer that he'd conclude shortly and invited her to the cafeteria for coffee.

Jennifer listened to her talk about how God had led her to start *Woman of Virtue* as she gave her a tour of the shelter. She was encouraged to hear how she overcame the initial challenges of starting a non-profit. Jennifer didn't feel alone. Miss Smith also shared her testimony of being homeless at one point after an ugly divorce, but through her perseverance, God had landed her back on her feet and overwhelmed her with His grace and favor, sending donors her way to launch her non-profit.

"I pray the Lord will send that kind of grace and favor my way," Jennifer said optimistically.

"He will, Jennifer. In His timing."

They walked into the cafeteria, and one of the workers came out to bring them tea. David came in shortly after to join them. Jennifer smiled and tried to cover it with her hand.

"David, this was wonderful. Hearing you open up about your relationship with your mother touched me...caught me off guard, to be honest, but in a good way. I got to see another side of you. The Bible study was wonderful and powerful. May have to get you to come down to meet the girls."

"Ah, I'd love to. I give all the glory to God. It was all Him. I'm just the messenger." He turned and saw the café worker come out with a cup of coffee. "Thank you."

"You're right. Nothing but God's grace."

After they all finished up in the cafeteria, David told Jennifer he would meet her outside, so she waited on the front porch. However, she was still able to see him and Miss Smith through the window. She watched closely. She saw David kiss Miss Smith on the cheek and hold her hands. She hugged him once more and rubbed his back.

It seems in some way she gives him what he never experienced as a child.

She quickly looked away when she heard the front door open. Miss Smith came over to hug Jennifer once more and gave her a business card. Jennifer and David walked to their cars afterward.

"Thanks again for inviting me. You're some kind of special, David. Please don't stop being you!"

"I am who I am, unapologetically in Christ. Nothing's gonna change that."

"Good." She smiled and rubbed his back.

"Let's do something tomorrow." He walked her to her car.

"I'd love to."

"I'll give you a ring before bed to let you know what I have in mind."

"Okay, David," she whispered in a soft tone.

That next morning, David called and arranged a time for them to meet up at the National Harbor in Maryland. She agreed to it, got off the phone, and dashed out of her condo to shop for an outfit at her favorite boutique in Georgetown.

While holding up a red high heel, a hand touched her shoulder. She turned around and saw Samantha's bubbly, penetrating blue eyes zooming in on her. Jennifer flinched like she'd seen a ghost.

"Oh, hi, Samantha. Imagine running into you again," Jennifer mentioned.

"Hi, Jennifer. I haven't heard from you since the hospital. Where have you been? Is everything okay?"

Jennifer answered, "Around," and signaled to the sales associate to box her shoes so she could continue browsing the store.

There's something a little off with this woman. I can feel it. "Everything's okay?"

Samantha interlocked her arms with Jennifer's, completely unaware she was trying to get out of the store as quickly as possible.

"We have similar taste." She reached around Jennifer and grabbed a dress off a rack.

"Not really," Jennifer countered under her breath and selected the dress she was considering.

"Yes, we do. I heard ya." Samantha winked. "I'm so glad that I ran into you. I've been wondering if you linked up with David yet." She was on the prowl about David again, and this time around, it irked Jennifer's nerves.

Jennifer eased out a laugh of discomfort and answered, "Why?" She was convinced that Samantha seemed more interested in getting to know the bestselling author than being friends with her.

"You haven't? He's hot and a good catch; no ring on his finger." She fanned herself.

Jennifer's eyebrows almost reached to the top of her hairline. She understood that Samantha was unhappy in her marriage, but she needed to focus on her husband instead of other men. She let out another awkward laugh. "I'm picking up a few things now for our get-together tomorrow evening." *Take that!*

Samantha's smile immediately turned brittle as her enthusiasm took a dip. "That's great!"

"Isn't it?" she answered with over-the-top excitement.

It was obvious Samantha wanted David, although she was still married. Happily married or not—married was married. Samantha's interest in David left an unsettling feeling in Jennifer's gut. She glanced over her shoulder for an escape route and noticed a man coming from behind, standing a few inches taller than Samantha. He was well-groomed and had brown eyes that fit his symmetrical oval face. He had the look of a model.

"Is that your husband?" She nodded in the man's direction.

She was relieved to change the subject.

"Yes." Samantha's smile turned even more brittle as she spun around to face her husband. "That's my hubby. All right, Jen. I'll catch up with you another time. Call me. A gal gets lonely on the weekends. Buh-bye."

"Thanks," she said, having zero intention of ever contacting her. Samantha needed to get her life worked out ASAP!

∽

A CRISP AIR swept off the riverfront where white yachts and small boats assembled in front of the marina. Jennifer shivered, instinctively wrapping her arm around David's waist to keep warm. She savored the muscular build and warmth of his body against her lean, petite frame. Being so caught up at work and focused on starting a non-profit had consumed her for so long, she'd forgotten how it felt to be this close to a man. The sun went down by the time they finished dinner. David laughed, leading Jennifer by the hand to a bench on the boardwalk.

They sat and listened to the trickling, calming waters, both feeling a special moment emerging from the night. She rested her head against his shoulder, capturing the full bright white moon. She solemnly confessed in a dreamy tone, unconsciously rubbing his hand, "This feels like a date."

"Does it?" David pretended not to have the slightest idea.

"It does." She held his hand. "Everything seems so natural, so effortless, and so right."

"I think it's better that way." David looked down into her eyes, surrendering to a smile. "I mean, for things to be natural and effortless."

"Seems like you take your time to get to know someone." She traced the veins on his hand. "But I could be wrong."

"You're right. I do want to take my time to get to know you. I really like you and would like to see where our acquaintance takes us."

"I like you too, but you know."

"Yes, I know you're not ready for a relationship."

"Is that okay with you?" Her eyes zoomed in on David's face.

"Yeah—that's fine, Jennifer." He squeezed her. "No rush."

"You're so sweet." She rose to her feet and pulled David up by the hand. "Let's dance."

"Where's the music?" David walked around the boardwalk. "I don't see a band and uh—there's no music."

"Hold on a sec." Jennifer closed her eyes and hummed a tune he had never heard before.

She saw David's eyes close as a soft smile graced his lips. She pulled him into her arms and held him close, gently tugging on his earlobe while she rested her head against his chest. That peaceful presence she recognized as God returned.

Wow. I need this!

The chill of the night and the cool breeze from the water no longer affected her. The spirit of love tucked her into its arms. She glided her thin fingers against the grain of his stubble, wanting to kiss him so badly, but she couldn't. She would've gone against what she'd said minutes ago. She could tell he wanted to kiss her so badly, too, just by the way he fastened the grip of his wide hands around her waist. There was a heated intensity in his eyes that set her heart on fire, consuming her from the inside out. Instead of kissing her lips, he planted a peck on her cheek and continued to hold her.

David.

She felt a part of her heart yielding to him, unraveling uncontrollably. If he'd kissed her, she couldn't have resisted him. She didn't have the strength. She tried to hide the surrender in her eyes by looking away, but it was too late. She gave herself away. He knew getting a kiss was possible; however, he decided not to do so. He shifted his eyes and let the intensity between them simmer slowly down. She appreciated his decision to not cross the boundaries of their newfound friendship.

He capped the night off by kissing Jennifer's hand and thanking her for allowing him to have dinner with her. She was delighted that he expressed himself with such sincerity, admiration, and gratitude. This made her feel special in the way a queen feels when her king kneels and kisses her hand in public. In return, she thanked David for treating her to dinner.

They walked back to the bench, and Jennifer grabbed her purse. She slung it around her shoulder and the ultrasound sonogram accidentally flew out. She froze in shock.

"You okay, Jennifer? You look terrified." David, being the gentleman that he was, quickly tracked it down before a breeze could take it into the river. "Got it." Before he could say something else, she caught up to him and snatched it out of his hand.

She sighed deeply and walked toward the waters, glancing up into the black skies. She closed her eyes, doing her best to hold back her tears, but when she felt David's hand rub against her back, followed by a hug, she could no longer conceal them.

"Is everything okay?" he asked.

"Back up and give me space." She stretched her arm out and pushed at his chest.

His face twisted at her in confusion. "Did I miss something?"

What did I just say? She reached out to him. "I'm so sorry, David. Had a moment."

"But what made you say that?" He grew with great cooncern.

"I'm sorry, David. It's just. . ."

Inside, she felt every bit of her pain rushing to the surface. Now wasn't the time to reveal the abortion. Besides, she wasn't ready to share that painful chapter with him.

I don't need him judging me anyway.

"No problem, Jennifer. I don't know what just happened, but I'm here for you, and whatever I can do to accommodate or support you in any way, I'll do that."

She stepped away from him and buried her face into her hands.

What did I just do? I feel so embarrassed.

While she soaked in shame, the gentle touch of his hand met her lower back.

"I'm here for you," he tried to comfort her.

She lowered her face into her hands. Hearing those words made her cry all the more.

John 4:18 says, "There is no fear in love. But perfect love drives out fear because fear has to do with punishment. The one who fears is not made perfect in love."

If Jennifer had never had any notion of what this scripture meant, she did at that moment. It wasn't to say David was in love with her, but she felt the love of Christ through him. This was all far left for her. How could something good make her so uncomfortable?

Well, she reflected, *when hurt and dysfunction have become the norm, what's good for you is uncomfortable. Fear works in the heart that way. It pushes you away from the things of God and encourages you to return to what's unhealthy for you.*

If she was going to experience what her heart longed for, she needed to let go of fear. She turned and hugged him. His words touched her heart and his presence made her feel safe. And the fact that he cared and could discern on some basic level what she was going through really meant a lot to her. His presence was beginning to become the antidote to her solitude of healing.

"Thank you, David. I think I needed to hear that."

THE FOLLOWING MORNING, while Jennifer was getting dressed to meet up with David for brunch in Old Town Alexandria, her mother called to find out how the outing had gone.

"Oh, we had a great time. We danced on the boardwalk at night and he invited me to a Bible study at a women's shelter where he volunteers. He was transparent about his relationship with his mom and taught from Proverbs 31. This man is beautiful, anointed, and totally on fire for God. This is insane!"

"Wow, Jennifer. I've never heard you call a man beautiful."

"Wait. Did I say that?" She giggled.

"Yes, you said that." Her mother laughed back. "Sounds like the kind of man we've talked about and you prayed for."

Jennifer became quiet for a moment. "I know. To be honest, it scares me." She started to mention something about the sonogram flying out of her purse but decided not to. She didn't feel like reopening that conversation with her mother. She immediately heard the excitement in her mother's voice as she went back to recapping the night out with David. Jennifer expressed how she found someone who genuinely cared about her, which made her mother extremely happy. Her mother knew she hadn't opened up to any man since Robert.

On her way out the door, she noticed a medium-size white envelope stuck halfway out of her mailbox. It was sealed with clear tape and nothing was written on the outside of it.

"Another message?"

Immediately, her heart started thumping and she grew anxious. Using her fingernail, she peeled the tape off and found a note inside. It read *I miss you.*

"Robert," she seethed, tearing the note into shreds. "How did he get my address? Things are starting to get weird," she mumbled under her breath.

Steam drifted from the shredded mozzarella sprinkled over sautéed spinach, red and yellow peppers, mushrooms, fresh tomatoes, and two peppered sunny-side-up eggs—Jennifer's choice for brunch. Three Cajun-grilled jumbo shrimps next to cheese grits occupied David's plate. The bistro in Old Town faced a narrow street and brownstone apartments. The intimate space was conducive for a quiet, intimate conversation that would spill over to a casual walk on the brown cobblestone streets. The food was just as good as the conversation that fed their souls. David talked about the very first time he wrote a story at nine, where he journeyed to planet Mars to find a treasure chest and found life there and helped create a geopolitical system with the citizens on the planet. Jennifer saw how passionate he was about writing, as he continued to stare off into the sky going on about this story. Jennifer smiled inside. She was happy for him. For her, there's something attractive about a man going after his dreams and fulfilling them. It spoke to his ambition, strength, perseverance and his relationship with God. Character and integrity were important to her. And David listened to Jennifer talk about the first time God spoke to her about starting a non-profit organization. He could see her eyes glistening and her cheeks redden with excitement. He admired her connection with God and her ability to hear from Him. He too saw her fire and dedication in see her calling come to pass.

After finishing brunch at the bistro, Jennifer walked quietly with her purse glued to her hip. She tended to clench the strap of it whenever something ate away at her. She wanted to tell him about the note, but she sure didn't want to give him the impression that someone from her past was trying to creep back in on them. She held it in instead. David had asked about her hobbies and interest as he worked on the smoothie that was left over from the bistro. Talking about her competitive spirit of playing volleyball and board games struck up a match of Checkers and Connect Four.

"I'm ready when you are," she confirmed, shoving an elbow at him.

Sharing her hobbies of painting, clay molding, and playing the violin in her spare time made her feel comfortable and special. It let her know that he was actively engaged and interested in her. Other guys she dated hadn't bothered to ask her about the little things. She knew that being attractive to someone is totally different than getting to know someone. David was into her—not just her looks.

And David told Jennifer about his love for live music, specifically acoustic.

"What do you like about acoustic music?" Jennifer stuffed her hands into her tan trench coat.

"You can really hear the vocals." David talked with his hands. "The voice is the music for me. It's an organic sound. It's peaceful."

"Never looked at it from that perspective before. You seem like a really interesting, multi-layered person."

"I invite you to peel off the layers." David rubbed Jennifer's back. "And since you play the violin, maybe I'll take you up on some lessons?"

"I would love to," she said smiling dreamy.

Coming upon Waterfront Park, Jennifer spotted a wooden bench that offered enough shade and sunlight. She pulled out a white photo album from her large purse and gripped it closer to her chest.

David seemed to know she needed a little prodding because he leaned his head against her shoulder and said, "I'd love to explore your memories."

She nodded and flipped the album open. In the first photo, her feet dangled from a piano bench while her mother hunched over her to help position Jennifer's fingers on the keys.

"What song were you learning to play?" He asked.

"*Once Upon A Time* by Mozart," Jennifer answered reflectively. "Maybe I could play something for you one day?"

"The piano, too. I don't know much about classical music, but I'd love to hear you play a little something."

One scenic picture caught David's eye. Her mother had snapped a shot of Jennifer beneath the bluest skies and perfect sunshine in the backyard of her garden. Jennifer's hair lifted as she ran in circles with tulips, daisies, and banana shrubs in one hand and a white, blue, yellow twirl lollipop in the other.

"Does your mother still have this garden?"

"She does. I love it!" Happiness filled her eyes. "I sit in it when I return home for vacations. It's where I go to spend time with God. Sometimes we worship God together there."

"Are you and she best friends? You seem really close."

"We are. Been that way since I can remember. She knows everything about my life. I go to her about personal matters or advice concerning major decisions."

"And what about your dad? I didn't see any pictures of him."

She became quiet for a moment. "Can we get into that another time?"

"Yeah, sure. No problem. But I think we have something in common. Photos are missing from my album, too."

Jennifer rubbed his hand and held it for a second, gently stroking it. His eyes lowered a little in surrender, and she matched his yielding.

Physical touch is one of his love languages.

She leaned her head against his shoulder and clenched his arm in a way to comfort herself. He rested his head against hers, causing a smile to ease out tenderly.

I like this.

She just knew he was in tune with her. Sometimes a woman wanted a man to interpret the unspoken and act upon what the Lord revealed to him. She could tell that he knew they both needed each other at this moment.

It was times like these that fertilized the ground for love to grow and blossom in due season. Love rests on God's timing—not our own.

"Are you afraid of water?"

"I'm an island gal. Of course, I can swim," she said with sass, cutting her eyes candidly at him. "Why'd you ask?"

"Let's go paddling tomorrow in the city."

"Aww. That'd be fun."

"Good. I'll pick you up tomorrow at one. Are you out of church by then?"

"Yep. I go to the early morning service anyway. I like to have the rest of the day for myself."

"Same here. Text me your address."

"Yes, Mr. Bradshaw."

It was comfortably warm this Sunday. David pulled up to Jennifer's place ten minutes early. He opened his Bible to read until she came out. He prayed and asked the Holy Spirit to speak to him. He was led to turn to Proverbs 8:17. As he read, "I love those who love me, and those who seek me early shall find me," the presence of God came over him powerfully. He quickly took out his journal and jotted down what was revealed to him.

You want face-to-face fellowship Jesus, so do I, Lord," he said to himself. His eyes watered as he saw Jennifer come out in white jean shorts and a beige tank top. An off-white light cardigan sweater was tied around her waist. She was donning oversized tan sunglasses. Her hair was up in her usual bun.

Man, she's gorgeous!

He slid the pocket Bible in between the seat and frantically checked the side of his car door for napkins and found none.

God, can you say, let there be napkins? He reached into his glove compartment with urgency. He'd run out completely. He sure didn't want her to see him teary-eyed.

She opened the car door before he could get out to do it for her. He was welcomed by a wide smile and radiant skin.

"I'm speechless." He gave her a long hug.

"What do you mean?" She blushed, squeezing him back.

"You're just beautiful." He inhaled her perfume that held sensual notes of pomegranate and the lotus flower. "That's all."

"Aww, thank you." She blushed more.

Their noses nearly touched when they released each other. He tried to smile long enough so that the corner of his eye would catch that tear. It didn't work. She'd already seen it.

"Thank you. You're pretty handsome yourself. Ever considered modeling? You have the look. High cheekbones and all."

He sported a gray fitted crew neck T-shirt, navy blue chino shorts, and white canvas sneakers. Gold frame aviator shades rested at the crevice of his shirt.

"I appreciate it."

"Is everything okay? Is this still a good time?"

"I'm okay. Why do you ask?" He took a swipe at his cheek to dry things up quickly.

"Come on, David. You know how I know things." She laughed.

"Yeah, I know," he quipped and joined in with her laughter. "I had an experience with the Lord."

"That's awesome. Tell me about it." She fastened her seatbelt.

His soul lit with fervor to have a conversation about God. He couldn't with the other women he had dated in the past. He was often met with confused, empty stares and awkward silences. His dating experiences had taught him that women who professed to be Christian didn't always have a relationship with God. Their lifestyles contradicted scripture. He wanted a woman who lived a life that was set apart. However, if he was candid with himself, his actions didn't always align with Christ-like living. He needed to embody what he desired. He understood a surrendered life to Christ equaled a godly relationship. He needed to fully surrender, and in some obscure way, her presence challenged him to do that—to raise the bar and deepen his walk with Christ so that he could be a holy and righteous husband. Only a holy and righteous man was fit for a virtuous woman.

"I feel the Lord is inviting me into deeper and greater intimacy with Him. The invitation to fellowship and friendship."

"Like seeing Jesus face to face?" she asked animatedly.

"Yes, Jennifer." *She gets it!* His voice weakened with holy reverence. "He spoke to me through Proverbs 8:17."

She grabbed his hands and prayed, "Father, I thank you for placing this awesome desire on David's heart. He has a passionate desire and a hunger to know you and have an intimate relationship with you. Prepare his heart for what he's asking for. Clear all distractions and heal all wounds."

What was happening in that instance couldn't be planned: This was something they both longed for from the depths of their hearts, which was fellowship with the person they saw as more than a friend. When David heard her say "wounds," he held her hand tighter. An avalanche of emotions rushed to his head. Her prayer was like light entering the secret, dark places of his soul that no one seemed to have penetrated. Maybe his heart wasn't ready to release the things that had kept him stuck for years. But in this instance, he was in agreement with her. Praying with someone who believed in the power of prayer and who understood the magnitude of what you were asking added faith and power because Jesus tends to show up. He is present when two or more are gathered in His name.

"It's in your name, Jesus, that we pray, amen!" she finished. "Whoa!" She opened her eyes and released his hands. "That was powerful . . . never prayed like that before. As I was praying, I could feel the special invitation Jesus is extending to you. I'd love to experience something like that. Maybe you can show me how to have that kind of relationship once you get there?" She rubbed his hand.

"I'd love to lead you to where Christ is drawing me."

"And I'd love that, David." She gently squeezed his hand.

~

THEY ARRIVED at Cordell Boat Paddling in DC. As David was walking over to grab the red lifejacket, Jennifer ran past him to snatch it.

"Seriously?" He laughed.

"Thought you'd look great in yellow, my sunshine." She covered her mouth laughing.

"I'll be anything you want me to be." He snapped the ultra-extra-bright happy yellow jacket on casually.

"My handsome sunshine!" She poked fun at him.

They put their shades on and paddled at a slow pace. Well, he was doing all the paddling. He'd turn to look at her from time to time, catching the reflection of the surroundings off her sunglasses. He could tell by her contemplative expression that something was on her mind, but he didn't care. He didn't want to interrupt her moment. Seeing the wind lift the loose strands of her hair from her bun, and how the sun dazzled against her majestic skin, was a sight to behold. His mind kept taking him back to her presence.

"Tell me, David. I find you intriguing. Last night, I thought about how you knew you wanted to be a writer at such a young age. What really sparked that?" she asked. "Some people are drawn to certain things that have either hurt them or they haven't experienced."

Gathering his answer, he looked out on the waves of water moving back and forth.

I don't want to lie to her, but I'm not ready to dig into the specific details of my past.

"Writing was something that I always enjoyed doing. I always had an imagination when I was younger. Stories would just come together in my head. I'd see them play out like a movie on the screen. They helped me get through tough times. And sometimes I'd draw them out in the sand when my mom used to take me to the playground."

She'd no idea how penetrating her questions were. He tried his best to not go into detail about his relationship with his mother. He was always reluctant to talk about his past no matter who he was with at the time.

I'm sure she picked something up at the Bible study.

He was all too familiar with judgment and misunderstanding. It was hard for him to be vulnerable, and when he was, he got hit square in the chest with cold words that made him feel embarrassed, humiliated, and rejected. Winter would set in, and it'd be a while until summer returned.

"You know hearing you talk about discovering your gift at such a young age is a blessing. Takes others years to find theirs. You can take a break now," she said, referring to the paddling.

"I'm off the hook, huh?" He stretched his arms back and let out an exaggerated sigh that couldn't hold up long enough because she tickled his ribs.

"Someone's ticklish." She continued at him.

"If you wanna stay dry, I think you better stop." He couldn't stop laughing.

"I think I'll take your word for it, but life's something else," she contended, getting back on topic. "You have this idea in mind of what you want to be or how things are going to pan out. Then the unexpected and unplanned happens."

"That explained why you zoned out for a bit."

She faced him. "I apologize for that."

"No, it's fine. What were you thinking about?"

She returned her attention ahead. "I wanted to be a ballerina, star in a play when I was younger. I wanted to be an actress like Dorothy Dandridge and all the other greats."

"No way." It was refreshing to learn a little more about her.

"Yeah, I did. I was in a few plays in middle and high school."

"What happened?"

"God chose a different path for me."

"Nothing wrong with that. Kids are supposed to dream and have an unfiltered fearlessness about life. It's better to dream before the fear comes."

"Never thought of it like that. Just learned something new."

AFTER THAT DAY, they met up for breakfast and lunch frequently. They read magazines and books over tea together. One day at Book World while David was ordering their drinks, Jennifer bought his fourth book and requested his autograph when she returned to him. "I'm your number one fan." She saw his face brighten with pride when he penned his name on her copy. The saleswoman who had teased her months ago about having a crush on David had fun with her again. She didn't say anything when she saw her with David but had this huge, knowing grin smeared across her face. Jennifer put her index finger against her mouth, playfully shushed her, and interlocked her arm in his. They sat together on the bench talking.

"Some of your stories seem so real." She glanced at the side of his face.

"Some of my inspiration comes from what I hoped to experience in prior relationships."

"That's so sweet. Your stories are really romantic." She clenched his arm and laid her head against it.

"Yeah, I guess they are. I also write about things that I'd like to experience with my wife one day."

As he talked, she felt the vibration of his voice in her chest. She grew weaker and weaker inside. If he'd asked for her heart, she couldn't have resisted.

How can this man be so endearing and amorous?

"You're very different, David. You just don't find men who are as expressive as you are or who write about the things you do."

"I get that a lot." He lifted her chin up. "Think it's a bad thing?"

"It's a beautiful thing." She smiled, catching the reflection of the ceiling lights in his eyes. "It demonstrates strength with the ability to communicate and articulate what you're thinking and feeling. God crafted you this way." She clenched his arm tighter. "I believe any woman looking for fulfillment and transparency would appreciate these things in a godly man."

"Thank you, Jennifer." He kissed her cheek.

"You're welcome, my love." She didn't realize what had just come out of her mouth. She saw him grinning a bit. "Oops. I didn't mean to say that."

"I know you didn't." He winked.

"I want you to meet the girls. Would you mind stopping by during lunch tomorrow? Maybe teach a short writers' workshop?"

"I think that'd be fun. I haven't hosted one in a while. Text me the address."

THE RED BRICK wall was decorated with paintings, words of affirmations, and declarations written with different colored chalk. The colors of the portraits varied. Some were painted in dark grays, purples, and reds, which resembled the thoughts, emotions, and moods of the girls. Others were painted in pastel and bright colors that offered hope, faith, and possibility. Two blank canvases rested upon an easel with palettes next to it. This was a therapeutic tool Jennifer often used for the girls.

When David walked in, his face lit with excitement. He was met with a welcome sign from the girls that waved like a banner. Jennifer smiled at the surprise on his face. They embraced each other and she introduced him to all the girls present. She gave him a quick tour around the building, introducing him to her colleagues and showing him her office.

"This is my mom again." She pointed to the picture on her desk.

He picked it up. "Now I can see where you get your looks from. The photo album didn't do much justice, but now I can really see."

"Oh, stop it." She hit him on the arm. "This is a more recent."

"Just stating facts. Your sister?" He put down the picture of her mother and picked up another.

"Yep. That's Nish. My younger sister."

"You have a beautiful family," he said, placing the frame down.

She saw him squint his eyes a little.

I think he's about to ask me about my dad.

"Well, let's go back to the fine arts & entertainment room. Everyone should be ready now."

"Sure," he said, following behind her.

Jennifer was impressed with how the girls were quietly seated and ready for David. His seat was front and center. Jennifer sat in the back. She listened to him describe how he started a story.

"You need a hook," he urged emphatically, throwing a punch with his right arm.

He's funny, she thought.

This caused laughter throughout the room and from some of the staff members who stopped by to eavesdrop. As he continued, she was amazed again at how he captured an audience's attention.

I can see us doing ministry together.

She sure was taking mental notes. After he finished up, she asked if he had a little extra time to grab a bite to eat.

"My treat," she insisted, batting her eyelashes.

"Yeah. I got some extra time."

They both had a taste for Thai and found a bistro nearby. Jennifer chose a seat by the window, which David didn't mind. She bounced ideas off his head about her non-profit. He pulled a napkin from the dispenser, took out a pen, and jotted down some ideas of his own.

"Thank you, David." She was engaged, beaming ear to ear about his ideas. He even gave her some prayer points for her non-profit to ensure its success.

"This was great." She forked the last shrimp into her mouth.

"The Cherry Blossom Festival is coming up soon. I think we should go." He moved his hand on top of hers.

"Hmm. I think so too, Mr. Bradshaw."

At the National Cherry Blossom Festival Park in DC, they took pictures of the cherry blossom trees, not to mention a huge number of selfies as they stood next to the beautiful foliage.

"If one of your eyes is roaming in this picture, I swear I'm cropping you out!" David joked, making the couple who was taking the picture for them chuckle a bit.

"You are so mean," Jennifer said, giving him a playful slap on the arm.

After taking pictures, David led Jennifer by the hand toward the river. She spotted a brown picnic basket at the center of the red picnic blanket. She threw herself into David's arms. She was smitten by the way he continued to court her.

She lay underneath him as he fed her diced mangoes and pineapple. She noted how beautiful the cherry blossoms were.

"I want to share a poem with you." He took out a piece of paper and unfolded it. "I wrote it last night after we went boat paddling."

"Oh, really?" She sat up excited and faced him.

"Jennifer, you are a divine encounter. One of the most beautiful things that I've witnessed about you is not just your external beauty or your mind, but your spirit. An artist couldn't sketch a picture accurately enough to portray your beauty. A writer couldn't fashion such words so eloquently. Only the hand and voice of God could accomplish that."

Her sweet smile encouraged him to continue.

"Your presence is a gift. You awaken my spirit when I am around you. The thought of you alone puts meaning and life into these very words. You are so soft and so tender, so sweet and so compassionate. I'm comfortable whenever I am around you. I can be myself. I am often lost in your smile and your alluring eyes, so much so that my mind wanders in and out of conversation with you, yet I am attuned to all that you say, that which is above and beyond the surface.

"You are the true definition of a lady, elegant and classy in dress, in your etiquette and speech, just the kind of woman I'm drawn to. Your beauty defies age. You have replaced that which I thought I could never find again—twice as beautiful, twice as open, twice as inviting. You care for me. You believe in me.

"The impact of your presence is a powerful one. My heart is full of joy because I have found a woman of purpose, a woman of virtue, and a woman of God. You are a Proverbs 31 woman. The impact of your presence is unsurpassable." David kissed her hand.

Jennifer couldn't hold back her tears. His romantic gesture had put another dent in the hard shell that coated her heart. If she wasn't careful, he'd be through those walls, and she wouldn't even care.

"Wow, David. Thank you. That was really sweet of you. I'm sorry for responding like this." She wiped her eye.

"It's fine." He handed her a tissue. "Thanks for allowing me to spend time with you and for allowing this moment to happen."

"I thought chivalry was dead." She giggled, drying her eyes.

"Not with the right person." He smiled through his eyes. "If you're free tonight, I have another surprise for you."

"What's that, Mr. Bradshaw?" she asked. "Are you trying to sweep me off my feet, earn extra brownie points?"

"Just treating you the way you deserve to be treated. Have you ever been to Dave's Kitchen?"

"Uh, what's Dave's Kitchen? Never heard of it." Her face scrunched up.

"Oh, you'll see. It's one of the best restaurants in town."

CHAPTER 7

*J*ennifer arrived at David's condo the next evening and saw a valet parker dressed in a tailored black suit and skinny tie standing out front. She reached to open her door, but the gentleman waved his hand to stop her. She snatched her hand back, completely impressed by what David had arranged so far. The valet then told her the front desk attendant would escort her inside.

"Okay. Thanks," she responded in a shy tone, crunching her toes together in the open-toe tan pumps she sported for the evening.

Minutes later, the front desk attendant came out and commented on Jennifer being the special woman David had been talking about. Jennifer couldn't hold back her smile. She thanked him, sensing a special night was on the horizon.

The front desk attendant seated Jennifer on the oriental auburn sofa in the lobby and poured her a glass of sparkling water. Afterward, he offered her fruit from a platter. "Make yourself comfortable. David will be down shortly."

"Thank you," she said, completely taken aback by the red-carpet treatment.

Jennifer had never been out on a date where her car was valet parked or where she was escorted inside her date's lobby. She was so impressed that she texted pictures of the lobby and the refreshments David had left for her. Her mother replied that she was jealous and that she'd never experienced anything like that before—even after being married for thirty-plus years.

There's still hope, Jennifer texted back with a smiley face.

She took out her hand mirror and checked to see if she needed to reapply her clear lip-gloss. She wasn't the kind of woman who wore much lipstick or makeup. She preferred her natural look, very much like her mother. They both had skin that glowed from inside out.

Minutes later the elevator sounded. David stepped out in a forest-green, fitted V-neck T-shirt, straight-fit denim jeans and brown wingtip shoes.

"Wow." Jennifer was so awestruck she could hardly keep her jaw from dropping. She cleared her throat and rose to her feet. He walked halfway over to her with a confident, wicked smile. He knew his presence affected her. She hugged him, inhaling the crisp, subtle scent of his cologne. Immediately, that warm sensation traveled throughout her body, soothing her soul.

"I wasn't expecting this first-class treatment."

"Ah, it's nothing." David led her outside.

"So where are you taking me?" Jennifer saw the valet parker pulling up in David's car.

"It's a surprise. I think you'll like it."

She took his word for it. She felt happy and relaxed. She loved spontaneity and pleasant surprises.

About twenty-five minutes later, they drove up to a huge greenhouse. Her eyes grew big when she saw white lights illuminating the paved pathway that led to the entrance of the glass enclosure.

"Oh, David." She quickly looked at him and back at the greenhouse. "This is beautiful. Is this yours?"

He smiled in a way that said he knew she was pleased.

"Nah. A friend of mine owns it. Let's go inside." He moved his head in the direction of the greenhouse.

They parked out front, and David got out of the car and

came around to the passenger side to open the door for her. Her heart took a snapshot of what could be. She saw David blending into her life as a confidante and friend. Then as a boyfriend, someone who had the potential of becoming an amazing lifelong partner.

"Jennifer," David said with his hand extended to her. "You there?"

"I'm sorry. I'm just so taken by the scenery." *Yep. Just the scenery.* No way would she admit to planning their wedding in her head.

"It's okay." He smiled and helped her out of the car. "Maybe we see the same 'future,'" he said with an impish grin.

"What do you mean?" She was all nonchalance and innocence, but she got the feeling she hadn't fooled him. His piercing eyes could see right through her at this point.

"Oh, nothing."

He knows what I'm thinking!

She returned from the vision of her future and grasped David's hand. She stood in front of him, rising to the tips of her toes like a ballerina. She looked deeply into his eyes. Neither spoke. That muted moment spoke blissfully of a wonderful night unfolding before their eyes.

"Ready?" David kissed her hand.

"Yes, David." Her eyes was shining.

Inside the greenhouse, Jennifer walked ahead of David. In awe, she observed the colorful display of plants and flowers, reeling from the aromas swirling around her. David warned her to be careful in her high heels.

Jennifer glanced back with a sassy look. "Excuse me, sir! I am a pro."

"Work it, Jennifer," he joked and stood back, watching her as if she were walking the runway.

She laughed and strutted her stuff for a moment before a saccharine fragrance sauntered across her nose.

"I smell banana shrubs," she said, veering to the right from the center of the aisle and finding the banana shrubs. She stopped, closed her eyes, and deeply inhaled.

"Yes, I remembered them from the photos you showed me," David murmured, coming up next to her.

"Tulips, too," Jennifer said with excitement.

"I'll keep that in mind." David hooked Jennifer's arm in his and drew her back to the center of the aisle.

In the middle of the greenhouse stood a pedestal. On it was a big bouquet of vibrant white, pink, yellow, and orange roses. Ascending tall in the middle was a red rose. She stared at the vivid floral arrangement, captivated by the elegance of its beauty.

"What's this, David?" she asked softly.

David walked to the other side of the pedestal. She could tell by his slow pace that he had something special to say. She pressed a hand against her chest and braced herself, holding her breath.

"What we have between us is beautiful, complete, and whole on its own," said David in formal tones.

"David," she exhaled. His name came out as a whisper.

"Each color is vibrant and beautiful," David continued, visible to her beyond the bouquet between them. "The orange and yellow roses are symbolic of the wonderful friendship we're cultivating. The white and pink ones represent the way your beauty springs forth with virtue and purity among the other roses in this universe. The red rose is what our friendship could potentially blossom into. You're a beautiful and special woman, Jennifer," he said, clearing his throat.

When she heard his voice becoming choked up, unable to contain the emotions pouring into the atmosphere, her heart melted until it was no more.

I can't keep myself together.

She stood still, consumed with the spirit of love infusing her soul. It took her a moment to find strength in her legs and voice again. There was nothing but pure joy. She'd never seen a man express himself in such a way.

This is beyond me.

"Thank you, David. That was powerful." A tear escaped the corner of her eye and ran down her cheek. "Are you using your creative writing skills on me or something?" She chuckled.

"Not at all," he assured her.

"I'm just overwhelmed," she said. "I have never been treated this way before. I'm speechless. You make courting a reality to me. Quite the impression."

"Thank you for allowing another special moment to happen." He beamed at her. He came over, took her by the arm and said, "Now let's go to the best dining establishment in town."

WHEN THEY LEFT THE GREENHOUSE, David noticed a red Mercedes coupe parked off to the side in the parking lot. He tried to make out the face of the driver but couldn't. The tints were too dark. He saw Jennifer look at him, bemused.

"I hope that's not the person who left that note on your windshield."

"Uh, that would be creepy."

"Have you gotten any more notes?" He slowly started to drive off, keeping his eye on the car.

"I haven't," she said, also trying to see who was in the vehicle.

"Someone probably saw the light and thought some special event was going on tonight." He shrugged the bystander off and peeled out of the parking lot.

As he was driving back to his place, she playfully hit him on the arm.

"Dave's Kitchen, huh?" She recalled the other day that he'd mentioned his cooking skills.

"Yep." He winked at her.

As soon as David opened the front door, the spicy scent of curry and salmon met her. Her stomach growled as the smell of conch curry, baked salmon sprinkled with lemon and garlic butter layered over carrots and asparagus, and brown rice hit her. She was even more impressed that he'd researched a classic Turks and Caicos island dish.

"A man who actually listens. Earning brownie points tonight, huh?" She gave him a flirty wink.

"It's a pleasure. I remember you mentioning you were from Turks and Caicos, so I did my research." He shrugged. "I'll show you around."

He gave her a quick tour of his place. He watched her eyes marvel over the earthy refined décor in living room. He saw she was impressed with the round copper plates and the silverware that was neatly wrapped in white napkins tied with thin black ribbons. And the bottle of sparkling apple cider rested in a stainless bucket of ice with two tall wineglasses beside it. Next to the wine cooler were two grooved carafes. One was filled with water. The other appeared to be some kind of punch. That topped things off.

"This is a nice setup you have here." She grazed her hand over one of the dining room chairs. "I really like it."

"Thanks. I hoped you would feel comfortable here. You look nice tonight." He gestured to her outfit. "Nice shoes, too. And I think soft pink compliments your skin complexion," he added, pointing at her finger and toenails. "It's one of my favorite colors on a woman."

"That's good to know. You clean up pretty nice yourself. I like your GQ style."

He struck a match and lit the candles on the table to complete the romantic ambiance. "You can get comfy in the living room while I bring out dinner. Oh, let me take your purse, or do you wanna hold on to it?"

"Thank you, but I'm okay. Do you mind if I keep you company in the kitchen for a while?"

"Not at all." He extended his arm and she took his hand, walking with him.

He put the white cooking apron over his head, and she tied the strings behind his back. "Aww, that is too cute," she said when he faced her. She traced the stitched red letters of "Dave's Kitchen" on the front of his apron.

"The apron and mittens were a gift from last year," he explained, sliding on the matching mitts to remove the salmon from the oven. "I figured I'd put them to use sooner or later."

"I have to say, that's a very nice gift." Momentarily, she wondered who'd given them to him.

"Thanks. I'm glad you like them." He pulled off the mitts and took her hand for a moment.

Her eyes cut at him. "Who taught you how to cook?" she asked like a detective in an interrogation room.

He leaned back against the counter and crossed his arms. He laughed for a moment before speaking again, giving her a look that said, *I see where you're going with this.* "I learned at the women's shelter. Bible study isn't the only thing I do over there."

"Did Miss Smith teach you?" she asked.

David nodded. "She taught me all the basics of cooking. I also took a few cooking classes here and there." He finished arranging the food, untied his apron, and put it on the counter. "Now I scorched a few meals in my early stages, but eventually, I got the hang of it." He laughed. "She was the one who got the apron and mitts for me. Just wanted to make that clear in case you thought I was harboring another woman around here. Now get yourself into the living room and get comfortable."

She smacked him on the arm and let out a chuckle. "Am I that obvious?"

"Uh, yeah." He went back to the stove.

"Okay, I'm going into the living room now."

IT HAD BEEN some time since she'd had a man cater to her like this, so she wasn't going to put up a fight when he told her to get comfortable. Given that he volunteered at the shelter, she knew he was a naturally kind and selfless person. She remembered her failed attempts at getting her ex-fiancé to participate in a walk to raise awareness about breast cancer and other community service events. With Robert, something always came up. She was willing to bet a hundred bucks that David, if asked, would be happy to participate in a walk. He'd already done so much to raise money for cancer. She did wonder, though.

But why does he work with women?

On the sofa, she spied the edge of the black remote underneath the overstuffed chair. "Men, I tell you." She rolled her eyes, flipped the pillows face up, and powered the television on. Not finding anything of interest to watch, she turned the TV off and observed the mood and colors of the room more closely.

Definitely a bachelor's pad. She ran her hand across the dark brown rough fabric of David's sofa. *He could use a little life in his living room but so could mine.* She stood and walked toward the brown five-shelf studio stand, examining a picture of an older man who strongly resembled David.

"Is this a picture of your father?" she called, bringing it closer to her face.

David stuck his head around the corner. "Yep. That's my dad."

"Nice. I see where you get your handsome looks from," she said, too quiet for him to hear.

"Dinner will be ready shortly," he said after ducking back into the kitchen.

She continued to look at the other pictures on the bookshelf and noticed a picture shoved clear out of the way.

I wonder why this one is in the back.

She reached for it and saw a woman whom David also resembled. She looked toward the kitchen, getting ready to ask if it was his mother, but decided against it. In her spirit, she felt it wasn't the time. Near the photo was a clear vase. It was filled with brown, orange, and green leaves. Chalkboard rocks were in another vase. Written on them were the words *discipline, strength, understanding, unconditional love, wisdom, healing, faith, trust,* and *keep writing.* It gave her even more clarity as to David's character.

"This is encouraging. Maybe I should do something like this myself," she said under her breath.

David sneaked up behind her. "Dinner's ready," he whispered, startling her. He held out his hand and led her to the dining room area.

"Are you enjoying yourself tonight?" He took the salmon off the platter with a spatula and placed it on her plate.

"Yes, I am. Thank you. This looks and smells amazing." She grabbed the apple green bowl of brown rice mixed with peas and gave them both generous servings. "David, I am moved by all of this. Makes a gal feel special."

After dinner, David cleared the table and they went into the living room. He went to the fireplace and tapped the touch screen on the audio player above it. Christian jazz music streamed gracefully from the speakers.

Jennifer's arms wrapped around David's back. She closed her eyes and rested her head against his chest. She fell into the rhythm of the music, to the beat of his heart, and into the peacefulness of his presence. This night felt just like the night at the National Harbor. She was overwhelmed by all that David had done for her in such a short period. After being with her ex-fiancé for nine years, he had never done anything special like this. David was a gentleman who'd cooked an amazing dinner for her. He loved Christian jazz music, too. That was the icing on the cake. One fond memory she had of her dad was that the two of them used to listen to jazz music together. She and her sister would dance and sing along with their father.

"Jennifer?" David whispered into her ear.

The deep overtones in his voice stirred her. "Yes, David." She opened her eyes and stared into his, noting a sweet heat there that made her insides tingle.

"Thanks for the dance."

"You're welcome, Mr. Bradshaw. I appreciate how you treat me. This is different. In a good way, of course."

David cradled her face in his hands. She saw the fire of passion in his eyes and his lips parting just a little in preparation for a kiss. She savored this kinetic moment. She wanted to kiss him.

I can't. I can't get attached like this.

She was well aware of what could happen if she did. Instead, she rested her head back on his chest. She closed her eyes and admitted to herself that David had found a way to paint himself into the portrait of her life. He was journeying deeper into her heart.

The music stopped and they stood motionless in each other's arms for a few more minutes. Then Jennifer stepped back. "Okay, Mr. Bradshaw. I'm going to get going now."

"I think that's a good idea." He kissed her hand and released it.

"You're so sweet," she said, feeling completely relaxed. She wondered if David had a similar picture in his mind of the two of them deeply involved in one another's lives.

"I think we see the same thing again," he said.

Her heart jumped. *He read my mind again.* He was so in tune with her. "I feel the presence of God again. It's stronger."

"I feel it too, Jennifer. I'll call downstairs for your car." David turned away and went to make the phone call.

In a way, she did not want to open the conversation about them feeling the presence of God. She'd rather allow things to flow without overanalyzing anything.

"Okay." Jennifer seated herself on the sofa, nervous anticipation fluttering within her chest. She didn't want to leave, which was exactly why she needed to.

"We should do this again sometime," he said, returning to her side and kneeling next to her. He lifted her foot and slid her heel back on, then reached for the other.

"You're right," she said, breaking apart inside. The touch of David's warm hand against her foot made her tempted to stay, to go to a place she wasn't ready for yet. "It'll be my treat on our next date," she said, trying to brush off the heavy tension coiling within her.

"Date?" David sat back on his heels and crossed his arms with a grin.

"Oh, I'm sorry. That's right. I forgot. This isn't a date. We're building a friendship."

"Right, Ms. Washington. Friendship," he said, gesturing his fingers in the form of a quotation.

"Right! Friendship." She laughed instantly, mimicking his hand movement.

"I'll walk you downstairs." He sighed out a laugh of his own.

David walked Jennifer through the sliding glass doors. The valet returned just in time. He jumped out and quietly waited with the car door opened.

"Well, Jennifer, have a good night. Call or text to let me know you got in safely." He hugged her tightly one last time before helping her into her car.

"I will."

David shut the door gently and Jennifer rolled her window down. "Thanks for everything. Loved the greenhouse and dinner was amazing."

"Maybe we'll be able to go again for another special occasion." He winked, waved, and walked back into the building.

The confidence in his stride made Jennifer beam from ear to ear. She loved his confidence and assertiveness. Very attractive in a man.

On her way home, she smelled a very familiar scent emanating from the back seat. "What's that smell?" She turned around. Her eyes grew wide. "Oh my gosh, David. How in the world did you manage this?"

There, sitting perfectly pristine in the middle of her backseat, was the bouquet of roses from the greenhouse, along with banana shrubs and tulips.

How did he?

Every romantic movie she'd seen or book she'd read now became believable. David took her fantasy and made it a reality. Her mind couldn't keep up with her emotions. "God, did you answer my prayers?" She just couldn't believe this.

She arrived home and carefully removed the bouquet of roses from her car. "Hmm, what's this here?" She spotted a small envelope that was stuffed into the flower arrangement and took a seat on the front steps of her condo. She opened the envelope and found a note that read:

Dear Jennifer,

This was a wonderful night. Forgive me if things feel like they're moving beyond the speed of a friendship. Know that I'm not rushing you into anything. What I did tonight was genuine, sincere, and completely uncondi-tional. You owe me nothing in return. However, what I'm starting to feel for you cannot be denied. I enjoyed your company and conversation. I think you're a great woman with a beautiful spirit. I'm looking forward to how our friendship will evolve.

I hope you enjoyed your time with me as much as I did with you. Have a good night, Jennifer.

-David

Jennifer laid the card down beside her. Words couldn't describe how special he'd made her feel tonight. She stared into the infinite black skies watching stars flash their brilliance across the universe. The moon was tucked amidst smoky gray clouds that seemed to configure two hands clasped over one another. She cupped her hands over her mouth as her vision became blurry. The awesome presence of God returned. The spirit of love seized her, rocking her side to side, but fear was there too. The men she dated always showed promise of something special in the beginning, but the initial phase of excitement and the new possibility of love would wear off. And the real version of them manifested. It wasn't that they were imperfect. The wolf would emerge out of the coat of the sheep and begin to mistreat her. She couldn't take another hit of disappointment.

She remembered the day she'd confessed these words and was wrong years later.

"Mom, I think Robert is the one," Jennifer said to her mother after their third date.

"I was wrong then, and I'm probably wrong now. This can't be real." She read the card over and over again. She searched for some deception or ambiguity in his words but found none. His actions supported everything he'd declared in the letter. She put the card back into the envelope and stuffed it into the bouquet. She'd never experienced anything like this before. She couldn't believe David. It all had to be one huge show. Her past wouldn't allow her to fathom that love was a possibility for her.

She thought of Leyanie and reminded herself that she needed to be careful. Friendship was a wonderful thing, but it couldn't take the place of her daughter. She decided to stay at the hospital that night and remain by Leyanie's side.

Sunlight illumed through the skylight window in Jennifer's workroom and bathed the brown wooden floors and green plants that grew tall in white and brown flowerpots. The bouquet of roses, banana shrubs, and tulips David had given her were on the countertop. She'd walk past them and admire the arrangement for moments. *He makes me feel special.* Against the white walls were paintings of white sand beaches, boardwalks that focused on the importance of nature, and scriptures that reminded her of God's place in her life. She'd painted them all. Painting was therapeutic for her whenever she needed to clear her mind. But this time, the white canvas was blank like her imagination. Nothing came to mind. Jennifer sat hunched over on her wooden stool in a white sports bra and stonewash overalls for nearly a half hour. She dipped the brush into the green paint and stroked aimlessly. Her heart and mind were at war about David.

It's hard to open my heart to him. She moved the brush up and down. *There's gotta be something wrong. And why am I looking for something wrong?*

She knew embracing a negative perspective would give life for things to go wrong. Dipping her paint brush into another color, she received a call from one of the nurses at the children's hospital.

"Hello," Jennifer answered.

"Jennifer." The nurse tried to speak, but her voice cracked so much.

Jennifer could tell something was wrong. She quickly threw on a pullover jacket and rushed out the door. She had just spent the night with Leyanie. What could have gone wrong between leaving the hospital that morning and now?

Once she got inside the hospital, she jumped into the elevator and pressed the 11th floor button several times. She paced back and forth feeling anxious, becoming hot from the rush of her emotions. She tried to cool down by fanning herself, but her efforts were in vain. When the elevator door opened, she saw David and Max standing in front of Leyanie's room. Sadness filled their eyes. She saw David coming over to comfort her, but she waved him off and went over to the nurse. The lead nurse, who was the closest to Leyanie, looked like she'd been crying for quite some time.

Jennifer asked what was wrong. "Where is Leyanie?" Two other nurses immediately came up to Jennifer and prepared to calm her.

"Leyanie passed away before I called you, Jennifer. We knew it was coming, but it still feels so sudden." The lead nurse held Jennifer's hand. "She left a letter for you. She died with it in her hand. We didn't want to remove her until you saw her."

"Where is she? I want to see her." She tried to break away from the two nurses.

"We're going to let you see her. We just need you to first calm down," the lead nurse said, restraining her.

"Okay. Okay. Okay. I'm calm."

They released their grips from Jennifer and allowed her to walk into Leyanie's room. She found the white linen bedspreads were pulled up to her neck. And her eyes were peacefully shut with a smile on her face. Jennifer took Leyanie's hand, which was still warm, and pressed her face against it.

"Leyanie, wake up. Please wake up. You're sleeping. I know you are." She pressed her hand to her cheek, hoping it would move. "God don't take her from me. She's my Kayla."

She took the letter out of Leyanie's hand and opened it.

Jen, you are an amazing person. I thanked God for you every day. You gave me life as mine was diminishing. Thank you for not breaking our vow. I never wanted you to feel sorry for me. I didn't ask to have cancer. Sometimes God uses unfortunate conditions for a greater purpose that we may later understand. It reminds me of the sacrifice of Jesus Christ. He died for our sins that we may all have a relationship with the Father through Him. I'm in no way comparing myself to Him and what He did on the Cross. What I'm trying to say is death draws us closer to the Son. It also brings families and friends closer together. I never knew who my parents were or if I had any siblings. In a way, this hurt me. To see the other kids' families come to visit hurt at times. I wondered who mine were and why they never came to visit me. I had hoped they would come. But you, Jennifer, you became more than a visitor. You became my family. You were my mother and sister. Better, you were a friend in Christ. God drew you to me, and I know he's going to use my death to bring you closer to Him.

I felt God say it was time to move on. My body could no longer take the pain. I know that you are living with pain, but you don't have to. You must let go like I did, Mom. Surrender your pain into the hands of God, and you will experience heaven on Earth. I'm sure Kayla is with our Father in Heaven. Maybe I'll get a chance to see her.

With all of my love. Your daughter,

Leyanie Washington

"She used my last name." Jennifer knelt at her side then stretched out on the floor. This broke and crushed her spirit even more. *I don't understand. My heart bleeds.* Grief pinned her down for minutes. Once she was able to stand on her feet, she grabbed the light brown teddy bear that had "Jesus I love You" stitched on it from the chair in the corner. She placed it beside Leyanie and kissed her warm cheek again. "Goodbye, Leyanie. I love you. I will see you again."

Jennifer left her room. Max and David were still in the hallway. Max immediately ran up and hugged her at the knee. She couldn't help becoming emotional again at the sight of the sadness in his eyes. She rubbed his back. "She no longer has to suffer. She's in a better place now, Max."

"I'm going to miss her," he said.

"I know, Max. We all will," she said.

David moved toward her, but she put her hands up to shove him away and started to make her way to the elevator. She saw the hurt register on his face, but she felt too much pain to stop. All she could think about was the night before and how she'd spent the majority of it with David when she should have been with Leyanie much sooner.

"I don't want to talk. This is all too much for me now. I think we should continue in our separate lives." She pressed the elevator button.

"What do you mean continue in our separate lives?" David crossed his arms against his chest.

"I have other things to focus on. I don't need distractions." She stoically faced the elevator.

"Distractions?" David jerked his head back with one of his eyebrows arched up. He sighed angrily.

She could him trying to hold back his frustration. "Yes, you would be a distraction in my life. Goodbye."

It hurt Jennifer deeply to tell David that. A destructive hurricane of negative thoughts hit her hard. It was the feeling of breaking up with Robert all over again, but David was different. Maybe this was why it pained her so much. He was what she'd never had. She knew he'd worked hard to earn her trust. He'd courted her before they had a chance to become an official couple. He'd invested time in her. He'd engaged her in ways that no man ever had. He understood her spirit and put into words things she couldn't articulate for herself. He was romantic in every meaningful and non-pretentious way. How could she allow fear to win when she had prayed so fervently to meet a godly man?

Easy. Guilt for splitting her focus between David and Leyanie had brought out all her demons. She didn't know how to handle the fallout.

LEYANIE's white dress nearly matched the color of her casket. Her teddy bear was tucked under her arm. The same smile was on her face as the day she passed away.

"Leyanie, I love you," Jennifer said holding the letter she'd given her. "I'm going to miss you so much."

Behind Jennifer were some staff members and her friends from the hospital, Leyanie's case manager from years ago, her friends from children's church, along with Max and David. They all came out to the church Jennifer and Leyanie attended in McLean. Today, Jennifer wasn't sad. She was more at peace. Leyanie no longer had to suffer. Jennifer felt someone's presence next to her. It was Max reaching up to hold her hand, and she gently squeezed it back. They both said their goodbyes.

As everyone left, David came up to offer some words of support. While she appreciated it, she didn't want to have a conversation with him. She silently thanked him and left the church.

CHAPTER 8

$\mathcal{M}$iami's cool morning breeze fanned against Jennifer's face, but she dreaded the hot humidity the afternoon would bring. She'd left northern Virginia a week after Leyanie's funeral. She needed to get away from everything. Kayla's and Leyanie's passing weighed heavy on her heart again, and the inner conflict she had about David remained prevalent. She also wanted to spend her birthday with her mom and sister. She needed her family too.

At the airport, she spotted her mom standing a few vehicles away. Catherine had on a white sundress, a pink shirt and oversized sunglasses. Jennifer flagged her down. Her mother welcomed Jennifer into her arms with a big hug like the little girl she used to be. She was happy to see her daughter again. Jennifer was just as thrilled to see her mother. They were the best of friends. Jennifer complimented her mother on how good she looked.

"I see the juicing, vegan diet, and cardio workout plans I suggested are paying off." Her mother returned the compliment.

On their way home, the only sound that could be heard was cars rocketing by. Jennifer paid no attention to anything in particular while she stared out the side window. She completely forgot her mother was there.

"How was the funeral?"

"Everything went well. I'm glad she doesn't have to suffer anymore."

"She doesn't. It was brave of you to adopt her and love her like your own."

"Mom, you're about to make me cry all over again."

"I'm sorry, dear." She patted her hand.

"It's okay."

"How's David doing?"

"Don't wanna talk about it," she said under her breath.

"Well, all right." Her mother digressed.

When they reached home, her mother helped Jennifer with her bags. Approaching the front door, Jennifer paused, caught up in painful memories from the past.

"Since you're living in my house"—her father raised his voice—"you're going to do what I say. These are my rules. Got it?" He pointed his finger in Jennifer's face.

Jennifer pushed his hand away. "You don't intimidate me."

"You don't have to be intimidated to take this." He smacked her across the face.

The sound of her father's hand against her cheek was loud enough for her mother to hear it from downstairs.

Jennifer's mother ran upstairs. "Don't put your hands on her!" she screamed, stepping in between them. "Jennifer, are you okay?" Catherine saw the left side of her face was red.

"You're going to regret this!" Jennifer yelled at her father in rage and ran from the room.

"Jennifer, are you okay? Is the door locked?" her mother asked.

"No, it's unlocked." Jennifer gripped her bag fiercely. "Something came to mind." That awful memory was still fresh even after all these years. "Where's your husband?"

Catherine let out an exasperated sigh and rolled her eyes. "Somewhere around here."

Jennifer unpacked her bags in her old comfy room while her mother prepared mango-peach iced tea. Jennifer's favorite. Not much had changed in her room. The walls were still robin's-egg blue, and all of her childhood teddy bears were perfectly lined in order from smallest to biggest, just how she'd organized them as a little girl. The screen of her fifteen-inch television was layered with dust, and the VHS tapes she'd collected of her favorite movies and musicals were all neatly stacked.

In her closet, a brown shoebox was on the shelf. Inside of it was a small, pink journal. The journal contained notes from her past experiences and relationships. She thumbed through it, seeing a wallet-size picture of her and Robert. She took it out and glared at it for a few seconds. She found the promise ring he'd gifted her underneath shoe stuffing paper.

"Jennifer, I got this ring to prove how much I love you. You're the woman I want to marry." Robert slid the ring on her finger.

She'd been so happy that day. Everything in their relationship had gone right up to the point of receiving the promise ring. Before she could linger on that moment, her mother called from the patio.

"Coming," she said, tossing the journal and ring back into the shoebox.

Outside on the patio, Jennifer sank into the wicker chair next to her mother with the ultrasonogram in her hand. She studied it for a few moments.

A few minutes later, Jennifer's father opened the sliding glass door to the patio. He stood tall in a fishing hat, poking at his teeth with a toothpick. He spat out whatever was between his teeth and walked toward Jennifer and her mother. They could feel the patio shake as he walked. He quickly snatched the ultrasonogram from Jennifer's hand and opened it.

Jennifer glanced up at him. His grim, deep-set eyes stared. He crossed his arms and smirked, apparently to savor this moment. He shook his head again and went back inside. Jennifer's heart broke just a bit more. She ran to the sliding door and screamed, "You're a sick, evil man."

"Ignore him," Catherine said.

"I so regret not having her. Every day this haunts me," she said, coming back to the present.

Jennifer looked up at her mom with hopelessness in her eyes. Life appeared to be crashing down on her all at once. Guilt from the abortion, Leyanie's death, and the dwindling foundation she'd established with David were all caving in on her.

"Mom, I just can't do this anymore. I can't. This is too much for me. I lost Kayla. Now I've lost Leyanie. My life has been all about losing. When do I win?" she said in a rage of anger.

When the pressures of life pound on top of you, it's difficult to sense and hear what God is saying in tough times. Jennifer sure did feel this way in the moment. But a moment is just a moment. God is still there in the silence.

Catherine hugged Jennifer to her. "Jennifer, don't say that." She glanced away. "I should've stood up for you. It was your right to keep her." She teared up. "I was so afraid of your father, so worried about how he would treat you and the baby if you tried to keep her. I just didn't have the strength to support you or do what was necessary at the time. And I'm sorry about Leyanie. I know how much you loved her."

Jennifer's arms wrapped around her mother's neck. "Mom, it's okay."

They both released their pent-up feelings from the abortion. Jennifer had always wanted to have this conversation with her mother, but she'd never felt it was the right time. She also didn't want a fight to break out between them. They were best friends. However, Catherine needed to get some guilt off her chest as well. While tough conversations were difficult to have, they were necessary for moving forward.

Her sister came out onto the patio a few minutes later and found them crying.

"She's going to be fine," said Catherine. "She's going to be fine."

Anisha seemed content with her mother's response. She looked on a few minutes and turned away.

That evening, Jennifer went out on the front porch with her laptop and sat on the swing. She felt well enough to start revising her grant proposal. In the process of doing that, she opened pictures saved on her computer, staring at moments capturing her and David. She caught herself adoring the sheen of his smooth chocolate skin, high cheekbones, and full lips when they were at the Cherry Blossom festival. Hearing the screen door creak, she quickly minimized the picture to a thumbnail size. She tried to close her laptop but didn't succeed in time. She laughed, giving herself away again.

"Is that David? He's extremely handsome," Catherine said. "Can I take a look at your pictures?" She peered closely.

"Yes, that's him." She enlarged it and turned to her mother with dreamy eyes.

Her mother took the laptop from her to get a better look. "He's handsome."

Jennifer agreed. That was something she would never deny.

"Are you thinking about David?"

"I am. I cut him off."

"Why?"

"I need to just focus on the non-profit. I don't need distractions." She grabbed the laptop from her mother and closed it.

"Okay, but from what you shared about David, he seems focused and has his priorities in line. I can't see how he would be a distraction. I don't think it's necessarily him."

Jennifer looked down the narrow road that faced their house. She searched her soul.

"What do you think it is?"

"You feel unworthy for what you've prayed for, and now that you have it, you're pushing him away. I think you feel guilty for spending time with him, but Leyanie would have wanted you to continue living whether she had passed or not."

Jennifer faced her mother, and their eyes locked for seconds. That truth hit her hard.

She's right. For once, she had to be honest with herself. *But why do I feel unworthy? It goes deeper than the guilt I feel at not being near Leyanie's bedside twenty-four/seven.*

"And if the man who's courting you is a distraction to God's calling in your life, that means he's not a part of it," Catherine said rubbing her back.

"What's going on out here?" Anisha's face emerged against the screen door. You could see the imprint of her forehead bulging out. When they didn't respond, she came out to the porched and squeezed herself between them. She snatched the laptop out of Jennifer's hand to surf the web and saw David's picture. "I'm going to be nosy this time. Ohhh, this must be the lovely David Bradshaw. He's way cuter than Robert."

Jennifer burst out laughing. "Yes, that's him, and I agree."

"What's the deal between you two? Better not lose this guy." Her sister knew how tough it had been for her to date after Robert.

"I don't feel like retelling the story right now, but we're not on speaking terms."

"Well, I'm here for you, sis, if you ever wanna talk."

"Thanks, Nish."

LATER THAT NIGHT, Jennifer fell asleep and slipped into an enthralling dream:

Birds soared high in the gray skies above the riverbank. Crickets chirped. Ladybugs marched on the long blades of green stems. Bumblebees buzzed, swarming over quiet, dark waters. With each step Jennifer took beside the stream, small splashes in the water rocked to the rhythm of her pace. A strong wind surrounded her, nudging her to direct her attention to the waters. She saw black, blue, gray, and purple rose petals around four medium-sized pictures that were facedown. Suddenly, the strong wind swept across the surface of the water and flipped the pictures face-up. She saw a picture of Robert and her father when he was a young boy. The other two were photos of an infant baby girl and a girl that resembled her at twelve.

"Love again," a gentle voice whispered from the strong winds.

"How?" Jennifer asked.

"When the clouds move." The voice faded away.

"I don't understand." Jennifer shook her head, confused.

The winds calmed and all life around her stood still. The pictures were facedown again.

Walking farther along the riverbank, she saw turquoise, green, yellow, orange, white, pink, and red rose petals lined perfectly in the center of the water. The same strong wind engulfed her, flipping the pictures up again.

The voice repeated softly, "Love again."

"How?" Jennifer threw her hands up in frustration.

"When the clouds move. Now come." The voice faded away swiftly.

Jennifer trembled as she kept walking until her feet sank into warm sand. She flexed her toes, savoring the balmy grains between them. She noticed the sand was black with dark blue crystals embedded in it.

"Where am I?" Jennifer glanced back at her footprints that seemed to stretch miles away. "How long have I been traveling on black sand?"

"Far too long," a little girl exclaimed.

Jennifer saw the girl in the distance and squinted to make out her face. Jennifer thought the girl looked very familiar, resembling her when she was twelve. "Is everything all right? Are you lost?" Jennifer yelled.

"Come." The voice resounded with a roar of thunder.

Jennifer flinched, taking her attention away from the girl. She trembled in terror but continued walking forward, glancing back to see if the girl was still there. She vanished. Jennifer turn back around and kept walking until she stumbled upon a hill. From the base to midway up the hill, the sands were brown. Closer to the peak of the hill, they were dazzling white. And the strong wind gathered around her. She closed her eyes and every hurtful moment of her life flashed before her.

"Oh, God." She slowly opened her eyes again. In the blue sky, the four pictures were suspended in the air, and before her, once again, stood the little girl who resembled her.

"Where did you come from?" Jennifer knelt. "You look like me. I mean, when I was twelve."

"Because I'm you." She smiled and hugged Jennifer. "It's time for you to let me move on, so you can be the woman God called you to be."

"Huh? I don't understand," mumbled Jennifer.

"Dad said some hurtful things to me, but now it's time for you to heal." The little girl skipped away mysteriously.

Suddenly, a sweet fragrance wafted through the air. It was so therapeutic and comforting to Jennifer that she closed her eyes, enjoying this ecstasy that couldn't be ascertained in the natural world. This fragrance was not made by human hands nor from any natural resource on the Earth.

"Love again," the voice instructed.

Jennifer opened her eyes and saw a man about six feet tall. He walked toward her in a glistening white robe. The robe was so bright, Jennifer had a difficult time looking at him. The man touched her eyes and she was able to see clearly. Jennifer saw that there was someone else. The man held the hand of a girl who resembled her, but not her twelve-year-old self.

"Beautiful, isn't she?" He spoke gently with admiration.

"Jesus?" Jennifer trembled with fear and fell to her knees. Though she'd seen many paintings and depictions of what people thought Jesus might look like, nothing came close, and yet she knew it was Him.

"Fear not!" Jesus' voice roared like a thousand waves but filled her with peace rather than trepidation. "I am He." He lifted Jennifer to her feet by the hand. "See. This is your daughter, Kayla. She's with me now."

This revelation horrified Jennifer. She'd always believed there was a chance to see her daughter again, but feared it as well.

How would she explain herself? What would she say? How would she feel?

"I can't. I can't look at her." Jennifer covered her face in shame. "I abandoned her. I took her life."

"I understand, Mom. It's okay." Kayla gently moved Jennifer's hands from her face. "I know you regret not keeping me. I'm with Jesus now. It's so beautiful in Heaven. I've so many friends here. Leyanie is one of them. She says hi. She's with Esther now."

"Esther? Like Esther from the Bible?"

"Yes, Esther in the Bible," Kayla giggled.

"Wow! Tell Leyanie I miss her." *This is surreal.* All of Jennifer's senses were engaged as she stared at her beautiful daughter. "Kayla!" Jennifer cried and wrapped her arms around her. "My baby. I love you!"

The bond between a mother and daughter is like no other. The maternal connection, warmth and love begins when a baby is formed and growing in the mother's womb. This was something Jennifer got to experience in this moment with Kayla. Not to imply that what she shared with Leyanie wasn't special; however, Jennifer emptied her entire being into Kayla when she hugged her. Jennifer felt every fuzzy feeling that she had when learning she was pregnant with Kayla. Jennifer embraced Kayla with all her spirit, every thought and emotion she had of raising her in a godly way, to changing her diapers, sending her off on her first day of school, getting manicures and pedicures together, and doing the other things a mother would enjoy with her daughter to build fond memories.

"I love you too, Mom." Kayla kissed Jennifer lightly on the cheek.

Hearing those words weakened Jennifer in an abundance of joy.

Then Jesus spoke again: "Your sins were forgiven years ago when you repented, but the accuser of the brethren persuaded you to think otherwise. I also came to heal the little girl in you and to remove the guilt from the abortion. See!" Jesus touched Jennifer's forehead.

"I'm healed. Now you are too." Jennifer's younger self returned.

Jesus continued to speak calmly: "This is a time to let go of your past with Robert. This is a time to reconcile with your earthly father. I've already dealt with your father's heart. He has finally surrendered to My love. My love that heals. My love that reconciles. My peace that exceeds beyond human understanding. My love brings salvation, so you are now made whole, Jennifer!" Jesus gently placed her hand over her heart. "I give you a new heart."

Jennifer felt something heavy depart from her: the deep condemnation and paralyzing guilt. "Thank you, Jesus. I feel light!" She knelt at his feet and began praising and worshipping Him.

"I now give you John 3:8: The wind blows wherever it pleases. You hear its sound, but you cannot tell where it comes from or where it is going. So it is with everyone born of the Spirit. The strong winds you felt earlier signified The Comforter. He was guiding you, Jennifer. Fear not!"

"I understand." Jennifer wept. "Jesus, what does 'when the clouds move' mean?"

"It's when you will recall this dream later today. Rest now."

Jennifer woke up with her heart beating so fast.

"Something happened," she said, hearing her phone vibrate on the nightstand. She picked up the phone, wondering who had contacted her at this time of the morning. It was a "Happy Birthday" text from Robert, along with him asking if they could meet up at the beach later today. She wondered how he'd figured out her number since changing it a few times. She decided against responding, grabbed a blanket her grandmother had made her a few years before she died, and went outside on the patio.

Shortly afterward, as she was sipping a cup of vanilla chamomile tea on the chaise lounge chair, Catherine came outside. She looked as if she hadn't slept much either. Before she could ask Jennifer why she was outside at this time of the night and wish her a happy birthday, Jennifer immediately jumped to her feet and said in a panic, "I think I saw Jesus in a dream, and I remember seeing pictures of Dad, Robert, and myself, when I was like nine years old or so—and Kayla."

"Kayla? No way."

"I did. She looks just like me."

"Aww, Kayla." Her mother cried. "That's wonderful Jen."

"I know. It was hard to believe. I can't remember the rest. Wish I'd written it down when I woke up. I think Robert's text coming in distracted me."

"Robert texted you?" Her mother was surprised.

"Yeah, he did," she said, deflated. "He wants to meet up. How does he even know I'm back home? Creepy."

"That is creepy. You have to change your number."

"Again," she said, interrupting.

"Yes, again, but I can't make sense of your dream. Maybe God was revealing something to you about healing or reconciling. I don't know, dear, but dreaming about Jesus sounds like a wonderful birthday gift." She rubbed Jennifer's back.

"I believe so too." Jennifer leaned her head back, thinking about that possibility. "Thanks for the birthday wishes. Feels good to be back home."

Jennifer realized how much she'd needed this trip. They sat outside for a bit longer enjoying the peace of the early morning. To Jennifer, it felt like they were the only two people in the world. Her thoughts then wandered to the text message Robert had left.

I wonder why he wants to meet up.

Later on, Jennifer woke up to the sound of sizzling turkey bacon and the smell of blueberry pancake mix lingering in the air. She continued to snuggle in bed, savoring the anticipation of breakfast. She walked to her bedroom window and opened it, pressing her face against the screen, letting the sunlight soak into her skin. She saw two squirrels chasing each other up a palm tree. It gave her a quiet joy she hadn't felt since leaving home.

"It's good to be back home," she said, hearing her phone vibrate. It was Robert calling again. She felt nauseated as it continued to ring before stopping. She decided to give in and call him to figure out what exactly was going on. When he answered, a whirlwind of mixed emotions swamped her. He still had the same baritone voice.

"Hi," he said. "Thanks for calling me back."

"Sure," she answered with timidity. In some ways, she still felt small and was reminded of all the pain he had caused. It came flooding back—even after her amazing dream. How could she forget so quickly?

"Hey, I just wondered if we could chat a little bit. Don't have much going on so . . ."

"What do you want, Robert?" she asked blunt.

"Just fifteen minutes of your time. That's all." His voice wavered in plea.

She took the phone away from her ear.

What does he want? Nervousness slashed across her heart. *Feel like I need to say something to him. Maybe my dream has something to do with this. I need to go.*

"Yeah, sure." Her voice had changed. This time she spoke with confidence. "Noon at South Beach is good."

"Great. See you then."

She knew whatever they'd end up talking about would have a life-changing effect.

She rummaged through her closet, searching for an outfit to wear. She tried to listen for guidance from the Holy Spirit as to what to say to Robert but wasn't discerning anything. She frantically tossed clothes over her head, staring at herself in the mirror. She tried on one outfit after another growing more frustrated as the time drew near. She sat on the edge of the bed feeling conflicted.

Anisha walked into the bedroom and glanced at all the clothes on Jennifer's bed and around the floor. Picking up jeans and shirts, she wished Jennifer a happy birthday.

"I'm surprised you missed breakfast this morning. You always stay in your room when something is on your mind. What's up?"

Jennifer continued tossing clothes around. "Robert called. He wants to meet up." She quickly cut her eyes to her sister to note her reaction.

"And what does that creep want? He's trying to get you back again. Huh?"

"And that would be unsuccessful, again," she said emphatically, shrugging her shoulders. "But I think we need to have a conversation." She went back to sifting through her clothes.

Catherine entered the room in the middle of their conversation but quickly made a U-turn when she saw her daughters talking in private.

"Is this a date?" Anisha flung a navy T-shirt and Bermuda khaki shorts in the air.

"No. We're just meeting up to talk." Jennifer leaned against her sister's shoulder.

"Don't make it so difficult on yourself. You're not trying to impress him or anything. Keep your outfit simple. You're not going there to look good. You're meeting up with him for a bigger purpose and to speak whatever truth you need to communicate to him."

Wow, Nish is right.

"You're right about that. I think there is a bigger purpose. I'm not trying to impress him. I don't want him back. I don't want to see him, but I feel like there's something that needs to be said."

"I kinda sense that too." Anisha picked a cute shirt and some shorts and handed them to her.

She gave her sister a grateful smile before putting them on.

"That'll work," Anisha said.

"Thanks. Now what's on *your* mind?" Jennifer asked. The only time Anisha sat on Jennifer's bed was when she had something serious and personal to talk about.

Anisha went over to Jennifer's dresser and picked up the pink and white jewelry box, admiring it for a moment. "Wanted to stop by and talk to my big sis."

"Aww, how nice." Jennifer came beside Anisha.

Looking at Jennifer's reflection in the mirror, Anisha said, "I know I don't tell you this often, but I love you."

"Aww, I love you too." Jennifer leaned her head on her sister's shoulder.

"I want you to know I look up to you, and I support everything you do. You're like a role model to me."

"Thanks, Nish. You're so sweet."

"I'm no relationship expert, but I do think that you should listen to what God is saying to you. He'll give you the courage and strength you need to make whatever decision it is that you need to make. I believe, deep down inside, you already know what He's leading you to do. Don't let fear keep you from the great things that lie ahead and from the things that you're meant to have in your life."

"Wow, Anisha. Where did that come from? I'm speechless," Jennifer said, patting her sister's hand. She was touched beyond words that her sister cared so much.

"Don't think I'm not watching you." Anisha winked, smiling at the surprised expression on Jennifer's face. "Anyhow, that's all I wanted to say."

That was nothing but God. Jennifer gave her a big hug. "Thanks, Nish."

"You're welcome. Call me if Robert steps out of line. You know I have your back." She balled her hand into a fist.

"You know I will!" Jennifer laughed and picked up her journal. "I'm going to the beach a little early to have some me time before Robert arrives."

"Okay. See you later." Anisha kissed her sister on the cheek and left.

Anisha had no idea how much Jennifer had needed to hear those words. Hearing the love in Anisha's voice touched her heart. Jennifer knew what was going to happen later.

Jennifer headed into the kitchen to grab a bottle of water before leaving out. As she opened the fridge, her father walked in to get one himself. They brushed shoulders a bit, causing her stomach to tighten. He grunted and cleared his throat, reaching around her. And he mumbled something that she couldn't make out. She scrunched her face a little, wondering what that was about.

"Umm, Jennifer. Umm."

She moved away from him and gripped the bottle with one hand, the cap in her fingers.

"Yeah?" she said, numb and detached.

"I'd like to talk. Are you heading out or something?"

She crossed her arms and quipped, "I am."

"When you get back, I'd like to talk with you." Her father's voice

185

seemed to carry some perkiness. "Maybe we can hang out for a bit. Like we used to."

She slightly turned her head away and tried her best not to smile. "Okay. We can."

"I'll be waiting for you out back. Happy birthday."

"Thanks, Dad." She grinned and left the kitchen.

Jennifer got in her car feeling this trip back home was all orchestrated by God.

A SOFT BREEZE caressed her face as waves brushed against the shore. She removed the pink rubber band from her ponytail to shake her hair free and dug her heels deep into the cool, damp sand. She closed her eyes and meditated on God. She was reflecting on everything He had done in her life, from things she had accomplished, challenges she had overcome, and what had happened since returning to Miami.

"Father, I know there was a bigger purpose for my return."

Suddenly, the fine hairs on her arms stood tall, and a strong wind gathered around her. Her eyes quickly opened. She saw clouds slowly moving by.

"When the clouds move," she uttered. She remembered her dream of walking along the riverbank and seeing the rose petals in the water. She opened her Bible, paged to John 3:8, and read from her Amplified Version. "The wind blows (breathes) where it wills; and though you hear its sound, yet you neither know where it comes from nor where it is going. So it is with everyone who is born of the Spirit."

"I get it now." Jennifer jumped to her feet and threw her hands in the air in celebration.

The revelation of the dream landed peacefully on her heart in the way a dove plants its feet quietly on a tree branch. The same way she experienced the presence of God when she saw David returned. This time it was so intense that tears streamed in joy. "Jesus," she uttered from the abyss of her soul. "Holy Spirit, you were guiding me in my dream on the sands until I met Jesus. It was your presence. It was You.

You are the wind that blows," she said, dropping to her knees and lowering her head in worship. She lifted her hands in grateful praise. "You were guiding me to all the truth."

Jennifer's hands lifted and she began speaking in her heavenly language, praying fervently. She tapped into a spiritual side of her that had been latent for a while. Continuing in prayer, Matthew 6:15 appeared in her mind. She turned to the scripture and read, "But if you do not forgive others, nor will your Father forgive you."

After reading this scripture, she thought about the rose petals in her dream and how the sands she walked on were black, changing to brown and white. It all became clear.

"Oh God, please forgive me for not forgiving him," she whimpered.

The dark colored rose petals that had surrounded the three medium-sized pictures of her, her dad, and Robert, represented the pain and anger that had festered within her from the time she was a child and on into her adult years. The lighter colored rose petals symbolized the moments she was on the brink of forgiving her father.

The black sands she walked on were how long she'd carried resentment in her heart and guilt from the abortion. "It's time for me to let go," she confessed. "This is why I'm back in Miami. I'm here to reconcile my relationship with my father, but I feel like there's something else that needs to happen." She looked over her shoulder, overhearing a group of women mention Proverbs 31 when they walked by.

This is surreal. Confirmation after confirmation. God, you're so amazing.

More revelation poured into Jennifer's spirit. She was overwhelmed with all God was revealing to her but in a good way. "This is who I am in Christ." She stood tall and held up her Bible high in the air. "I am a virtuous, God-fearing woman. I lost sight of who I was in You, Jesus, by not walking in Your love and living life through the eyes of my father and Robert who never accepted me. I'm not the same woman who dated Robert."

And at that, her identity in Christ was starting to become clear.

Not long after she said those words, she heard a monstrous engine from behind. She turned her head and saw Robert getting off his black motorcycle. He sported a black leather jacket and aviators. Doing a double take, she noticed flowers in his hand. She put her Bible aside and brushed her hair away from her face.

This isn't going to go well. I can feel it.

She smiled half-heartedly and crossed her arms when he came up to her.

"How are you, birthday girl?" he said with enthusiasm and handed her flowers, hugging her. "Thanks for meeting up with me."

"Thanks for the flowers," Jennifer said, holding them close to her and breathing in their fragrance.

"Let's take a walk." Robert stood at six foot three. Compared to Jennifer, he was a giant.

"Yeah, sure. Is everything okay? Seems like you have something serious to tell me." She studied his stark expression closely.

Butterflies circled violently in her stomach. She knew the conversation wasn't going to go smoothly—no better than rough sand rubbing in between her toes. She believed Robert still loved her and that he wanted her back in his life.

"I have some things to tell you as well," she said.

"What's on your mind?" he said.

Jennifer suggested that they take a seat by the rocks to talk. By his sullen expression, she could tell he was preparing himself for a conversation he didn't want to hear. She leaned against one rock and removed her sunglasses and got right to it.

"Robert, you know how much I still care for you."

He threw his arms up in irritation. "Oh, here we go again," he puffed.

"What exactly were you expecting? You show up with flowers and we forget about why we broke up in the first place? Maybe live happily ever after?"

"I was hoping enough time had passed."

She waited for him to explain, and when he didn't, she continued,

"I've thought about you often since we broke up. I've wondered what life would've been like if we'd gotten back together."

"What does that mean?" He crossed his arms and teethed the sunglass frame.

"I don't feel the same about you as I once did." Jennifer tried to be as gentle with her words as possible. "Our relationship was toxic and unhealthy."

"What do you mean?" His nostrils flared.

"I lost myself dating you. You don't lose yourself in love. I believe the person God has for you confirms your identity in Him. Love builds you up. And I don't think love makes you feel insecure. Robert, you made me feel unvalued and like I wasn't enough. I know I wasn't the perfect woman, but no woman should feel they're never enough despite their efforts and shortcomings. This is what life was like with you."

"Huh?" he said, puzzled.

"I allowed you control over my self-esteem. I let you put me down, let you push me into an abortion, feeling guilty if I didn't have Kayla. What you call love was controlling, manipulative, and condescending." She paused for a moment. He tried to speak, but she stopped him. "I'm not done yet."

"Whoa! Okay." He lifted himself off of the rock and stood in front of her.

She had never stood up to him like this before.

"I am a Proverbs 31 woman. I know my worth, and I met someone who sees that."

"Proverbs 31?" He was confused. "What's that? Umm, never mind. Met someone new?"

"Yes. I met someone who has believed in me since day one, someone who understands me and never judged me. Someone who's a God-fearing man and someone I pushed away."

"Who? The guy from the hospital?" He sighed, irritated.

She didn't answer.

Robert put his aviators back on and tugged down at the bottom of his jacket. Jennifer was all too familiar with the angry look on his face.

"I'm freeing us from one another, so we can be open to experiencing love with someone else. I'm sorry, Robert, but I don't see myself being with you. I don't see a present or a future with you."

"But you can see yourself being with this guy, right?" He got up.

Jennifer didn't respond again. She hoped her silence was enough to answer Robert's question. Jennifer knew if she told him she wanted to spend the rest of her life with David the stake would drive further into his heart.

Nonetheless, he made a brave attempt to plead his case. "Jennifer, how could you say this to me? I came back for you. I'm a changed man!" His face looked completely lifeless. All hope had left his spirit.

"And I'm a changed woman for another man. I'm sorry, Robert. I know we should move on."

"Stop it! Just stop it!" He waved her off. "This is some crap!"

"Robert, we came here to be set free from one another. Don't you see that?" When he didn't respond, she said gently, "Robert, come here."

"Why?" he asked, coming over.

"You're a good man." She hugged and patted him on the back. "I believe you'll find a woman meant for you and you only," she said releasing him.

He removed his aviators and finally faced her with tears welling up in his eyes. She had never seen him cry before. She saw his desperation.

"Jennifer, what's wrong with me? Tell me what's wrong. I can fix it," he pleaded. Tears flooded through his ego and edgy persona.

"You can't fix something that's not in the will of God. Potential remains potential when something is outside the will of God. It will never become a promise. We will not work. I know this in my heart. Take care of yourself." She started walking to her car.

"Jen," he called after her.

"Yeah?"

He shoved his hands into his pockets and looked down.

"Yes?" she said opening her car door.

He shook his head and waved her off.

When the will of God speaks there's nothing you can do to argue against it.

Jennifer fastened her seatbelt and shifted into drive. From her rearview mirror, she saw Robert standing with his head lowered, arms hanging loosely at his sides. She pressed her foot against the brake pedal, stopping the car before exiting the lot and broke down. She needed this cry. It was the cutting of the soul-tie. She released every part of him from her soul. Sometimes the conversation you needed to have with your ex wasn't about getting back with them, reflecting on good or bad times, what could've happened or should've happened, but communicating that it was okay that things hadn't worked out, and it was okay to let go and move on. Closure and peace come that way. It seals the past and cuts the soul-tie. She felt a huge part of her heart had just broken off and drifted out to sea. But she knew this was the best decision she could make—for herself and Robert.

Jennifer wept most of the way home and pulled into the driveway. She saw her mother sweeping the front porch. Jennifer couldn't help but smile. Before she could even reach the steps, her mother asked, "So how did it go?"

She gave her mother a long hug. "It's over. It's really over now and it's time to move on."

"I'm so proud of you, sweetheart. I knew you had the courage to say whatever you needed to say to him."

"You know, when I woke up this morning, I had no idea what I was going to say to Robert. But when Anisha encouraged me to listen to what God was communicating to me, I knew what I had to do. I just needed confirmation."

"I'm glad you had the strength to finally put the past behind you."

"I am too. Where's Dad?"

"In the back yard." Catherine pointed with the broom.

"Okay." She kissed her mother quickly on the cheek and walked to the back.

She made her way around the house and heard the sound of an electric trimmer.

Jennifer yelled, "Hey, Dad!"

"Hey, Jen," he said, shutting off the trimmer. "Give me a sec." He went inside the house and returned with a tray containing a chocolate mousse cake with lit candles on it and a pitcher of mango-peach iced tea with glasses. "Gotcha some tea and your favorite cake. Happy birthday!" He put the tray on the table, cleaned his hands against his jeans, and poured two glasses.

"Thanks, Dad." Jennifer smiled like the nine-year-old girl who'd wanted her father's approval.

Her father placed the plate with the cake on it in front of her and sat down across from her. She nodded at him and smiled, wary of what was up. He smiled back and took a sip of tea. "For years, I've been ashamed to look at myself in the mirror, knowing how I treated my beautiful daughter. I know I've said some really brutal and discouraging things to you." He looked down. "I apologize for making you feel guilty about the abortion."

Jennifer couldn't help but cry. She dropped to her knees and released every emotion that had been buried within her since she was a teenager. Her father knelt at her side and hugged her. If she'd ever needed her father's love and touch, it was now. They say the first introduction a woman has of a man is her father. And the way he loves her becomes a defining moment of how she perceives and expects other men to treat her. There's some truth to that statement. Jennifer was drawn to men who were controlling and borderline verbally abusive like her father. But that was all over now. Seeing the change in his heart and hearing his apology gave her peace to trust again. She remembered when Jesus had told her He was going to deal with this heart.

She looked him in the eye and saw her father cry for the first time ever. Not in a million years would she have thought of hearing an apology.

"Dad..." Jennifer tried to respond, but he continued as if he had no control over the words that spilled out.

"You didn't deserve that. Please find it in your heart to forgive me. I'm sorry." He squeezed her hand and looked earnestly into her eyes. "From now on, I'm going to be there for you, no matter what. I promise I will. I love you."

"Thank you, Dad," she said, choked with emotion. "I love you, too." She gave him one more squeeze and returned to the chair opposite him. "And I forgive you, too. Our relationship all these years made me so sad. I missed you, Dad. I missed not being able to talk to you about the struggles and the joys. My life didn't feel right without you in it. It means everything to me that you're going to be a part of it now."

"And I will, Jennifer. I will. And I'm going to support your non-profit."

"Can we pray?" Jennifer eyes gleamed as if she were tiptoeing on ice with this request.

"Pray?" He arched his eyes.

"Yes. Pray."

"Uh, sure," her father said willingly, extending his hands to Jennifer's.

"God, Your love is so powerful that I can't find the words to describe it. But I know You made this day possible. Thank You so much for healing my and my dad's relationship. I pray You restore all the years we missed with each other."

As Jennifer continued to pray, a gentle wind came in between them. She didn't bother to open her eyes. She knew Holy Spirit was present. Her father's hand started to shake and he started weeping.

"I know He's real," her father confessed. "Jesus is real!" he shouted. "I accept you, Jesus Christ as my Lord and Savior. I thank you, God."

At the sound of these words, her heart overflowed with joy. She didn't have to ask if he wanted to accept Christ as his Lord and Savior. God had already worked on his heart.

Jennifer gave thanks when her mother and Anisha came outside. Catherine gasped and covered her mouth when she heard her husband saying the name of Jesus. Anisha was shocked too. Her eyes opened wide. They all came around and hugged him.

"I didn't see that coming," he said.

That day, they were all filled with joy. They were a happy family, together again.

Jennifer's father went inside and grabbed his saxophone. When he returned, Anisha and Catherine sang happy birthday while her father played along. Afterward, he played her favorite song, *My One and Only Love.* She thought about David and the time they'd spent together that night.

Jennifer realized that returning home was exactly what had needed to happen. Her relationship with her father was restored. And not only that, he had given his life to Christ. To top things off, she was now a free woman, available to fully embrace her dreams and accept God's gift to her of the man whom she had come to love. David Bradshaw.

Later that afternoon, she gave David a call, but he didn't answer. She decided to leave him a message in the hope that he would forgive her, and they could try again.

CHAPTER 9

 $\mathcal{I}$ n the kitchen, David shoved his phone across the counter when he saw Jennifer's call and scrubbed away at a white plate that was already spotless. He saw that she left a voicemail and deleted it.

"That excuse sounds like crap to me. *I need to focus on my career,*" he kept repeating. "Why can't she just woman-up and be honest? I'm not buying the whole *I need to focus on my career* crap."

He scrubbed the plate harder and harder until it squeaked. Then he flung it against the wall, shattering it into pieces.

"God, I don't get it!" He slowly picked up the pieces of the plate, hoping he'd succeeded in breaking his fantasy of Jennifer. Still, he replayed their time together over and over in his head, failing to understand what had so drastically changed on her end. He tried to pinpoint where he might have messed up but couldn't put his finger on it. In his eyes, he had done everything right.

"I wasn't a distraction." He'd presented himself as a gentleman and a good prospect. He'd respected her boundaries and honored her request for accepting no more than a friendship.

Letting out a weary sigh, he dumped the broken pieces of the plate into the trash can, feeling an inner prompting to get alone with God. *I feel Your presence, God.* He stopped, holding the dustpan in his hand. *I don't know what You're saying,* he thought, throwing it in a corner and heading to Kelsey's house before he was tempted to destroy anything else.

David drove down Ballston Avenue and came to a red light. A woman waited at the corner with a young boy. She lifted him, kissed him on the cheek, and carried him across the street. David's mother's face flashed before him. *My mother.* He pounded his fist against the horn. He startled the mother and caused the young boy to cry. Feeling guilty, he waved them on and mouthed the word *sorry.* The more he thought about his childhood experiences with his mother, the angrier he grew. Jennifer severing their friendship didn't help. Infuriated, he slammed his hand against the steering wheel and peeled off.

He finally arrived at his old friend's house and slugged through Kelsey's front door, holding his hand in pain. The familiar melancholic energy accompanied him.

"I don't get it," David said, locking eyes momentarily with Kelsey. "I just don't get it. It's always the good ones."

Kelsey must've seen something in his expression as he looked at David. Maybe David looked just as he had when Maria had cheated on him. Kelsey went over to the freezer and filled a zip-lock bag with ice and handed it to him.

"Sit down, young man." He pointed to the sofa and sat in his rocking chair. "Let's start with what happened."

"Thanks." He sank to the sofa and said, "Why can't I win?"

"What happened, David?"

"So many roadblocks, man. Her ex, Leyanie passing away, and my stuff."

"Leyanie passed away? Oh no," Kelsey said, cutting him off.

"She did." His voice weakened. "Why did that kid have to die? It was the worst possible thing to happen to Jennifer."

"That's tough, Dave. Tough. I'm sure it's taking a toll on Jennifer, and the ex popping back up in the picture further complicated things. That's a lot of confusion, overwhelming, and emotional fallout." He leaned back. "I think you should focus on your relationship with Christ. She's dealing with a lot."

David dropped his head and rubbed his eyes.

"Reconciling with your mother is also important."

David shot up from the chair and paced around the living room with clenched fists.

"There's nothing wrong with me."

"David, you're trying to force love to happen while you're wounded." Kelsey's eyes followed him back and forth.

"I'm not wounded," David said belligerently. "I'm fine. Look at me. I have everything that I need. I can get anything that I want."

"You may be a successful writer and established financially, but you can't purchase love solely on romance, a good time, and conversation. David, you need time to heal from the past. Once that happens, you'll truly know what's missing from your life and what you need—not what you want. You'll have a sense of clarity and emotional independence to live life without the need for someone else to make you feel loved. Eve didn't complete Adam. She was an addition to him. God joined Eve to Adam to be a helpmate, to fellowship with, to be a companion and a friend—someone with whom he could worship God with. Besides, you sure didn't read about him complaining that he was lonely. Why? Because his walk and fellowship with God fulfilled and sustained him. And yeah, you could argue Adam probably had no concept of a romantic desire, but I would counter-argue that the first longing for love that God instilled in man was the need and dependence for Him, and the first kind of marriage He instituted was the one between man and Himself. All other relationships that follow rest on the one you have with God."

All sorts of cosmic Big Bang Theories of love exploded and fell apart in David's head.

"You gotta understand this," Kelsey continued. "Your desire to experience love will come from a healthy place rather than brokenness. Satan has access to your brokenness, and he will use it to create an unhealthy need for love. He wants you to seek marriage with Jennifer, or whomever, while you're broken and without putting God first, because he knows it will fail and push you further away from God."

"Broken?" David mocked him. "I think I need a vacation."

"Is that the only thing you heard?" Kelsey gritted his teeth and shook his head in frustration. "Son, I'm not trying to get on you, but a vacation is not whatcha need. You need to start spending time with God again and find your mother!"

David waved him off. He was sick of hearing Kelsey constantly saying that. Kelsey knew it, but he persevered.

"Your past will continue to ruin your present if you never face it. I'm telling you this because I love you like my son."

"Find God?" David yelled. "I have God."

"You have an intellectual understanding of who He is, but you haven't experienced Him in a revelatory way. God wants to be first in your life before anyone. He also wants a personal encounter with you. I'm talking about intimacy. Sadly, something the Western Christian churches don't know much about."

David tried to calm down, knowing Kelsey was only trying to help him. "Yeah, I hear you."

"Do you?" Kelsey shuffled his feet before crossing one leg over the other. "Do you?"

"Hey, listen. I've gotta get out of here."

"Wait a minute." Kelsey got up and grabbed his arm, but he jerked away. "You're acting just like your father. Your stubbornness is going to be your downfall if you don't change."

David stopped dead in his tracks. Change was something his father had a hard time doing.

He could still hear the swooshing sound of the oxygen machine that pumped air into his father's lungs. He remembered the look of regret on his father's face as tears streamed down against the thin frame of his cheeks. No one could get his father to quit smoking. His friends from church had tried to no avail. He was a stubborn man, and David took on that part of him. David's father eventually died of lung cancer a few months after they started building a relationship, which was just around the time he had graduated from college.

Kelsey's right, but I don't care. "Yeah, yeah." David wagged his hand at Kelsey, heading to the door.

"David," Kelsey called after him.

"Kelsey, you're not my father." David slammed the door behind him.

He sped off down the highway, knowing what he had just said to Kelsey was wrong, and that he was right. David glanced into the rearview mirror, resenting that he was becoming more and more like his dad.

He returned home that evening and moped at the edge of the bed. He rubbed his head, feeling bad about how he'd left Kelsey's house and guilty about not putting in the effort to find his mother.

"I just can't do this," he said, overwhelmed. "I just can't."

He turned to a music station and closed his eyes. He heard a tune that sounded familiar. That fond memory of Jennifer singing angelically into his ear as they slow-danced on the boardwalk at the National Harbor came to mind. The lyrics penetrated his heart to the point that he reached his hand out to touch her face. He clenched nothing but air. He wanted to see his reflection in her eyes. He wanted to hold that which made his heart beat off rhythm. Where gravity was no more because she was a part of his world, but she wasn't there. He opened his eyes and realized seeing her face was only a mirage. He wanted to give her a call, but his ego wouldn't allow him. To prevent himself from thinking about Jennifer further, he opened his laptop to log on to Facebook.

Skimming through status updates and friend requests, he saw a message from someone named Samantha. It read that she would be on later to chat if he wanted to. He looked for pictures of her and discovered a photo album titled *Bad Girl*. The erotic pictures of her posing seductively in thin T-shirts and boy shorts aroused him.

I can't be on here.

He logged off and took a cold shower. He couldn't take being teased any longer. However, temptation had already lured him down its murky path. He went back to her page after showering and found her available online.

He typed her name, and she responded immediately. David asked how she'd found him and who she was.

Her reply: *"I'm rereading* Intimacy. *And all I can say is wow; you have a way with words. I'm sure you hear that a lot."*

"Thank you, but are you the Samantha that showed up at the hospital that day?"

"Maybe. LOL."

He scratched his head, considering what he was getting himself into. Nonetheless, he couldn't resist inquiring about the *Bad Girl* photo album.

"Your husband doesn't have a problem with that?" He leaned back in the chair and crossed his hands behind his head. He was hoping she would say she didn't have a husband.

"How do you know whether I'm married or not lol?" Samantha typed.

The edges of David's lips lowered. He hoped she wasn't. *"I don't, but I just threw that out there to see if you were. Are you?"*

Samantha answered that she was. David smacked his head in disappointment. *"So you're off-limits?"*

"Hmmm, not necessarily."

David rocked toward the computer screen in shock. The idea of linking up with a married woman excited him. After Jennifer's hot and cold routine with him, he wondered if maybe he just needed to look for something that wouldn't require him to invest too much of his heart. He'd been with women who were in a relationship, but not a married woman. He asked if they had an open relationship. She answered no, but she was open to relationships, and her husband was never around. Samantha then asked about his relationship status. David started typing, and Jennifer came to mind. He wasn't in a relationship with her; however, the feelings he'd developed for her sure did make him feel like he was.

Nonetheless, Jennifer telling him she wanted to move on were the last words he'd heard from her. He was nothing but a distraction to her. Right after he replied that he was single, Samantha planted a thought in his head about possibly linking up. David considered for a moment.

I can't do this. I can't do this. He closed his laptop instead of replying yet pondered the idea of seeing Samantha.

The next morning, David was awakened by his cellphone vibrating on the nightstand. Jennifer was calling. He put the phone down and rolled back over to sleep. That afternoon, she texted him while he was working on his mystery novel. She asked him if he had time to talk. He didn't respond. He powered off his phone and threw it on the sofa. About forty-five minutes later, he went downstairs to the lobby to retrieve his mail. As he shuffled through it, he found a postcard from Maria, posing in a white bikini by a waterfall in Venezuela.

I miss you was written inside a heart drawn with red ink.

"Never again," he said under his breath and balled up the postcard.

The front desk attendant came over and noticed the picture in the trash. "I haven't seen Mamacita Maria in a while."

Shortly after, a car pulled up outside. "You've got to be kidding me." He saw Jennifer's white Mercedes. He went outside before she could come in. "What are you doing here?" He was both surprised yet disinterested to see her.

"Hey, I've been trying to get in touch with you." She stepped out of the car and moved in to embrace him. But she paused, seeing the post-card in his hand.

David kept his arms folded, so she took a step back.

"David, I'm so sorry for ending our friendship and the directions things seemed to be heading in. I just had a lot of personal things going on in my life that I hadn't told you about." She paused. David was trying to keep his expression neutral. "Um, I came here to apologize to you," she continued. "I didn't mean what I said. I just had a lot going on in my life, but that's all over now."

"Thanks for coming down, but it wasn't necessary." David started making his way back inside.

"And what does that mean?" She pushed strands of hair behind her ear with one hand.

He turned around. "I heard you loud and clear when you said I was a distraction and that we should continue in our separate lives. I think we should do that. I moved on."

Jennifer was speechless.

"I really can't take all of this back-and-forth stuff. One minute you're telling me you don't want to build a friendship, then you're building a friendship with me but giving me all the signals that you want more, and then you cut me off like I don't matter. Like my feelings don't matter. I don't need any added stress in my life. I've got personal issues and a life of my own."

Jennifer nodded, giving him a guilty look filled with shame. "I know. I . . . You're right. I haven't been fair to you throughout this process. You have every right to be hurt and confused and angry with me, and I'm asking you to forgive me. I needed to get myself right first. I needed to go away and clear my head, learn what I want and what I need. I promise if you give me another chance, you won't regret it."

David shook his head, completely unmoved by her heartfelt apology or her request for forgiveness. "It's just too late, Jennifer. I can't do this anymore."

His heart stung at the moisture that welled within her eyes, but he stilled his emotions and firmed his resolve, keeping his face a disinterested mask.

"Oh, okay." Jennifer moved away and grabbed the handle on the car door. "I don't want to take up any more of your time. It was good to see you." She gave him a pallid smile and opened the door. "And I see you've moved on." She nodded at the postcard in his hand.

David looked down but didn't bother to explain. "You take care."

She lowered her gaze. "Thanks. You too."

David headed back into the lobby. He heard Jennifer's car door slam shut. He sighed but kept a poker face, telling himself he didn't feel anything for her anymore.

During happy hour, David strolled into Madison's as if he'd just stepped off the front cover of a *GQ* magazine. His hair and beard were neatly trimmed. The classic tailored charcoal gray suit fit him perfectly. He pictured himself looking dashing as Daniel Craig, who wore sharp, tailored suits in the most recent James Bond movies. He'd chosen what he believed to be his finest cologne, one that would help him accomplish his goal tonight.

David and Kelsey made eye contact. They grinned at each other, but Kelsey's eyes held a slight hint of disappointment. Kelsey knew he was on the prowl.

David approached the bar, drummed his fingers on the counter, and nodded at Kelsey. Before Kelsey could say anything, David apologized for the way he had stormed out his house the last time they'd talked. Kelsey kept silent. He continued to wipe shot glasses down with a white towel hanging loosely from his shoulder.

Kelsey shook his head. "Some things never change. Want the usual?"

The statement zapped David's energy. "Yeah. Sure."

While Kelsey got his drink, David faced the entranceway. He rested his elbows on the bar, scanning the lounge for new faces. A gentleman walked in with a tall blond woman latched on to his arm.

Wow. She's hot! David watched the woman lean over to him and say something in his ear. She let go of his arm and came to the bar while her date found a table. He was mesmerized by the sway of her hips.

Lord help me. Wait, that's the woman from the hospital . . . that's gotta be the same Samantha from Facebook.

"Here you go, Dave." Kelsey placed David's drink on the bar. "Dave," he called out again. "Dave!" David was miles away from everyone and everything except the woman he couldn't stop staring at. "Dave!"

David spun around. "Sorry about that. Thanks." David understood his agenda wasn't confidential.

"He's at it again," Kelsey mumbled.

David caught a whiff of the woman's fresh, sweet, subtle fragrance when she came up to the bar. He nearly melted. She eyed him like a lion before ordering two martinis. "Enjoying your evening?"

"I am. You're Samantha." David leered at her.

"I am." She sat next to him and slowly crossed her legs.

"I'm David." He shook her hand, noticing the huge, clustered diamond ring on her wedding finger.

"Nice to officially meet you." She smiled seductively.

"Wait a minute." His jaw nearly dropped. "Are we friends on Facebook?"

"We sure are. Thanks for accepting my request." She winked.

"No problem." David released her hand. "That must be your husband over there?" David shifted his eyes in the man's direction.

"Yes," she said with diffidence. "I'll see you around later." She grabbed the drinks and walked over to join her husband at the table.

His eyes were glued to her lush hips. When he looked up, he saw her husband glaring at him. David didn't look away or flinch. He returned the same expression before turning his back to him.

"Be careful, Dave," Kelsey warned him. "She's no good."

"I'm cool." David yanked down on the hem of his jacket and fixed his handkerchief.

The evening progressed with the music going from upbeat to a slower pace. People rushed to the dance floor with their partners and draped themselves around one another. David debated whether he was going to join the fun until he felt a light tap on his shoulder. He ended up with a pretty woman he'd seen frequenting the bar on multiple occasions.

David held her lightly in his arms. The woman stared at him, wanting to make eye contact, but he was too busy exchanging seductive stares and come-hither smiles with Samantha. She was several feet away, dancing with her husband. David knew he had Samantha in the palm of his hand, and that she had him in hers. They continued to flirt with each other until her husband turned Samantha's back to David. David redirected his attention to his dance partner. The woman David was dancing with finally got the idea that he was distracted and abruptly left him stranded on the dance floor. David wasn't upset. Her departure was timely. Samantha's husband had just left her on the dance floor to take a call outside.

"May I?" David extended his hand, knowing full well what her response would be.

"Yes, you may." Samantha leaned closer into David's arms. "I've been waiting for this opportunity all night. The way that poor woman stalked off, I tried my hardest not to laugh. You're such a heartbreaker." She laughed into David's ear.

"Not at all," he whispered into hers.

Samantha pressed her body against him. David lavished in the warmth of her soft skin. He wasn't getting any mixed signals with this one. Kind of a relief after everything he'd been through with Jennifer. David's temperature rose as he surrendered to the heated intensity in her eyes. He dipped to one side to catch a glimpse of her feet and caught a peek of her cleavage along the way.

"Your husband is going to come back and catch us dancing. He probably won't react well."

"He wouldn't care," she said, yanking on his black skinny tie. "David, can I tell you something?"

She roped her arms around his neck and massaged his earlobe with her fingers. He closed his eyes, enjoying the molten heat he felt with her touch. Her lips pressed against his neck as she whispered, "The first time I saw you, I wanted you, wanted this so much."

David felt himself losing control.

"Well, when exactly would you like to make this happen?"

She leaned back to consider him with a sultry smile. "How does this weekend sound? I'm always home alone on the weekends."

"Oh?" David got excited.

"I'll take it from here." Her husband grabbed David by the shoulder and shoved him away from Samantha. "Get lost, Mr. Romance Novelist." He smirked and took Samantha's hand.

"Oh, honey, I was just about to come out and check on you." She threw her arms around him. "Honey, he was just keeping me company while you were taking that phone call. Is everything okay?"

"Thank you, Mr. Bradshaw, for taking such good care of my wife." He kept his focus on David.

"No problem. The pleasure was all mine," David replied, gritting his teeth. "How do you know my name?"

"Writers know about other writers," he said with a sinister grin.

"Hmm," David said. "Well, you two enjoy the rest of your evening." He headed to the bar, feeling a little embarrassed by his behavior. He never allowed himself to be seduced that way, especially in public and going after a married woman. He tried to push down the uneasiness he felt.

Kelsey shook his head again in disapproval as David returned to the bar. All he could do was shrug his shoulders.

"You're treading unstable territory, David. Messing with married women is not a road you want to travel," Kelsey warned.

"It was just a dance," David said, giving him an annoyed look before sipping his drink.

"Looked like more than just a dance to me. Y'all were nearly having sex. Nothing but your clothes were stopping you."

David downed his drink and thought for a moment. He knew Kelsey was right. He was playing with fire, with a woman who seemed to enjoy taking risks. He took one final look. Samantha was seemingly enthralled with her husband. "I'm outta here. Catch you around, Kelsey."

Kelsey called David on his way home, but he wasn't in the mood for more lecturing. He powered his phone off, needing some quiet to put things back into proper perspective.

"What was I thinking back there? She's married." But the memory of Samantha's touch and curvy frame begged his conscience to step aside and let his emotions run the show.

He logged on to Facebook when he got home and there was already a message from her. She thanked him for the dance, left her number, and invited him out for a cup of coffee on the weekend at one of her favorite cafés in Falls Church called Bellevue Café. Before responding, he browsed through more of her photos, growing more motivated to link up with her.

He powered his phone on and texted, *"Coffee sounds good. And I'll send you a text to let you know."*

Right after he sent that text, a voicemail notification popped up. He listened to the stern tone of Kelsey warning him again about getting involved with a married woman. "We know what happened to Samson, David. You must succeed where he failed."

For a moment, David thought about how Delilah seduced Samson and became his demise. He started to reconsider meeting up with Samantha, but after one more perusal of her photos, he couldn't resist the temptation of seeing her in person again. He saved her number without a second thought.

That Saturday morning, David arrived at the Bellevue Café. He saw Samantha sitting in the back near the restrooms. He lowered his blue baseball cap, carefully glancing around for any familiar faces. With each step he took, he could feel his heart thump harder and harder against his chest. The risk of meeting up with a married woman, and in public, finally hit him.

This is crazy. He stopped walking.

"Over here, David." Samantha waved.

He waved faintly and walked sluggishly over to her. He moved stiffly into the chair and nervously rubbed his hands together. Samantha had pulled her hair back into a ponytail, just the way Jennifer did.

Jennifer. Her face quickly flashed in his head. His lip coiled up in a leer.

"David, are you there?" She waved her hand in his face. "Seems like you're looking through me." She propped her chest up in her black tank top to make it difficult for him to keep his eyes off her.

He shook his head and pinched his nose, coming back into the present, and apologized for the scatterbrained moment.

"Good to see you again, handsome." Samantha gave him a enticing little smile and winked.

His eyes maneuvered below her chin.

Help me, God. "Great to see you again as well," he said with a shaky voice.

She noted that he seemed a bit uncomfortable and uptight from the last time they exchanged pleasantries. He fibbed that he was a little sore from a workout, which set him up for her to say she gave marvelous deep-tissue massages.

"That'll fix you up." She reached for his hand across the table and began massaging it.

"I'm sure it would. I got a taste of that on the dance floor." He half grinned and forced out laughter through his teeth.

A waitress came over and took their orders.

"I still find it hard to believe that a great guy like you is still single." She moved her hand on top of his.

He closed his eyes, feeling moved by her touch. Then he sighed, contemplating telling her about Jennifer. He figured, why not get a woman's perspective?

"I did meet someone several months ago, but that situation ended quickly."

"Aww, what happened?" She placed her hand on top of his.

Lowering his face, he answered that some personal things happened with her, that a dear friend of hers passed away, and that she had some other things to focus on. "Honestly, I think it was another man," he continued, moving his thumb on top of hers.

"That could've been the case. Women use that excuse all the time." She mirrored the movements of his fingers against the back of his hand. "How long did you two date?"

"Not long—maybe a month or so. We weren't even really dating. We were just friends who had some romantic feelings for each other. The attraction and interest were there."

"That was quick. Is it Jennifer?" She gave him a sinister stare.

She knows. "Jennifer who?"

"Come on, David. You two were at the hospital together, and I know the chick is a huge fan of yours." She rolled her eyes disgustedly.

"How did you end up going to the hospital?" One of his eyebrows arched up.

"I kinda do a little volunteering, too, but enough about her. Sounds like she passed up an opportunity to be with you. Her loss."

The waitress delivered their hot teas. Before David could say anything else, Samantha laid out ground rules for their situation. She let David know her husband wasn't home often and that he didn't talk to her much when he did manage to make it home.

"It's like his mind is somewhere else. I try to do little things, like wear lingerie, dress sexier when we go out to dinner, bring him lunch, make him breakfast, things like that. He just doesn't appreciate anything I do." Samantha's face turned red and she covered it with her hands.

"Hey, look at me." David gently took her hands and moved them away from her face. "There's nothing wrong with you."

"Sometimes I want to throw in the towel . . . even after fifteen years." She started to give in to a cry.

"That's a lot of time invested." David tried to sympathize.

"I know." Samantha's eyes met David's. "Sometimes a woman just wants to be touched. She wants to matter. She wants to feel alive. She wants to be desired and wanted."

"I agree. Women deserve all those great things. A woman's mind and body, spirit and soul must be nurtured with love, affection, and attention. Negligence pushes her into a dark place when she was created to exist in light."

"Wow, David. You are a painter of words. I'm so lucky I get to experience the writer in person." She grabbed his hand again.

"Well, I write and speak from the heart." He kissed her hand.

Samantha got up and moved around the booth, seating herself next to him. "You have a good understanding of women."

"I just pay close attention to what they say. That's all. And I ask God for understanding and wisdom. That's my way of preparing for marriage."

"I'm sure." She squeezed his hand. "Michael is out of town next weekend. I was wondering if you could come over to hang out—maybe catch a movie or something."

Michael? David contemplated. He wondered if this was the same Michael who authored *1994. This can't be.* "Make it a movie night, huh?" David chuckled, reading between the lines.

"Come Saturday. Let's make it eleven p.m. Here's the key." She slid a small white envelope across the table to him. "I have a yoga class that evening and dinner with some girlfriends afterward, but I should be home by then. I don't live far. I'm in DC."

David stuffed the envelope into the inside pocket of his sweat jacket. "I'll be there at eleven p.m. sharp."

HEAVY RAIN BEADED against the brown windowpane. Flashes of white lightning ripped through the dark skies, and thunder crashed in the distance. David shuddered, pressing his nose against the cold window. Through his reflection, he watched the water rise on the black pavement.

"Maybe this isn't a good night to go anywhere," he said, feeling a bit of trepidation. The answering machine beeped. He peered over his shoulder at the gray digital clock. The bright red numbers read 10:00 p.m.

"David, I know you're grown enough to make your own decisions, but I'm telling you this because I love you. Stay away from that woman. She's no good." There was a great sense of urgency in Kelsey's deep, guttural voice that caused David to hearken to it for a moment. He pondered again if it was worth driving to Samantha's house in Georgetown in the stormy weather.

"I'll be all right," he muttered to himself. He got dressed and snatched a coat.

66 East Highway was pitch black. Tires slashing through the rain and the rhythmic swooshing of his windshield wipers eased David into a meditative state. At this point, he was able to speak from his heart.

"I don't know about this." He saw his breath in the cold air of his car. At once, red and blue lights flashed from behind. His back stiffened and his foot slowly eased off the gas pedal. Two state trooper cars shot by, going after another car. He sighed, relieved. His intuition spoke to him, screaming at him to turn around. Only minutes away from his destination, he told himself, *I'm already here. It's too late to turn back now.*

A lavish brick house was on a hill surrounded by tall trees and wooded areas. David's halogen lights erased the darkness and beamed on the eyes of a deer that reflected a yellowish purple hue as he drove up the long, curvy driveway. He parked behind a smoke-gray BMW. The license plate read MD456.

"Must be his car," David murmured, cautiously stepping out of his vehicle.

At the front door, David's hands were shaking. He tried to push the key into the lock before the flickering porch lights went completely out. He fumbled the key, dropping it at the foot of a thinking Socrates statue. He looked like a bumbler in a theatrical comedy searching for the key using the light on his cell phone. Locating it, he spotted Samantha through the tall glass door and flinched. But when he saw the tight lavender boy shorts and thin white T-shirt she had on, he quickly stuck the key into the lock and went inside. Lust consumed his fear and marched him upstairs. It was too late to turn back. He opened the door and Samantha ran to the top of the stairs. She gave him a saucy look before disappearing.

The stairs creaked as he walked up them slowly. Against the white wall, he could see the reflection of flickering fire and her shadow. He peeked into the bedroom lit with candles lined around the king-size bed. Samantha lay in the center. He removed his shirt and slowly crawled onto the bed like a lion stalking its prey.

"You're such a beautiful work of art," she said as she examined David's chiseled body.

She kissed him with urgency and maneuvered on top of him. A large mirror big enough to capture the king size bed was suspended above them on the white ceiling.

Whoa!

He'd never seen anything like this before. For a second, he wondered what could have happened to Samantha and Michael's love life. The mirror suggested they were experimental in their marriage. But soon after, talks with Kelsey warning him about Samantha flashed in his mind.

I shouldn't be here.

Right after, Jennifer's face popped up like a notification on his cellphone. David's temperature went from hot to cold.

"What's wrong?" Samantha asked, seeing him disengage.

"Shish. I hear something. Footsteps."

Samantha pulled the sheet around her chest. David quickly put his shirt back on. They listened intently to the footsteps, which stopped above them. David's heart pounded. Samantha clung to him like a starfish on a rock. Seconds later, a bullet pierced through the mirror, striking the champagne-colored satin pillow next to them. White feathers exploded into the air.

"Watch out!" David yelled, grabbing Samantha and rolling her to the floor before the sharp pieces of glass could cut them.

David hurried off the bed while Samantha frantically searched for her clothes.

"That's gotta be Michael," she whispered.

"What's he doing here, and why does he have a gun?" David balled both of his hands into fists.

A grinding noise came from the far side. A draft of wind whisked into the bedroom. The candle flames flickered out just as a tall silhouette appeared against the wall. Samantha grabbed David's arm and hid behind him like a shield. David stepped forward with Samantha latched to him.

"Who's there?" He ducked, looking left to right, trying to see in the dark shadows. He stood up straight only to find the barrel of a black 9mm handgun with a silencer pointed right at him. Ghostly eyes devoid of life emerged from the darkness.

"I told you I'd see you again," Michael said through gritted teeth.

"Honey, please put down the gun," Samantha pleaded with a shaking voice.

Michael's eyes narrowed, and a dark vein bulged to the surface of his forehead.

"Put the gun down! No one needs to get hurt! This was clearly a mistake on my part." David raised his open palms in surrender, trying to plead with Michael. "Hear me out—"

Michael fired a shot that went past David's head.

"Stop, Michael!" Samantha lunged at her husband and grabbed his arm.

"Get off me!" He shoved her against the bed.

David sprinted out of the room and downstairs, falling to the bottom. From the top step, Michael fired another shot that shattered the front door. Glass fell in a cascade, showering him with shards that created shallow slices along his exposed skin. David leaped through the frame and rushed to his car. He jumped inside and shifted in reverse. Two bullets hit the hood. Another struck the passenger side window. Bits of flying glass swatted the side of his face.

"Michael, stop!" he heard Samantha scream.

Driving in reverse, David rammed into the curb, smashing the back of his bumper. In the rearview mirror, he saw Michael aiming at him. He ducked below the dashboard and swung the car around. Michael fired two more shots. Both hit the front windshield. David raced down the driveway, nearly hitting the curb again, and sped out into the street. He glanced behind again and saw nothing but darkness. He strapped on his seatbelt and tried to relax his tense shoulders. As soon as he thought he'd gotten away, round halogen lights appeared like nefarious eyes through the night. David stomped on the gas pedal, but Michael's car was gaining on him. David pressed harder on the gas pedal, climbing to 110 mph. He frantically searched for the 66 West exit, but he couldn't find it. He turned left into a residential neighborhood instead and skidded across the narrow street. Another shot hit David's taillight.

God, help me!

He swerved and smashed into garbage cans and blue recycling bins until he slammed into a light pole. Porch lights turned on and dogs barked obnoxiously. Dizzy and slumped over the half-inflated airbag, thick red blood ran down the bridge of his busted nose. He blinked chips of glass off his eyelids, catching a glimpse of Michael slowly cruising by, pointing the barrel of the gun at him. David inhaled a ragged breath and closed his eyes.

CHAPTER 10

*S*tellar Loft museum in DC was unusually crowded on a Thursday afternoon. Locals and tourists walked the marbled floors and flooded the stairs. Jennifer chaperoned a group of girls from the non-profit she worked at into the museum after attending a Christian musical.

Did someone say David? She heard someone mention his name as they passed by in a huddle of people.

Samantha.

She saw Samantha standing in front of a group of women with her arm in a sling. She talked animatedly while the group of women was glued to what she said. Jennifer slowed her pace and moved to the other side of a large Egyptian-like statute. She told the girls to read up on the history of an artifact while she listened.

"We almost died," Samantha said, laughing evilly. "What a night."

Jennifer's stomach plummeted with dread.

I feel something happened between her and David.

Samantha and the women begin to inch near Jennifer. Jennifer frantically looked around for an escape so Samantha wouldn't know she was there. She quickly stuffed her hand into her purse, pulled out a large magazine, and stuck her face in between the pages.

"Michael nearly killed him," Samantha said.

Jennifer held her face tight in between the pages. She kept her eyes down until Samantha's voice faded away and peered up after a few minutes.

Good. They're leaving. She saw them move toward a different room. Jennifer got up and signaled to the girls that it was time to leave. She tried to lead them discretely through the crowded museum, bumping into groups of tourists.

So many people here. Come on, move.

"Excuse me, please," she said, parting a path through the sea of people. It was a full-blown exodus, and she was the female version of Moses.

Lord, I've got to get these girls out of here.

Reaching the entrance, Jennifer saw Samantha make her way around the corner.

"Hurry up, ladies." She placed a hand on one girl's back and gently guided her forward. Pushing through the double doors, she made eye contact with Samantha but pretended to look through her.

I think she saw me.

She clenched her teeth. Jennifer got the girls in the non-profit van and made a quick stop at a fast-food restaurant to get dinner for them before dropping them off at their homes.

On her way out of DC, she noticed a red Mercedes coupe with tinted windows following behind her. She shrugged it off and kept driving, but pretty soon she noticed the vehicle behind her kept taking the same turns she did.

"I think this person is following me." She sped up a little faster, steadying the wheel. Her eyes switched back to the rearview mirror again. "I've seen this car before. I think at the greenhouse with David." She turned on to 66 West, and the car kept driving straight. "What the heck was that about?"

Jennifer got to her front porch and checked her mail. Shuffling through several envelopes, she found another note. Her mouth dried up, and her hands became so fidgety that she dropped the mail. Looking both ways, she picked it and opened the envelope.

A message read *David is still mine.*

"This has to be Samantha." She didn't have proof, but Samantha was the only woman she knew who had an obsession for David and knew about her acquaintance with him. "I'll probably have to call the police if this continues."

In the evening, she spent time reading scripture, praying, and listening to worship music. It helped calm her down. She curled up at the corner of the sofa. She rocked her knees back and forth, thinking about David. Fond memories of spending time with him flashed before her now and then. She remembered how they had slow danced on the boardwalk at the National Harbor as she sang into his ear. She recalled their time at the National Cherry Blossom Festival, photographing beautiful trees and blossoms. To top things off, he had surprised her with a picnic and a poem that brought her to tears. She couldn't forget about their date at the greenhouse, the Caribbean dish he had prepared afterward, and leaving a bouquet of roses with a letter stuffed inside in the back seat of her car.

"I still wonder how he pulled that off." She smiled in remembrance. Chivalry was a foreign language to her in today's age, but her standards understood its antiquity. And her hope became the beneficiary of believing that such men existed. David Bradshaw had made his presence known in her life.

"God, I miss David." She felt a powerful yearning for him. Although she wanted to see his face, see his smile, to have another good conversation and laugh with him, she refused to contact him. She believed if they were meant to cross paths again and reconcile, it would happen at the right time. "It's all in Your hands, God."

A WEEK LATER, Samantha called Jennifer and asked to meet up at the grocery store in Vienna. Silence came over Jennifer.

I don't think this a good idea.

"Is there anything I can help you with, Sam?" Jennifer asked. She didn't want to see her.

"Just need some company . . . going through a really tough time. I could use some encouragement from a woman of God." Samantha's voice sounded candid and honest, and Jennifer wondered if maybe she was wrong about her.

"I guess. Gotta grab a few things myself. I'll meet you over there. Meet you there in thirty."

Jennifer pulled up to the grocery store and found a parking space at the midsection of the lot. Gathering her purse and putting some personal things into the compartment of the armrest, she glanced up in the rearview mirror and saw a red Mercedes parked far on the opposite side of the lot. The windows were tinted.

"I think that's the same Mercedes." She waited a few minutes to see if anyone would get out, but no one opened the door.

Jennifer strode to the entrance, clenching the strap of her purse, looking back and forth between the entrance to the grocery store and the car. Walking through the sliding doors, she saw Samantha sitting in the café area. Her arm was in the same sling. She used her other hand to slide her finger up on the screen of her cell phone with a huge grin. Jennifer paused for a moment to watch. Just then, Samantha broke away from her phone and turned in Jennifer's direction. Jennifer waved when they made eye contact and walked over.

"Hey, Sam. What happened to your arm?"

"Ah. Hurt it lifting some heavy furniture."

"Husband wasn't around?" Jennifer slowly turned her head and tilted her ear to listen closely.

Samantha laughed sarcastically. "Was gone for the weekend and didn't want to get another man to do a hubby job."

"I see," she said in a low tone.

They got their shopping carts and pushed them to the produce section. Jennifer felt an awkward vibe the entire time but tried her best to play it off.

"What's on your mind, Sam—said you wanted to talk about something?" Jennifer began inspecting papaya.

"Uh, I think I kinda worked things through last night . . . think I'm good now. How's David?"

"Well, it's good you were able to resolve whatever you were dealing with, and I don't know where David is at the moment. You seem to be interested in him."

"Jennifer, I have something to tell you," Samantha said with a serious expression.

"What's that?" Jennifer laid papaya in her cart.

"Let's finish up shopping and we can talk in the café area."

"Sure thing."

Samantha went the opposite way to complete her grocery list. Jennifer walked off wondering what Samantha wanted to talk about it.

She's going to tell me something about David.

There was a sense of urgency in her tone and expression. Jennifer prayed in her head, asking the Holy Spirit to guide and lead her in the conversation. More importantly, for God's will to be done.

After Jennifer finished up at the cash register, she walked toward the juice bar and saw Samantha sitting at a table in the corner, crying her eyes out. She hurried over and moved Samantha's hands away from her eyes, asking what was wrong.

"I hate myself." She sobbed. "I'm so disgusted with myself."

Jennifer eased into a chair. "Why do you say that?"

"My mother envied me. Everywhere we went people would tell me I was beautiful. I would watch her snarl at me, and she would yank me by the ear when we got in the car and tell me I was ugly. My dad would lock me in the basement for hours with the lights off. Guess that was his way of instilling the fear of the Lord in me." She curled fingers llike quotation marks." Jennifer, I dealt with this all through high school."

Jennifer couldn't help but tear up. "Fear of the Lord?"

"My dad used that stupid Bible to discipline me."

"Oh no, Sam. I'm so sorry. That's not what Jesus is about. He's a loving person. Religious people condemn others and use scripture to fit their preferences. I see why you reject God. You associate shame and punishment with him." She sighed.

"Everyone had the perception of me being this confident woman coming from a stable home with loving parents. I always walked with my chin high and my back straight while inside my self-esteem wanted to crawl under a rock and hide."

"Did you tell anyone?" Jennifer asked with heaviness in her heart.

"I couldn't." Samantha sniffed. "My parents probably would've kicked me out and disowned me. I couldn't tell anyone that my uncle fondled me, that I was drugged and taken advantage of at the beginning of my modeling career. Jennifer, is beauty a curse?"

"I don't think beauty is a curse. I think sometimes it draws superficial things and ungodly relationships into our lives." She clenched her jaw and ground her teeth. A wave of righteous anger rose within her. "It is so unfortunate that you went through this."

"Hey, it's a part of life." Her head tilted a little.

Jennifer came closer and placed a hand on her shoulder. Samantha's eyes slowly rolled up. Jennifer could see her pupil just a little over her arched eyebrows.

"Is there something else you want to say?" Jennifer asked.

She lifted her chin. "I think you need to stay away from David. He's mine."

Jennifer pulled her hand back, shocked at the sudden change in Samantha's demeanor. One moment Samantha needed a friend and now she was snarling in Jennifer's face?

"Excuse me? What did you say?"

"You heard what I said. Stay away from him," she screamed.

"I think you need help." She pushed her chair away with the back of her heels. "There's a Christian counselor I know in the city. She could help."

Samantha shook the table violently and stood up. Jennifer rose up, too, and stepped back. She braced herself for the unknown, shocked and baffled at Samantha's behavior.

"I don't need a counselor, especially a Christian one. I don't believe in Jesus! You all hide behind some religious figure to keep yourself saintly. If Jesus was real, He wouldn't have let this happen to me. Would He?" Samantha screamed and slammed her hand on the table.

This woman is crazy! "Samantha, I was just trying to help," Jennifer pleaded.

"I don't need your help." Samantha's eyes turned red. "Just stay away from David. I slept with him."

Jennifer saw the young man at the juice car shut the blender off, and customers stopped to give their attention to the drama. Her heart started to beat rapidly, and her body turned numb. A store manager came over to confront them.

"Don't touch me." Samantha pushed him out of the way and left the grocery store when he asked if everything was okay.

Jennifer watched Samantha walk away and took a moment to gather her thoughts. "God, heal her," she prayed.

She pushed her grocery cart to the parking garage, feeling disappointed and mortified.

I can't believe David slept with her. I can't believe him.

A tear left the corner of her left eye. She opened the trunk of her car and started emptying the cart. In the distance, she heard screeching tires against the pavement. She dropped one of her bags and broke her jar of honey. She glanced over her shoulders and saw a red Mercedes with tinted windows speed by. "That's gotta be Samantha's car."

A few exits way from her home, she saw a red Mercedes behind her.

"She can't be following me. After that scene she just made, what else is left to say?" She called her mother to tell her about the suspicious activity. Her mother suggested she call the cops, but Jennifer decided against it. "Maybe it's just me. Chat with you later." She turned to a Christian contemporary music station and sang while keeping her eye on the car until it turned down another street after she got off the highway.

When she got home, she didn't turn any of the lights on. She dropped her groceries on the counter in her kitchen and went into her bedroom. She slowly parted her long beige curtains and peeked out to see if the red Mercedes was in sight but didn't see it. Feeling stressed, she got into the shower to decompress.

Closing her eyes, she relaxed under the stream of hot water thinking about life. David came to mind again.

"I can't believe he slept with Samantha. That dog! Hypocrite! I knew he was too good to be true."

She also thought about Leyanie again and started crying. She poured shampoo into her hand and massaged her scalp. After a few seconds of washing her hair, there was a squeaky noise against the shower door. She didn't bother to open her eyes because she knew she was the only one home. Then she heard the noise again. She opened her eyes.

"Who's there?" She cleared the water from her eyes only to find David's name spelled out in bright red lipstick on the shower door. "Oh my gosh." She flinched. She slowly turned the water off and stepped out.

"Who's there?" she shouted with a shaky voice, putting her robe on, listening. "God, please protect me," she whispered breathlessly, trembling with more fear than the faith she had in her prayer. She opened the bathroom door and peeked her head out. "Who's here?"

She crept into her bedroom and headed for her cell phone to call the police. When she turned the light on, she saw Samantha stretched out on her back in the middle of Jennifer's bed with her arms crossed behind her head. She batted her eyelashes and rotated her head in Jennifer's direction like a toy doll.

"I did say I'd see you shortly." She giggled.

Jennifer jumped back and eyed the doorway. Samantha got up and paced around. "Don't think about leaving." She took out a small, chrome handgun from her purse.

Jennifer trembled so hard her teeth started tapping together. She looked at the nightstand for her phone.

"Looking for this?" Samantha held up Jennifer's phone.

"Samantha, what do you want?" Jennifer asked in as calm a voice as she could manage.

"David. Where is he?" Samantha put the gun aside and tossed the phone up in the air a few times, catching it.

"I don't know." She gave Samantha an incredulous look. "We

haven't spoken to each other in a long while." Her thoughts raced in different directions as she tried to figure out how she was going to get out of this perilous situation.

"Sure. Oh my God, I can still feel his body next to me. That night was so special." She clenched her hand between her crotch. "It isn't over between me and him! I know I said I wanted nothing more to do with him, but I miss Mr. Bradshaw so much. I wanna relive the past." She closed her eyes and moaned. "You're so missing out." She giggled again.

"I think you should leave." Jennifer pointed to the doorway.

"I am," she bubbled, basking in the detailed architecture of her handgun. "Pretty, huh? Jennifer, just stay away from David. That's all you have to do."

Samantha lunged toward Jennifer and put the gun to her temple. Jennifer stood quiet and terrified. But in seconds, Jennifer looked Samantha directly in the eyes. Inexplicably, the terror left her, and she said with great confidence and serenity, "I command you, in the name of Jesus Christ, Samantha, to put that gun down and go home to your husband."

Samantha paused for a moment and slowly lowered the gun to her side. She sat up on the bed and covered her ears with her hands. "He's not there!" she sobbed.

"David isn't the answer to your problems—or any other man. Or Michael, for that matter. I know what it's like to mask the pain that's burning deep inside, and I know about trying to find something to distract yourself from it. I understand your parents weren't good to you, but there's a Father who can heal the pain. He can fix all the things in your life. You can only find Him through Jesus Christ. That's what I did. Jesus freed me to be the woman I am now. He also freed me to love again. Samantha, you can fall in love again with your husband, but you have to give your heart to God first."

"God?" Samantha sat down on the edge of the bed and laid the gun beside her. "God exists?"

"He does," Jennifer said with absolute confidence.

"How do you know?" Samantha looked into Jennifer's eyes with surrender.

Jennifer sat next to her and pushed the gun out of her reach.

Just then, she heard the still gentle voice of the Holy Spirit saying, "Put your arms around her." Jennifer flashed her eyes and slightly jerked her head back. She never head Holy Spirit speak this way before.

Okay. She put her arm around her. "Samantha, I know because I've always felt His presence around me since I was a little girl. His presence is an incomprehensible peace. It's an inner knowing."

Samantha hung her head, and Jennifer took the opportunity to surreptitiously retrieve her phone from the bed. She pressed a number to activate the burglar alarm. The silent alarm notified the police. She rubbed Samantha's back and spoke encouraging words to her until the police knocked on the door. Samantha saw blue and red lights flashing outside the window.

"What do I have to do?" Samantha was desperate.

"Just repeat after me." Jennifer took her hands. "Father, thank You for sending Your Son Jesus Christ into the world. He sacrificed His life for me. He died to save me and to redeem me from the power of sin. Because of You, Jesus, I have salvation. I believe in my heart You died on the Cross for my sins, and three days later, You rose from the dead with all power. I receive You into my life. I receive You into my heart as my Lord and Savior. Thank You, Jesus. Amen."

Samantha sobbed every word of the prayer. She accepted Jesus Christ as her personal Lord and Savior.

"I feel this warm sensation coming over me. I feel the peace you're talking about," Samantha said, overwhelmed inside. Her eyes filled with tears as she hugged Jennifer.

"Guess this is it, huh?" Samantha said listlessly, looking at Jennifer.

"You're going to be fine." She patted Samantha on her back.

"Forgive me for sending those anonymous notes. Robert and I tried to keep you and David away from each other."

"What?" Jennifer covered her mouth with both hands. "You and Robert were in on this?"

"I'm sorry. We tried to break you and David up. He sent notes to him, and I sent some to you."

Jennifer thought about the day she had said her goodbyes to Robert, and it appeared he'd had something to say, but hadn't said it.

"I don't know how David's doing. My husband went after him that night he was at my house."

"What happened to him?"

The police rushed into Jennifer's bedroom with guns pointed and ordered Samantha to put her hands behind her head. They talked to Jennifer about Samantha. Jennifer said she didn't want to press charges, but she believed Samantha needed a psychiatric evaluation. She spoke calmly, but inside she was traumatized. When the police left, she checked her closet and every other room in her condo. She made sure all her doors were locked. She snuggled up in her comforter and cried.

"God, I can't believe this happened. I couldn't have done this without You." Never in a million years did she think she'd experience being stalked and having a gun pointed at her head. She called her mother and sobbed as she told the story of what had happened, crying so hard her mother had to keep asking her to repeat herself because she couldn't understand what her daughter was saying.

Her father got on the phone. "Jennifer, what's wrong, honey?" Hearing his voice made her cry all over again.

"Someone invaded my home, Dad."

"Come home," her father said immediately. "I'll take care of the flight."

The next morning, Jennifer flew home to Miami.

During her three-and-a-half-week visit, Jennifer spent a great deal of time with her family and extended family. Her uncle, who was a Christian therapist, met with Jennifer to help her work through her traumatic experience. During a week of daily sessions with him, she made an excellent recovery.

She flew back to Northern Virginia. She researched Samantha's whereabouts through a guy she dated who was a policeman in DC. She found out that Samantha had been admitted to a psychiatric hospital in Maryland. Knowing this made her feel safer at home. However, she was still left with unanswered questions and explanations. She wanted David to give an account of his side of the story. And at the same time, she wanted to apologize to him for the notes he had received from Robert.

He's going to feel like I dragged him into a love triangle.

It had been a month of no contact with him. She tried to give David a call but discovered he'd changed his number.

"Wow, he really moved on."

Later, at her computer, she found his email address no longer worked, either. She was shocked. She had no way to find him except to go to his condo, and that was out of the question. However, she put her pride aside, determined to get answers.

About noon the next day, she drove up to David's place. She didn't recognize any of the lobby associates. "Is, umm, David Bradshaw here?" she inquired of the petite woman behind the desk.

"I'm sorry. You are?" The woman replied with sass and attitude.

"An old friend of his. Jennifer." She propped her pocketbook on the counter.

"He's not here," she said brusquely and made herself busy with a sheet of paper on the desk in front of her.

"Well, excuse me. If you see him around, tell him I stopped by to check on him," Jennifer said, irritated with the woman's rude behavior.

"Sure," the woman replied, not giving Jennifer eye contact.

"Rude," Jennifer mumbled under her breath as she walked away. "She probably has a thing for him."

The thought crossed her mind that David had an affair with Samantha, but she brushed that thought from her mind. Jennifer was concerned about his well-being and his whereabouts, and she didn't care whether he wanted to hear from her or not.

"PUT THE GUN DOWN! I didn't mean to!" David yelled, tossing and turning in his hospital bed. He could still see the barrel of the gun pointed at him.

"He's awake!" a nurse said to her coworker.

They came into David's room. One dabbed sweat off his forehead with a white towel. The other returned with a cup of room temperature water.

David squinted, struggling to make out their faces. They were all a blur.

"How long have I been here?" He grunted from the throbbing pain in his ribs. "Ah!"

"Take it easy. You're still healing. You've been in a coma for a little over a month now." The nursed dabbed his head with a towel.

"Coma? A month? What's today's date?" David tried to sit up again.

"December fifteenth, and yes, a coma. Your head slammed against your steering wheel when you hit a light pole. I guess the airbag didn't come out in time. I'd sue the maker for that mishap. An expensive car you had. You broke a few ribs and fractured your leg in two places. You also had a doozy of a concussion."

"Two places?" David moved his legs, feeling the left one was heavier than the other. He looked down at his leg to see it in a cast.

"Yes. You fractured your femur and fibula. But we were mostly worried about the coma, so we're so happy to have you back. The cast will be off before you leave."

"So that explains the sharp headache I have now?" He reached behind his head.

"Yes, David. Take it easy. You had a bad concussion. It's a miracle you survived. You should see your car. It looks like crinkled paper in the front. Someone must've been watching over you. We tried to get in touch with the family but couldn't find anyone. We located someone's name, Kelsey."

"Kelsey?" David squinted confusedly.

"Says he's like a father to you. We'll get you more water and something light to eat." The nurse left.

David rested his head on the pillow. He lay in a state of shock and disbelief until he dozed off.

A few days later, he was fully conscious. His strength had improved tremendously. He was able to eat and use the restroom without assistance, which he was most grateful for. Washing his hands in the bathroom, he noticed the scar on his forehead and nose. He went to touch it and a quick flash of the car chase and crashing into the light pole came to mind. A sharp pain stabbed at the front of his skull, causing him to stumble back against the wall.

"David?" called the nurse, who was standing at the ready outside the bathroom door in case he had any problems. "Are you okay in there?"

"Coming." David limped out, holding his head. "Ah!" he gasped. "My head hurts."

"David, you need to rest. Lie down now." The nurse helped David to bed.

The gentle touch of the nurse's hand on his forehead made him smile. "Thank you, Mom," he slurred.

"Mom? Excuse me?" The nurse laughed. "I have more than enough kids—all grown up and moved out. But I can adopt you as my son." She winked.

"I'm sorry." David rubbed the back of his head.

"I'll get you some pain medicine. Oh, expect a visit from the police soon. They could stop by any day now. They want to question you about the accident." She started to make her way out the door.

"Where's my cell phone?" David patted his side as if he had pockets.

"In your locker. You want it?" She paused with one foot in between the door.

"Yes, please." He gave her a distraught look.

She left quickly and brought it back, handing it to him. "Thanks." Once he had the phone, David quickly browsed for calls and text messages. He saw missed calls from Kelsey. "I gotta give him a call. May I have a pen and notepad?"

He got Kelsey on the phone and asked if he could come by the hospital right away.

"Coming now." Kelsey hung up.

The nurse returned a few minutes later with a pen and notepad, aspirin, and a cup of water. David steadied the notepad against his leg and penned:

Tragedy has a way of teaching us life lessons we should have learned before. Temptation has a way of overriding our power to make the right decisions. There are no happy endings with lust. I'd like to share a personal experience with you that nearly cost me my life. I share this experience not to gain your sympathy—only to have your understanding, and to prevent you from making the same kind of mistake that I made. I had an affair with a married woman.

David wrote away until he heard the stomp and squeak of heavy boots outside the door, followed by two hard knocks. David quickly set the pen and notepad down beside him. "Come in." He winced in pain.

Kelsey entered and removed his brown plaid newsboy hat, camel scarf, and black leather gloves. He stared at David contemplatively for half a minute before scooting the chair next to the bed. He knew why David was in the hospital. Before Kelsey could get a word out, he confessed, "I almost slept with her." He shifted uncomfortably in his bed. "I can't even say her name." He clenched his hand in a fist.

Kelsey rested his hands on top of each other. His appearance was stolid.

David wasn't quite finished spilling his heart out. "Look at me. I shouldn't be in the hospital. The messages, the signs—I ignored them all. I should've taken your advice." David turned his head, embarrassed. "I listened to your voicemail that night."

The two men sat silently for a while as the sounds of honking horns, the shifting of gears of city buses in busy streets in DC, and kids marveling at the snow was enough to scale back the tension. Minutes later, they heard two hard knocks at the door.

"Come in." David assumed it was the nurse. Instead, he saw two navy blue uniforms, shiny gold badges, and clean-shaven faces. He tensed, sitting up to brace himself for questioning.

"Mr. Bradshaw, how are you feeling?" The elder officer, who looked to be in his fifties, flapped open a small notepad. The other officer appeared in his early twenties.

"Fair," said David.

"I'm Officer Penset and this is Officer Sharp. We're with the DC police department. We have a few questions for you."

"Penset and Sharp. Interesting names." David nearly cracked open a laugh, but no lines formed around the police officers' mouths.

Officer Penset stood by the bed and asked their questions. Officer Sharp took notes. David told them he had been carjacked at a gas station by two masked men. They got into his car and told him to drive, threatening to kill him if he didn't give up his wallet and vehicle. He refused, and the last thing he remembered was heading for the light pole. Kelsey avoided eye contact with the police officers. He kept quiet and to himself during the investigation. They seemed satisfied with his story and didn't question him any further.

"Tough decision, Dave. Tough!" Kelsey said after the policemen left.

"I had to. I can't let this get out in the press. It'll ruin my reputation, career, and everything I've built." David shook his head. "Can't imagine Miss Smith finding out about this or anyone else."

Especially Jennifer.

"Telling the truth is more important than your reputation. The truth gives you peace in public. A lie holds you captive before those who admire you. And a lie keeps vengeance awake. David, it's time to change. You have to surrender yourself to God, so the pattern can stop, and . . . " Kelsey hesitated, wagging his finger at David.

David had heard this lecture about how fragile life is plenty of times from Kelsey. He knew he wanted to tell him again to get his life in order and get to the business of finding his mom. But Kelsey didn't say this. All he said was that he had something to give David once he returned home.

"What is it?" David asked curiously.

"Patience. You'll see." Kelsey left and shut the door.

The sharp sound of the door closing lingered in David's ear. A great sense of urgency overcame him. He knew his next course of action would be a defining moment for him.

A week later, David was discharged from the hospital. He was instructed to take it easy until he was feeling one hundred percent. He wasn't too upset about staying in. After all, he wasn't quite ready to reenter the public. He'd also be able to fully focus on completing his mystery novel. Now, because of his near-death experience, he had a trove of material, theories, and motivation to write. But as the sleepless nights of waking up in cold sweats tallied up, progress with writing was minimal. Everything that happened at Samantha's was still fresh in his mind. He needed some closure. He called her, knowing he was taking the huge risk of putting his life in danger again. To his surprise, she answered. She asked if he was okay.

"I'm still alive." He coughed. "How are you?" He heard nothing but sobs on the other end. She ignored his question and said it wouldn't be a good idea for them to see or contact each other in any way. David agreed and apologized for his actions and for endangering her life and her marriage. She ignored his apology and said her final goodbyes. He stared at his phone for a few seconds, realizing that if he never talked to her again, the memory of her and his near-death experience would remain with him forever.

The next morning, he pondered in front of his fireplace with a pillow clenched under his arm. He listened to the crackling of burning wood, staring into the flames, watching gray, lit ashes float and disintegrate against the black smokescreen. He stared down at his Bible on the coffee table, as if expecting it to jump into his lap and open to a page. He drifted off to sleep but was awakened shortly by a voicemail coming from Kelsey on the answering machine.

David shuffled slowly into the kitchen with his walker to prepare tea for him and Kelsey. As water filled the green Chantal kettle over the faucet, he winced in pain. "God, why did I put myself in this situation?" he said aloud, steadying the kettle on the stove. "I should've listened. I know You were warning me," he continued sadly with deep regret, tears rolling down his face.

Shortly after the water began to boil, Kelsey arrived.

"It's unlocked!" David shouted from the kitchen.

Kelsey came in coughing into a handkerchief. "Boy, it sure is cold out there. How's it going?" He stuffed his arms into his armpits walking towards the kitchen. "Healing okay?"

David turned around gradually. He was unable to make any sudden movements. "Slowly but surely."

"Let me get that for you." Kelsey reached over David and took two gray mugs out of the cabinet. He poured water into each one and dropped peppermint tea bags in them, along with cubes of brown sugar. Kelsey picked up the cups and followed behind David into the living room.

"I meant to ask you if you'd heard anything from Samantha." He swooshed the cubes around, so they would dissolve faster.

"I did. We both agreed to move on." David eased down into an armchair and Kelsey got comfortable on the sofa.

"Good." Kelsey nodded.

"You know, it's time for a change," he said, teary-eyed. "I can't continue living like this anymore."

"What kind of change?" Kelsey stirred his tea, leaning into the steam to warm his face.

"It's like I'm always looking for love outside of myself when I need to find it within. Like I'm searching for validation from women to define my worth and value. I'm looking for someone to complete me. It's been that way in all the relationships I've had. The sleeping around, pretending like I'm happy . . . it all has to stop. I'm going to be abstinent until I get married."

"What?" Kelsey nearly spat out his tea. "Hold." He laughed. "Never thought I'd hear the 'a' word from you."

He cocked his head to the side. "A-word. You're a total fool." He laughed back. "Yep, it'll be hard, but I want to save myself for that special woman." He looked Kelsey square in the eye.

"Wow, David. I'm proud of you, man. I am. I think it's worth the wait. I have a book for you to look at. It's not a Christian book per se. Eat the meat. Toss the bones."

"What book?" David eased the hot cup to his lips.

"*The Art of Loving* by Erich Fromm." Kelsey handed over the book. "A friend of mine recommended I read it when I was around your age. It helped me out a lot. I think it may help you, too. You have to get some closure or some sort of understanding about why the relationship between you and your mom is the way it is. There's always a reason behind our actions, good or bad."

David started to browse through the book.

"Dave, in this book I believe you'll find some answers to the questions you have about yourself and how life was for you as a child. You also may come to an understanding about all that's holding you back from being the man you're capable of being. And I'm thinking," he said pondering with this head down, "maybe God is protecting Jennifer from what's in you."

"Whoa!" David froze up. That hit him hard. He felt that. The presence of God came over him again. This time it was more invigorating and powerful. "Didn't think of that." He put the book down and returned his attention to the fire in the fireplace.

"And this isn't a replacement for the Word of God—rather a supplement. Spend some time in the book of Matthew. I strongly feel that's a good place to start. Chapter six in particular." He put his hand on his hip. "Yeah. Chapter six. I gotta get going, kid. I gotta get to work. See ya around." He got up.

"I know. Thanks for stopping by, and thanks for the talk." He stood up and hugged Kelsey.

"Anytime. Take care of yourself—I mean that." He patted David on the back.

"I will."

At the door, Kelsey turned to David and said, "And, Dave, keep this in mind."

"What's that?"

"Jennifer, or any other woman you meet from here on out, can't fix what's broken within you. Only God can do that. The love you discover within, through Him, can heal what's pulling you apart and warring within your soul. Only the love of God can complete you. No other love."

CHAPTER 11

*D*avid finally opened *The Art of Loving*. He struggled through portions of it over the next couple of days. Mainly, grasping some of the concepts of the "theory of love" and "love being the answer to the problem of human existence." During phone conversations, Kelsey helped bring clarity to some of the questions David had but left others for him to figure out on his own.

"Those who have truly healed from their ailments have gone the distance in God to find the truth." Kelsey left those words for David to ponder before he hung up.

Deep in thought, David peered out the window. He looked down at the busy streets and houses decorated with Christmas lights. He was determined to make sense of the chapter of *The Art of Loving*. Finally, something clicked. He discovered that all along, his loneliness derived from his mother's lack of love, nurturing, and affirmation—all of which caused him to seek those things from the women he dated. Most recently, Maria and Samantha. He also realized that the absence of his mother's love prevented him from loving himself.

"I got it. I got it," he chanted quietly and pumped his fist. David now had the key to unlocking the door of his past that would free him in the present. After this epiphany, he jotted down notes about how to move forward.

As he was writing, his eyes locked on the Bible next to him. He opened it and paged to Matthew 6 and stopped at verse 15 and read, "But if you do not forgive others their sins, your Father will not forgive your sins."

He dropped to his knees and moved his hand over his heart. The scripture hit him so hard with the conviction that he started to cry. He laid prostrate on the floor, knowing in his heart that he had to forgive his mother while his mind continued to give every reason not to. "I hear You, Father. I hear You."

Seconds later, Miss Smith called. She asked if he'd be able to make it to the appreciation day event at the women's shelter later that afternoon. He'd completely forgotten. "Yes, I'll be there." He got off the floor as quickly as he could, gulped down two aspirins, and showered.

Strong winds blew past David's ears, sounding like air inside of a seashell. His stiff joints slogged through the thick, sticky snow on the walk way to the shelter. "Miss Smith needs someone to clear this," he said, climbing the stairs slowly, gripping the handrail and balancing himself with his metal cane. When he came inside, the front desk receptionist hardly recognized him. His fully bearded face was mummy-wrapped in a red-and-blue striped scarf.

"Haven't seen you around, ladies' man," she gently teased.

David couldn't have managed a chuckle if he'd wanted to. The tag "ladies' man" no longer had the same ring to it. "I'm no ladies' man," he said solemnly. "Just a man who's striving to live a simple and complete life in Christ—nothing more." He nodded, limping to the cafeteria with his cane.

The chattering in the cafeteria grew louder when he pushed through the heavy brown double doors. His mouth watered at the smell of tenderloin steak, seasoned mashed potatoes with gravy, and sautéed green peppers and onions.

Haven't had a meal like this in a while.

He hobbled through the crowd, half smiling at the women who were leaning against the wall talking or huddled in circles. They regarded him with concerned faces. He could hear them asking what happened to him. His head sort of stooped in shame. Finally, he spotted Miss Smith seated at a table with several other women. The shiny silver 9/11 commemorative brooch on her red sweater caught his attention.

David drew near to Miss Smith.

"Hey, David, how have you been?" She studied him as he hobbled over with his cane. "What happened to you?" she said, alarmed.

"I was in a car accident." He steadied himself with the cane for balance.

"Oh my! Thank God you're alive. Excuse me for one second," she announced to the women, wrapping things up and fixing David a plate.

When Miss Smith returned, she wanted to know about David's accident. He tried to cut through the steak but couldn't. His ribs were still sore. She grabbed the knife and started cutting it for him, waiting to hear David's explanation. He smiled to himself, envisioning his mother doing that as a kid. He wanted to tell her the truth about the car accident but couldn't. He shrugged his shoulders, stuffing mashed potatoes into his mouth, and settled for telling her he fell asleep at the wheel. Miss Smith switched into mother mode.

"You know better than that now. You know how to use better judgment." She rolled her eyes and shook her head in grave disappointment. "Can't believe you, David."

"I know, Miss Smith. I know," he said, puppy-faced.

David felt horrible having to conceal the truth from someone he loved, someone he cared about, someone he trusted and who had been like a mother to him.

"Have things gotten better since we last talked?" she inquired.

David felt a sharp pain in his abdomen. "Yeah, things have gotten a lot better." He grunted.

"Are you sure? I'm talking about between you and your mother. Have you gotten a chance to reach out to her yet?"

The fork hit the plate and David scooted his chair away from the table. "I plan to in a few days."

"Listen here, David." Her eyebrows narrowed as she pinched her lips together.

"I apologize for being rude, Miss Smith. I'm starting my search for her tomorrow." He stared at his plate.

"Good. Good for you. Been waiting to hear those words for the longest time."

Before she was able to probe for details about exactly when he was going to search for her and where he planned to start, a woman entered the room and announced that they were ready to begin the next portion of the ceremony. He quickly finished what was left on his plate and followed them upstairs.

After Miss Smith finished giving out the awards for women's appreciation day, she invited him to come to the podium to say a few words. As he'd never been able to tell her no, he slowly rose to his feet and took center stage.

"I had an experience not long ago that finally woke me up to find my mother." His head lowered. He could still see the barrel of Michael's gun pointed at his face and the moment he slammed into the light pole. He face twitched a little, making him stumble back a little.

Some women in the audience gasped.

"Are you okay David?" One of them asked.

Putting his hand up, he indicated that he was fine and continued. "Sometimes God has to allow us to make mistakes and feel the pain of it, so we'll turn back to His will." His voice started to crack. "I want to get it right this time around. I strongly feel I don't have time to waste in reconciling with my mother. I have this eerie feeling deep within me that scares me, to be honest. My mistakes have cost me some things—things I'll probably never get back again." He paused for a moment and patted his eyes with a tissue. "And, I lost someone who still has a special place in my heart, and I've been praying that God gives me a second chance with her. You met Jennifer a few months ago."

Sniffs from the women echoed throughout the auditorium.

"Maybe you lost something before you came here, but that doesn't mean it's the end. God made time and He redeems it as He pleases. And whatever is broken, God can heal if it's in His will. After I find my mother, I plan to reach out to Jennifer. I'm not sure what the outcome will be, but I believe it to be worth the effort. And at least I'll know I made a genuine effort to repair things with her. I could find peace in that. I believe Jennifer is in the will of God to take as my wife. I just have that kind of faith. I appreciate you all for allowing me to come down here and speak with you. It's been an enriching and healing experience for me. I'm learning that love truly needs to be a part of your life. You have no idea how you all have aided in my healing process with your love and your presence. I think that's all I have to say." David chuckled out of nervousness, bringing his speech to a close.

Miss Smith approached the podium and embraced David in a huge, long hug. Everyone got up and gave a standing ovation. She pulled the microphone closer to her, creating a squeak of feedback.

"Excuse me!" She laughed. "David, we have something special we want to give to you for your time, dedication, and help." She looked out into the audience and signaled for one of the women to come to the stage. A woman approached her and gave her a large bag. "Thank you," said Miss Smith. She handed the white bag to David.

Inside, he found a small box, gift-wrapped in royal blue wrapping paper tied with a white ribbon. In the box was a black fountain pen and matching cuff links. Both were engraved in gold with his initials.

"This is nice," he said quietly, holding the items up for everyone to see and then placing them on the podium. He opened another box, gift-wrapped in green paper. A brown leather toiletry case was inside. "I'm speechless. Thank you," he said, looking out at the women in the audience. He tore the red paper off the last gift and found a bottle of cologne. "Thank you so much, everyone. This means a lot to me." He hugged Miss Smith, truly surprised by all the nice things that had been given to him.

"I am completely taken aback by these wonderful gifts. It seems as though someone's been snooping around in my bedroom," he said into the mic, laughing. The women in the audience joined in the laughter. "Thank you, everyone. I appreciate it. Thank you." He bowed his head.

After he said his goodbyes, Miss Smith walked David outside. He wrapped his scarf around his neck, bracing himself for the cold weather.

"David, I'm proud of you. I am." She dabbed her eyes with a tissue. "Thank you so much for stopping by." She wrapped her arms tightly around herself as a cold breeze engulfed them.

"You're welcome. And thank you again for allowing me to be here to speak to you all." He bowed his head.

"I'm glad you're ready to make that change. I'm excited for you. You're going to be okay." She patted him on the back.

"Yeah, I think it's about that time. I'm ready to free myself from all that's been holding me back." He tightened the scarf around his neck and face. "I'll be in touch with you." He hugged her.

"Okay. Take care of yourself." She waved.

Miss Smith was the closest thing he had to a mother, but now David knew it was time for him to make things right between him and his biological mother.

At home, he searched his attic for the envelope Aunt Jamison had sent him when he was in the orphanage. "It's gotta be in here some-where." He rummaged through box after box. "Got it!" It was falling apart.

He dialed the number with urgency. After each ring, he grew more nervous and cotton mouthed. An automatic response came on after the fourth ring to leave a message after the beep. He called again and someone answered.

A screeching, elderly voice said hello from the other end of the phone. David swished his tongue around to gather some saliva to speak. He introduced himself and asked if she were Aunt Jamison. He heard a heavy sigh interrupted by a cough.

"Who are you?" she asked.

"David."

"Diane's son?"

His eyes slightly squinted. *Diane's son.* "Who's Diane?"

"Your mother."

He froze and took the phone away from his face. He didn't know what to say.

"We have some catching up to do, David. I kept you a short while when you were a little boy."

"Kept?" David puzzled over the word. "I was in an orphanage. Why didn't anyone look for me?"

Another silence surfed the airways. "We will catch up, David."

"I need to find my mother. Where is she?" he asked with great urgency.

"Hmm. It's been years since I've talked to her. I don't think I have a new number for her, either. I may have to ask around," she said, frazzled. "I know she moved to an apartment in Reston a few years ago. I'll give you that address. She might still be there."

After David took down the address, his aunt invited him to her house in Arlington. "I should have the number by then. But come. I haven't seen you in years."

"Okay. Sounds good."

David drove to Reston that evening to see what he could uncover. He didn't know what to expect. He didn't know what he was going to say or do once he saw his mother. He knew for sure that he wanted to see her face, hear her voice, touch her hands, and give her a long-overdue hug.

He pulled up to the apartment complex at the address Aunt Jamison had given him and limped up to unit 1 with this cane. After two hard knocks, an elderly woman answered the door hunched over with her walker.

Her droopy eyes peered up to look David in the face, and she pointed the cane at him. "Is that you, Eddie?"

"No, I'm not Eddie," David said twisting his face.

"I'm sorry. My hearing isn't good." She put her hand to ear. "You'll have to speak up."

"Eddie? I'm not Eddie!" David raised his voice a little. He felt sorry for the elderly woman whose sense of memory and hearing were diminishing.

"Oh, okay. Who are you, then?" She stepped back and gripped the cane.

I think we're about to square off. "I'm looking for Diane," he said loudly.

"That name sounds familiar." The woman rested her hand on her hip. "I think her mail used to come here."

"She's no longer living here?" David said hopelessly.

"No." She put her hand on her doorknob.

"Well, thank you. Sorry for disturbing you." David walked away. *Hopefully Aunt Jamison will come up with something tomorrow.*

He drove home, less optimistic than before about finding out where his mother had relocated. Aunt Jamison was his only hope at this point.

The next day, David parked on the street in front of his aunt's yellow house. Stopping just shy of the doorstep, he recalled as a kid that seeing her black shutters had reminded him of huge eyes. He would get scared and hide behind his mother's leg when they visited. Some of his memories as a kid began to come back.

Before he could reach for the screen door, a howling wind flung it open and the rusted, aluminum wind chimes sang off-key. He knocked twice and stepped back. The blinds in a nearby window rolled up. He could see pale skin through the frosty window.

"She's white." He jumped back. The doorknob rattled, and the door slowly drew back. A short, frail woman with fully gray hair and gray eyes appeared. She examined David from head to toe.

"Well, my, my," she said in a whispery voice. "David. Look at you. You're so tall and handsome. Come in, come in." Aunt Jamison led him to her antiquated living room.

"How old are you, now?" Her hands shook as she talked.

"I'm . . ." David said awkwardly.

Before he could answer, she bear-hugged him. "Lord, I haven't seen you in so long."

"Thirty." David coughed, wincing from the strength of her embrace.

"David, it's so good to see you." She released him and noticed his cane. "What happened to you?"

"I was in a car accident, but I'm okay." He smiled.

"You be careful in this snow." She wagged her cane at him.

Offering him a seat, she sat thigh to thigh with him, patted his hand and held it. "You're not married yet? No hot young gal snatched up a handsome fella like you?"

David laughed, amused by her sweet, sincere concern. "Someday, Aunt Jamison. Someday."

"I'll fix us some hot tea." She got up and ambled off to the kitchen.

A gray cat jumped on the arm of the beige sofa and walked slowly toward him. The cat's eerie yellow eyes watched him closely, appearing ready for an attack. Then it purred, head-bumped, and brushed up against his arm a few times before leaping off at the sound of the rattling heater against the wall.

His aunt returned with a white tray. "Sophia always jumps when she hears that heater. Here you go, David." She placed a white teacup and matching saucer on the coffee table in front of him. And resumed her place next to David with a teacup and saucer of her own. "I think she likes you." She winked at the cat.

I can't tell. "Thank you," David said cheerfully. "Can you tell me about my mother?"

She looked through the beige curtains hearing the snowplow came up the road. Her hands trembled as she lowered the teacup to the saucer. She gave him a long stare as sadness filled her eyes. He braced himself for whatever he was about to hear.

"I'm ready, Aunt Jamison."

"I'm not your aunt by blood, but I loved you like you were my kin. I met your mother when we were both living in an orphanage."

"Orphanage?" David asked, confused.

"Yes. Your grandmother, who is now deceased, gave your mother up for adoption when she was seven years old. I don't know why. Your mother never talked about it much. Anyhow, it was difficult for your mother to find a steady foster home. She never got along with any of her foster parents. Most of her life she moved around, never really finding a place to call home."

Hearing this grieved his heart. He shut his eyes for a moment. "I had no idea she was given up for adoption or lived in an orphanage."

"Unfortunately, she was, and that's when she and I became close. It took her a while to warm up to me, but I gained her trust. We eventually grew a bond, like sisters. When she had you, I knew that she wasn't quite ready to be a mother. She was always in the streets, bars, and clubs, looking for love in all the wrong places. You know how that story goes."

"Sounds a lot like me," David admitted. "That's what I've been doing. People who are hurt, broken and wounded look for love outside of themselves. They turn to people instead of God."

"God?" Her eyes glimmered with approval.

Catching on, he replied, "Yes. I believe in Jesus."

"Good." She silently clapped her hands. "Go on." She flicked her index finger for him to continue.

"I turned to relationships, Aunt Jamison. I looked for love in women instead of turning to God." He lowered his head in shame.

"It's okay, David. You can put an end to that pattern. No one but God can fix what's broken. You have to seek God. I tried to get your mother to see this, but she wouldn't listen." She sighed. "I can see that's why you're here today."

"Why I'm here today?" he asked, slightly puzzled.

"I think you'll get it by the end of this conversation."

"Wait." David sat up, interrupting her. "Do you know anything about my father? I had no idea who or where he was until later on."

"Your father was a good man. Your mother pushed him away."

He repeated what she said, confused.

"You were only an infant, so you don't remember any of this. Your father tried to be a part of your life, but Diane kept him away from you. She thought he was out cheating on her while she was pregnant with you and even after she had given birth to you. But the reality is he was working his butt off to support the two of you."

"This is all making sense now." He thought about *The Art of Loving* book when he read how the absence of a father and his love from his daughter's life could affect her later on as a woman and a mother.

Sympathy started to sink into his heart.

"I went so many years without having a relationship with him because I thought he didn't want me." He threw a fist into his other hand. "I was angry at him for a long time, but when I finally found him, it was too late." He could no longer hold back his tears of pain.

"Your father loved you very much." She stopped in the middle of her statement. "Wait. Too late?"

"Yes, it was too late. He died of lung cancer." David covered his face with his hands.

"Died . . . of . . . lung cancer?"

"Yes, I found him. Got to know him in the hospital." His voice cracked.

"Oh, David, I'm so sorry to hear this," she said sympathetically, rubbing his hand.

"It's okay. Go on with what you were saying."

"David, despite all this surrounding you, I just knew that you'd grow up to be something great. You asked why anyone didn't come for you. I didn't come to you because I got sick. I couldn't have taken care of you for long. I had to give you up. If it were up to me, you would have been with me."

"So that's how I ended up at the orphanage? Another pattern, I see. My mom was there."

"Felt so bad, but I prayed for you throughout the years. I prayed God would watch over you. I couldn't take you to anyone on your mother's side of the family. She was a little rough around the edges. She cut everyone off from her—family and friends."

"Thanks for letting me know. And thank you for praying for me. For a long time, I thought nobody wanted me."

"That's not true, David. I kept you for a little while . . . up until you were about nine years old."

"I think I remember now. Your house did look vaguely familiar when I was walking up the driveway."

"Ha!" She laughed. "You remember a bit. You would hide behind your mother's leg whenever she bought you over." She laughed. "You were a loving, special kid. You had an imagination—a very unique one at that. You always had a book in your hand, and you were always scribbling up some type of story. No one could understand your handwriting, though. Only you could." She smiled.

"I write for a living, Aunt Jamison," he said proudly.

"You do?" She covered her mouth in excitement.

He nodded.

"What do you write about?" She leaned closer to him.

"Love," he said with confidence, knowing Aunt Jamison was going to insert her experience and wisdom.

She grinned. "What's a young man like you know about love?"

"Enough to write about it." He smiled politely. "God gives understanding."

"Ha! I see." The cat crawled into her lap and eyed David again. She petted it absentmindedly.

"Do you know how I can find my mother?" David kept his attention on the cat and gripped the handle of his cane tighter.

"Oh, it dawned on me this morning that I may have something. I'll be right back."

She returned with a small, yellow phonebook. "Let's see here . . ." She licked her fingers to flip through the pages. "Here we go." She wrote down the number and address and handed him the piece of paper. "I pray she's at this address."

"Thank you, Aunt Jamison." David took the page and looked at it. "She's in Durham, North Carolina?" His eyes widened a little.

"Possibly. How about you dial the number now to see if it works before you make that trip?"

David dialed the number fast and waited with anticipation but received no answer. A canned voicemail greeting came on that gave only the number, not the name of the person. "Mom. This is David. Your son. Umm, I'm trying to get in touch with you," he said, making eye contact with Aunt Jamison again. "I want to see you. Hope to hear from you." He ended the voicemail by leaving his number.

"No luck, I see." Aunt Jamison sipped her tea.

"At least the number is in service. I may have to chance it and drive out there if she doesn't call me back. I'll try again tomorrow. I gotta get going now. It was good seeing you. I promise to keep in touch." He got up, keeping his attention on the cat.

"Please do." She stood up to walk him out.

"I will, Aunt Jamison. I will." David headed for the door with her trailing alongside.

"David?" She called his name somberly.

"Yes?" He waited for what she was going to say next.

"You were broken for the very thing you longed for, which is deeper intimacy with God and true love." Her voice reverberated with wisdom.

"Huh?" David was perplexed.

"I see the pain, David."

Tears instantly formed in his eyes as he put his head down.

"Everything that you've gone through God permitted it to happen. It's drawing you closer to Him for some greater purpose."

"I could kinda see that."

"And the transformation has to take place to receive the things of God. I know you're going to marry a beautiful woman one day, one who will compliment you in every way that you imagine," Aunt Jamison continued. "You have a beautiful spirit and a warming soul— two ingredients that only an extraordinary woman of spiritual substance would be able to understand and handle, receive and appreciate. You don't belong with the shallow, David. So just be patient and embrace the breaking process. It's going to hurt, but it's worth it. She's coming soon."

Every word hit him so profoundly, causing more tears to flush from his soul. *Wasn't expecting this.* He frowned slightly, wondering what had prompted her to share these words. His tingling toes crunched in his boots, feeling God's presence again. It was in the way he experienced it with Jennifer.

"The love of God has to heal me," he said meditatively.

"Yes, it does."

"Thanks, Aunt Jamison. Now I see why I'm here."

"Told you that you would get it by the end of this conversation." She rubbed his hand and winked at him. "Take care of yourself." She hugged him. "And please keep in touch."

"You, too." David embraced her back with a kiss on the cheek. He walked down the driveway, turning to wave goodbye before getting into his vehicle.

For the next three days, David tried contacting his mother by phone. He received the same results. No answer. "Guess I gotta make a trip to Durham."

CHAPTER 12

*H*eavy snow wasn't quite the perfect background he wanted to see driving on slushy roads. He revisited the conversation he'd had with Aunt Jamison that made him reflect on the course of his life. From how subdued he was as a child to growing up, becoming a timid teenager, and eventually blossoming into a self-confident, successful, and self-assured man. He was proud that he'd pulled himself out from under the rock that could've kept him hidden forever. Today, he was ready to heal and to put his past differences with his mother behind him.

"I am coming for you, Mom." He turned onto the highway.

Five and a half hours later, he arrived at a white apartment complex. Some buildings were spray-painted with black, orange, blue, and red graffiti. The parking lot was riddled with deep potholes, newspapers, ragged clothes, and shoes. Birds pecked through black and white trash bags near oversized green rusted dumpsters to gather whatever food they could. He saw sneakers slung over light pole lines. He glanced at the address once more before getting out of his truck to make sure he was at the right place.

"Yep, this is it. Here we go," he muttered under his breath. He got out of his truck and traipsed through the snow with his cane.

Inside the building, pieces of newspapers and mail cluttered the cold hallway. He knocked, sweeping the debris away with his cane. A dog barked viciously from behind a doorway, and a rock the size of a fist smashed through the window by the entrance. "What the heck?" he said, startled. A group of teenagers scattered when they saw him coming down the hallway toward the entrance. "Kids." He groaned and swatted the rock out of the way with his cane. He trod up the creaking wooden steps and found the apartment he was looking for. Giving two hard knocks, he stepped back.

"Hello, is anyone there?" He put his ear to the door, hearing the squeak of sofa springs and footsteps.

"Who is it?" A grumpy, husky voice of a woman answered.

"David," he said.

"David?" she yelled. "Who's David?"

"David," he replied. "Your son, David. Mom, it's cold out here." He adjusted his scarf and stomped his feet to get the circulation going in them again.

The door opened. There stood his mother. Dark circles were patted around her eyes. Wrinkles lined her sullen face. Her frame was small. She gasped, moving her hand over her chest as if seeing a ghost.

"Hi, Mom." David lingered in the doorway, anticipating a "Hello" or "How have you been?" or, even better, "David, I've missed you." Instead, he was greeted with the same coldness in her eyes that had widened the distance between them when he was a child. "May I come in?" he asked hurriedly. Being in her presence made him feel like a kid again, trying to be polite to please her. "It's cold out here." He tried to cup his hands and blow hot into them.

She shrugged and backed into the apartment, which felt almost as chilly to David as the hallway. His mother ambled into the compact kitchen. She lit a match and put it to the burner on the small, boxed stove, and filled a pot with water. She leaned against the stained countertop, apparently trying to warm her hands by stuffing them in her armpits and waited for the water to boil. David stayed at the entrance to the kitchen, wanting to hug her, but he could feel the thick, invisible wall between them.

"Mom, I just wanted to come by and talk to you, see how you're doing." He cupped his hands and blew warmth into them from his breath again. "It's been years, you know." She peered into the pot to check on the water. "Mom, I want to make things right between us. It's been too long since I've last seen or spoken with you. It just doesn't feel right going through life without you in it. I don't know what it's like to have a mother."

She turned the burner off, poured water into a chipped yellow cup, and dropped a green tea bag into it. She shoved the cup over to David, still avoiding eye contact with him. Some water spilled over.

"Thank you for the tea. I need it, so cold outside," he said, raising the cup to his lips and blowing to cool it down. "Mom, I'm ready to put whatever happened between us behind me," he said, taking small sips. "Whatever grudges we had in the past, I'm ready to be done with them. I talked with Aunt Jamison."

His mother quickly looked up, meeting David's eyes for a second, but returned to staring at the discolored beige tile floor.

"I understand why our relationship is the way it is. She told me everything, everything about your upbringing and why my father wasn't in my life. I understand now. I'm not holding that against you."

Tears welled up in her eyes, and she covered her face with her hands. She appeared ashamed and embarrassed.

He felt a desire to hold her again but didn't. He kept talking to her. "You know, as angry as I was with you in the past, every time I saw a son with his mother, I could imagine that being us. I wished I could have experienced that same kind of love and affection that they did."

She turned her back to him, walked into the tiny living room, and stood before the window, flanked by dangling, chipped, tan blinds.

David put the cup down and came up behind her. "Mom, do you have anything to say to me? Don't you want to know what's been going on in my life? How I turned out?"

She said nothing and didn't move, facing the window.

"I've written three novels. I'm an international bestselling novelist.

I'm successful. I write mainly about love, but I'm giving mystery a try now. And guess what?" David's eyes got bigger with excitement. He became like the kid who was happy to show his mother he got an A on his test. "And maybe one day, one of my novels will be adapted into a film. Wouldn't that be great?"

He noticed that she was listening, despite keeping her back turned to him. He hoped that hearing how well he was doing would spark something inside of her and she'd talk to him. He hoped his words would provoke a sense of pride that her son had accomplished so much. But there were no sweet, tender words of "congratulations" or "I'm proud of you, son."

"I'd love to buy a home for you someday." His voice wavered, seeing that his efforts weren't any traction, but he persisted. "And guess what? I met this amazing woman, but things fell apart. Her name is Jennifer Washington. Who knows, maybe we'll get back together. I would love for you to meet her if we do."

She folded her arms across her chest and stared out into the wintry scene. He noticed snowflakes drifting and sticking to the ground.

"Mom, I love you." He came around in front of her and opened his arms. "I want you to be a part of my life. I forgive you." His voice wavered by pain and hurt in his heart.

Her arms never moved. They stuck to her side. There was sorrow in her eyes, but she winced when she felt David's arms wrapped tightly around her. Her body trembled.

"I forgive you." His voice lost strength.

His mother sobbed but said nothing.

"I said I forgive you, Mom." His voice cracked.

He released her when she flinched and hung his head low.

To pour your heart out only to have it hit cold cement instead of reaching a warm place of reconciliation knocks the life out of you.

"If you want to call me, you can." He slipped a piece of paper with his number on it into her palm. He made his way to the door and paused for a second. He turned around to see if she would say anything, but she faced the window again. He inhaled a deep breath of disappointment, released it and left.

Outside, he stopped on the way to his truck and looked up at her window through the falling snow. "I forgive you," he yelled out, startling the line of blackbirds sitting on the power line. She immediately shut what was left of the blinds.

David stepped into his truck, slammed the door, and pressed his face against the cold steering wheel. "God, this hurts so much. Why? Why? I tried, Lord. I tried," he said, losing his breath.

He returned home in a grim mood. He was no closer to understanding why his mother was so unresponsive to him, especially after he'd gone to all this effort to find her.

"God, I don't understand," he mumbled. "I don't understand."

When he arrived home, he poured a glass of liquor. He swished it around and tossed it out. "No more drinking for me." He grabbed several bottles from the cabinet and poured them all down the drain. "I can't deal with my problems this way anymore." He fixed a cup of tea instead and wrote the night away in front of the fireplace.

The following day, he went to Kelsey's and told him what had happened with his mother. Kelsey was saddened by the news.

"How am I supposed to move on?" David smacked *The Art of Loving* book against his hand then pointed it at Kelsey.

"David, you may not ever get the kind of answers or closure you feel you need to move on. You have to understand that some people, even family members, may never be close to us in the way we expect and want them to be. But we have to love them anyway. Unconditionally. That's the way God wants us to love. Love is what God commands of us. Love keeps us free from walking in what others are bound by. She's bound by hurt and bitterness, David. God have mercy on her," Kelsey said with sorrow and compassion.

"I don't know. I did what I was supposed to do. I reached out. I found her. It's not supposed to end like this. I gotta get out of here."

"David. Pain is often the beginning of something new. I don't know what the new is, but I feel it's coming soon."

David folded the book up, threw it on the floor and glared at him.

Dejection filled Kelsey's eyes. He gave David a quick stare before his head sunk low. He rubbed his forehead, knowing his words of wisdom never reached the door of David's heart.

"I'm out." David slammed Kelsey's front door behind him.

CROWS SQUAWKED ABOVE tall oak trees, icicles hanging from the tips of their branches. Squirrels dashed about frantically at hearing David's heavy footsteps in the snow. He reached his father's tombstone and brushed the snow off it. He knelt and thought about all the years his father hadn't been a part of his life. He envisioned seeing his father's face in the crowd when he received his undergraduate and graduate degrees. But there wasn't one man cheering him on, embracing him with a macho hug and high-fives like his college buddies. He thought about his first date when he was twenty. He'd second-guessed himself on whether he should open doors for her or how to engage and initiate conversation. He'd felt both awkward and embarrassed and had no one to show him how to court or be a gentleman to a woman. Whenever he visited his college friends' houses or spent Thanksgiving or Christmas with them, he'd picture familiar faces that looked like his, even though he was among loving people who welcomed him as if he were their own. He took a hard swallow before speaking.

"Dad, I just wanted to come out here to share a few words with you. I now understand why you were absent from my life for so long. All those years I held a grudge against you because of a lie. I'm sorry for being so angry with you. I can remember it like it was yesterday." He looked up at the gray sky. "On your deathbed, you told me to love my mother no matter what because she's the only mother that I'll ever have. Dad, I tried to. I tried, but she doesn't love me back." A ball of emotion welled up in his throat. "What am I supposed to do? How can I move on?"

Right after David asked those questions, he heard a man and woman approaching. He kept his attention directed at the tombstone, but he was able to see them from the corner of his eye, standing before a grave about twenty feet from him. He listened to the woman pay respects to her mother. Then she admitted to the man next to her that at one time, she didn't think she could love again after her ex-fiancé had broken her heart. She told the man that her mother's support and prayers helped her through a difficult time and opened her eyes to see it was possible to love again.

"I didn't think I could. God healed me." She leaned her head against the man's shoulder.

David closed his eyes and prayed. "How could I drift away from Your presence, Father? I need You to heal me." He leaned his head against the tombstone and told his dad he loved him.

The following day, David lounged the morning through in front of the television, mummy-wrapped in a comforter on the sofa. A leather notebook was on the coffee table. A silver scribe pen layed on top of it. Nothing was coming to mind. Reaching for the pen to scribble something with hopes of generating an idea, he heard knocking at the door. It was Kelsey.

Kelsey shimmied in, clapping his hands together to generate heat from the below temperatures outside. Without saying anything, David went straight to the kitchen to prepare something for him to drink.

"Tea or hot chocolate?"

"Hot chocolate?" Kelsey coughed, pulling out a teal handkerchief from his gray overcoat.

"Teal?" David said, glancing at Kelsey.

"What's wrong with this color?" Kelsey asked about to break into laughter. "What? Martha gave it to me."

"Guess I'll let it slide this time," David said, maintaining a serious tone.

"Hey, you might get married in teal, wise guy."

"Yeah right." He smirked.

"Doing any better?" Kelsey asked, inspecting David's living room. It was a bit tiddy than the last time he visted him.

"Yeah, I'm okay." He poured hot water into a red Christmas decorated mug and ripped open a white hot chocolate packet.

"Couldn't find a better mug than that?" Kelsey broke into full laughter.

"Guess today's your lucky day," David said with a teasing grin.

"There goes my Davey." Kelsey clapped his hands.

David burst into laughter and told Kelsey to never call him that again. They laughed until they heard knocking at the door. David asked if Kelsey had invited someone over to join them because he sure wasn't expecting anyone. Kelsey said no. He was just as surprised as David.

"I better go get that." David handed the mug to Kelsey.

He looked through the doorway peephole and saw Jennifer. He turned to Kelsey and whispered, "It's Jennifer."

Kelsey whispered back, "Jennifer Washington?"

"This isn't funny," David whispered.

"Well, you always say her name." Kelsey wiggled in his seat excited for him. "Let's go!" He pumped his fist.

David opened the door and invited Jennifer in. The expression of worry and anger was transparent. David made eye contact with Kelsey. Kelsey stood up, prepared to leave.

"No, please don't leave on my account," she said. "No intentions to stay long."

Kelsey's eyes quickly shifted from left to right. He fixed his lips like he was about to whistle and lowered his head like a mother who disciplined her son.

Before David could get a word out, Jennifer stepped to his face and asked if he had any idea what he'd put her through. David started to speak, but Jennifer talked over him.

"You put my life in danger! Do you know that?" She was filled with rage. "Samantha followed me home, broke into my condo, and put a gun to my head over you. Do you have any idea what your actions caused?"

He didn't dare to look her in the eyes.

"Did you sleep with her?"

"I-umm. I almost," he said clearing his throat. "I almost did. And, I'm sorry for putting your life in danger." He reached out to hug her, but she stepped away. "I'm sorry, Jennifer."

"Your apology doesn't fix anything.' She covered her mouth, crying. "I've never gone through anything like this before."

David dropped to his knees and hugged her around the waist. "I'm so sorry." He looked up at Jennifer. Her arms were crossed, and no sympathy could be seen from her eyes. However, what was visible was the long look of goodbye.

"You changed your phone number and email address. Now it's time to change mine. Goodbye." She removed his arms from her around her legs and left, slamming his door.

Kelsey helped David up and returned to his seat. David sat with his hands pressed into his face.

"David, she has the right to be angry and hurt. The wisest thing you could do is to let her feel every justifiable emotion during this time. You both are dealing with some tough things. Perhaps it's best to go separate ways for now."

"For now?" David looked up. "I'm going to lose her."

"You can't lose anything in the will of God if your response is obedience. I honestly can't tell you if you two are meant to be together or if she'll ever let you back into her life. What I do know is that God is drawing you away from each other and toward Him."

David mashed his face into his hands again. He was so devastated by his actions that he could hardly speak. Kelsey tried to talk to him, but David had mentally checked out.

"Dave, I'm gonna get going. I'll let you be with God. I'll keep you in prayer." Kelsey walked out.

STANDING at the peak of the green hill in Shenandoah Valley, David unscrewed the silver cap of the cooper flask. He inhaled the earthy smell of fresh grass before swallowing another swig. "Slipped out of the grace of God again," he said as the whiskey oozed down his throat, soothing his body against the chill. Through his obscure vision, he could see his log cabin at a distance, which looked like a dark speck in the vast green land dotted with tall oak trees. He'd rented a cabin to get away from everything. He wobbled down the hill, mumbling incomplete sentences as he returned to writing.

A brown leather-bound Bible, a laptop without wi-fi, an old gray radio, and a longneck wired lamp were all that occupied the small wooden desk. The wood floors creaked when he walked. Gusty winds were easily heard whistling from the walls. At night, the wild creatures created a natural soundtrack. This was the perfect location for solitude and the luxury of not being distracted by people or technology. However, the blank document on his laptop glaring back at David had won the staring contest for weeks. And the thought of not talking to Jennifer again ate away at him the way termites eat wood.

He tried to read the Bible but couldn't concentrate. He tried praying. Neither was that successful. His mind wandered and wandered. He'd paced the room reliving Jennifer's goodbye and his mother's refusal to make amends with him. So much pressure compounded on top of David that he yelled, "God" and flung his chair across the room. "I can't take this anymore, Lord. Help me! Make yourself known to me," he yelled from the abyss of his soul and lay prostrate on the floor with his eyes closed.

Suddenly, the temperature in the room went from cool to warm. There was a shift and vibrancy in the atmosphere that let David know someone or something had entered the room. Soon, footsteps came up from behind. He wanted to get up to see who was coming, but couldn't. He knew the door was locked. Fear paralyzed him. He dared not open his eyes and get up to see who it was. The footsteps reached his ears.

"Fear not!" A calm yet strong voice boomed throughout the room. "I am the Alpha and the Omega. The Beginning and the End. The First and the Last."

"Jesus." David called His name, trembling. "My Lord, I cannot face you." David closed his eyes tighter and curled up in a fetal position. Every bone in his body couldn't remain still. His strength left him as a dead man.

"Stand to your feet," said Jesus.

David got up with his eyes still on the floor.

"Look to me, David," Jesus comforted him.

David slowly lifted his head until their eyes met. At the sight of peace in Jesus's eyes, fear instantly left him. He felt love emanating from Jesus' presence. Instinctively, he reached over and hugged the King of the universe.

"Jesus," he cried.

"David, I've heard your cries. I have listened to your prayers." Jesus embraced him back. "I meant that I would never leave you or forsake you. I have been with you the entire time. I love you more than what you could describe with words, yet I talented you to fashion them creatively. I love you more than what your earthly father or mother could ever give. My peace I give you. My peace I leave with you. Be strong, mighty man of valor. Be of courage. I am always with you, even in those moments when you are scared, feel alone, and unloved. Know, I first loved you, David." Tears streamed down Jesus' face. "I knew you before you formed in your mother's womb. I love you deeply, David."

He hugged Jesus tighter, literally feeling pain, unwantedness, and insecurity leave him. Jesus gave him his love in exchange for his surrender.

David stepped away and sank to his knees in reverence. Tears engulfed his eyes to the point that he could no longer see clearly.

"Oh, I worship You, my Lord. I love You, Jesus," David said in a loud voice. "Hallelujah." He gave Him the highest praise.

"I love you too, David. My love covers a multitude of sins. I have forgiven you. I am always praying for you. I'm sending you examples of what love looks like in a marriage ordained by my Father. Be of courage. Love how I love, and you will see the fruit of my love manifest in your life as it impacts others around you."

Jesus began to walk away and paused. Turning around, He said in a solemn voice. "It's going to hurt, but it's My will."

"What do You mean, Lord?" David asked.

Jesus walked through the wall and was gone, but His peace and presence remained in the room.

The quiet serenity and tranquility in and outside the cabin were sublime. Nature knew to reverence the Creator when He manifested Himself: Winds ceased. No owls hooted or wolves howled. He stayed up that night and wrote everything his brain could process from his encounter with the Lord. That night, he had the most peaceful rest he'd ever experienced and new material for another book he would write about his encounter with Jesus.

~

DAVID PUSHED the yellow orange-striped kayak to the water and hopped in. He paddled out early in the morning to spend time with the Lord. He slowly paddled, beholding the picturesque landscape. The blue sky was the perfect background to the craggy mountains arranged like a painting. He stopped paddling to marvel.

"God, you spoke what I see into existence. I imagine what the Heavens look like." David closed his eyes and meditated on his encounter with Jesus last night. He was still in shock and disbelief. As he continued to revisit that moment, he heard water splashing in the near distance. He saw a man and woman in a red kayak waving at him. They appeared to be a couple in their late 40s. David squinted his eyes and hesitantly waved back. They slowly paddled up to him with relieved looks on their faces.

"Alex and Susan?"

"David is that you?" they said. "What are you doing out here? Could have called. It's been what, seven years?"

"I think. It's been a while, though. Just spending some time with the Lord Jesus Christ."

"Can we invite you to our house for some breakfast? We'd love to catch up," Susan said.

"Did you guys talk to Kelsey or something?"

David politely accepted the offer, took down the directions to their cabin, and paddled back to land.

He drove up to Alex and Susan's cabin home in the red Jeep he'd rented. A tall, lean, brown German shepherd was out front chasing a white squirrel around a grouping of trees. Alex hacked away at a thick log with an ax. Susan stood nearby, hugging a stainless-steel tumbler. When David got out of the truck and walked toward them, the German shepherd immediately charged in his direction. He jumped back into the truck and locked all four doors as if the dog had hands to unlatch it. Susan yelled to him that Jack was harmless. Jack ran around the truck, barking playfully, wanting David to come out to play with him. He finally hopped out and knelt to pat his head. There was a fond look in Jack's brown eyes. His long pink tongue wagged before it licked David's face. Jack pushed his wet nose against David's and baited him to throw a white ball not too far from them. He entertained Jack for a few minutes before joining Alex and Susan.

Alex chopped one more log in half and took the mug from his wife. He thanked her for bringing tea and puckered his lips goofily to kiss her. She puckered her lips back and met him halfway. They both laughed at each other and completed their moment of affection. David was both amused and envious of this sweet interaction. He'd never had a chance to see his parents together.

Inside the kitchen, fried eggs, baked beans, brown tattie scones, black pudding, Lorne sausage, grilled tomato, and black tea was on the table. Jack continued to take a liking to David, wagging his tail. He followed him and stayed by his side around the kitchen table. Alex and Susan were laughing, getting a kick out of it.

"He senses the peace of Christ in your spirit, David," Susan said. "Must've been with the Lord."

"He sure does. Jack recognizes good company." Alex patted Jack's head. "Trained by the Holy Spirit."

David burst into laughter. "I came out here to spend time with the Lord. Actually, I had an encounter with him last night, so powerful!"

"We know what you're talking about. He frequently visits us."

"That's so awesome. Would love to experience that when I get married. And I may have to get myself a dog."

Alex held Susan's hand, and Jack stood up straight on two legs, giving his paw to Alex. David gathered they were about to have prayer before eating, so he took Jack's other paw into his hand. Jack seemed to have shut his eyes to pray.

No way. A praying dog. I have to get a pet.

Alex prayed, thanking the Lord for their salvation, life, strength, and health. He thanked the Lord for Susan, for blessing him with a beautiful wife, companion, helpmate, and friend in her. He also prayed for God to continue to bless their house and marriage, and that they would forever keep Christ at the center of it.

After Alex prayed, he kissed Susan on the cheek before pulling her chair out and fixing her plate. *This is what Jesus was talking about. An example of love!* He tried not to make himself too obvious about gawking at Alex's gentlemanly treatment, but Alex was very much in tune to his reaction, giving him a shrug and a wide smile.

"What's been going on, David?" Alex asked, placing food on David's plate.

"I'm writing now," he said in a quiet voice.

Alex and Susan made eye contact with each other. David's eyes shifted quickly from left to right, knowing they weren't satisfied with his answer.

"We would love to hear about your writing, but we want to know about you." Susan tapped David on the hand. "How are you doing?"

"You guys talk to Kelsey or something?"

"We haven't. It's been a few months since we have. We do plan on having a family gathering soon."

"Well, if you have time," David replied, "I can tell you my story."

"And we have time." Susan gave him a warm smile. "We know the Lord led you to us today."

"He sure did." Alex grabbed his wife's hand. "He showed you to us in a dream last night. That's how we know you've been with the Lord."

David couldn't believe it and asked if they were sure it was him. They both said yes with confidence.

In the living room, they all gathered around the fireplace with cups of hot cocoa. Jack jumped up on the hunter green sofa and plopped his head on David's lap. Alex and Susan got cozy on the sofa in front of them. Before David tell them about his life, he surveyed the living room. Two long black barrel musket rifles with a chrome and walnut finish hung on the wall next to a deer's head. Navy blue hats sowed in with the Arms of Scotland yellow and red flag draped over the antlers. Next to the deer's head were first place hunting trophies and a Masters in Christian Counseling degree in a plaque with Alex's name on it. David turned to his left. Susan's name was scrawled in cursive on a vanilla doctoral degree in Psychology and Outstanding Teaching awards. David was impressed. He imagined what it would have been like to grow up in a home where both parents were present in the household and established in their respective careers. Oddly enough to him, he didn't see any pictures of children. David blew away the steam rising from the mug and told his story.

He confided in them about his parents and how God gave him a mother in Miss Smith and a father and mentor in Kelsey. "We bump heads sometimes. I can be stubborn," David said, rubbing Jack's head. "Let's say Miss Smith is the comforter and Kelsey is the sandpaper." He laughed. "They're both what I need. I can't thank God enough for them." He touched on his prior lustful relationships with women, most recently Samantha. He turned to the fireplace and peered at it for a few seconds. "I almost slept with a married woman and her husband walked in on us." He placed the mug coaster on the coffee table and put his head down. "And put a gun to my face. He could've killed me when I crashed into a light pole. He drove by pointing the gun at me."

"Amazingly, you're still alive," Alex said, turning to his wife, then to David. "Definitely the grace of God."

"I agree. Learned a lesson."

"David, we heard something in your voice when you talked about your mother." Susan placed her hand on her husband's lap.

"What did you hear?" David asked, feeling exposed. "I mean, I had a real encounter with Jesus last night. He came to me. He talked with me and wrapped His arms around me. He took the pain away."

"But you've taken it back," said Susan.

David got up and paced around the living room. Jack jumped up with pointed ears and eyed David closely as he walked from left to right. He confessed that he just didn't understand why she continued to reject him after all these years.

"That's the part I don't get." David moved closer to the fireplace. "I don't get it."

"David, you may not ever get the kind of closure you think you need to move on," said Susan, referring to his mother. "Sometimes knowing a person's choice of refusing to open up to us is enough to let go. Whatever is haunting your mother is deeply rooted."

"Many of us have come from unfortunate backgrounds." Alex moved his hand on top of his wife's. "We both have in some way. Love can change and heal all things."

"Yes, it can." Susan looked at her husband lovingly. "We know God is a healer. And sometimes He sends healing our way through others. He sent Alex into my life to help heal me. I know what it's like to not have a close relationship with your mother."

"And God sent Susan into my life to heal my wounds too. I never knew my dad," said Alex.

David returned to the sofa and Jack settled back down again. The Lord bringing Alex and Susan into each other's lives to become one in marriage and to also help each other heal echoed in David's heart.

"God, I miss Jennifer." The moment he confessed those words, the Spirit of God returned, and he felt his soul gravitating toward her. "I screwed things up with her. I put her life in jeopardy. The woman I almost had an affair with invaded her home."

Susan gasped and place her hand over her heart. "Oh no."

"I know," David said heavy breath.

Alex and Susan both agreed it was understandable for Jennifer to react the way she had and encouraged David to give her some time.

By the time they were finishing talking, the evening had come. He couldn't stop thanking them for their hospitality, listening ears, and wisdom. He felt like he was part of the family now. Alex and Susan assured him that he was.

The next day, Alex cooked roast beef and fresh vegetables. He also baked an apple pie and prepared a bonfire outside for them to sit around after and enjoy dessert. Jack once again waited by David's side. Alex and Susan were entertained by it. They joked about David kidnapping Jack.

"My suitcase is big enough." David laughed. "You know, I admire the way you love Susan."

Susan's face blushed red. She didn't say anything right away, but her eyes were filled with every emotion of awe as her husband took her hand into his and kissed it. She grabbed his hand, pressed it against her warm cheeks, and confessed that the height of her love for him lengthened, and the breadth of her affection widened each day.

David could see the passion and love beaming off her face. He wondered what it would be like for a woman to love him like this. He was more intrigued about their relationship and asked how long they had been married.

With excitement, they both answered, "Thirty-five years and our love for each other still burns strong."

"What's the secret?" David asked.

"Friendship," Susan said.

David gestured as if he were pulling his hair out. He couldn't reconcile how it sounded so simple.

"Well, of course—" Alex's left eyebrow arched up as he started to elaborate.

"There we go," said David. "I knew there was a catch." He clapped his hands.

"No catch, David." Susan gave him a motherly stare. "Besides a friendship, you need great chemistry that gives life to a great conversation."

"Companionship is important, too. And we trust each other," said Alex. "During difficult times, the friendship, the companionship, the fellowship and . . ."

"Fellowship," David interrupted. "What do you mean by fellowship? This is getting good." He gulped down his hot chocolate.

"To have fellowship is to be in the company of someone whose heart burns after Christ-like yours does." Alex placed his hand over his heart. "You can study and discuss Scripture together, pray together, worship together, and praise God together."

"Whoa!" David raised his left hand and gulped down his hot chocolate. "I don't use this word often because it's cliché, but that's deep."

"It's the Holy Spirit that joins believers together to fellowship. David, a relationship without fellowship is an unequally yoked one." He moved his hands like a professor who taught with his hands.

"I get it. I get . . . Makes sense." David shook his head in agreement. "But continue."

"The unconditional love we have for each other holds us together," Susan said, clenching her hands to illustrate her point.

"You have to love through intense disagreements and deep disappointments." Alex grabbed her hand and held it tight.

"And forgive, no matter how deep the offense is." Susan gripped his hand back.

"That person, whom you can sit in silence with—enjoying their company because there's a conversation happening without words is someone worth spending the rest of your life with," Alex chimed in.

"That's how strong and profound a spiritual connection is." Susan didn't miss a beat.

David was amazed at how tuned in they were to each other, complementing each other's thoughts and completing each other's sentences. This was the kind of connection he'd longed for.

"We love each other dearly." Alex gazed at his wife. "You have that connection when two become one flesh."

"That's beautiful. Awesome," David said, looking at Susan then Alex. "Thanks. I have more new writing material now." He rubbed Jack's head.

"Write on!" Alex said, and everyone laughed.

David's excitement turned into a hush. He confessed that he needed to contact Jennifer. But they caution him to be patient. "I will." David reclined back. "I will."

Alex capped the night off with prayer, thanking God for sending David into their lives. They were grateful for his company. He also prayed over David's life, his relationship with God, and for him to walk in love. Then David led in prayer. His heart was filled with gratitude for crossing paths with a God-fearing couple.

~

DAVID HEADED BACK HOME EXCITED, renewed, and transformed. His encounter with Jesus, then meeting Susan and Alex had energized his spirit. He was ready to embrace all God had anticipated for him to experience in His will.

However, God's timing is not our timing.

A month and a half after returning home, David tried contacting Jennifer. He discovered she had changed her number. He also emailed her. The message bounced back. Popping up at her place was out of the question at first.

The letters of *A New Light* were in purple, yellow, orange, red, and blue. David stood at the beginning of the swerved white pavement surrounded by grass. He wondered if he was out of his mind for coming down to Jennifer's job to find her. The closer he got to the entrance of the building, the harder his heart pounded. He stopped short of the door and started to walk away.

What the heck. I have nothing to lose at this point. He turned back around, swallowed his fear, and continued.

"I'm looking for Jennifer Washington," David said to the young lady sitting behind the desk. Her lips lifted and scrunched together. She asked David who he was to which David replied by giving her his name. "Hmm. Your name sounds familiar. Have you been here before?"

"I have." He perked up. "I did a workshop several months ago."

"Hmm. Sorry, I don't remember you. Maybe I wasn't here around that time."

"It's fine, but is Jennifer around?"

"I can't give out that information. I'm sorry."

David raked the back of his head with his fingers, annoyed, and thanked her. He hopped back into his car and drove over to the café to see if she was there. She wasn't. He did catch up with Monica for a few minutes. It'd been a while since they had seen each other.

Monica came from behind the counter and greeted him with a hug. Before she could get out a question, David told her about the car accident, but assured her he was okay. She was content with that answer. However, he wasn't prepared when she asked about Jennifer. David couldn't answer. Monica knew something was up.

"Umm. Jennifer and I parted ways," David said in a hollow tone.

"Parted ways? What do you mean? What happened? Haven't seen you around." Monica went back behind the register and leaned over against the counter on her elbows.

David glanced around. He didn't want to lie to Monica. And he didn't want to tell her about Samantha. He settled for telling her they were at two different seasons of life.

Monica was unconvinced.

"I understand this is personal, David. As you told me many times, you lost nothing that wasn't in the will of God for your life."

David snickered at Monica. She was dishing back wisdom he'd given her in the past, particularly about her ex-boyfriend.

"It feels different when your advice comes back to you." David looked up at the menu. "But thank you, Monica. I needed to hear that."

"I'm sure it does." She laughed at his reaction. "Chai tea?"

"Nah." David shook his head. "Something different. I'm gonna try to do some writing tonight. I'll take a double shot of espresso over ice. Gonna be up for a while."

DAVID STOPPED by Aunt Jamison's house after leaving the café. She was excited to see him again. He smiled when she welcomed him with a hug and a tender kiss on the cheek. Looking over her shoulder, he saw the gray cat sitting on the same arm of the sofa where he had last sat. The cat's head lifted, and she purred when she saw David.

Where's Jack when you need him?

He sat on the opposite side of the sofa while Aunt Jamison went into the kitchen to pour a glass of water. When she came out, she stopped and examined David for a moment. "You had an encounter with Jesus. I can see His imprints on your heart. Tell me about this experience."

"You can?" David was shocked and surprised.

He took the glass of water and sank back, sharing his encounter with the Lord. Aunt Jamison was so taken aback that she cried and laughed at the same time.

"I only saw Him once in a dream."

"But there's something I don't understand, Aunt Jamison." He sat the glass down on the table and got up.

"What's that?" She watched him pace back and forth along with the cat.

"He said something's going to hurt."

"Maybe He's talking about your mother, David," Aunt Jamison said with heavy concern.

"Uhh," David sighed. "I don't understand."

"It'll come clear soon."

David left Aunt Jamison's house worried and confused. He didn't quite understand Jesus' last words.

The next day, David decided to go to the gym. His leg was feeling much better. Heading toward the stairway to the free-weights area, he saw Jennifer on the treadmill walking a slow pace.

"Jennifer," he said under his breath. His foot suspended in midair as he was about to take a step.

Her headphones were plugged in and she was focused on the television screen suspended in front of her. David looked around at the cycle area. It was crowded. Once again, he found himself in a position where he could get embarrassed. He bit down on his fingernails, then retied the string to his gym shorts.

I can't do this. I can't do this, he repeated in his head.

A gym team member came up from behind and tapped David on the shoulder. He asked David if he was okay. He laughed and jokingly played it off like he was, but in his head, the outcome of approaching Jennifer meant life or death.

He got on the treadmill next to her and accidentally pressed the incline button. The treadmill slowly rose. He tapped the button to lower the machine, but it wasn't working.

"Stupid treadmill." He pointed at the machine.

Jennifer was still in her own world. Finally, he was able to lower the treadmill.

As it was lowering, he tapped Jennifer's shoulder. She looked at him, eyes widening in shock before turning away and going back to watching television. He left and returned with the TV remote. He turned the television off.

"What are you doing?" She angrily pulled out her earbuds. "And what do you want?" She spoke loudly enough that several people turned to look. The attitude was there. David could feel their eyes on him. He was initially embarrassed, but then realized he didn't care what anyone thought.

"I apologize for what I put you through."

"I thought you were a decent person. I was wrong. You have no integrity." Jennifer spoke without looking at him, still walking on the treadmill.

"Can I please have a word with you? If you don't ever want to talk to me or see me again, I'll have peace with that."

She paused the treadmill. "You have five minutes," she said in a firm voice and tightened her ponytail. "I have to finish my workout."

They found a small bench in a quiet corner of the gym. David confessed that he'd had a vulnerable moment with Samantha. "I never slept with her."

"It doesn't matter! That crazy woman stalked me and popped up in my bedroom while I was in the shower. You put my life in jeopardy. What kind of man are you? You have no standards. You're completely selfish!"

Tremendous degradation fell over his face. He could feel her love for him was completely gone. "I'm sorry that I put you through this. I can make things right."

"No, you can't make things right. Goodbye, David." She stood up and walked away.

He started in the opposite direction toward the exit. He was no longer interested in working out. But when he heard his name called, he felt a leap of hope.

"Yeah?" he said with optimism.

"This isn't going to end like one of your romance novels. Rip this chapter out of your book."

This was a fatal arrow to the heart that hit directly in the middle. He could say nothing after that statement. His eyes shifted down and he turned and walked away.

CHAPTER 13

The white cathedral-framed windows of Miss Smith's red-brick house complemented her white picket fence. Red, yellow, orange, and violet flowers and lilies sprouted along with her manicured lawn. It had been a while since David had visited her at her home. Miss Smith was watering plants near the driveway. He got out of the car and asked her how she was doing. She shut the hose off and gave David one of those motherly hugs. "What rock did you climb out from under?"

Before David could go into talking about his time away in the cabins, Kelsey came around from the back of the house with a bag of fertilizer in his hand. David immediately started laughing from his belly. "What the heck?" He turned to Miss Smith, and back to Kelsey. "I've been gone that long?"

"David, where have you been? We called and stopped by so many times." Kelsey dropped the fertilizer. "By the way, I quit smoking."

"We," David repeated, laughing again. "Wait. What? You quit smoking? Congratulations. About time." He clapped.

Miss Smith asked about how things were since the car accident and Jennifer. Kelsey looked down at the mulch and started spreading it away. David stuffed his hands into his pockets and cut his eyes over his shoulder.

"Can we go inside to sit down and talk?" David suggested in a serious tone.

"Sure," said Miss Smith.

In her living room, David sat quietly before them. Kelsey knew why. He and David made brief eye contact with each other. Miss Smith still didn't know what had happened to his leg. He couldn't hold it in any longer. He turned to her and confessed he had nearly slept with Samantha. He talked about Jennifer being stalked by her and a gun held to her head. Her mouth opened wide and the palms of her hands pressed against her cheeks. She couldn't believe.

"Not you, David."

David admitted again that he had.

Miss Smith gasped in disbelief while Kelsey remained tight-lipped. She couldn't believe any of it. David was the innocent young man who she had come to know as a son. A young man who wanted to settle down with the woman God had for him. David hoped Miss Smith wouldn't judge him.

"David, I still love you and believe you have a kind heart. Everyone at some point has made the wrong decisions. I do hope and pray Michael and Samantha's marriage heals, and that he finds it in his heart to forgive you rather than seeking further revenge. And Jennifer." Miss Smith shook her head. "She's hurt and traumatized, but Samantha's actions are not your fault. Samantha has to pay for her behavior, including stalking Jennifer and holding her at gunpoint. It may take a while for Jennifer to see that, and it will take God for her to let you back into her life. Her trust and perception of you have been shattered."

"I know," David said.

"And don't think I didn't realize you told a fib." She threw a pillow at him. " You hurt your leg at the gym okay."

"I know, and I apologize. But something good did come out of this. I had an encounter with Jesus in Shenandoah Valley."

"You mean the Messiah?" Kelsey stuck his thumb between his bottom lip and chin.

"Yeah," David said emphatically.

"You mean the King of Kings and the Lord of Lords?" Kelsey scooted to the edge of the sofa.

"Yes!" David shook his head up and down confidently.

"You mean the way, the truth . . ." Kelsey stood up.

"And the life. Yes!"

Kelsey knelt and high-fived Miss Smith. They were both laughing.

"I am serious," David said. "I saw Him the way I see you. His eyes are so peaceful. Love radiates from His being."

"Wow, David that's awesome. I know you're a good storyteller. Sorry, I didn't believe you."

"Oh, stop it." Miss Smith hit Kelsey on the arm.

"Okay. Okay. Okay. I'll stop. That's wonderful, David. Been waiting for something like to happen in my own life."

"It could happen. Jesus seemed to be happier to see me than I was with Him."

He told them about running into Alex and Susan. Kelsey was happy he had.

"My lady and I plan to go up to 'em," said Kelsey.

"My lady." he repeated. "This is crazy."

David just couldn't believe they had hooked up. This was so weird to him. However, he was happy that Kelsey had found someone again. Miss Smith as well. And they could see David's heart was full of gratitude. He had been healed, transformed into a better man, and God was preparing him to have what was in His will.

Wisconsin Avenue was busy as usual on Sunday afternoon. Near a shoe store, David circled his thumb on his mp3 player as a pair of tan wingtips caught his eye. In the reflection of the window, he saw a woman on the opposite side of the street. She had oversized sunglasses on and a navy cap. A long ponytail hung out the back. He turned around and saw that it was Jennifer.

"Jennifer!" he called out, but she didn't look in his direction. "Jennifer!" he yelled again, but she boarded a city bus that immediately took off. So did David.

He ran across the busy street, cutting off cyclists and taxi drivers. Horns honked, obscene words were hurled at him, but all that mattered to him was Jennifer. He sprinted down the sidewalk, maneuvering through the crowds until the bus stopped at a red light. He jumped up and down alongside the bus and waved his hands to try to get Jennifer's attention. She was looking down and didn't see him. The bus took off again. David sprinted after it.

The bus came to another red light. This time, David stood in front of it. He jumped and waved his hands in the air. The bus driver mirrored his motions and gestured for him to get out of the way. He ran to the door of the bus and banged on it, begging the driver to let him aboard. As soon as the door flung open, two policemen approached him and asked him to get out of the street.

"Let me explain," David grunted as Jennifer stepped off the bus.

"David, what's going on?" She removed her headphones.

"Trying to get your attention," David said.

"Step back, miss," said one of the officers. "He could be dangerous."

"Really?" He cocked his head to the side at the police officer.

"Nah, we're just messing with ya, but you put yourself in harm's way and could've caused an accident. And this is a sensitive area. We gotta stay alert."

"Well, she's worth it," David said.

"Shoot your shot. Good day." The officers walked off.

Jennifer tilted her head and looked away.

"Okay, Jennifer, now that I have your ear, can we talk?" David asked, dusting himself off and standing up.

"I thought I told you to move on. What do you want?" She propped her hands on her hips.

"Just hear me out," he pleaded, holding his hands up in supplication.

Jennifer crossed her arms and sighed. "Okay . . ."

They strolled to a park nearby, silent along the way. David found a bench and extended his hand out for Jennifer to sit. He got on one knee and held her hand. Jennifer's face relaxed, turning somber.

"Jennifer, I am so sorry." He squeezed her hand. "I apologize for putting your life in danger. My stupid mistakes put the people I love and care about in harm's way. Jennifer, I'd never intentionally do anything to harm you. I'd give up my life for you. You're the only woman I've ever met who I've felt God's presence with and believed so strongly in. I'll give up everything to be with you. Jennifer, I am so sorry."

Jennifer stared at David with watery eyes. She put her hands to her temples and lowered her face into her palms.

"David," she said, as tears streamed down her face.

"Jennifer, please forgive me. I am so sorry. I love you. I'm in love with you," he confessed without thinking.

Those words didn't just leave his mouth. They left his heart. He felt relieved and at peace. He'd never expressed those words and felt so sure.

He laid his head in her lap and wept for the pain he'd caused her. "I'm sorry, Jennifer. I'm truly sorry."

"All right, David." Jennifer lifted his face with her hands. "I accept your apology. I have something I need you to forgive me for."

"Uh, what's that?" he said with concern.

"Robert sent you anonymous notes a while back."

"Yeah, that was him? I'm sorry he interfered like that."

"He and Samantha tried to pull us apart. Samantha was already stalking me long before you had an affair with her. She would have pulled that gun on me no matter what. You aren't to blame for that, and it isn't fair of me to do so, especially when my ex targeted you."

"They tried to pull us apart, but it didn't work. I appreciate you telling me this," he said, adoring the woman he loved more than ever at that moment.

She kissed him and he planted one back. He closed his eyes, and he let his head fall back into her lap. He hugged her around the waist as she slowly rubbed his back. He savored this moment, sighing in relief as his heart lightened. Jennifer Washington was back in his life. His prayers and patience had paid off.

After that day, they spent quality time together. Their bond grew stronger, along with their love for each other. David helped finish decorating Jennifer's condo by painting the walls in her living room and bedroom. He even installed cherrywood floors in her living room.

"That's so attractive," she said as she watched David carefully lay the flooring. "I could get used to having a handyman around the house." She winked.

Jennifer helped him pick out new paint and furniture to liven up his place. They also started attending church and praying together over the phone—sometimes in person—throughout the week. Inviting each other into their personal, spiritual space exposed many layers of each other they hadn't known existed, causing their attraction to each other to heighten.

FISH SWAM IN CLEAR PONDS. Far away, deer fed on berries amidst towering fir trees. Birds glided high in the sky above David and Jennifer as they navigated the rocky ledges of Great Falls Park. The warm sun and gentle winds made the weather perfect for rock climbing. They reached the top and Jennifer squatted next to him, loosened her hair tie, and grabbed a bottle of water from her red and black backpack. She took a swallow and gave David some.

"Thanks. It's peaceful up here, isn't it?" he said, gulping it down.

"It is. This is where I like to come to clear my mind sometimes. Although I could do without the bugs." She plucked a small black beetle off her leg.

David pointed at a bug on her shoulder, causing Jennifer to swat herself. He laughed hysterically. She couldn't be mad. His sense of humor and charming ways were winning her over. Without thinking, she leaned over and kissed him on the lips.

Then he palmed the back of her head and matched her passion. If there were any rebellion or uprising of resistance, peace had settled the cause of fear. There was an overlapping of emotions that brushed against the shore of her spirit. And her spirit then received David into its arms. He released her and they looked at each other through the window of their eyes, cracking half-smiles.

"I enjoy your company," she murmured while her lips were on his.

David raked his hand through Jennifer's hair and stared at her for a few moments more. "Jennifer, you are amazingly beautiful."

"Thank you, David." This was the happiest she'd been in a long time.

"There's something I'd like to say to you."

"Sure, Mr. Bradshaw." She kissed him again and took the water back.

"I waited a long time to say this." He brushed her hair away from her face. "I knew when I saw you, I wanted to marry you. I never experienced the presence of God with anyone I laid eyes on or dated before. It makes you that special. You know," he said, stroking the strands of her hair, "I could forever enjoy your company and conversation."

Her eyes lit up, then her head dropped. She became quiet. David didn't say anything right away. He waited to see what she was going to do or say. Finally, her chin raised. Tears streamed down her cheeks.

"I feel I can trust again, David." She raised her head and said with relief. "You make it safe to trust. There's no fear in love." She uttered this as if it was an epiphany.

For love was created to cast out all fear, to experience its abundance of joy, peace, patience, kindness—forever pushing out all likeness of envy, boasting, pride, anger, dishonor, keeping no records of wrong—always embracing the truth, even when it hurts. For love protects anything from the outside that threatens it. And when things appear bleak or are falling apart, love takes everything you've put in to build something meaningful with each other and holds the foundation together again.

"You make it safe to trust again, too." He kissed her. "I want to make this official."

"I would love that, David." She kissed his forehead.

He took her hands. "Thank you for allowing me to court you. I hope that this relationship will be a successful, meaningful, and long-lasting one. I hope we can be honest and transparent, respect each other and talk things out when issues arise. I desire for us to be the best of friends, to fellowship with one another, as well as be the best of lovers. I commit to practicing patience when challenges arise. And be faithful to one another mentally, emotionally, and physically," he said, squeezing her hands softly.

"Wow, David. That was sweet. No guy has ever done anything like this before. Then again, you are different. And that's why I love you." She kissed him. "You're rare and special."

"I love you, too," he said from the depths of his heart again. "This is the first time those three words have left my mouth while knowing the love is mutual."

"I mean it, David. I also pray that our friendship and newfound relationship flourishes in the way God intends it to. I give you my heart because I know you'll take care of it. I have absolute trust in you. And you can trust me with your heart because I'll guard it with all the love I have in me. But, babe, I need to tell you something."

"What's that?" David asked, excited.

"No sex before marriage." She made a bratty face like a toddler.

"I agree," he said with ease.

"Thought I should be honest. We have to be on the same page and not put ourselves in compromising situations to sin against God, if you know what I mean."

"Yes, I know what you mean." David winked.

"After I broke up with my fiancé, I made a vow to dedicate my body to God. I vowed to wait until I met the love of my life. I wanted to purify my spirit to restore my innocence so that I can share myself with the man God has for me. My body is sacred. Yours is too. What's special isn't given away to anyone."

"Yes. 1 Peter 1:16 tells us, 'But just as he who called you is holy, so be holy in all you do; for it is written: Be holy because I am holy.' Holiness is a lifestyle. I decided to be abstinent a while back."

"You're not just saying this because of me, are you?" Her left eyebrow arched up.

"Not at all, Jennifer. I wanted to change my ways. I'd rather share myself with the woman God has for me." He maneuvered his thumb on her chin.

"That's good, David. I'm glad that you made that decision for yourself." She kissed him. "So, we'll have curfews."

"I agree. Whether out on dates or at our places, hanging out, we can't be together past ten."

"This is great, David," said Jennifer. "How about we have dinner at my place tonight to celebrate our relationship?"

"Sure. Wait. I feel my phone vibrating." David reached into his bookbag. "Aunt Jamison? Bad news?" David stood to his feet. "What happened? What? How?" David dropped to his knees and slumped on the ground. Jennifer rushed to his side and asked what had happened. "My mother is on life support. She had a heart attack and hit her head against the bathroom sink."

"Oh no, David," Jennifer gasped.

"I need to pray for her salvation."

Jennifer was slightly confused. "Do you mean for healing?"

"No. I feel the Lord telling me to pray for her salvation. Can you pray with me on her behalf?"

Jennifer didn't hesitate. She grabbed his hands while David led in prayer. He prayed with a great sense of fervor and urgency—pleading for the Lord to forgive her for any sins of unforgiveness, bitterness, or resentment and take her into Heaven.

THE TRIP TO DURHAM, NC was a quiet one. David wasn't very talkative with Jennifer the entire ride. He respected the fact that she gave him space.

At the hospital, the hallways were quiet and the lights a little dim. David and Jennifer held hands entering his mother's room. She was in a coma. He pulled up a chair next to her bed while Jennifer sat near the door in a meditative posture of prayer.

The beeping of the oxygen tank lowered his spirit even more and made him think about his dad. With praying hands, he looked at this mother with watery eyes. There was an ache in his soul that disturbed him. He was completely numb for a few moments until his lips slightly parted to say something, but he remained quiet. He just looked on. A white blanket was pulled up to the neck of her fragile frame. Her eyes were shut. He leaned over and placed his hand against her arm. Then he took her hand into his and pressed his cheeks into it.

He took out some oil and prayed over it, dabbing some on his hand. With tears in his eyes, he placed his hand against her forehead. Before he started to pray, he looked over his shoulder when he heard Jennifer's footsteps. She kissed him on the cheek and rested her hand against his shoulder, closed her eyes, and prayed silently.

"Father, this hurts so badly." He started praying for his mother.

As soon as he uttered those words, he remembered what Jesus had said: *It's going to hurt.*

"Yes, I remember, Lord," he said quietly to himself.

More tears fell off his cheeks, and as Jennifer prayed for him, he felt the warmth of Holy Spirit.

"I ask you, Lord, that you be with my mother, and that you give her peace and comfort in her body," he continued. "I ask you, Lord, to forgive her for all sins in her life and to forgive others who have hurt her. I pray for her salvation, Lord. I have no idea if she's saved or not, but I ask to receive her into your Kingdom. It's in your name, Jesus, I pray. Amen!"

After he finished, he turned to Jennifer and hugged her.

"David, I know the Lord heard your prayers. I felt it. Your mother will be fine." She rubbed his back.

~

INSIDE THE SMALL Baptist church were a handful of people gathered. David didn't recognize any of the faces that were sitting in the white fold-up chairs except Miss Smith and Kelsey, who had driven down for support. Jennifer seated herself behind them while David approached the white and silver casket. His mother's cold face was stiff as a wooden puppet. It was the same expression he had come to know as a child, an adult, and now in her final departure.

"You weren't supposed to leave without answering me. You weren't supposed to leave without saying goodbye." He shook the coffin, rocking his mother's lifeless body.

All the peace he'd had at the hospital had dissolved.

"Come back!" David yelled.

Kelsey, Miss Smith, Jennifer, and Aunt Jamison stood up and gasped. The pastor and members of the mortuary staff came up and took his clenched hands away from the casket, trying to calm him down. No matter how long he stared helplessly at her, he realized that no words of "I'm sorry, son" or "I love you" were going to emerge from her lifeless lips. Neither were her eyes going to open and look upon him with love and care. Nor were her arms going to reach out to give him a motherly hug. At this moment, he had to make peace with what was never going to be.

Kelsey came up from behind and placed his hand on David's shoulder. "David, your mother doesn't have to suffer anymore, and neither do you. You did what you could do to patch things up. You've tried your best, son. You have to let go now."

"I know, Kelsey. You're right. I had a moment."

Miss Smith took him gently by the arm and ushered him back to his seat. She tried to comfort him, but he held himself stiffly, locked inside his grief. Even Aunt Jamison's tender touch and words had no effect on him. David wiped his face with his black handkerchief and peered forward, focused on nothing in particular. He didn't blink or move. Still as a statue.

〜

JENNIFER HEARD bits and pieces of Miss Smith and Kelsey's conversation. She saw how Kelsey and Miss Smith were much like a mother and father to David. Jennifer leaned forward and spoke David's name. He turned and rested his face against hers.

Kelsey smiled and said in Jennifer's ear, "You have a special place in David's heart. A place not too many people get to explore. Make sure he's okay." He moved away from Jennifer and said loudly to David, "David, I'm around if you need me."

"All right, Kelsey." David got up and hugged him. "And thanks for coming too, Miss Smith."

"I was honored to. David, I'm very sorry for your loss." Miss Smith enveloped David once more and kissed him on the cheek. "And it was a pleasure seeing you again, Jennifer."

Jennifer smiled, watching Kelsey and Miss Smith leave the church. "You're lucky to have both of them." She reached out to take David's hand.

He rubbed his thumb along the back of her hand and gave her a watery smile. "I'm blessed to have them, and I'm blessed to have you too."

THE TART on David's tongue became more acquainted than the tingle of winter fresh toothpaste. And his hair was unkempt, standing taller than usual. His nightclothes were musky. Empty wine and liquor bottles and potato chip bags were scattered around his living floor, the sofa, the dining room table, and the kitchen counter. He raised another glass of cheap whiskey to his chapped lips and downed it in one gulp. At times, he glanced at his phone to see if Jennifer had called.

"I know I said I needed some time, but she could at least call to check on me."

Life didn't matter much now. The sunlight that had seemed to burn away his despair when Jennifer entered his life had now faded into darkness. Daytime looked as dark as night. Nights were darker than the black, endless skies he'd often gazed into for some kind of explanation.

God, what happened to me? I need to snap out of it.

David finally came out of his stupor and reached out to Jennifer. They met up at the café.

He shuffled in to see Jennifer and Monica talking. He waved to them and headed toward the back. He took a seat and crossed his arms. Jennifer walked over with two cups in her hand.

"Hey, David." She handed him his drink.

"Thanks." He pushed it aside. "It would've been nice to hear from you, you know."

"I was giving you space to grieve."

"I know that, but you could have called or stopped by to check on me. What's up with that?"

Jennifer gave him a confused look. "I don't understand why you're acting this way. I wasn't going to interfere or do anything that would upset you. I'm sorry, David."

He got up, pushed the chair away, and made his way toward the door. He stopped in his tracks when he made eye contact with Monica. She watched to see how he was going to respond. She didn't know that his mother had passed, but he knew she had looked up to him as a mentor and big brother. He was doing it again. He was allowing his abandonment issues and emotional pain to get in the way of his happiness. He turned back around.

"No, Jennifer. I apologize for taking my anger out on you." To his relief, she gave him an understanding smile and beckoned him back.

"I have no idea what it's like to lose a mother without being able to reconcile with her. I could imagine how much this has hurt you."

"Jennifer, I have something to tell you, something I've been embarrassed to tell anyone."

"What's that?"

"I grew up in an orphanage. My mom left me with my Aunt Jamison when I was seven, but she didn't keep me long. She got sick and couldn't take care of me. She couldn't leave me with any family members because my mom cut them off, so she took me to an orphanage."

"Oh no, David." She walked over to him and held his hand.

"I dealt with abandonment and rejection issues, so when I didn't hear from you, those feelings returned. I apologize for that. Please be patient with me."

"It's okay, David. I'm here for you."

"I appreciate that."

"I have something I want to tell you."

His face filled with concern and curiosity—all at the same time. "I'm listening," he said bracing himself.

"I had an abortion. I so wanted to keep Kayla. But you know what, David? Jesus came to me in a dream and comforted me. He healed me from all the pain from my last relationship—with my dad and the guilt of the abortion."

"Wow," said David, thinking about his encounter with the Lord.

"And I met Kayla." She gently rubbed his hands.

David couldn't believe it. "Say that again."

"I know. Kayla is in Heaven." She hugged him.

"I have to tell you about meeting Jesus too."

"Yes, I would love to hear. I know we have both been through trying times, but we're going to get through this by the strength of God."

Hearing those words did something miraculous to him. Love met his soul in an uncanny way. He was no longer headed down a long, dark hallway, shackled at the wrist and ankle by abandonment, anger, and rejection, while the voices of what could've been or should've happened in the past shouted at him that he'd never be free. Jesus had reaffirmed that to him through Jennifer. Her words prevented him from receiving a lethal injection that would have slowly ended his life. Healing had kissed brokenness on the cheek. Sorrow waved a permanent goodbye. They hugged and kissed each other. Monica started clapping, along with everyone else in the café.

~

THE NEXT SIX months of their relationship were magical. Love flowed uninterrupted, but that didn't mean rain and thunderstorms were exempt from the forecast of their relationship. When Jennifer spent time at David's place, she would get a little jealous of the attention David gave to emails and Facebook messages from his fans that were mostly women, but he always knew what to do whenever he felt the tension. He'd pin her down, interrupt her complaints with kisses, and tickle her until she nearly peed her pants.

"Stop, David. I know you love me. Now stop." Jennifer couldn't get enough of him.

He'd have it out with her sometimes, too. She wasn't accustomed to being with a man who was as affectionate as David. She rarely reciprocated it. David understood this because of her relationship with her father. From other talks they had, he also knew her exes were emotionally distant but physically present.

"I can't tell if you love me," David would complain.

"I'm sorry, my love." She'd sit on his lap and kiss his forehead repeatedly until he gave in to a smile.

Many late nights, David was at his desk writing. Jennifer poked fun at him for courting his manuscript instead of her. He'd fire back that his constant attention to her wasn't necessary if they were in the same room together. He'd gotten used to writing in the same room as his ex, Maria, and previous women he'd dated without interference. Through their growing pains of learning each other's love languages and knowing when they needed space, they were able to keep the love and respect afloat during wintry times. They both made adjustments to accommodate each other and were mindful to always express themselves in the language of unconditional love. God was with them.

He carved out afternoons after church to help rewrite and strategize Jennifer's proposal for her non-profit. One day, he came up with a name for it while they were having a picnic outside at a park on the grass.

"What do you think of Kayla's Place?" he said, leaning up against her shoulder as she studied a strawberry and put it into her mouth.

She turned her head to look at him. "You know what, I love that. That's it. Thank you, David."

"No problem, my love. I know some investors who are good long-time friends of mine. I'll connect with them and I'll talk to Miss Smith. She's going to help too. Of course, you have my support too."

Jennifer returned home to Miami with David to formally introduce him to everyone as her new boyfriend. Although they knew about Samantha, they embraced him with nothing but love and respect.

"This is the young man my daughter has been spending her time with. Let's go around back and talk." Jennifer's father hooked his arm roughly around David's shoulders.

Her father took David to his shed and showed him his gun collection. He selected a rifle and shot at three tin cans that were set up in the backyard. He hit all three dead in the middle. "This is my favorite rifle, David. You know."

"I see. You know, sometimes you gotta shoot your shot." David laughed awkwardly.

"I'm sure you get my drift." He loaded up more ammunition, ignoring David's sarcasm.

"Don't worry. Jennifer's in good hands." He placed his arms around his shoulder.

Jennifer's dad pretended to look at him with disgust but quickly erupted into laughter. They both enjoyed a hearty laugh.

David and Jennifer's father returned to the house to find several people sitting around the table. All eyes turned to them as they approached. Catherine and Anisha had prepared a special dinner for Jennifer and David and had invited extended family over to meet him. David had the time of his life. He seemed to click with everyone in the family. This was something he'd longed for: love, family, and unity.

Throughout the week, David found himself doing yard work and other chores around the house. He didn't mind. He cherished these moments with Jennifer's dad, wishing he'd had this opportunity with his father.

During brunch with the family, he got a call from his investor friends. Jennifer saw the excitement on his face as they talked.

"Jennifer, they're all in."

"No way." She stood up and hugged him. "I can't believe it. Thank you so much, David. You're such a blessing."

"I don't mind helping, my love." He kissed her hand.

Everyone at the table found them to be adorable and congratulated her. Her mother, father, and sister were extremely happy. To the point of tears. They knew how long Jennifer had waited to find the right guy.

That evening, Jennifer's family bought her a cake and invited more family over to celebrate. David's heart was filled with joy to see her dreams come to pass.

A day before they left, Jennifer's father invited David out for fishing, which he'd never done before with Robert. Her father prayed, and they set sail. In the fishing boat, they held their poles in the water. Keeping alert to any nibbles, Jennifer's father asked David about his relationship with his parents. David shared with him what he felt comfortable disclosing. "I could relate to not having a close relationship with your mom," Jennifer's father said. "I also grew up in an environment where love was absent, which hampered my marriage and relationship with my daughter for a long time, but God healed us." David could see why Jennifer had been hesitant to get close to him at the beginning of their friendship.

"Mr. Washington, I have something I want to ask you." David shifted in his seat.

"What's that, David?" He steadied his pole. "I think I got something."

David saw the line jerk in the water. Reeling in a fish the size of a football, he asked David what was on his mind. David shared how thankful he was to be with his daughter.

"Uh-huh. I'm listening," He held up the fish like a trophy. "This is a nice one."

David confessed that he loved her dearly and that he'd love to take her as his wife.

Jennifer's father turned to him and asked if she had any idea of his intentions. He was sure that she knew.

"Hmm." Mr. Washington took the hook out of the fish's mouth. He stood there holding the flapping fish, lost in thought. "Well, my daughter seems to be very happy with you. I haven't seen her like this in a long time. I assume you're good for her."

"Good things have happened in my life, too. She's helped me heal from my past. She's redefined what love is to me. I've never met a woman with such a beautiful soul and spirit as Jennifer's. I promise to take care of her."

"I'm sure you will." He turned to David. "Son, you have my blessing." He patted David on the shoulder.

"Thanks, Mr. Washington. I appreciate this. This means a lot to me. You know, to have your approval." David examined the fish that was now in the bucket.

"God's approval is what matters, son." Jennifer's father winked at him.

David nodded slowly in agreement. "Yeah, you're right. God's say matters most."

David pulled out the engagement ring he'd bought several weeks ago and showed it to Jennifer's father. It was a huge cluster diamond ring.

"That's a nice rock you got there. She must be special to you."

"Oh, she is." David laughed. "She's worth more than this ring though."

"Better not drop that in the water," he joked.

They returned home before the sun went down. David helped to scale and clean the fish and went downstairs to shower afterward. He came back upstairs just in time to join everyone at the dinner table. He took a seat next to Jennifer with an enormous smile on his face. Jennifer narrowed her eyes at him, but his smile was contagious.

"Umm, David, are you okay?" Jennifer's face scrunched up.

It took David a few seconds to respond because he was laughing. "Yes, I'm fine. Your dad is quite the comic."

"He is. That's one reason why my mom married him."

CHAPTER 14

*T*he full moonlight reflected a glowing trail on the river's surface. Jennifer sported a white dress that David bought for her. They held hands and walked the boardwalk in front of the marina at the National Harbor.

"Beautiful, isn't it?" She relished the bright lights of the shopping centers, pubs, and luxury hotels. David agreed. She thanked him for taking her back to Grace Mandarin. "We had a great time that last time we were here."

David didn't respond. He stared out at the water smirking. Jennifer wanted in on what David was thinking, but he didn't bother. He kissed her hand and kept on smiling. She tugged on his ear, realizing his weird behavior had been going on all week. She tilted her head up sideways and asked him what he was up to.

"I just love spending time with you. Can a man just be a man?" He put his arm around her.

"Yes, David," she said jovially. "Thanks for this dress. Good pick." She gave him an elbow to the side.

David pulled her by the waist to the center of the boardwalk. "Shall we dance?"

"Where's the music?" Jennifer looked around.

David cleared his throat and started humming *"My One and Only Love."*

She laughed as he hummed on. Her eyes closed. His chest became a pillow of comfort. His arms around her waist was a blanket of security. The warm soft kiss on her forehead and the vibration of his voice against her ear was a preview of what was to come. God's presence came upon her again, stirring her spirit with vigor. Tears pressed against Jennifer's eyelids.

"I love you, David." The words left her heart before they left her mouth. She said them with life.

"I love you, too, Jennifer," he said as God gave him the utterance.

David stopped humming, but the presence of God kept them moving. They slow danced a little while longer and continued their walk and talk along the boardwalk.

The cherry blossoms at the National Cherry Blossom Festival were blooming more beautifully than ever. The view from the yacht they cruised on was spectacular, and the brunch they served made everything seem like a fairytale to Jennifer. After brunch, they snapped pictures of all the festivities in the park. David pointed up ahead, handing Jennifer a pair of binoculars from his backpack. She saw couples of all ages lined up next to each other at the edge of the river. They held up huge blowup pictures of David and Jennifer. Some of the photos were in color. The others were in black and white. Jennifer immediately recognized the first picture from the recent night out at Grace Mandarin. The second picture was from their coffee date at Blue Café. The third photograph was the evening they went painting in Alexandria.

"These pictures are from all the nights we went out. How did you do this?" Her face blushed red.

"A man can't reveal his tricks." He laughed.

After the cruise, they stood at the edge of the riverbank, looking at the pictures they'd taken together during the day. David picked up a fishing rod leaning against the wall.

"Going fishing?" Jennifer asked. "I see my dad got you hooked."

"No." David nodded upriver.

Jennifer saw a small white boat sailing their way.

"What's this?" She blocked the sun with her hand to get a better look.

"You'll see." David waved to a guy on the yacht who was controlling the boat with a remote control.

When the boat got near, David lowered the hook to it. Jennifer saw a scroll of papyrus paper tied with a red ribbon. He snagged it and reeled it up.

"I see my dad taught you well."

"I learned a little something. Go ahead. Untie it." He handed it to Jennifer.

Jennifer opened the scroll. "*The Impact of Your Presence.* Wow, I remember this poem you read to me. You make a woman wanna cry."

"That moment was special for me, too." He kissed her.

The next day, Sunday evening, Jennifer waited in David's living room. She didn't know what he had planned for the night. Soon, he appeared from his bedroom. She'd seen him dressed up plenty of times. Tonight, the tan sport jacket he wore over his white button-up shirt and the dark denim jeans impressed her.

"You are a beautiful man, Mr. Bradshaw." She gave him a standing ovation.

"We're continuing this trip down memory lane." He came up to her and wrapped his arm around her waist.

"Memory lane?" She was curious.

"It'll make sense later tonight." He led her out by the hand.

Leaving David's condo, they passed boutique stores and shopping centers down the narrow road, which Jennifer began to recognize, along with other landmarks. Twenty minutes later, they arrived at their destination.

"The greenhouse!" Jennifer gushed. She saw the same lights that lit up the walkway and the ceiling light shining at the center. "This entire week has been like déjà vu." She latched on to David's hand when he helped her out of the car.

"Has it?" He pretended to be clueless.

He led her by the arm down the center of the aisle. He was calm and his voice was solemn. At the center of the greenhouse, she saw a bouquet of roses sitting on top of a wooden stand. It was in the same location the first bouquet had been years ago. This time, the roses were all red. There was something else that caught Jennifer's attention. She saw a dazzling color spectrum shining in between the roses.

"What's that, David?" She faced him.

David walked around to the other side and pulled out the red rose in the middle of the arrangement. A diamond-clustered platinum ring was around the stem. Jennifer gasped, and her hands flew up to cover her mouth. The presence of God returned. This time it stirred more powerfully than before.

"Oh my God, David," she said, regaining her voice.

He knelt in front of her and took her by the hand. She watched her king gracefully kneel and raise his head.

"Jennifer, I can't convey more . . ."

"David," she cried.

"Baby, may I finish?" He laughed lightheartedly.

"Yes, I'm sorry." She brushed the tears away from her eyes with her thumb.

"Jennifer, I can't convey more adequately in words how I feel. I've never so loved a woman as I do you. You are the very essence that brings life into my world. You are my healing. You are my love. You are my laughter and my joy. You are my perfection. You are a divine expression of God's love and grace in my life. I'm thankful for you." His voice became choked up.

Jennifer's hand trembled as more tears flowed down her cheeks. She was completely consumed with the spirit of love—taken captive by its power.

"If you could hear the sound of unconditional love, it would sound like a symphony filling the ears of those who listen. God is with us. If you could see love's movement, it would dance gracefully like a ballerina around challenges, forcing them to kneel at her feet. Let's continue to pray together. If you could feel love's power, it would halt the hand of anyone attempting to tamper with it. I am your protector.

"Thank you for giving me a chance to dine with you. During these last five days, I recreated all of our past dates, leading up to this wonderful moment. I want to spend the rest of my life with you. Jennifer Washington. Will you marry me?"

"I would love to spend my life with you, Mr. Bradshaw." She sobbed through her joy. "I love you."

David slid the engagement ring on her finger. "I love you too, Jennifer." His voice began to break.

The sun radiated through the waving Turks and Caicos flag that was tied to two tall wooden poles. White and gray seagulls mewed, circling high in blue skies and sailing above the placid clear water. It was the day of David and Jennifer's wedding. The ceremony was being held on the island of Turks and Caicos.

Seated on the white-padded chairs were Kelsey and Miss Smith, holding hands. A few women from Miss Smith's shelter were also in attendance. Next to them were Aunt Jamison and some of David's friends from the literary world. On the opposite side of the aisle were Jennifer's parents, sister, some of her extended family from the Island, and many friends from her previous job.

The pastor who had married Jennifer's parents in Turks and Caicos stood at the altar. He wore a white linen shirt and pants. On a small, white, silk pillow were two platinum wedding bands. Engraved inside Jennifer's and David's wedding bands was *Love is 1 Corinthians 13*. Their initials were also on each other's bands.

The chattering in the audience stopped when David walked across the sand. It was strewn with white and red rose petals. Jennifer's father escorted her from the left. Seeing David in a tailored teal suit, a white solid collared shirt with a coral handkerchief made Jennifer blush on sight. David's heart pounded. He was overwhelmed with the spirit of love when he saw her approaching. Her diamond earrings and necklace made him admire her beauty even more. Her sparkling clear rhinestone sandals were a perfect match for her short shantung strapless dress.

My God, she's beautiful, David, thought to himself. Then he laughed when he saw Kelsey pointing at the color of his suit. *He was right.*

Jennifer stood next to David. They smiled at each other before facing the pastor.

"This is a beautiful day the Lord has joined David and Jennifer together. Let us bow our heads in prayer."

"God, we thank You for Your presence. We thank You, Lord, for David and Jennifer. You have ordained their lives to become one, according to Your perfect will—yet they are imperfect. We understand that, because of Your unconditional love, we must love each other the way You love us. Because of Your unconditional love, You have given us Jesus Christ, who is our perfect model to mirror in our daily lives. We understand that it is through Your power and unconditional love that marriage can stand up against any obstacle; that we can be faithful in mind, body, and spirit. It's because of You, Christ, we can love when we don't feel like loving, to accept the things about each other that we might not like, to love everything about each other, including our past and our scars. It's because of Your unconditional love that we can hold one another through trying and difficult times and love selflessly and sacrificially. We pray Thy will be done on earth as it is in heaven. Amen."

The pastor continued. "Marriage is the most sacred of all romantic relationships. It is a lifetime commitment to love each other in the most exalted form. A marriage takes teamwork, praying together, and supporting each other to be a better man, a better woman, a better wife, a better husband, a better mother, and a better father. Marriage is about loving each other the way that God loves us, and the way Christ so loves the church—with a love that is holy, unconditional, forgiving and relentless—never giving up. We find all of this in 1 Corinthians 13, which I see engraved on the wedding bands.

"David and Jennifer, if you have wedding vows to exchange, now would be the appropriate time to do so."

David looked into Jennifer's eyes and held her hand tightly. "Jennifer, the letter you found in Leyanie's room—everything in it came into fruition. It truly was a testament to my faith. I believed I would find a woman like you before I saw you. I know you read it, but I want you to hear the words directly from me." He cleared his throat and blinked away the tears from his eyes to see.

As he read, she grabbed his hand and closed her eyes. Every word had a greater impact from the time she'd read it. She held his hand tighter and cried. The words from this letter overflowed into her heart. She felt and received every word as he finished.

"Jennifer, I found you." He held her hand tightly too.

"I found you, too. Oh my God, David. I love you so much," she cried. "I'm not as poetic as you are, but here's a try." She unfolded a piece of paper. She laughed, glancing out into the audience. Light laughter spread through the crowd, but they grew silent again when Jennifer began to read.

"I admit I thought you were too good to be true, and so I prayed silently behind closed doors. I pushed you away and played hard to get. My fears went away, and my wounds healed, allowing me to love again. You made me believe I could love again, David. I'm glad God chose me to love you. When I kissed your luscious lips, it was a powerful moment for me. I mean, that wasn't the confirmation, everyone," she said, laughing. "But when you hold me, I feel God's presence. God sent me a strong and ambitious man who I know adores me and respects me—a man I can't take for granted. You are truly one of a kind. I love you."

"I love you, too, Jennifer." David moved his thumb across her eyelid to brush away her tears.

The pastor took the wedding bands and gave them to Jennifer and David. "Do you, Jennifer, take David to be your lawfully wedded husband?"

"I absolutely do," Jennifer vowed.

"Do you, David, take Jennifer to be your lawfully wedded wife?" The pastor turned to David.

"Without a doubt." A tear came down David's face.

"I now pronounce you husband and wife. David, you may kiss the bride."

More tears streamed from Jennifer's eyes as David kissed her. Their foundation was built on an altar of peace and security. More importantly, Christ! David and Jennifer had finally found what they'd been searching for.

They had found each other.

OPEN LETTER TO MY FUTURE WIFE

A few years ago, while blogging one day, the spirit of God suddenly came over me to write a letter to my future wife. I opened a new doc and started typing away. Every word came from a deep place. I was moved nearly to the point of tears. Sometimes it's how I respond to God's presence. In many ways, the letter was chronicling my journey to healing, becoming whole and maturing as a man in Christ and preparing myself for the woman God has for me. Preparation doesn't always look good or feel comfortable. The Lord has to remove certain things out of your character and life that could stifle or kill the love you will share with someone someday. I want nothing in me that would cause me to be insensitive, unfaithful, impatient or hurtful to my future wife. I want to be emotionally available, mentally present and spiritually mature to handle the responsibility of love.

I know the spirit of God crafted these words for a special woman. I don't know who she is, but I do know she's a woman that has been set apart for me because she has set herself apart from this world and committed her ways to the Lord. And this doesn't mean she's perfect. I'm not perfect. Knowing your weaknesses balances the scale. They keep you humble and from becoming judgmental. I believe when

Christ is at the center of your relationship, the perspective of how you see each other is a healthy and equal one.

The woman I will read this letter to is one who will able to speak my love language and feed my spirit. She will be equally yoked with me. She will be everything I need, as I know I will be that for her. My heart is set on loving my future wife in an unconditional way, which is beyond my emotions. I'm sure this will be a challenge, but when two are faithfully committed to each other, they will continue to grow in Christ together and their love will evolve in height, breadth, depth, and length.

After writing this letter, I decided to insert it into my novel and record it. I wanted my voice to capture what God imparted in me. I hope it will inspire men to write one of their own, as they're led by the spirit of God to do so. I pray the same for women. I pray this letter touches every fiber in you as you read or listen to it. I want women to know that godly men exist and that they desire true love. I want men to know good women aren't hard to find. Some are still healing.

Scan to listen to the letter

THE AUTHOR NOTES

·

Healed for Love is a story that I thoroughly enjoyed writing. All I had was an idea in mind of how I wanted to story to begin and end. I saw it in my head. The challenge was filling in the middle. I remember seeking advice from a friend I attended seminary with. He told me "let the story write itself," and I did. The journey of moving from scene to scene, chapter to chapter was a fun and exciting experience. Everything flowed naturally without force.

Writing *Healed for Love* was also both a learning experience and cathartic for me. I've never taken any creative courses or workshops. Blogging and reading articles in *The Writer's Digest* magazine of tips of crafting plots, characters, dialogue and scenes played a tremendous role in developing my creative skills. I also read a romance novel called *The Bridges of Madison County*. I wanted to learn how to write a love story and in third person. I also credit the editors I worked who gave me constructive criticism and feedback in my development. I'd like to note that I believe within every creative writer is the natural instinct to create a story and the characters that belong in them. By instinct, while writing *Healed for Love*, the inclination of when to show vs tell, where to evoke emotion in certain scenes or focus on the elements in it to lift the reader into the shoes of my characters was all there. I know there's room for improvement.

Healed for Love helped me heal. I met someone after seminary while studying philosophy at George Mason University. Philosophy really unlocked the creative writing side. Something just clicked. I was able to organize my thoughts and get them down on paper. Anyhow, I crossed paths with a woman from the Turks and Caicos. Out of respect, I will not mention her name. She caught my attention one day at the Skyline gym. I became fond of her. We became friends and no more than that. I told her if we ever stopped talking, I would write about my encounter with her, and I did. I poured my disappointments of things not working out with her into the story. However, through numerous revisions, the story became less and less about her and me. That's how I knew I'd healed, severed the soul-tie and moved on. And in the process of moving forward, I decided not to date or pursue anyone for a year. I focused on myself, as God drew me to Himself. He held up the mirror with His word and showed me all the ugly things about myself that I needed to change, heal and who I needed to forgive. It was uncomfortable, a bit embarrassing and a humbling time. It was a season of maturing. It takes maturity to understand that God is not hurting us when He corrects us. He wants us to heal, cultivate an intimate relationship with Him, and become whole and everything He created us to be inside of His will. Some of me is in David Bradshaw. I believe many people will be able to identify with David and Jennifer Washington

Made in the USA
Middletown, DE
27 June 2021

43242619R00172